SAVAGE NATURE

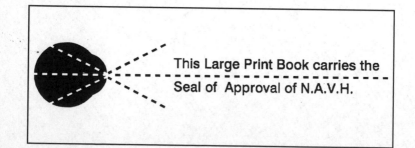

This Large Print Book carries the
Seal of Approval of N.A.V.H.

LEOPARD SERIES

SAVAGE NATURE

CHRISTINE FEEHAN

THORNDIKE PRESS
A part of Gale, Cengage Learning

GALE
CENGAGE Learning

Detroit • New York • San Francisco • New Haven, Conn • Waterville, Maine • London

GALE
CENGAGE Learning

LIBRARY OF CONGRESS CATALOGING-IN-PUBLICATION DATA

Feehan, Christine.
  Savage nature / by Christine Feehan. — Large print ed.
    p. cm. — (Thorndike Press large print romance) (Leopard series)
  ISBN-13: 978-1-4104-4306-9 (hardcover)
  ISBN-10: 1-4104-4306-X (hardcover)
  1. Shapeshifting—Fiction. 2. Bayous—Louisiana—Fiction. 3. Louisiana—Fiction. 4. Paranormal romance stories. 5. Large type books. I. Title.
PS3606.E36S25 2011
813'.6—dc22   2011031375

Published in 2011 by arrangement with The Berkley Publishing Group, a member of Penguin Group (USA) Inc.

Printed in the United States of America
1 2 3 4 5 6 7 15 14 13 12 11

For my mother, Nancy King,
whom I miss every single day

FOR MY READERS

Be sure to go to http://www.christinefeehan
.com/members/ to sign up for my PRIVATE
book announcement list and download the
FREE ebook of *Dark Desserts.* Join my
community and get firsthand news, enter
the book discussions, ask your questions
and chat with me. Please feel free to email
me at Christine@christinefeehan.com. I
would love to hear from you.

ACKNOWLEDGMENTS

As always when writing a book, I have several people to thank: Melisa Long, for information on the bayou and the Cajun people. Thanks so much for taking the time to talk with me. Brian Fechan, who always drops everything to work out tough fight scenes and discuss difficult scenarios. Domini, as always, you make the book so much better! I appreciate you all so much!

1

The swamp had four distinct seasons and within each she had moods as well. Tonight she wore a mantle of purple, all different hues, dark swirls that filled the night sky and lighter lavenders that crept through the cypress trees. The moon illuminated the veils of moss hanging to the water's edge, turning them a pale, silvery blue. Crimson and blue made up the color purple, and it was evident in the splashes of dark red slashing through the trees to pour into the duckweed-carpeted water below.

Saria Boudreaux smiled as she carefully stepped from her airboat to the blind she'd set up, building it day by day, a little at a time, so as not to disturb the wildlife around her. She'd grown up on the edges of the swamp and there was nowhere she was happier. The blind was set up alongside an owl's nest and she hoped to get night pictures, a coveted coup that could possibly bring her a great deal more money. More and more, her photography was allowing her an independence from her family's store that she hadn't thought possible.

Going to school had been rather difficult — she'd been miserable — until she'd discovered the world of photography. Most of her childhood had been spent running wild in the swamps, fishing, maintaining the crab pots, even helping hunt alligator with her father when her brothers were gone — which had been most of the time. She wasn't used to authority in any form, and school was too structured, had too many rules. She couldn't breathe with so many people around her. She had nearly fled into the swamp to avoid the rules when a kind teacher had pushed a camera into her hands and suggested she take some pictures of her beloved swamp.

There was a bit of a moon tonight, so she wouldn't need the dim light she had used the last few nights to reveal activity in the nest. The babies made eager sounds as an adult approached, and as it descended, Saria tripped the camera's shutter release. At once there was a burst of light, much like a lightning strike, as she set off the electronic flash. Used to lightning, the birds never seemed to be bothered by the occasional bright flare.

She caught a glimpse of talons and a beak outlined against the night sky as the owl dropped down to the nest, and her heart sang. At night the swamp had a different music to it. The bellow of alligators could literally shake the earth. Movement was all around her, in the air, under her feet, in the water and through the trees. The natural rhythm even changed from daylight to dark. Sometimes, lately, she thought maybe she'd been spending too much time in the swamp. Her night vision seemed vastly improved, so that even without the flash of the camera, she often caught sight of the adult owls returning with their catch.

Flickering light caught her eye. Someone had to be poaching, or night fishing around Fenton's Marsh. Fenton Lumber Company owned thousands of acres of swamp and leased it to most of the families that she knew. Seven of the families living in the burrow each leased several thousand acres to hunt, trap and fish, making their livings almost entirely in the swamp. Some of the men, like her brothers, worked on the Mississippi to bring in money as well, but their lives centered around the swamp.

Fenton's Marsh was considered rather sacred and off-limits to her people. She found herself scowling at the thought of anyone poaching there. Jake Fenton, the original owner, was well-respected by those living there. It was hard to gain the trust and respect of anyone living in the swamp, yet all the families had liked the older man and often invited him into their homes. He'd become a regular fixture in the swamps. More than once, several of the alligator hunters had allowed him along, a huge privilege when it was dangerous work and a greenhorn was never welcome. He had given them generous leases and no one would jeopardize their livelihood by biting the hand that fed them. Fenton was dead, but everyone knew that the marsh contained oil, and his great-grandson, Jake Bannaconni, would be developing it one day. Out of respect for Jake Fenton, they left that marsh alone.

The adult owl took off again, the rustle of movement attracting her attention briefly, but she refrained from trying to get any more shots. The lights in the swamp made her uneasy, and she didn't want the flashes from her camera to give her away. She shifted position, easing the cramping in her hip, reaching almost unconsciously for her gear. She had meant to spend the night and go home in the early morning light, but the uneasiness was suddenly full-blown fear, and there weren't a lot of things Saria was afraid of.

She had begun the climb down from her blind when she heard a ragged scream. The sound was human. Male and ugly, harsh — and terrified. The swamp came alive in an instant, birds protesting, frogs and insects going silent, the normally rhythmic world evaporating into chaos. The scream ended abruptly, a ragged, cut-off note of agony.

Chills slid down her spine as she quietly slipped into her boat. Had an alligator managed to kill the person hunting it? As she pushed off into the carpet of duckweed, a screaming roar of absolute fury cut through the swamp. Spitting growls and deep roaring reverberated through the cypress grove. The world around her froze, every creature going still. Even the alligators fell silent. The hair on her arms and the back of her neck stood up. Goose bumps rose. The breath left her lungs in a rush.

A leopard. She knew the legends and myths of leopards in the swamp. The Cajuns who spoke of seeing one of the elusive creatures referred to them as "ghost cats." A few naturalists said they didn't exist. Others claimed they were Florida panthers out of the Everglades, looking for new territories.

She knew the real truth, and they all had it wrong.

Saria sat very still in her boat, her body trembling, her hand feeling for the reassuring knife at her belt. She'd carried that knife from the time she was ten years old and she'd discovered the truth. Using careful, deliberate movements, she extracted her gun from the case beside her and checked to make certain it was in perfect firing order. She had begun practicing at the age of ten and was a deadly shot — which had made her invaluable when hunting with her father. She could hit that small quarter-sized spot on the back of an alligator's neck to kill it every single time.

She moistened her suddenly dry lips and waited there in the dark, heart pounding, hoping the trees and the root systems hid her. The slight wind carried her scent away from Fenton's Marsh. The roars faded into the night and the silence stretched for what seemed hours. She knew the large predator was still close — the night was far too still.

She had tried to tell herself for years that she'd had nightmares, and maybe she'd actually convinced herself it was true until she heard that sound — that roar. And now she could hear a rasping call and then a sawing cough. She closed her eyes and pressed

16

her fingertips to her temples, biting down hard on her lower lip. The sounds were unmistakable. She could pretend away many things, but not that. Once heard, it was never forgotten. She'd heard those sounds when she was a child.

Remy, her oldest brother, was sixteen when she was born and was already considered a man. He worked on the river, as did Mahieu by the time she was walking. The boys were in school and worked afterward for long hours while her mother slowly succumbed to some wasting disease and her father retreated further and further into the world of alcoholism. By the time she was ten, her mother was long gone and her father rarely spoke. Remy and Mahieu and Dash were all serving in the armed forces overseas and Gage had just joined. Lojos, at eighteen, ran the store and bar nearly single-handedly and rarely had time to do more than grab a handful of food before rushing out to work.

Saria had been responsible for the house and the fishing lines, running wild in the bayou without supervision from that time on. The boys had come home for a mini reunion before they scattered again, back to the service. They were barely aware of her existence, eating the meals she provided, but not really paying attention to the fact that she cooked. She had desperately wanted attention and felt alienated and left out — not angry exactly, but rather sad that she didn't really fit in with them.

The night had been warm and humid and she hadn't been able to sleep. She was so upset at the way her family treated her — as if she didn't exist, as if she was beneath notice. She'd cooked and cleaned and taken care of their father, but like him, her brothers must have blamed her for her mother's slow sink into depression and then death. She hadn't known her mother when she was the vibrant woman they all remembered; she'd been too young when she'd died. At ten, she'd been resentful of their relationships when she felt as if she didn't quite belong. She had gotten up and opened her window to let in the comforting sounds of the swamp — a world she could always count on, one she loved. The swamp beckoned to her.

Saria hadn't actually heard her brothers leave the house, they all moved in eerie silence — they had most of their lives — but when, resentful and hurt, she'd gone out her window to find solace in the swamp as she had hundreds of nights, she caught sight of them slipping into the trees. She followed, staying well back so they wouldn't hear her. She had felt so daring and a little superior. Her skills in the swamp were already impressive, and she was proud of herself for being able to track them without their knowing.

That night had turned into a surreal nightmare. Her brothers had stripped. She'd sat up in a tree with her hands over her eyes wondering what they were up to. Who would take their clothes off in a swamp? When she'd peeked through her fingers, they were already shifting. Muscles contorted grotesquely, although later she'd admitted they'd all been fast and smooth at it. Fur covered their bodies and they were horrifyingly real as leopards. It was just — scary gross.

They had made those same noises as she heard tonight. Chuffing. Rasping, sawing coughs. They'd stretched tall and raked the trees with claws. The two smallest had gotten angry and erupted into a furious fight, swiping at one another with claws. The largest roared in fury and cuffed both hard enough to send them rolling, breaking up the fight. The sound of that ferocious roar had shaken her to her very core. Her blood went ice cold and she'd run all the way back to the house and hid under her covers, her heart pounding, a little afraid she was losing her mind.

Leopards were the most elusive of all large cats and the true shifters were more so, keeping the knowledge even from family members who couldn't shift — such as Saria. She'd tried to find out about them, but there were only obscure references in the library. She had convinced herself she'd made up the entire thing, but there had been other signs she couldn't altogether ignore, now that she had seen them.

Her father often rambled on in his drunken state, and she had listened carefully to the strange references he made to shifters. Surely they couldn't really exist, but sometimes her father made random remarks about running free as he was meant. He'd stumble off to bed and then next morning there would be rake marks on the side of the house, or even in his room. He would be sanding the wood down and resealing it when she woke up. If she asked about the scratches, he refused to answer her.

Sitting in the swamp with only the night to protect her, she knew a leopard was a cunning predator and once on the hunt, he would find her. She could only hope he hadn't noticed those first few flashes of her camera and come looking. It seemed like hours before the natural rhythm of the swamp began to come back to life, insects humming and the movements reassuring if not comforting as creatures once again began to carry on with their lives.

She stayed very still while the terrible tension drained out of her. The ghost cat was gone. She was certain of it. She immediately left the safety of the cypress swamp and made her way to Fenton's Marsh. Her mouth was dry, her heart pounding in terror at what she might find, but she couldn't stop herself.

The body lay half in, half out of the water, right at the edge of the marsh. She didn't recognize the man. He appeared to be between thirty and forty, now lifeless and bloody. He'd been stabbed in the stomach, but he'd died from a suffocating bite to his throat. She could see the puncture wounds and the raking claw marks clearly on the body. Blood leaked into the water all around him, drawing insects and interest from alligators.

She pressed her fingers to her eyes for a moment, sickened that she didn't know what to do. She couldn't go to the police. Remy was a homicide detective. He was the police. And could she turn in her own brothers? Would anyone even believe her? Maybe this person had done something terrible and given one of her brothers no choice.

Saria made her way home slowly, dread filling her as she tied up her boat and stepped onto the dock. She stood for a moment, observing her home. The bar was dark, as were the house and store, but she knew with that strange warning radar she always seemed to have that she was not alone. She circled the house, determined to avoid her brothers. As she reached for the back door, it jerked inward and her oldest brother filled the doorway, towering over her, a handsome, dark-haired man with serious, watchful green eyes. Startled, she stepped back before she could stop herself. She knew he would catch the fear flickering in her eyes before she had a chance to cover it up.

Remy's eyes narrowed, inhaling, as if drawing her fear into his lungs. He swallowed whatever he'd been about to say, concern replacing impatience. "Are you hurt?" He reached to take her arm, to draw her into the house.

Saria stepped back out of reach, her heart pounding. Remy frowned and raised his voice. "Mahieu, Dash, get out here." He

22

didn't take his eyes from her face. He didn't even blink. "Where have you been, *cher?*" His tone demanded an answer.

He looked so big. She swallowed, refusing to be intimidated. "Why would that suddenly matter? You never wanted to know before." She gave a little casual shrug.

There were no footsteps — her brothers moved silently, but both Mahieu and Dash stood shoulder to shoulder behind Remy. She could see their eyes moving over her, taking in every detail of her no doubt pale face.

"Were you with someone tonight, Saria?" Remy asked, his voice gentle — too gentle. He reached out and just as gently caught her arm when she shifted as if she might run.

She wanted to cry at the gentleness in his voice, but she knew Remy could go from gentle to lethal in moments. She'd seen him handle suspects on more than one occasion. Nearly all of them fell for his gentle routine. She wished he was really all that kind and caring with her, but until recently, none of her brothers had noticed her.

She scowled at him. "That's none of your business, Remy. Nothing I did mattered to you while I was growing up, and there's no need to start pretending it does now."

23

He looked shocked. She saw it on his face right before he went all Remy on her, no expression whatsoever. His eyes went flat and hard, kicking her accelerated heartbeat up another notch. "That's a hell of a thing to say to me. We practically raised you. Of course we're goin' to be concerned when you stay out half the night."

"You *raised* me?" She shook her head. "No one raised me, Remy. Not you. Not Dad. I'm a little too grown for any of you to suddenly decide you're goin' to start wonderin' what I'm doin'. And just for your information, since you know so damned much about me, I go out into the swamp nearly every night. I have since I was a kid. How the hell did you possibly miss that with all your concern?"

Dash studied her face. "You tangle with somethin' out in the bayou, Saria, or someone?"

Her heart jumped. Was that a taunt? She didn't know if there was some double implication. She took another step back. "If I had a problem with someone, I'd take care of it myself, Dash. Why are you all suddenly interested in my life?"

Remy rubbed the bridge of his nose. "We're *famille, cher*. If you're in trouble . . ."

"I'm not," she interrupted. "What's this

all about, Remy? Really? Because none of you have ever questioned where I've been or whether or not I was capable of takin' care of myself. I'm at the bar alone for days at a time. None of you ever questioned whether that was dangerous or not, although I was underage runnin' it."

Her three brothers exchanged long, sheepish looks. Remy shrugged. "Maybe we didn't, Saria, but we should have. I was sixteen when you were born, feelin' my oats, *cher,* burnin' through my youth. You were a babe. So maybe I didn't pay attention the way I should have, but that doesn't mean you aren't mine. *Famille* is everythin'."

"While you all were out feelin' your oats, I was takin' care of our drunken *pere* every night. Paying bills. Runnin' the store. Makin' sure he ate and had clean clothes. Orderin' for the store. Fishing. You know. *Grown-up* things. Keepin' the place runnin' so you could all have your fun."

"We should have helped you more with *Pere,*" Remy admitted.

Saria blinked back unexpected tears. Remy could be so sweet when he chose, but she didn't trust his motivation. Why now? She risked a quick glance at her brothers' faces. They were all watching her intently. They were utterly still. Their eyes had gone

25

almost amber with the pupils fully dilated. It took every ounce of courage she possessed not to turn and run.

"Now I'm grown, Remy. It's a little too late to start wonderin' about my life now. I'm tired and want to go to sleep. I'll see you in the morning." Not if she could help it.

Remy stepped aside. She noticed they all inhaled as she walked by, trying to read scents off of her. She smelled like the swamp, but she hadn't touched the dead body, just went close enough to shine her light on it and see.

"Sleep well, Saria," Remy said.

She closed her eyes briefly, just the simple gesture giving her another attack of nerves.

Six Months Later

The wind moaned softly, an eerie, lonely sound. A snake slid from the low-hanging branches of a tupelo tree and plopped into the water, swimming away, no more than a ripple in the dark water. Overhead, dark clouds, heavy with rain, boiled in the evening heat.

Saria stepped from the pirogue to the rickety dock, pausing to inhale deeply while she cast a careful look around, studying the shore and grove of trees she had to walk

26

through. Years earlier, one of the farmers had planted a Christmas tree farm that had never quite taken off, although the trees had. The town, small as it was, had grown to the edge of the farm, and the variety of cedar, pine and spruce trees were beautiful but had grown thick, creating a forest effect behind the cypress grove on the water's edge.

Moss hung in long silvery webs, swaying gently from the twisted cypress branches lining the river. The grove was fairly large, and with the gray mist spreading like a fine veil, the cypress trees lining the water appeared spooky and ghostlike. Behind that, the thicker farm trees loomed, a silent dark forest. Icy fingers crept down her spine as she stood there on the wooden planks, a good distance from civilization.

Night often came fast to the river, and she had waited for her brothers to leave, checking on the fishing lines and crab pots before she took off to come to the mainland. All the while, she'd had the feeling someone was following her. She'd stayed in close to the banks of the river as much as she could. Someone — *something* — could have kept up with her and certainly could be ahead of her now. Her brothers had gone out in the bass boat, leaving her the old pirogue, which was fine with her as a rule, but something unseen in the night made her wish for speed.

Lately she'd been uneasy and restless, her skin too tight as if it didn't quite fit over her bones. Itching came in waves as something seemed to move beneath her skin. Her skull felt too large, and her jaw and mouth ached. Everything felt wrong, and perhaps that contributed to her gathering fear that she was being watched.

Saria sighed, moistened dry lips and forced herself to take that first step toward the farm of trees. She could bypass it, but it would take time she didn't have. Her brothers were going to be back and they'd be angry if they caught her going off by herself again. They'd been as edgy as she was, and to her dismay, had taken to checking up on her continually. The last couple of weeks the attention had grown worse until she felt as though she were a prisoner in her own home.

She began walking, touching the knife strapped to her belt for reassurance. If someone — or something — truly was stalking her, she was prepared. She walked in silence, along the narrow path through the grove, toward the old church.

Behind her and a little to her left a twig snapped, the sound overloud in the silence of the grove. Her heart began to pound. The mist thickened with each passing moment, slowly drawing a veil over the dark clouds and sliver of moon. The fog turned the crescent a strange, ominous red. She quickened her pace, hurrying through the variety of trees.

Saria emerged from the grove of Christmas trees straight onto a sidewalk leading through the small town just off the Mississippi River. A large holding wall helped to prevent flooding. Most of the land had been built up to help with the flooding as well. She walked quickly down the walkway along the river. The wind sent waves lapping at the wall and piers. She took another cautious look around but didn't slow her pace. The church was just ahead, and she felt a pressing need to get inside.

In spite of the night, the air was very hot and heavy with moisture, promising rain soon. She felt sweat trickle down between her breasts, but wasn't certain if it was the oppressive heat or sheer fear. She breathed a sigh of relief when she gained the steps to the church. Deliberately she paused there, covering her hair with the lace wrap that had been her mother's. While she did, she turned and surveyed the street. Quaint gaslights lit the street, glowing a strange yellow in the mist. She felt the weight of eyes watching her, but she couldn't spot anyone overly interested in her.

She turned her back to the street and walked up the steps to the church door. Right between her shoulder blades she felt an itch, and the hair on the back of her neck stood up. She pulled open the door and slipped inside, her heart pounding. The interior of the church was dimly lit. Shadows clung to the walls and created dark valleys between the empty pews. She dipped her fingers in holy water and made the sign of the cross as she walked slowly toward the confessional. The statues stared down at her with empty, accusing eyes. She had been here several times since she'd found the first body, but she couldn't bring herself to confess, not even to Father Gallagher, not even now that there had been two more.

She felt guilty, no doubt about it, although she'd tried to get help and that had only put her in danger. Now, the priest was her only hope — if she could get up the courage this time to ask him. She waited her turn, closed the confessional door and knelt on the small padded bench provided. She bowed her head.

The darkness and privacy screen of the

shadowy confessional prevented Father Gallagher from identifying which parishioner had just entered the small booth. He knew it was a woman by the faint fragrance of lavender and wild honey. The scent was extremely subtle, but, in the stifling heat of the confessional, the fragrance was a welcome change from the sweat that sometimes was faintly sickening.

"Father," the voice whispered.

He leaned closer, alarmed by the note of desperation in her tone. Over the years he had learned to recognize real fear.

"It's Saria," the voice continued.

He knew Saria, had known her since she was a toddler. Bright. Intelligent. Not given to flights of fantasy. He had always known her to be a cheerful, hardworking girl. Maybe too hardworking. She came from a large family, like many of the Cajuns attending his church, but she had stopped coming to mass and confession years earlier. About six months ago, she had returned to confession — but not to the service — coming faithfully every week, but not confessing anything of importance that might have made her suddenly need to come back to the church. Her whispers made him think perhaps there had been another reason for her once again coming to the confessional.

"Is everything all right, Saria?"

"I need to slip a letter to you. It can't be mailed from this parish, Father. I've tried, and the letter was intercepted. I was threatened. Can you get it out for me some other way?"

Father Gallagher's heart jumped. Saria had to be in trouble if she was asking such a thing, and he knew from long experience that the people in the bayou as well as up and down the river were hardworking, large clans that often kept troubles to themselves. She had to be desperate to come to him.

"Saria, have you gone to the police?"

"I can't. Neither can you. Please Father, just do this for me and forget about it. Don't tell anyone. You can't trust anyone."

"Remy is a policeman, isn't he?" he asked, knowing her eldest brother had joined the force years ago. He didn't understand her hesitation, but he had a sinking feeling in the pit of his stomach. His comment was met with silence. He sighed. "Give me the letter."

"I need your word as a man of God, Father."

He frowned. Saria wasn't dramatic either. This strange conversation was completely out of character for her sunny personality. She feared very little. She had five very large brothers who would probably skin someone alive if they tried to hurt her. They'd grown up rough, big strong boys who had turned into formidable men. He couldn't imagine why she wouldn't go to Remy. He had been head of the family since her father's death some years earlier.

"Should I be afraid for you, Saria?" he murmured, lowering his voice even more and pressing his ear to the screen. The situation would have seemed surreal and dramatic had it been someone else, but Saria had to be believed.

"Somethin' bad is happenin' out in the bayou, Father, but I can't call the police. We need someone else. If you can get this letter out without anyone from here knowin', he'll do something. Please, Father Gallagher, just do this for me."

"I give you my word I won't tell anyone, *unless*," he emphasized, "I think it is necessary to save your life."

There was another small silence. A rustle of paper. "That's fair. Please be careful, Father," Saria whispered and pushed the flat envelope through the opening. "No one can see you with that. Not in this parish. Not in this ward. You have to take it far from here to mail it."

Father Gallagher took the envelope, not-

33

ing it was sealed. "Say three Hail Marys and the Lord's Prayer," he whispered, reminding her to keep up the charade of confession if she wasn't actually going to confess any sins. He waited, but she stayed silent, and he blessed her, tucking the envelope into his robes.

Saria crossed herself and left the confessional, going up to the front pew to kneel before the altar. There were several people in the church and she took a slow, surreptitious look around, trying to see if anyone could have followed her. She didn't see anyone suspicious, but that didn't mean anything. Most of the people she knew attended the church and could pretend, as she had done, that they had legitimate business there.

Just a short distance away, the Lanoux twins lit candles. Dion and Robert had recently lost their grandmother, and it stood to reason they might be in church. Both men were stocky with roped muscles and dark, thick curly hair. Handsome men, they had quite the reputation as ladies men in the community. She'd found both of them to be gentlemen beneath their rough-and-tumble ways and she liked them both.

Armande Mercier sat beside his sister, Charisse, fidgeting while she prayed piously in the second-to-last pew. Charisse's head was bent, eyes closed, lips moving, yet twice when Armande sighed heavily and ran his finger around his shirt collar she sent him a sharp glare. He sent Saria a glance and quickly looked away, unusual for Armande. He was probably the biggest flirt in the ward. She found him selfish but charming, and he definitely protected his sister, whom Saria was quite close to. Saria's brothers often gave Armande a free beer when he came to their bar, feeling sorry for him having to take care of his tyrant of a mother and his extremely shy sister.

The two elderly women in the back were well known to her as was the older man, Amos Jeanmard, sitting in the corner, his walking stick close. She had gone to school with his daughter, Danae, and knew his son, Elie, who was older by a few years. She knew them all, just as they knew her. They'd always been friends and neighbors — members of one of the seven families on the edge of the swamp where she resided. She'd gone to their homes, attended weddings and funerals with them. They supported her family bait shop and grocery store. Many of them were customers of the small store and bar the Boudreaux family owned. Now, they terrified her. She had even grown to fear her own kin.

She made the sign of the cross and left the church, anxious to be gone before Father Gallagher was finished hearing confession. She didn't know if she could face him and not give herself away. The stress was getting to her, and her stomach had begun churning. She ran lightly down the steps and headed back toward the dock where she'd left her boat.

The night seemed darker, the shadows longer, reaching for her as she hurried toward the grove that would provide the shorter route back to the dock. Quickly, she moved along the narrow path through the thick stand of trees. The hairs on the back of her neck stood up, goose bumps raised along her arms and she shivered, cursing under her breath as she hesitated, nearly turning back toward the lights of town muted by the fog. As if on cue, the rain began to fall, a downpour of warm drops that soaked her instantly. The deluge drove her into the grove where the overhead canopy might protect her a little from the onslaught. She hurried along the path, head up, searching for anything that might be causing her warning radar to go off.

A large shadow shifted in the trees. Her heart jumped and then began pounding.

Something seemed to move, pushing against her flesh from the inside out, leaving behind an itch as it receded. Her skin felt tight and her jaw ached. She became aware of her hands hurting. She looked down to see her fingers curled tightly, sharp nails pressing into her palm. Behind her, cutting off her escape to town, she heard a soft chuffing noise and her blood ran cold. Her heartbeat accelerated out of control, thundering in her skull. Her breath came in ragged gasps.

She took a cautious step toward the dock, her hand slipping the knife from her belt. The hilt felt solid in her palm and she curled her fingers tightly around it like a talisman. Her own brothers wouldn't kill her, would they? Her mouth was dry.

She tried to listen as she hurried, but her own heart and her gasping breath filled her ears, the thunder a terrible roaring, drowning out everything else. The veils of Spanish moss swayed, creating an eerie, ghostlike presence in all the trees. The branches, twisted and gnarled, reached out in the dark like ghoulish hands. She'd never been afraid in the groves of trees along the river. She'd never feared alligators or the swamp even at night. She was careful, as her father had taught her, yet now terror gripped her.

She knew better than to run, knew it

would trigger the leopard's instincts, but she couldn't stop herself from picking up her pace, moving as fast as she could through the pouring rain without actually running. She heard a whoosh, like the rush of a freight train. Something hit her from behind, slamming into her back so hard, she felt as if her bones had shattered. The heavy weight of it drove her down so she hit the ground hard, landing with her hands pinned under her, the knife still firmly in her grip, but completely useless. She felt hot breath on the back of her neck and tensed, ready to fight. The thing was far too heavy to push up. She couldn't get her knees under her, and the moment she started to struggle, it sank teeth into her shoulder.

Saria opened her mouth to scream, but got a mouthful of mud. Tears burned her eyes as she waited for it to kill her. Claws gripped her hips hard, warning her not to move. She went still beneath the heavy weight. For a moment neither moved. Very slowly she turned her head. The leopard shifted to bring his head beside hers. She found herself staring into yellow-green eyes. Wide and unblinking, the thing stared back at her. There was intelligence there, and a warning. Breath blew hot against her skin.

She shuddered as the large head drew near her face. The mouth yawned wide and she closed her eyes, certain those terrible teeth would close around her face. The rough tongue lapped once over her face, removing the stream of tears. She drew in a breath and then felt fire raking down her back, ripping through her shirt. She screamed again, struggling to throw him off. His claw dug into her flesh and carved four deep grooves from her shoulder blades to her waistline.

Deep inside of her, something wild lifted its head as if awakening. Adrenaline pulsed through her, rushing like a drug through her veins, strength and energy pouring into her, lending her phenomenal strength. She shoved up hard, gathering her legs under her enough to create a small separation, just enough to roll. At the same time, she brought the knife up, slashing toward the leopard's jugular.

The cat's front paw flew toward her knife hand, the heavy body pinning her as the great claw shifted, and to her horror, fingers caught her wrist and slammed her hand back into the muck. That human hand, coming out of a leopard's body, terrified her. It was grotesque and wrong and not at all romantic like a young child had envi-

sioned. Deep inside her own body, something shifted and moved, pushing aside fear
to ignite a burning bright anger.

As they stared at one another, fury smol-
dered deep inside her body. She could
almost feel something inside of her, living
and breathing, furious that the leopard
dared to touch her. Her skin itched and her
jaw ached. Her entire body hurt, probably
from the vicious hit when the cat brought
her down.

"Go ahead," she bit out, trying not to sob,
trembling with a combination of fear and
anger. "Just do it."

He held her down with his heavy paws,
breathing against her neck again. She closed
her eyes and waited for the death bite. Unlike most large cats, leopards preferred to
bite the throat of their prey and hold until
the victim suffocated. Slowly, almost reluctantly, the large leopard backed away from
her. She peeked out from under her lashes
and watched it as it steadily backed up, one
silent paw at a time. All the while, those
yellow-green eyes remained on her face.

She didn't dare move, afraid she would
trigger more aggression in the animal. Long
after he disappeared into the fog, she lay on
the ground, shaking, tears running down
her face. It hurt to sit up, her back on fire.

The rain soothed the fiery streaks. The bite mark on her shoulder oozed. Infection was a real threat in the swamp. She couldn't go to a doctor, and if she went to the *treateur,* what was she going to say? That a leopard attacked her in the cypress grove just outside of town? The woman would have her committed.

She sat in the rain, listening. Already the regular sounds of the night were resuming and deep inside her body, whatever had stirred subsided. For several long minutes, she sat in the mud with the rain pouring down on her, weeping. Her stomach lurched unexpectedly, and she rolled painfully to her hands and knees and retched again and again.

She was a Boudreaux and she'd been taught since birth not to trust outsiders. Her family was shrouded in secrecy and she was cut off from the world. She could leave the river — but she knew no other way of life. Where would she go? Who could she turn to? Saria lifted her head slowly and looked around her.

This was her home, the wilds of the river, the bayous and lakes, the swamps and marsh. She couldn't breathe in a city. She wiped at the mud on her face with her sleeve. The movement caused a spasm of fire to chase down her back and small flames to burn over her shoulder. Her stomach lurched. Stifling a small sob, she pushed herself up with one trembling hand. Exhaustion set in. She stumbled her way to the dock, every step painful. She was afraid the leopard had broken something in her back.

It was difficult to step onto the pirogue, but she did a lot of deep breathing as she reached for her pole to push off. Her back muscles were on fire with every movement. She looked back at the grove as she thrust the flat-bottomed boat away from the dock. Her heart jumped. Red eyes stared back at her through the mist. He was still watching her. She stared right back at him as she pushed out into the current and let it take her back downriver. The red eyes suddenly disappeared and she caught a glimpse of the big cat running, using long leaping strides, weaving in and out of the trees, heading into the swamp.

Trying to beat her home? Did she believe any of her brothers would harm her? Could one be a serial killer? She'd found a second body three months ago, and now a third. She'd tried to mail the letter out herself, but found it taped to the bottom of her pirogue, scaring her nearly to death. Her brothers were tough men, all capable of killing should the need arise. But wantonly? Any of them? She shook her head, not wanting to believe it was possible. But the evidence . . . Maybe if she just told all of them when they were together, just blurted out that she'd found bodies, it might be possible to tell from their reactions.

Saria found it impossible to think the rest of the way home. Using oars or a pole required back muscles, and her body protested every movement. She didn't even care to see if the leopard cut through the swamps and beat her home. There were several boats tied up to the dock and music blared out over the water. Lights spilled out over the river. A couple of men were standing outside the bar, but neither looked up as she tied her pirogue to the dock.

The bar was open, which meant at least one of her brothers was at home. She would have liked to peek in and see just which one was there, because that would rule him out as a suspect, but she didn't dare take a chance of anyone seeing her.

The house was nestled back in the trees with the river running on one side and surrounded by trees on the other three sides. She used to find comfort in the trees, often climbing them and surveying the world from the heights as a child. Now she searched the branches frantically for signs of a large cat as she went around to the back of the house, hoping to avoid her brothers if any others were at home.

There were no lights on, and she paused on the back stairs, listening. Her hearing seemed more acute sometimes, like a switch that went on and off, as did her night vision. Right now, she could hear only her own ragged breathing. She crept into the dark house, not bothering with lights, trying not to make a sound as she made her way through the small rooms to her bathroom.

Saria stripped off her ripped jacket and examined the slashing tears before she shrugged out of her shirt. The shirt was soaked with blood. She held up the remnants, looking at the gashes that could only be made by a large cat's claws. The sight of all that blood and the tears made her feel sick. She balled up the shirt, threw it into the sink and turned her back toward the full-length mirror. The glass was cracked in places, but looking over her shoulder, she could see the grooves marring her skin. They looked angry and red — definitely an infection waiting to happen.

She touched the puncture wounds on her shoulder and burst into tears. Saria stood in the shower, shaking, the hot water pouring over her, rinsing away the blood, her back and shoulder stinging horribly. Her legs gave out and she sank down onto the floor of the shower stall and cried, letting the water wash away her tears.

She drew her knees up and hugged herself tight, ignoring the burning along her back. Why hadn't the leopard killed her? Clearly he knew she'd found the dead bodies. She breathed deep to keep from vomiting. She had no idea what to do, other than scrub to remove all scent from her body and then get rid of her clothes. Leopards had a great sense of smell, and she didn't want any questions.

Forcing her body back up, she reluctantly took the soap and poured the gel over her back, using a scrub brush to work it into her wounds. She had to stop several times and breathe deep to keep from fainting. It hurt beyond anything she could imagine. She rinsed off and repeated the scrubbing with the bite on her shoulder. She patted her body dry and rummaged in the medicine cabinet until she found iodine.

Saria bit back a scream as the iodine burned through the gouge marks on her back and the puncture wounds on her shoulder. She pushed her head between her knees, breathing deep as blackness edged her vision. Bile rose and she fought hard not to get sick.

"Fils de putain." She hissed the words between clenched teeth, struggling to keep from landing facedown on the floor as the world around her darkened and white spots fluttered in front of her eyes.

It took several minutes for her world to right itself, and she was able to straighten again without her legs going rubbery on her, although her back protested with a fierce burning. She breathed through it and carefully bandaged the puncture wounds on her shoulder. She couldn't do anything about her back and knew whatever she wore would be ruined, so she pulled on an old shirt and soft sweatpants.

She couldn't just go to bed and hide beneath the covers, she had to get rid of her shredded clothes. She picked up the jacket and shoved it in the sink with the shirt. Her brothers would smell them if she didn't do something about the blood before she threw them away. The only thing she could think to do was pour bleach over them, which she did. She left them to soak while she went to get water and some aspirin.

The scent of bleach and blood had permeated the bathroom by the time she returned.

46

This was not going to work. The bleach would definitely mask the scent on her clothes, but her brothers would be suspicious. She rinsed the shirt and jacket and cleaned the sink. She would take the clothes out to the swamp and burn them.

Saria tried to still her chaotic mind long enough to think the situation through as she slipped out of the back of the house and into the thick grove of trees toward the swamp. Why hadn't the leopard killed her? The shifter knew she had found the body. Wouldn't it have been simpler just to kill her — unless the killer was one of her brothers and he couldn't bring himself to kill a family member.

"Saria! Where the hell are you, *cher?*"

Her heart jumped at the sound of Remy's voice calling from the back porch. Lately, he'd been checking several times a night to make certain she was in her room.

Swearing to herself, she hastily dug a hole and shoved the tattered remnants of her clothing into it. She had to answer. He would have seen her pirogue tied to the dock and he would come looking for her. "I'll be right in," she called as she buried the evidence. "I just was getting a little air."

"Hurry up, Saria, you shouldn't be out alone at night in the swamp." His voice was always gentle. That was Remy, but under all that soft, black velvet, there was steel. She knew he'd come after her if she didn't get inside.

She dusted off her hands and pushed up. "I'm coming. No worries. I'm tired tonight."

When she heard voices in the front of the house, she hurried in and made a point of closing her bedroom door loudly. She lay on her stomach, awake most of the night, listening for the sound of her brothers, but after their voices faded, there were only the comforting sounds of the swamp.

2

The sun dropped from the sky, a molten, fiery ball, pouring red and orange flames into the darkened waters of the Mississippi River. The air was heavy, nearly oppressive with humidity, just the way he liked it. Drake Donovan stepped from the barge with casual grace, lifted a hand to the men on board, and stopped for a moment there on the wooden walkway to admire the rolling river. With night falling, shadows delved sweetly into the ripples, giving the water a mysterious, beckoning feel. The pull of the river's secret places was strong.

Groves of trees, tupelo and cypress, graced the water's edge enticingly. He had seen many such inlets and isles as they approached the banks. Great blue herons walked in the shallower waters of the bayous, canals and marshlands, graceful figures drawing one's eye to the beauty of the surroundings.

He listened to the night sounds creeping in as he watched the first of the bats, dipping and wheeling in the air overhead, catching the insects drawn to the massive body of water. Not too far from the river's edge, a small fox darted toward a mouse scurrying into the leaves. An owl sat very still in the dusk, waiting for the sun to sink into the river, leaving the night to blanket the swamps and bayous.

The wildness in him reacted, rising with a great leap, demanding freedom. It had been so long. Too long. His thick five-o'clock shadow composed of tangible hairs embedded deep into the tissue supplied nerve endings with tactile information. Always, that guidance system would plug him into the air currents and enable him to read objects, and this time, unexpectedly, when he gathered information, his cat reacted aggressively, raking at him, snarling with his demands.

Drake lifted his nose to the airways, drawing the night deep into his lungs, drawing in — *her.* His heart skipped a beat and then began to pound. Every nerve ending in his body came to life. Need punched low and mean, a wicked, unexpected blow that staggered him. Her scent was alluring, captivating, unleashing a deep primal command impossible to ignore.

The animal in him leapt hard, challenging the man. Fur rose beneath his skin in a wave of demand, leaving behind a terrible itch. His jaw ached and he felt the slide of canines pushing into his mouth. He tried to breathe, tried to calm the lethal beast pushing so close to the surface. His muscles rippled, contorting before he could get himself under control. He'd experienced his cat's edgy need before, but not like this, not this dangerous — the temperamental leopard pushing so close he couldn't distinguish between man and beast.

His mind became a haze of red, primal instincts drowning out civilized man. Drake had always had enormous strength, holding back his animal side with more discipline than most of his kind, but this time the struggle for supremacy was more like mortal combat. Bones ached and his left leg pulsed with wrenching pain. Strangely it was the pain that allowed him to hold on. He was out in the open, a danger to any male — human or leopard — near him. He kept his face in the shadows and simply breathed in and out, relying on the simple mechanics of an automatic reflex to keep the wild animal caged.

"Just for now," he whispered — a promise

he intended to keep no matter the cost. His leopard had been caged long enough. "Wait a little longer."

The beast subsided, snarling his reluctant obedience; more, Drake was certain, because the alluring scent had drifted away on the night breeze than because the man was stronger. He wanted to follow that scent — he needed to follow it, but it was as elusive as the females of his kind were. The sexy fragrance was gone and he was left with a clawing need and an aching groin as the scent gave way to the normal smells of the river's edge.

"Mr. Donovan? Drake Donovan?"

He closed his eyes briefly, savoring the melodic sound of a woman's tone. She had the sultry lilt of Cajun country in her voice. He turned his head slowly, not believing any woman could match that voice. He didn't know what he expected, but he sure as hell hadn't expected his reaction to her. That same low, mean, wicked punch to his groin, the same assault on his raw senses he'd experienced earlier repeated itself even harder.

She stood several feet from him but he was instantly aware of everything about her. His senses were heightened by his leopard, he had no doubt about that, but this time his reaction was all man. She wore faded and ripped blue jeans and a short tee that clung to her curvy form lovingly. Her face was young, but her eyes were old. Her hair was thick, a dark blonde, but heavily streaked with silver, gold and platinum strands. Beautiful dark chocolate eyes spiced with golden flecks seemed at odds with the sun-kissed hair that was worn in a ragged, jagged cut that would never have suited anyone else, but somehow only enhanced her appearance.

Drake could barely breathe, knew he was staring, but couldn't stop himself. She stood there, just looking at him with a curious expression, waiting for an answer. Her lashes were long, and she had a tiny scar on her chin, and melting dimples. Her mouth was a thing of fantasy, full lips like a fasci-nating bow, her teeth small and white, although her canines were sharper than normal. He had a strange urge to drag her into his arms and taste her.

She regarded him with a mixture of reti-cence and wariness. "I'm Saria Boudreaux, your guide. You are Drake Donovan, aren't you?" She tilted her head to one side, study-ing him with concern. "If you don' feel good from the trip, it's all right, we can wait before we get you back on the boat. Maybe get you somethin' to eat?"

Her accent curled in his stomach. He could feel the reaction pulse through his groin. "I'm fine, Miss Boudreaux. I'll be staying at the Lafont Inn, as you recommended. You said it was close to the canals and marshes I'll be visiting?" He'd made certain the bed-and-breakfast she'd recommended was rarely visited and near the bayou where there were groves of trees, marsh and swamp. He'd rented the entire B&B on the chance he'd need his team as well as to ensure their privacy.

She nodded. "Call me Saria, it will be easier since we'll be spendin' a week together. Is that your bag?" She indicated his small war bag with a nod of her head.

He'd be damned if she carried it for him. He reached down and lifted it himself, sending up a silent prayer that his very full groin would allow him to walk. "Just Drake then. Thanks for meeting me so late." He *never* had such a reaction to a woman. It had to be the fierce need of his cat.

She shrugged and turned away from him, walking down the wooden sidewalk toward the grove of cypress trees dipping long shimmery beards of moss into the water. She made no sound as she walked, a graceful, silent sway of her hips so enticing his breath caught in his throat. He was not a man given to shocking, erotic images at the sight of a woman walking, but every cell in his body went on alert and he had the mad desire to leap on her, to pin her under him and devour her. He shook his head to try to clear madness from his brain.

It was his leopard; that was the only sane answer. He'd been injured too long ago and his cat had been unable to emerge. Recently the man he chose to work for, well okay — Drake actually winced before admitting it — his *friend,* Jake Bannaconni, had arranged an operation for him, grafting the bones of his kind to his bad leg in the hopes that he could someday shift. He wasn't quite healed, and when he was tired he still walked with a limp, but his cat was growing more restless as each day passed, eager to test out the new material in his leg.

More and more the leopard fought him to surface. He had purposely asked their guide to find a bed-and-breakfast in a remote area with the idea that he might try to allow the animal side of him freedom — it was that or go insane. He pushed down the voice of his surgeon warning him to take it slow. He'd taken it so damn slow he really was losing his mind, and his poor, unknowing, *beautiful* guide was in danger of being savaged.

He was a man who automatically noticed everything and there was no way not to watch Saria walk. He felt so damned old and she looked fresh and innocent and so far out of his league it wasn't funny — but still — she wasn't wearing a wedding ring and the wildness receded even more. He breathed normally now, years of discipline taking over. The small breeze caressed the wispy ends of her sun-kissed hair and his heart stuttered.

Saria turned her head and looked at him over her shoulder, a slight frown on her face, her eyes assessing him. She slowed her pace. "Are you all right?"

He gave her a direct stare, the kind that usually scared the hell out of people. "Why wouldn't I be?" He was gruffer than he intended but she looked so damn young and innocent and he wasn't having a great deal of success controlling the images of her naked body writhing under his — and that made him feel like a lecherous old man.

"You're limpin'."

There it was again, that little accent that seeped into his skin and made his cock jerk hard. And he wasn't limping. No way. He kept his stare steady, regarding her without expression. "I don't limp." He walked with ease now, fluid and strong, and damn it all, he'd gone from a lecherous old man to a decrepit one in her eyes. Faced with the sexiest woman alive, he had obviously forgotten suave and power.

Her eyebrow raised slightly. A dimple melted into that full, tempting mouth. She gave him a small half smile. "I'm glad we got that straight because the bed-and-breakfast is a distance away. We can cut through town and a sort of Christmas tree forest and maneuver the edge of a cypress grove. That will save a few steps."

He gave her a faint grin, not admitting a thing. "The quicker we get started, the better."

The setting sun dropped a fiery shower of light just before it sank fully into the river, bathing her in red and orange flames. The silken fall of her hair beckoned him, impossible to resist. He reached out and tucked a stray strand behind her ear, his heart pounding. He felt a rush of heat pour through his bloodstream. Blood roared in his ears, thundered in his head.

She was potent, no doubt about it. She went completely still when he touched her, but she didn't bat his hand away as she had every right to do. Her eyes went liquid and she blinked, locking her gaze with his. She looked untamed, unattainable, and everything male in him responded to that challenge. He felt the ripple of response run through his heavily roped muscles, felt the strength and power of his body. *She* made him wholly aware of his power.

He had the ability to leap huge distances with absolute agility. He could land gracefully in either form — cat or man. He could slink like fluid water over the ground, so silent not even the leaves dared move. Like his cat, the sheer power of his muscles enabled him to move fast to control prey. Those same muscles allowed him the stealth of freeze-frame motion, holding completely still until he disappeared into his surroundings.

He was power, and in that moment, he knew she was completely aware of it. The gold flecks in her eyes grew until they ringed the darker chocolate. She didn't look away. Didn't blink. His body went into overdrive, hard and full and suddenly aggressive. The woman triggered the same reaction in the man as the elusive female of his kind had done to his leopard. He would have to revise his opinion of her. Saria Boudreaux was more than the young woman he first thought her to be — much more — and he intended to uncover every secret she had.

Saria shivered as she stared into Drake Donovan's unusual piercing eyes. His steady, direct stare was disturbing. She had the feeling he could see right through her into her deepest thoughts. She blushed at the idea, thankful darkness was falling fast. Drake Donovan was an unusual man. He had stood so still that, although outlined by the river, she had barely managed to see him — and she had unusually good night vision. He seemed to have a trick of disappearing into the background around him.

It didn't make sense that he could fade into his surroundings so easily. He was an impressive if not striking man. His shoulders were wide, his chest thick and muscular. He had the strongest arms of any man she'd met. Ropes of muscle rippled enticingly every time he took a step. He had a wealth of thick blond hair and a face that was carved in strong lines. The moment she laid eyes on him, her heart beat too fast and a million butterflies took wing in her stomach. Even now she felt jittery.

She was used to being around men, even being alone with them. She worked the bar, sometimes alone, and she'd never before felt so aware of herself as a woman. She could barely breathe. The heat of the evening seemed just a little worse. She could feel sweat trickling down the valley between her breasts and it was a struggle to keep her breathing even. Every breath she took just brought his wild, unusual scent deeper into her body. She had never been so utterly, acutely aware of a man in her life.

He was so silent when he walked she couldn't stop herself from glancing over her shoulder every now and then to assure herself he was following her. He was the type of man she normally would avoid at all costs. She had seen other women around her succumb to physical attraction, or even genuine love, and all had ended the same way, doormats for demanding, needy husbands. That was *so* not going to be her.

She was not even close to his league and she wasn't stupid enough to pretend she was. He had a hard-won sophistication about him, and he carried authority as easily as he breathed. Physical attraction died fairly quickly when everyday life set in, and then where would she be? Donovan was the kind of man who ruled everything and everyone in his domain with an iron fist.

He wore his blue jeans low on his hips, and his thighs were strong twin columns. She couldn't help darting a couple of furtive glances at the impressive package in the front. Drake Donovan was perfect as eye candy, but she needed to pull herself together fast. He would eat a woman alive.

She searched a little desperately for something to say to him, feeling awkward. "Have you been here before?" She was a professional guide, for heaven's sake, yet she couldn't even make small talk.

"No."

She swore under her breath. A week with him. An entire week. The money was good, but she couldn't control her reaction to him and it was very clear he didn't want to even engage in polite conversation. She bit down hard on her lip and picked up the pace. Another quick glance over her shoulder told her he kept up with her easily.

"You seem a little young to be a guide in the swamps," Drake said.

Saria bit back her first retort. Great. Her first real hottie and he thought she was young. She kept her back to him, trying not to stiffen her shoulders. Who cared what he thought? Just because he was the hottest guy on the planet didn't mean a thing. She didn't want anything to do with him, but he could see her as a woman, not some little kid.

"I grew up here. If you aren't familiar with the swamp it can be very dangerous." She

61

couldn't help the little bite to her voice. "There aren't any landmarks out there. If you prefer another guide there are others available. You won't have any trouble gettin' anyone with the kind of money you're payin'." Like she could afford the loss of income. Pride was a terrible thing, she reminded herself, but she wasn't going to beg for the job.

"When we asked for someone who knew the swamp, plants and wildlife throughout this area, you came highly recommended by several people," Drake said. "And you did say it was possible we could extend the time if needed."

She couldn't help risking another small glimpse of him. *Mon Dieu,* he was beautiful. She could spend a lot of time with him — he was that easy on the eyes. And at least he was talking to her now. "Yes, if you let me know a few days in advance, I can arrange it." Maybe not. Every time she looked at him she lost her mind. There was something compelling about his eyes, those deep gold-green eyes framed with impossibly long lashes. He had a five-o'clock shadow that made him look even more rugged.

She made her way through the small town, avoiding getting too near the church, afraid of running into the priest. She hadn't been back to confession since she'd given him the letter, and now she didn't want to chance contact. The long streaks on her back and the bite mark on her shoulder were healing a bit, but they left enough of an ache that, along with the nightmares, she was convinced to mind her own business. She didn't want Father Gallagher asking her any questions. She'd managed to avoid her brothers, and now, by taking this job, she'd be out in the swamp for at least another week.

"You married?" Drake's voice was very casual.

Her heart jumped. "No."

"I didn't think so. No man in his right mind would let someone like you take strangers out alone into the swamp."

She touched the knife at her belt. "I can take care of myself." *Why had he asked?* She'd seen the way his gaze drifted over her, taking in *everything.* He couldn't have failed to note her lack of a wedding ring. Still, maybe some women didn't wear their ring. She let her breath out. Maybe under that expressionless face he was a little more interested in her than he let on. "Are you?" She couldn't image it. She couldn't image any woman holding his interest for long.

Silence stretched between them until she

stopped again and looked at him. He gave her a small smile that didn't quite reach his eyes. "I doubt I could find a woman who would put up with me."

Her eyebrow shot up. "Are you that difficult?"

"I imagine I might be, yes," he admitted. His voice dropped an octave — became soft, seductive, an intimacy she was totally unfamiliar with. "You'll be living with me for the next week. You'll have to tell me."

Her mouth went dry. Her heart jumped and damp heat collected. His gaze locked with hers and she immediately experienced the sensation of falling into him. It was bizarre, but she couldn't look away, as if he'd managed to take her captive in some primitive manner. His stare was both charismatic and alarming. Her heart began drumming a very real warning. Everything feminine in her responded to him, yet at the same time urged her to run.

She was lost in his gaze, so she witnessed the abrupt change. The green with golden flecks suddenly went antique gold. The round pupils dilated three times wider. He moved, or did he? She didn't think she'd blinked, but his body was close to her, almost protective, shielding her from something he'd seen without so much as turning his head. Icy fingers crept down her spine. Her warning radar exploded, and this time the threat wasn't emanating from the man in front of her. Maybe it hadn't been all along, but his predatory magnetism had confused her. Whatever the reasons, she hadn't recognized her alarms for what they were.

"A man is back in the shadows just at the entrance to the trees. He's watching you." His voice was pitched very low, nearly inaudible. Had she not had such good hearing, she would have missed the whisper. "Do you know him? Look over my left shoulder." He took another step closer, bending his head toward hers as if he might kiss her.

Her breath caught in her throat. Everything in her stilled. She placed the palm of her hand on his chest, right over his soundly beating heart, but whether to push him away or to steady herself as she raised her head, she wasn't certain.

She flicked a quick glance into the tree line and her throat nearly closed. Red eyes glowed back at her. Something was there all right — *someone.* They knew she cut through the stand of trees to the docks whenever she came into town. Had they known she was picking up a customer? She couldn't tell who it was, only that human eyes didn't reflect back light in that manner. Whoever was in the forest of Christmas trees was probably her attacker.

"We don' need to cut through the grove to get to the dock. This road curves around and then goes back toward the canals. It's a little longer but . . ."

"I think a stroll through the grove is just the thing," Drake interrupted.

She shook her head. "I don' know if you've been readin' about the ghost cats people think they've been spottin' in the swamps, but sometimes those things are more real than we want them to be. I'd just feel safer if we stayed in town."

"Look at me." He kept his voice low, and she swore the tone was almost a purr it was so soft and alluring, but he'd definitely given an order.

Beneath her skin, she felt an itch. If she'd been a cat she would have sworn he'd ruffled her fur the wrong way, but before she could stop herself, her gaze jumped to his. Instantly she was caught by that commanding, focused stare. His eyes were gorgeous, frightening and sexy all at once.

"You're safe with me."

His tone was just too intimate, too certain — so certain that when she stared into his eyes, in spite of her brain telling her to be logical, she believed him — and how dumb was that when she knew there was a leopard stalking and killing people? Drake Donovan might be a powerful man in his world, and clearly everything about him shouted he could handle himself — but not with a killing machine like a shifter. Cunning and intelligent, the shifter used both man and beast to bring down prey.

She swallowed hard, unable to escape those piercing eyes. He'd locked in on her and there was no fleeing. It occurred to her suddenly that he was telling her something altogether different than she'd imagined. She frowned, but he was already turning her gently but firmly back in the direction of the grove. Reluctantly she took a few steps, confused by Drake, confused by her reaction to him.

She scowled. Drake Donovan threw her off balance. She glanced into the deeper shadows. Nothing moved. No eyes stared back. Whoever had been there had shifted position. Still, she was uneasy and that wasn't a good sign. She dropped her hand very casually to the knife at her waist, unsnapping the safety flap with one thumb.

"We're fine," Drake said softly. "A man at ten o'clock and two more trailing after us."

Her scowl deepened. *She* was the guide. It was up to her to protect him in the swamp. This was *her* home turf and she should have spotted the others far before Drake became aware of them. He was messing up her warning system. She had the uncomfortable feeling he was setting off the alarms and she couldn't see beyond him. So why would she feel safe with him?

She flicked her gaze to the position he'd given her. Walking along the path merging with theirs was Amos Jeanmard. She glanced behind her and identified the Lanoux twins, Robert and Dion, one rarely seen without the other. They'd gone to school with her brother, Mahieu, but often dropped by the bar late at night to say hello. She suspected Robert flirted with her for fun, but that Dion was quite serious. From the look on his face, he wasn't happy seeing her with Drake.

She came from a society of people who were friendly but very private. The adults had long ago tried to point out to her father that she was a wild child, but when he hadn't responded, they all seemed to think they needed to keep an eye on her, from a distance of course.

"They're neighbors," she announced, relaxing a little. If a killer lurked in the

68

grove, he wouldn't show himself with so many grouped together. Once she got her charge settled into the bed-and-breakfast, she'd go back to the house and add to her supply of weapons. She wasn't going to endanger anyone, but she had to make a living.

Donovan was paying too much money and she needed it. She refused to be dependent on her brothers for income. That would give them some semblance of control over her, and now that she was grown, she wasn't about to let them have any say in her life. She flashed a smile at the Lanoux brothers. They had obviously quickened their pace to catch up.

Beside her, Drake reacted so subtly she couldn't put her finger on what he did, but the air charged with tension and he seemed at once dangerous, not at all the easygoing man he first appeared. His gaze settled on the two men and didn't waver. She *felt* the difference, felt him coiling in readiness, and suddenly she wasn't so certain anyone was safe with Donovan. His eyes glittered with menace and he very gently but firmly lifted her by the waist and put her behind him, facing the two brothers alone.

Dion and Robert were nearly as bad, splitting apart to come at Drake from either side, looking like professional fighters instead of the amiable men she knew them to be. She was fast losing control of the situation, the tension filling the air so thick it could be cut with a knife.

"These are my neighbors," she reiterated. "My *friends*." She curled her fingers around Drake's biceps as if that might hold him back. His body was warm, no, hot. She felt the ripple of muscle beneath his skin and an answering heat pulsed between her legs.

Drake hesitated, and then, to her relief, she saw him flash a brief smile. His eyes were as focused and she noticed that his body still shielded hers, but some of the tension in him eased. Not tension, she corrected herself — the Lanoux brothers generated that — but certainly Drake was coiled and ready should an attack come.

"Dion." Saria projected more friendliness than usual into her voice. "How are you? What are you doin' in town?"

"I could ask the same question of you, *cher*," Dion greeted, stopping just a short distance from them, his gaze running over Donovan, sizing him up. Apparently whatever he saw, he didn't like, because there was no friendliness whatsoever.

"I've got a guide gig." She willed Dion to understand it was lucrative and he'd better not blow it for her. "Drake, this is Dion Lanoux and his brother, Robert. They're close neighbors. Dion, Robert, this is Drake Donovan. I'm going to show him around the swamp and bayou."

"Really?" Robert's eyebrow shot up. "Why?"

"Robert!" Saria was appalled. "Mind your own business."

"You don' mind, Donovan, but I need to speak with Saria a moment," Dion said smoothly, and held out his hand to Saria.

She felt a sudden surge of power running beneath Drake's skin. Her eyes jumped to his face. He was looking at Dion, not Robert, and there was something very deadly in his expression. "Saria." His voice was very soft. "If you're afraid of them, you don't have to go with them."

He knew. She had thought she'd been so clever and careful. She'd hidden terror from her own brothers, from her neighbors, and yet this total stranger within minutes of meeting her, knew. She forced a smile, a little impressed that he was obviously willing to fight off both brothers on her behalf. "No, even though they clearly have forgotten their manners, they're friends." Maybe if she said it enough times, both sides would stop posturing and play nice.

71

Ignoring Dion's hand, she stepped around Drake, or nearly did. He shifted his weight slightly, cutting her off. His fingers just barely trailed down her arm to her wrist, settling with infinite gentleness. "You're absolutely certain, Saria? I assure you, there's no need to protect me." He gave her a faint grin.

Her heart nearly stopped and then began pounding. He was so gorgeous. And the way he touched her, feather-light — she felt it all the way to her bones. Heat rushed through her veins and she swallowed hard, trying not to give in to sheer physical attraction.

"You're wrong about that," Dion said, glaring at the sight of Drake's fingers loosely forming a bracelet around Saria's wrist.

She followed his annoyed gaze and had to fight to keep from blushing as she pulled away and very firmly stepped around Drake. "You could have used the phone, Dion," she said, "if it was so necessary to get in touch with me." She walked ahead of him, but stopped where she could keep an eye on Drake and Robert. If the twins had planned some underhanded sneak attack on her customer, she was going to let them know once and for all that she could take care of her own.

"Do your brothers know what you're doin'?" Dion hissed between clenched teeth. "That man is dangerous, Saria. You're in over your head."

She tapped her fingers on her thigh, wholly aware of Drake's interest. She was careful not to look at him. "This isn't any of your business, Dion, nor is it my brothers' business. I'm a licensed guide. In case you haven't noticed in the last few years, it's how I make my livin'."

Dion shook his head, stepping closer to her and lowering his voice another octave. "Not with this man. If he wants a guide, I'll do it for you. You have no idea what you're dealin' with."

"So tell me," she challenged. "He didn't roll over and play scared when you and your brother tried double-teaming him?" Fury burned through her. "If you know somethin' about this man, tell me now."

"I've been around men like him, Saria. You haven't. He's too still. He didn't even blink when we came up on him, and believe me, *cher,* normal men fear us."

She believed him. Robert and Dion were built strong and could fight fiercely. Others left them alone, knowing if you fought one, you'd be fighting the other.

She shrugged one shoulder. "Then I guess

73

I'll be safe out in the swamp with him."

Drake could hear the whispered conversation rather easily, as did his leopard. His cat was already far too close to the surface and once again he found himself struggling to keep the animal under control. Saria was surrounded by leopards, and if he hadn't known it before, he sure as hell knew it now: he didn't want *any* male, in *any* form near her.

The Lanoux twins, as well as the man in the shadows, whoever he'd been — and Drake couldn't tell until he managed to get over there and nose around — were certainly leopard. The older gentleman — Amos Jeanmard, she'd called him — who was watching them from the path with interest, was a leopard as well. He had stumbled into a real shifter lair where not one but several families grouped together to form a loose coalition. He hadn't known one existed outside of the rain forest.

He inhaled the scent of males in their prime, furious that another male had entered their realm. An outsider, possibly a rogue. He had no fear of them — both he and his leopard had been fighting since he was a child — but he hadn't shifted in a long while. The surgeon had been adamant that he take it slow and allow his leg to fully heal before he tried shifting again. That mattered little to his cat.

His animal raged, throwing himself at Drake, but Drake had been an alpha for many years, running teams of male leopards in the rain forest, where their primitive natures often edged out the civility of their human side. It took strength, patience and discipline to control them — all of which he had in abundance. More than anything, he had to get Saria away from the males. If he read her correctly — and he was very good at reading people — she was as independent as they came.

Ignoring the others, as well as the older man coming up behind him, he sent her a small, taunting smile. "If your man objects to you showing me around, Ms. Boudreaux, perhaps you could recommend another guide."

Saria turned, color creeping up her neck. He found it charming, even alluring, and he felt a bit guilty for manipulating her as color swept into her face.

Her eyes glittered, more amber than brown. "Monsieur Lanoux is *not* my man. *I'm* your guide, Mr. Donovan, and no one is takin' the job from me."

She pushed past Dion, stalking toward him, her shoulders stiff with outrage. She

75

actually shoved against Robert as she passed him, her shoulder hitting his. She was a little thing, but solid, and she had surprised, even shocked, the male. She rocked him, Drake saw with satisfaction. His grin widened, and he allowed admiration to flair for a moment in his eyes. He loved her accent and he noted it got stronger when she was angry, something well worth remembering.

Saria picked up his bag and pointed the way into the grove with it. At the same time, she glared at the brothers. "I'm quite capable of keeping us safe in the swamp."

"Your brothers . . ." Dion began.

"Mind their own business, as you should," she snapped back. "Good evening, Mr. Jeanmard," she greeted the older man as she continued walking down the winding path into the trees.

She was magnificent. Drake found himself smiling even as he recognized the newcomer was definitely leopard. He followed Saria, resisting the cat's desire to roar his triumph to the other males. *Sometimes, my friend, using brains is far better than brawn,* he soothed his cat. *We're close now. It will be soon.* The swamp called to the wildness bred into his bones.

"What was that back there?" he asked, knowing she would wonder if he didn't.

"Are they upset because you got the work instead of them?"

"I take customers into the swamp all the time," she said. "I don' know what got into them. They aren't related to me and we don't date, so don' worry about it."

Drake glanced to his right without turning his head. Dion Lanoux paced beside them several yards away, winding in and out of the thicker stand of trees. To his left, Robert Lanoux did the same thing. There was no doubt their cats had scented his. This was going to be one very interesting investigation. More than anything else, he needed to find out just how big the lair was, how many members, and if one of them had become a serial killer. He glanced at the woman leading the way through the grove. She walked with confidence, but she was nervous. Twice her hand brushed the hilt of the knife and she sent several surreptitious glances into the surrounding trees.

"I don't want to make trouble for you," he said.

She sent him a quick glance over her shoulder. Yeah. She knew the Lanoux brothers were in the grove pacing along beside them and she didn't like it one bit. She *had* to be the female his cat had reacted to. It made sense. *He* was reacting to the woman.

The men were edgy with a stranger in their midst. That might be natural, but to actually challenge one wasn't — unless a female was close to the emerging.

The Han Vol Dan, the period of time when a female shifter's leopard as well as the woman were both ready to mate at the same time, was the most dangerous time for all shifters. The male cats became edgy and restless, combative and difficult to control. Drake studied Saria. There was no sign of a cat now, nothing that gave away that a female leopard could be hiding beneath all that glorious skin.

It took him a good few minutes before he realized everything in him, every cell, every muscle, everything he was, reached for her. Saria Boudreaux belonged to him, and he was going to have to steal her right out from under the noses of every single male in what looked as if it could be a considerable lair. And he had to do it right in the middle of a murder investigation. No small task, but there was no question he was looking forward to it.

"What?" Saria glanced at him over her shoulder again.

He was grinning, he couldn't help himself. It felt damned good to be alive.

"Nothing. Just enjoying the evening —

and the company. You live in a beautiful place, Saria."

She sent him a faint, pleased smile. "It is, isn't it? Not many people appreciate it."

He followed her contentedly, and with the danger pacing close and the night closing in, he felt right at home.

3

Saria and Drake were being followed right out into the swamp, and their trackers weren't being subtle about it. His cat, always lethal, stretched languidly, claws out, ready for battle — even eager for it. For a few moments, Drake could only stand very still and fight the internal battle for supremacy. His cat became agitated as it scented the males racing along the banks beside him. The leopard went from mildly irritated to furious feline in a matter of minutes.

Drake turned his face up to the sky. The clouds rolled overhead, a turbulent blend of heat and moisture, threatening to break open. The weather suited his mood, stormy and unpredictable. He couldn't allow his leopard to emerge, not there on the boat with Saria so close to danger. Not with male leopards prowling the water's edge looking for a fight with him. He forced down the need to shift, using every bit of discipline and control he'd learned over the years to restrain his angry cat.

The ache in his jaw receded, but his bones hurt, particularly his injured leg. He shifted his weight to ease the burden on it while he drew in several deep breaths to chase away the mad desire to shift. He pushed the leopard back even more. His knuckles were on fire and the ends of his fingers throbbed. A soft growl escaped and he sensed Saria stiffen and throw him a look. He pretended great interest in his surroundings.

The boat skimmed over the soft green carpet of duckweed, taking him deeper into the misty swamp. Leaves had begun to fall away, making branches reach low over the dark waters, like large bony fingers ready to drag the unwary into the alligator-infested canals and bayous. They passed grass prairies as the moon rose, throwing a silvery glow across the dark waters. Cypress and willows hung over the banks. Tupelo gums rose up through the tangled vines and vegetation on the swamp floor. Egrets preened their white plumage, looking like no more than stick shadows against the dark sky.

Towering thunder clouds promised more rain, turning the sky even grayer. He used his cat's vision to pierce the veil, spotting a nutria watching them pass. An otter sat on a log, but his attention was centered in the grove of cypress trees on the edge of the swamp. It didn't surprise Drake when a large buck leapt off the bank and raced for safety, startled, no doubt, by the leopards following the progress of Saria's boat.

Drake looked for landmarks, but there were none. "You seem to know your way around, yet there's little to tell you which direction to go."

"You don' ever want to come back here without a guide," she cautioned. "I'm not just sayin' that to you so I can work. Most of these areas are leased and they'll shoot to protect their lands. They earn their livin's out here by trappin', huntin' and fishin'. It's a hard, satisfyin' life, but we get poachers and a few others that have business they don't want anyone to know about. That threatens our way of life."

"I hear you," he said to appease her. He could see she was genuinely worried — and ordinarily she had reason to be. But he was leopard and he could find his way anywhere — even in her swamp. He had supreme confidence in himself.

As if reading his thoughts, she continued with her warnings. "A lot of the land is spongy, and one misstep and you'd fall through."

He spotted a large cat moving fast through the trees near the bank and hid his smile. Leopards had an instinct about foot placement. They could swim and they were good arboreal travelers as well. He could maneuver the swamp as well as any native.

The landscape was beautiful. The trees, half submerged in water, rose up bare, twisted, bony and gnarled, the branches stretching up and out with great sheets of moss cloaking them. He kept his eyes on the leopard. Shifters could sustain speed and travel much longer periods of time than a large cat could, but still, not miles and miles, not in that form. Sure enough, one cat skidded to a halt and another who'd been waiting took up the chase. The word was out and the lair was calling in its defenders.

He had to turn away to hide his grin. They should have just asked Saria where she was taking him and saved them all so much trouble. Still, they would have followed to ensure the safety of the female. He would have. In any case, he was going to have company tonight. They knew exactly what he was, they would have scented the leopard in him and the fact that he wasn't intimidated wouldn't sit well with them, not with a female involved.

He glanced at his watch. He had a satellite link-up with Jake Bannaconni soon. He'd cut it close, catching the last barge, but he'd stopped off just to make one last trip to the surgeon. He was going to shift as soon as he had an opportunity. His leopard had been patient enough. Both of them were withering without being able to be true to their wild nature.

Mist gathered, moving in slowly through the stick-figure trees, thickening into a heavy veil of gray. Sounds changed the deeper they penetrated the swamp. He caught a glimpse of a hunter's camp, a small snug building used while fishing and trapping. The cabin represented a vanishing way of life, men living off the land, independent and fiercely proud. Families still tight-knit, hardworking people who supported each other to survive.

He looked from the cabin to Saria's face as she stood, one hand resting lightly on the helm. Her hair blew around her face, yet there was an elegant, regal quality to her in her simple blue jeans and face scrubbed clean of makeup. She embodied the spirit of nature to him. Strong yet fragile. Independent and still vulnerable. Elusive and so tempting. Her lips were slightly parted, her eyes shining. The wind put color in her cheeks. She glanced at him and laughed, clearly enjoying the ride over the water. The sound carried on the wind and became part of the rhythm of the swamp for him.

His body reacted immediately, hardening on the outside, melting soft on the inside. He'd never quite experienced the sensation of need before — and need was definitely part of what he was feeling. She moved him. The stillness of her. The simplicity and complexity of her. Saria's laughter was pure magic, wrapping him up in her spell.

"Are you from a large family?" He'd overheard the remark about her brothers, plural, so she had more than one.

"Yes and no."

She gave a casual shrug, maybe too casual. He went instantly on the alert. Her gaze had touched his and jumped away. She stared out over the water. She hadn't changed her stance, but he felt her withdrawal into herself. She wasn't thrilled talking family. Was it the natural reticence of their kind, or something more sinister?

"I've got five brothers but I'm eight years younger than my next siblin'. My mom died a couple of years after I was born, and before I really had a chance to know any of them, they were all workin' away from home. They sent money of course, but I wasn't really raised with them, so in some ways I'm an only child."

"That must have been lonely."

She frowned, shaking her head. "Sometimes, when they were home and would talk together, not really noticin' I was around, I felt left out, but for the most part, I had a great childhood." She sent him a grin. "I just did whatever I wanted."

He fell halfway in love with her for that grin of sheer camaraderie, as if she expected him to fully understand her way of life. He couldn't help but send her an answering smile. She was beautiful, giving him that little insight to who she was and what she needed. He tucked the information somewhere into his soul where he could never lose it. After walking through life these last couple of years feeling as though he were dead inside, she'd certainly awakened him with a vengeance.

He saw her head snap around and she stiffened, looking into the swamplands to their left. He looked carefully to the right in case she glanced at him. Yeah. He knew. There were two of them running together. He was definitely outnumbered, and if they came at him en masse, which was proving to be likely, someone was going to get hurt.

Drake risked a quick glance at her face. She'd gone pale. Her mouth set in a firm line and her shoulders straightened. He followed her gaze to the trunk in front of her. He'd bet his last dollar she had guns in that trunk. So his little guide was prepared to defend him. Warmth poured into him.

"Hang on." She sounded grim.

He took the hint and grabbed for safety. The boat turned abruptly, skimming through the thick carpet of duckweed into another canal. Reeds divided the narrow lane of water, taking them away from the swamp where the large cats, in a relay, had followed. A roar of fury sent birds screeching into the air — a male leopard venting.

His eyes met Saria's. "What the hell was that?" Surely the question had to be asked.

"There are bad things in the swamp," she explained. "Don' worry. I know my way around."

"I can see that. I'm not worried, Saria. I'm quite capable of taking care of myself — and you — if there's need," he assured. "And I hired you as a guide, not to put yourself in danger. If we get into trouble out here, I want you to cut and run."

She made some sort of sound that ended in a cough. He was fairly certain she'd hissed the word "bullshit" under her breath, but she covered the slip nicely. "Now, *cher*," she soothed. "I wouldn' have much business if I left my customers in the swamp to be eaten by gators, would I?" She sounded as if he wasn't quite bright.

"I see your point," he said, and couldn't help laughing.

She laughed with him. "I'm glad we're in agreement. The last three I left for alligator bait turned me in to the Better Business Bureau. Some trivial matter like losin' a leg or arm, nothin' big, you understand?"

"Imagine turning you in for a little thing like that."

The boat swerved again and they skimmed through a thin point in the weeds, taking them back across to the main channel. Without warning the water changed to a glossy dark blue. They were in open water and the lake was beautiful at night.

She pointed to a small, inviting cove. "See that little beach there? People swim there all the time. One of the biggest gators I've ever seen uses that area all the time to sun himself. His territory is just to the left. They're crazy to bring their kids here."

"Has anyone tried to trap him?"

"Trap him?" she echoed. "We don' relocate gators, Drake. We live off them, but yeah, we've all tried to get him. He's smart.

He takes the bait, bends the hooks, steals the bait and leaves us all lookin' foolish." There was respect in her voice.

A bluish gray settled around the trunks of the trees lining the shore, the muted color a cloak of mystery. It was difficult for anything to penetrate too far behind that thick veil. He studied the terrain as the boat swept around a curve and stands of cypress gave way to oak and pine. The trees sheltered a long, Victorian-era inspired chateau. Pale blue trimmed in white, the house blended with the gray-blue fog pouring in from the bayou. The wraparound porch was inviting and the balconies on the second story were large, enticing any visitor to sit and watch the water flowing over the rocks. Hammocks were slung in the trees a few feet from the water's edge in the cool of the shade trees. He could hear bullfrogs and crickets calling in invitation.

Saria beamed at him. "Isn't it a jewel? Miss Pauline Lafont runs the inn now. It was her grandmother's home first. Her mother turned it into a bed-and-breakfast and Miss Pauline has made a lot of improvements."

"It's everything you said it was," Drake agreed. Mostly the house had privacy. The place was old-style elegance, an era long gone. Quiet, hidden, an inviting jewel, just as Saria had promised when he'd contacted her through her guide advertisement. "Perfect," he added with satisfaction.

He hadn't yet told Saria he'd rented the entire bed-and-breakfast for two weeks with the intention of bringing his team in the moment he found anything. And he knew he was going to find something. He'd stumbled onto a shifter's lair right there in the middle of the Louisiana swamp. They were every bit as elusive and secretive as the shifters in the rain forests throughout the world — but it all made sense now.

Drake waited patiently as he was introduced to the woman whose family had owned the beautiful Victorian-style home for a hundred years. Pauline Lafont was a small woman with laugh lines around her eyes and a ready smile. He liked her instantly.

"Would you like the grand tour?" she asked graciously.

"I'd love it, ma'am," he said, meaning it. "The house is amazing." It was essential that he knew the layout of the house. Every nook and cranny, every hiding place, where Pauline Lafont slept and lived when she was not interacting with her guests.

"I'll leave you in Miss Pauline's hands,"

Saria said. "But I'll be back at dawn to pick you up."

He was reluctant to allow her out of his sight. If the leader of the leopard's lair knew she was close to the emerging of her leopard, he might not let her anywhere near Drake. "Can you just stay here so we can get an early start? It might be easier. In any case I'll want to go into the swamp at night."

"I've already arranged with Miss Pauline to stay," Saria admitted, "but I need a few more things from home. I'll be here before first light if I can't make it back tonight."

He couldn't kidnap her, as much as he wanted to. Instead, he locked his gaze with hers, knowing his eyes had gone pure cat, mesmerizing, holding her to him through sheer willpower. She had to have read the hunger in him, the urgent need, he couldn't suppress it, even when he told himself she needed — even deserved — a courtship. Even a male leopard courted his mate carefully. Bands of color widened, and heat leapt between them.

Pauline cleared her throat. Saria blinked rapidly and looked away. There was color in her cheeks.

"Miss Pauline," she said, not risking another glance at Drake. "I'll be back as soon as possible." Saria turned away from

91

them, keeping her head down to avoid looking at Drake.

"Saria," he said softly, unable to just let
her go.

She stopped, but didn't turn her head.

"Be careful. And come back to me." He
said it deliberately, using a velvet purr mixed
with a steely command.

"I will." Her voice was barely above a
whisper. He felt that soft sound vibrate
through his body. His fingers curled tightly
into his palms as she walked way, Pauline
trailing after her. His leopard was close —
too close. He could feel the stiletto-like
claws puncturing his palms. He breathed
the animal away.

Pauline walked Saria to the door and
stood for a minute watching her run lightly
down to the dock. "She's a smart girl that
one," she announced, obviously sensing his
interest. Pauline Lafont, he decided, was an
incurable romantic and the moment he'd
displayed his interest in Saria, she began
planning. At least someone was on his side.
"And sweet."

"Very competent in the swamp," Drake
said. "I was surprised by her. She's very well
educated, yet she chooses to stay here. I
would have thought most of the young
people would look elsewhere for employ-

ment." Saria hadn't looked back at him. He knew, because he watched her all the way to the boat. She hadn't so much as glanced over her shoulder.

Pauline nodded. "As a rule that's true, although most of us return when we're older. There's something about this place that calls us back. Saria comes from one of the seven oldest families in the area. They almost never leave the swamp even if they work away from it. Remy, her oldest brother, works as a detective in New Orleans. All of her brothers served in the military and most work on the river, but they always come home." She looked at him directly, imparting the knowledge as a warning. "She has *five* brothers."

"Big families around here," he commented, showing confidence. "Is it unusual for the children to come back to the swamp after they go to school?" Drake asked as he followed her, committing the layout of the large house to memory.

"I think most young people think there's something better for them. Certainly they want more," Pauline said. "Life in the swamp can be hard. They all get educations and move away, like I said."

"With the exception of families like Saria's?" He kept his voice casually interested.

Pauline frowned a little as she thought about it. "The seven families that live closest together seem to always come home," she admitted. "As far back as I can remember, they've done that — gone away to school and come back. The children take over their parents' businesses and lifestyle right here in the swamp. My sister, Iris, married into the Mercier family, and her children, Armande and Charisse, both went to college and returned. I never had children so my nephew and niece are very special to me — as is Saria. Charisse is extremely talented." Her voice tinged with pride. "She and her brother own the perfume shop in New Orleans together, but Charisse actually makes the perfume and sends it all over the world. The shop has become a tremendous success because of her talent. Still, they live in the Mercier family home rather than town."

"Instead of living in New Orleans itself?"

Pauline nodded. "Remy, Saria's brother, is a detective with the police force and he always stays in their family home. I was so surprised by them. Charisse in particular used to say she couldn't wait to get out of here to a city. The families are very close, but as I said, it's a difficult way of life."

"I can imagine," Drake said, infusing

admiration in his voice. He had grown up in the rain forest and understood the need to stay in the wild. The Louisiana swamp was as wild as the local leopards could find. "Seven families? Are you part of one of those families?" She wasn't leopard. He would have known. At her age, her leopard would have emerged already, but it was a way to keep her talking.

Pauline opened the door to the dining room with its gleaming floors and polished table. "Oh, no, but I've certainly known them all for years. They're very tight-knit. They participate in the get-togethers, but as a rule they stay to themselves. They're pretty isolated."

That made sense. Leopards, animal or shifter, as a rule were elusive and very secretive. Seven families would make this a large lair for such a small area.

"Which seven families?" Curiosity edged his voice, a deliberate attempt to lure her into talking more. "Names are so intriguing here."

"Let's see. Boudreaux of course. Lanoux, Jeanmard, Mercier, Mouton, Tregre, and the Pinet family. I think they all date back to the first settlers here."

Drake took the punch in his gut and breathed his way through it without showing a reaction. *Tregre?* He knew that name. He knew a woman from his own lair who had married a man with that last name. She'd come home a widow, with her son, Joshua. The same Joshua who was now employed on the Bannaconni ranch as a bodyguard to Jake's wife, Emma.

Joshua had never said a word to any of them about a connection to a family in the Louisiana area. Did he even know his father was from the Louisiana swamps? Joshua was part of the team Jake would send to back him up. Could he be trusted if he had to bring justice to his own kin?

Why had Elaina come home? He remembered her well. She'd gone to school in the States, married, and then a few years later, Joshua had been about four or five, had returned to the Borneo rain forest and her family. No one had mentioned Joshua's father. Elaina had never remarried. The web was becoming more tangled with each passing moment.

Drake climbed the stairs to his room after bidding the innkeeper goodnight and assuring her he wouldn't need to eat until early morning. The first thing he did was contact Jake Bannaconni on his satellite phone.

"We've definitely got a situation here, Jake," Drake greeted. "I have no idea how large it is yet, but there's a shifter lair here."

There was a small silence as Jake Banna-conni digested the information. "You safe?"

"For the moment. I expect a visit tonight. They know I'm here and they know I'm leopard. They aren't going to want me sniffing around their territory, and if it comes out why I'm here, I'm certain none of them are going to be welcoming."

"Have you figured out who wrote the letter to me?" Jake asked.

"Not yet, but the way it was worded, so carefully, yet implying they knew of shifters, it has to be someone in one of seven families. I've met my guide and the innkeeper, but they don't seem to have a clue about the shifters, although I can't really tell with either of them for certain. Your great-grandfather had to have known. He leased them his lands."

"Jake Fenton was a man who played his cards close to his chest," Jake said. "He was careful what he said to me, but he left me the properties and my guess was, he expected me to protect those people."

"Not if one of them has turned killer, Jake," Drake cautioned. "What did you know of Jake Fenton? Who was he?"

"He was my mother's grandfather. I asked him straight out once if he could shift and he said no. He admitted his family had deliberately tried to find women carrying the shifter genetics in order to produce a child who could shift. They were looking for a child who could find oil."

"Like you."

"Like me, but they didn't know what they had. My great-grandfather suspected I was a shifter," Jake said, "but I didn't ever admit it to him. He was the one who suggested I go to Borneo and seek out my people to learn about them."

"Did he ever suggest you come to Louisiana? Or reference this area in a conversation about shifters?" Drake prompted.

There was a small silence as Jake pulled up the memories of his talks with his great-grandfather. They had been few and far between and Jake had been young and very guarded. "I don't recall that he ever mentioned shifters in conjunction with Louisiana. He knew there was oil there. He bought the lumber companies out, not for the lumber, but for the oil," Jake explained. "I haven't spent a lot of time exploring there. In all honesty it wasn't on my list for another two years. I continued the leases. Fenton seemed to be friends with seven or eight families there and has given them the use of the land for hunting, fishing and trapping."

"Can you get me the names of the families?" Drake asked. "I can compare the names on the leases with the families I suspect are shifters. I'll bet my last dollar each family leasing the land from your great-grandfather is shifter. There seems to be a very real lair here. Sooner or later their leader will have to come out into the open. First he'll send his soldiers. Once he identifies himself, I can find out where this lair comes from."

"I don't like the sound of that, Drake."

"I've handled worse. What do you know of Joshua's family?"

There was a small silence. He'd managed to shock the unshockable Jake Bannaconni. "You vouched for him. That was good enough for me." There was caution in his voice.

"His last name is Tregre, one of the family names I suspect is on the lease. His mother brought him home to her family in the rain forest, so he may not even know them, but it's worrisome."

"Do you want me to question him?"

"No. I've known Joshua most of his life. He wouldn't betray us. His loyalty isn't in question, but then it might not be best for him to come here. I wouldn't want to put him in a position of choosing family over his team."

Jake swore under his breath. "He's one of the best we've got. I want to send the boys to back you up. And damn it, Joshua is family. *Our* family."

"I'm telling you, I don't doubt him. I don't want you to think he wouldn't die to protect Emma, the children or you for that matter. He's a good man. I just want to find out a little more about his father's family before I put him in a bad position. We should send word to Rio and ask him to do a little research for us." Rio Santana was the leader of a team of shifters in Borneo. They traveled around the world wherever they were needed. Drake trusted Rio implicitly.

"Maybe we should pull out of there, regroup and come back in force," Jake suggested.

Drake cleared his throat. "I can handle it, Jake. There's no need unless one of the leopards here has been killing innocents."

"What aren't you telling me, Drake?"

Drake cursed under his breath. There was no getting anything past Jake. The man was as shrewd as they came. "There's a female close to the Han Vol Dan. I caught her scent and my cat went crazy."

"And?" Jake prompted.

"So did I." That said it all. Everything. A warning. A challenge.

Jake went silent. Drake refused to be drawn in. He stayed utterly still, staring out over the water. Darkness had long since settled. Bullfrogs called back and forth. Crickets sang insistently. The heat in his veins crackled with the same power as the veins of lightning lining the black clouds tumbling in the sky.

"Drake, if you're dead, she isn't going to do you any good."

"I won't be the one dead."

"If these people are her family and try to protect her, she isn't going to be thrilled with you killing them," Jake cautioned.

Drake found himself smiling, and some of the tension eased in his gut. He had come from the Borneo rain forest in order to teach Jake the way of the shifter — and keep him calm and under control. It took a great amount of discipline and power to keep a male leopard under control, and Drake was renowned for his control, holding together teams of shifters in tense situations, yet his own student was now cautioning him.

"I guess she won't be," Drake admitted.

"I'll call you when I've checked out the body."

"The boys are on standby, Drake. Use them if you need them. And let me know if I can send Joshua. In the meantime, I'll contact Rio."

"Give my love to Emma."

Drake hung up the phone as he studied the layout of the grounds below the balcony. He had to know how the shifters would come at him and he had to be prepared. He didn't have a lot of time for recon. Saria had left him an hour ago, heading back to her home. He was reluctant to let her go, but there was no reason he could give to keep her there, and it was just as well that she wasn't in the middle of whatever battle was coming. He didn't want her to be afraid of him.

He took a breath and leapt over the balcony to the ground below. Landing in a crouch, his legs acted like springs, absorbing the shock. It was the first time he'd really tested his leg to see if it would hold up to the rigorous needs of a shifter. As tests went, the drop was a fairly good one, as he'd been on the second story. He landed a little harder than usual, which didn't surprise him, as he was out of practice, but the surge of wildness rising like a tidal wave did.

Beneath his skin, fur rippled and itched. His jaw ached with the need to accommodate the change. He wasn't going to be able to wait. His cat needed — and so did he. Elation swept through him. He didn't want to be cautious or patient. He wanted the absolute freedom his leopard provided. No, he *needed* the freedom to let his real nature out, that savage, primal nature that was more instinct than reason. He had been forced to suppress it for too long, and his entire body ached with urgency. Bones hurt. Muscles throbbed.

He dragged his shirt over his head and hastily bent to remove his shoes. Already his knuckles bent and the tips of his fingers burned as the skeleton designed for maximum flexibility lying dormant along his human frame stretched in anticipation. He clawed his shoes off and reached to peel back his jeans, shrugging out of them fast as the heat took him. Bones cracked. Muscles contorted. The wrenching, painful experience felt wonderful, a release, that first overwhelming flush of freedom.

Pain stabbed through his leg, robbing him of breath, but even that was welcome as he felt the bone shifting, reshaping, finally complying with his leopard's demand. His heart stuttered and deep inside he felt claws unsheathe, felt his feral nature leap to the forefront. He leapt toward it, embracing that side of him, grateful he was alone with no young males to keep in line. This first emergence after so long deserved to be untamed, uncontrollable, a rough, fierce — even violent shifting of pure foolishness.

He went to the ground, to all fours, letting the pain and beauty of the change take him. Roped muscles slid over his entire frame, his muzzle extended, mouth filling with teeth. Strong muscles and sinew formed over bones in a loose, supple, very pliable structure, giving him his graceful, feline sinuous movement. Fire pierced his leg, ran from hip to paw, flames licking over his bones, as they shrieked and protested that reforming, but he gloried in the ability, no matter what the cost to him. His fur went damp and dark as his body shuddered, trying to overcome the twisting of that last bone.

At last he stood, fully formed, a large, heavily muscled leopard, shaking itself, feeling every individual muscle, savoring the moment as it slowly absorbed the fact that after more than two years of not being able to shift — of believing it would never happen again — he had done it. He was large for a leopard — most shifters were quite a lot larger than their wholly animal counter-parts — but he weighed in close to two hundred pounds of solid muscle. Even for his kind, that was a large leopard.

Each leopard had a unique spotted coat, a beautiful blend of golden fur splashed liber-ally with dark rosettes so that when they remained stationary, the pattern created an optical illusion of moving spots. Thick, but loose, the coat provided ample protection in a ferocious fight. Drake was a vicious, skilled fighter, very experienced, and bore the scars to prove it. He was abnormally strong in a world of shifters who had enor-mous strength.

Deep inside where Drake really lived, at the very heart of him, was a smoldering fire the others caught glimpses of through his blazing green eyes. His piercing intelligence always shone there, revealing the cunning, shrewd mind. His leopard wanted to run, to hunt, to find his mate. The fierce need shook him, as the animal leapt free now, the scent of other males uppermost in his mind while the black fury of a male in his prime seeking his mate raged in his heart.

Drake allowed the leopard to run for a short time, stretching his legs, feeling the sheer freedom of the animal form, but he controlled where the beast was going, refusing to allow him to track after Saria. Before all else, he had to establish his territory, mark it well and often, claiming the land around the inn, so he had a legitimate claim should any male challenge him. That would happen. They would send their fiercest fighter. He would have to fight and take care not to kill his opponent in the heat of battle — just in case the challenger was someone related to Saria. His leopard understood and immediately set about claiming every square inch of land they went through.

He took his time, although he did feel a sense of urgency, but he was determined to make his claim on as much territory as thoroughly as possible. He raked trees, he scent-marked, he rolled in an ever-widening circle, covering all of the land surrounding the inn to the water's edge. There was no evidence of any other leopard and he hadn't expected it. Each of the families claimed their leased lands if they followed true to the shifter way of life. They would edge one another's territories and even share a corner or two, but they would avoid contact within those territories.

He pushed his claim into the surrounding swamp, taking note of the terrain. His leopard stored every smell, each shape of every branch. He climbed trees and left his scent along the twisted limbs, testing each for strength and also hiding places. He had come to find a killer and now everything had changed. He was here to claim a mate. Courtship with a female leopard was dicey at best. Like the cat, the human counterpart could be moody, temperamental and wildly seductive. Add in a killer and an entire lair of male leopards and he was in for a rough ride — just what his cat needed.

The leopard explored deeper and deeper into the swamp, penetrating into the interior and marking a larger and larger territory. He knew when the first wave of defenders came, his claim would enrage them. These shifters may not have been born in the rain forest, but the rules and instincts would be close if not the same.

He circled back toward the inn, committing every square inch of new territory to memory, burning the map of the swamp into his mind. His leopard's radar let him know where every creature was far before he encountered it. The animal instincts guided him over treacherous ground, easily finding solid land to maneuver. His ultimate goal was to claim Fenton's Marsh. No other leopard should have set foot on the property, but according to the mysterious letter, that was where the leopard was making its kills.

He made his way back to the inn where he leapt into the trees, using the branches as an arboreal highway from one tree to another until he was beside the two-story structure. His balcony presented a tricky jump, but he made it — which meant other leopards could do so as well. Reluctant to shift back into his human form, Drake paced across the balcony for several minutes before leaping to the roof. Again, it was a difficult maneuver, but he had to know how the other leopards might come at him.

Satisfied he'd done all he could as a leopard, he padded on cushioned paws back into his room to shift in the security of isolation. Pain streaked up his bad leg, robbing him of breath as his bones reformed with a wrenching crack. He lay on the hardwood floor for several long minutes, struggling for air, a fine sheen of sweat coating his body. When the pain ebbed a bit, he pushed himself up and tested his ability to put weight on his bad leg. He needed to be fit if he was going to fight a challenger and he couldn't be seen limping. That fact that Saria had somehow noticed bothered him. He had been so certain he was walking without favoring the injured leg. If she could tell, when he was keeping it under control, an alert leopard certainly would spot the weakness.

Drake let the cool water wash the primal heat from his skin. He had to use his brain now, think along the lines of attack his opponents would most likely use and prepare for them. The most important thing was to establish dominancy immediately to draw out their leader. Saria had complicated things immensely. A female in the throes of the Han Vol Dan had to be protected at all costs and every male in the vicinity would be edgy, moody and at times in a thrall — the most dangerous condition a male leopard could find himself in.

He walked naked through the spacious room, toweling himself off, testing his leg as he went. The fiery pain had subsided into a dull, throbbing ache. It would hold. Just to be certain, he placed weapons throughout the room and on the balcony. A knife went up under the eaves. He was a careful man and he knew leopards and their tempers. It would be best to be prepared for anything.

He dressed in a loose pair of drawstring pants, something he could easily rid himself of, and padded barefoot out to the balcony. Placing a chair close to the wall, but well back from the overhang, he sat outside and waited patiently for the company he knew would come.

4

Drake had learned many years earlier to take advantage of any downtime and get sleep. In the middle of the worst battles, when there was a lull, he often managed a little catnap. He allowed his eyes to close, but he put his cat on alert. His leopard would let him know when the enemy came.

He dreamt of her. Saria. Her soft skin. Her curves. The silk of her hair. The shape and feel of her fantasy mouth. He dreamt of taking her, a wild primitive mating that left him insatiable for her, desperate for her. Addicted to her. He stroked his hand over her slender legs and felt the inner heat of her thighs. He needed to taste her, to find her wild, exotic scent and devour her. He wanted to know every inch of her, every erotic place that made her moan and writhe beneath him, every single spot that would make her purr and tremble.

That soft junction between her neck and

shoulders called to him to claim her, to mark her. To put his personal brand on her. The need to let the others know she was taken was a living, breathing, urgent demand that would never let him rest until he'd managed to make her his. He heard the soft deep growl of warning, an insistent rumble that rose in volume, warning the other males of his kind away from what was his.

Drake's eyes snapped open, his mind clear immediately. The music of the night filled his every sense. He stretched languidly, a sinuous, feline movement, a ripple of sheer power. It had been a long time and he welcomed the coming battle, was even eager for it. The call of the wild was on him now, a thrall, an urgent need to defend what was his.

The leopards were out there, stalking silently through the fog, hoping to catch their enemy unaware. He knew they were unused to having to defend their lair or their females. They had been rulers of this territory for a long time unchallenged, unknown to outsiders. He was a shifter who had been honed in battles around the world. He fought whenever it was necessary — and sometimes when it wasn't. He was skilled, vicious, and very fast.

The territory he'd claimed had been open — and that was their mistake. They'd left him the loophole of a legitimate claim, and he was within the law defending it. By rights, they couldn't come at him en masse — they would have one fighter challenge him. He waited, stretching out muscles, testing his leg, readying himself.

His leopard waited in the silent, coiled way of their kind. He would have one moment of weakness, landing on his bad leg, but he'd tested the injury and knew it would stand up to a battle, especially a short one. He intended to dominate fast, to take control so there was no question the other would have to submit or die. He hoped his opponent chose submission. He wasn't altogether certain in his present state, with a female — *his* female so close to the Han Vol Dan — that he could control his leopard should the other refuse to submit.

A bellowing roar shook the night, the sound carrying across the lake and into the swamp. The insects went silent. The alligators and frogs ceased their calls, knowing a predator stalked the night. Drake had been waiting for that ferocious challenge. Instantly, he zeroed in on the leopard's exact location, his vision already banding into heat waves as he shed his drawstring pants, put one hand on the railing and leapt into the air.

His body contorted, a practiced shifting few could do. Fast and abrupt, Drake threw himself into his other form, embracing it, reaching for it, changing in midair so that he was fully leopard when he landed on the back of the challenging male. The wrenching sensation sent the blood singing in his veins, and made him feel truly alive. The sultry night, heavy with moisture, sank into his soul, the heat rushing through him and filling him with the joy of combat.

He dropped out of the night sky, an avenging warrior, slamming into the large leopard posturing on the rolling lawn leading to the bank of the river. He smashed into his enemy hard, the other cat grunting as the air left his lungs and his legs went out from under him. Merciless, Drake sank teeth into the back of the neck and claws deep into the sides, gluing himself to the other leopard as they rolled over and over toward the river.

Snarls filled the night as other leopards looked on, unable to aid their fallen champion. Rules held every society together and although primitive, they lived by the law of their kind and the newcomer had every right to defend his territory. Red eyes and bared wicked teeth gleamed as leopards loosely ringed the fighters.

Drake's opponent twisted desperately, using his flexible spine to bend nearly in half, frantic to get out from under those deadly teeth and the claws that raked his belly and sides, leaving deep, long furrows that would scar, if not kill. The teeth were merciless, and with every movement he made, they sank deeper in warning. It was clear he had to submit or die. There was no dislodging the huge beast from his back.

He submitted, hatred in his eyes, but with no other viable choice, he went still, allowing the stranger his victory — knowing it would be short-lived. The rogue had taken him by surprise, but the others would be more prepared. Shuddering, he lay still and waited while the newcomer held him.

Drake backed off with a warning snarl and slap of his paw to his opponent's bloody muzzle. The leopard lay on the grass, torn and bloody, trembling. He rolled and cautiously came to his feet, tail flicking, his eyes on Drake, a golden, wicked glare. Satisfaction gleamed for one brief second.

Drake leapt sideways and the leopard launching his attack missed him by a few scant inches. Drake whirled in midair, landed and pushed off hard, driving into the side of the newest attacker, knocking

115

him off his feet. He sprang, trying for a quick hold on the back of his neck, missed and sank his teeth in the ear and skull. His own leopard was furious at the second attack, making it more difficult to direct him away from a kill.

Bloodlust rose. Fury. A raging need to drive the males away from his territory or kill them to keep them away from his female. Drake's opponent had a darker muzzle and a dark stripe down the middle of his back. There were several scars indicating he'd fought battles, and Drake's leopard drove relentlessly into him, rolling him over so they bashed at each other with lethal, rending claws, snarling and growling as they boxed, standing on hind legs.

Drake drove hard, slashing at the exposed belly, and when his opponent curled up to protect himself, with lightning speed he sank his teeth into the neck. The snarls and growls of those watching faded into the background. The struggle now was to keep his leopard under control. He barely noticed the claws ripping into his flesh, or the teeth sinking into his shoulder as the leopard made a desperate attempt to free itself.

He growled and shook his opponent, blood staining his muzzle and the other's coat as he took a firmer grip on the throat.

"Submit, Dion," a voice called out. "Use your brain. He's goin' to have to fight his leopard to keep from killing you. You aren't makin' it easier. Damn it, you submit."

As if very far in the distance, Drake heard the human voice penetrating through the mindless fury, the demand to kill. He vaguely recognized the voice. The leopard beneath him shook with fury, raked at him again, sending a burn along his ribs. He growled deep in his throat, struggling to maintain a semblance of humanity when his leopard raged for a kill. It was his right. The opponent was in *his* territory. He refused to submit. Fury swept through him. He sank his teeth deeper. Using his enormous strength, he held his adversary immobile in a suffocation grip.

"Dion!" The voice rose in command and fear. "Submit now!"

The leopard beneath him suddenly went slack, the fight draining out of him, sides heaving, mouth open, eyes glazing.

"Let him go." The voice held a note of pleading.

Drake reached for calm, fought for control of his leopard. This fight had not been about territory, not with this leopard. It was the female so close to the Han Vol Dan that had triggered the fierce fight. His opponent

117

wanted him dead and his leopard knew it. The need to kill was a living, breathing entity and it took every ounce of discipline Drake had to fight his leopard back. Reason seemed just out of reach for several precious moments — moments while the other cat was without air.

"Robert, no!" A second voice rang out, sharp. Insistent. Commanding. "You pull that trigger and I'll have no choice but to kill you. Back off. He's gaining control."

"It will be too late."

"That was Dion's choice."

The voice held authority. Sorrow. The loss of a male in his prime was a blow to any lair. Drake took another firm grip and forced his leopard to back off. The cat did so reluctantly, snarling and growling every inch of the way, raking at Drake, spinning around to face the other leopards in the lair, roaring a challenge, dangerously close to a killing madness. Blood coated his sides and dripped down his flanks, matting in the thick fur, but he snarled and placed each paw carefully, watching his enemies, daring them to move.

Two men had shifted back into human form. Drake, through the red haze of madness, recognized Robert Lanoux and the older man, Amos Jeanmard. At a signal from

Jeanmard, the other leopards reluctantly faded into the shadows. The retreat helped to calm his leopard a little more, although it paced and went to ground, rose and paced again, never far from his downed opponent.

"We need to see to our kin," Jeanmard said. "Do you have control?"

It was a good question. Drake wasn't certain. He pushed harder at his leopard, fighting now for supremacy. His leopard whirled to face Robert, who had taken a step toward his fallen brother. Drake forced him back until reluctantly the leopard gave ground, one slow inch at a time. He summoned enough restraint to swing the leopard's head toward the leader of the Louisiana lair and nod.

Jeanmard gave a small, formal bow, more an incline of his head than anything else. "*Merci,* my lair to yours. Go to your brother now, Robert, it is safe to see to his injuries."

Without hesitation, Robert rushed to Dion's side.

Drake's snarling leopard backed off further, allowing the older man to approach the fallen leopard as well. The two humans crouched beside the bloody, mangled cat, leaving themselves open to attack by the furious leopard. Drake exerted more control, slowly backing away, although watching carefully, not quite as trusting as the two men. Their friends had to be close or they wouldn't risk their lives so easily.

Robert had a gun, a violation of their code. Had he been in the rain forest the repercussions of bringing a human weapon to a righteous leopard fight would have been severe. Drake had no way of knowing what Jeanmard would do to the man. It was a black mark against the entire lair, and Jeanmard in particular. A leader was expected to keep his leopards in line, and Robert had made him lose face. Had a member of Drake's team done such a thing, the retaliation would have been swift and brutal and public. When dealing with leading alpha males, sometimes the need for complete ruthlessness was absolute. In any case, Robert Lanoux didn't fight fair or with honor, something Drake would file away.

Drake, snarling and growling every step, backed away, facing toward the cypress grove where he knew other male leopards had retreated to the edge of the water to respect his territory yet protect their leader. Drake saw the clothes he'd left behind from his earlier run, shredded into small strips of cloth. They'd ripped the shirt and jeans completely apart and the shoes hadn't fared much better.

In a fury, the leopard slammed a massive paw across the torn clothing, sending strips of cloth into the air before gathering himself to make the leap into the branch of the tree nearest the house. He gained his balcony and padded inside before going to his belly and slinking back through the open doors to watch and listen, alert to any danger.

The leopards shifted into men and hurried out of the trees to aid Jeanmard and Lanoux recover their fallen kin. Dion was lifted up and rushed to a waiting boat. Drake waited a long time after the sounds of the boat retreating in the distance faded, holding himself still. He listened for the whisper of fur against trees, which would tell him he was being hunted. The crickets resumed their symphony. Frogs took up the chorus, calling back and forth. He heard the sound of the slide of an alligator slipping into the water.

Pain hit him then, and he didn't wait, didn't hesitate, shifting before he could think too much about the cost of the battle on his human body. He found himself on the floor, suppressing a moan. Fire burned over his belly and ribs. His bad leg screamed in protest and there were scores of bite and claw marks over his body. He lay there staring up at the night sky, just as the clouds burst and rain poured over him, washing some of the wildness out of him.

His heart beat too fast, and adrenaline poured through his body like the rush of a fireball. He breathed deep to clear his head, to get past the need for violence. A leopard was a perfect killing machine, and blending the cunning and temperament of a leopard with the intelligence of a human, his kind was extremely dangerous under the best of circumstances. He had barely managed to contain his savage beast, but he hadn't killed — at least he didn't think so.

With a groan he rolled over and pushed up onto his hands and knees, trying to ignore the screaming in his leg. His stomach lurched. He managed to make it to his feet, dizzy and weak. He'd lost more blood than he'd thought. Staggering, he made it back into the room, leaving bloody footprints on the mosaic tiles for the rain to wash away. The hardwood floor in the bedroom wasn't so lucky; the smears remained as he made his way through to the bathroom.

The hot water stung, yet felt good as it poured over him. He stood on shaky legs while the water cleansed away the last of the wildness. He sent up a small prayer that he hadn't killed Dion. The laws of his world dictated and he was within his rights, but intellectually, he knew Dion was simply trying to protect his world from a rogue — as Drake himself might have done.

He might feel regret about Dion if the man didn't make it, but Dion knew the rules of combat and he'd chosen not to submit until it was nearly too late. All of them knew how difficult it was to control one's leopard during a challenge. Coupled with a female nearing the emergence, he could hardly be blamed.

In spite of every injury, Drake rejoiced that his body had held up, he'd shifted in midair and he'd been damn fast about it. As a first time back after trying out his leg only once, his ability pleased him. He'd kept in shape, working out strenuously after he'd had plates and pins in his leg and couldn't shift. He'd been determined to stay in fighting shape, although he hadn't believed he'd ever have the chance to allow his leopard freedom. Jake and his surgeon had brought about a miracle. He'd ended the first battle almost before it had begun through sheer surprise.

Drake carefully assessed every aspect of his fighting technique. He'd been fast, but not fast enough. He needed more time for his leopard to run, to once again feel the strength and power in its body. He had experience on the members of the Louisiana lair, but the lair had numbers and if he'd had to fight them all, even one at a time, he would have been in trouble. Dion had scored some heavy gouges and he'd lost blood. Loss of blood meant weakness.

Toweling off carefully, he examined every wound. Cats could leave venom behind and infection resulted quickly. That meant the hated burn of the iodine. He poured it liberally into his wounds, breaking out in a sweat as he did so. Cursing with every stitch, he sewed up the three worst wounds, steri-stitched the others before putting an antibacterial ointment on each and covering them with gauze. All in all, he wasn't in too bad shape. He had no doubt that in the morning he'd feel every bruise, but right now, only sleep mattered.

He scrubbed away the evidence of blood, carefully locked up his room and laid down gingerly on his bed. Smiling, fingers linked behind his head, he drifted somewhere between awake and asleep. At once Saria was there, a smile curving her soft mouth, her eyes bright with mischief. He reached for her, wanting to draw her down onto the bed with him. His heart pounded and he tasted desire in his mouth and he groaned with need of her.

A single sound escaped. Penetrated his layer of sleep. Not her answering moan, not even a whimper of desire, but a soft whisper of movement. His eyes snapped open and he lay silent, with the taste of her in his mouth and his cat roaring. Something moved out on the lawn. He eased to his feet, conscious that other leopards heard as well as he did. Very carefully, he padded to the French doors on his balcony and opened them enough to allow his body to slip through.

Below him, the yard was mostly shadows, but with his night vision, he could easily make out Pauline Lafont moving around the yard in her bathrobe. She held a shotgun in one hand and a large trash bag in the other. She meticulously picked up every scrap of cloth from Drake's shredded clothes as well as his shoes and socks. She took her time, making certain to remove every tiny string and thread.

He stayed motionless, knowing she couldn't see him. She wasn't leopard, he knew that, he would have scented her leopard. She'd been forthcoming with information about the seven families that leased lands in the swamp and he hadn't scented one lie, but clearly, she was aware of the leopard fight. She must have heard the horrendous noise. Leopards in a fury weren't quiet about their rage. She had a shotgun for protection, but she didn't seem too frightened. A woman alone out in the middle of nowhere, far from help, with leopards fighting on her front lawn should have been terrified. Yet Pauline Lafont walked slowly around her property, meticulously removing all evidence of the battle.

She had to know about the shifters. Her family had lived in the area for a hundred years and obviously had lived beside the shifter families. They'd intermingled. She'd said her sister had married into one of the families — the Merciers. Was it possible her brother-in-law or a nephew had been present and she was destroying the evidence to cover up for them? It made sense. Family was family and no doubt they'd been protecting their own for hundreds of years — just as the lairs in the rain forest did.

Pauline shined her flashlight down in the trees where the fight had taken place. Two alligators, no doubt drawn by the scent of blood, slithered back into the water as the light hit them. She studied the splashes of blood before going back up to the house and retrieving a long hose. Again, she took her time, the shotgun in her fist as she sprayed down the areas where the battle had taken place. She was very thorough about it, obviously determined to remove all traces.

She methodically wound up the hose, picked up the garbage sack containing Drake's clothes before she took one last look around, nodded her head in satisfaction and went back into the house. Drake nearly turned away to go back inside, but he caught movement out of the corner of his eye. Someone else had been observing Pauline. The shadowy figure was in the trees and the wind was blowing away from Drake so he couldn't pick up a scent. His cat raised no alarm either, but there was no doubt something — someone — was in the tree just down at the water's edge, closest to the dock.

Drake eased his muscles into a slow, loose stretch. Every wound pulled, reminding him stitches didn't work well if he had to shift again. He kept his gaze riveted to the branch that had barely moved. It had gone quiet again. An alligator bellowed somewhere across the lake. The reeds shimmered like a wave. The leaves in the tree did the same. Whoever it was, he moved with the wind, inching his way down the tree to the ground.

The shadowy figure was smaller than he expected, crouching low, holding a rifle in one hand and a small case in the other. He reached under the balcony railing for the gun he'd taped there earlier. He was betting he was a better shot, but still, arrogance could get one killed. Had Robert Lanoux come back to finish the job? Robert was a large man with plenty of muscle. The figure crouching near the tree seemed too small. He eased the safety off and waited.

Saria Boudreaux sprinted toward the trees nearest the inn, staying low and out of the sliver of moonlight. Even in the rain he recognized her easily with just that small glimpse. His heart stuttered as she slipped into the darker shadows, watching the house and the cypress grove.

He pulled on the soft cotton drawstring trousers and a loose shirt from his bag as a precaution. Saria had been angling toward the trees closest to his room. He had no idea what she was up to, but he didn't want her seeing the evidence of a leopard fight.

It took her a few minutes before she raced to the tree just to the side of his balcony, the one he'd marked where the branch hung far enough over that he could jump into it without trouble. She used a strap around her neck and shoulder to free her hands from the case and rifle and she went up the tree fast. She was an adept climber and quiet, spidering up the branches easily and climbing high to reach parallel with the second story of the inn.

He waited, heart in his throat, terrified she might fall, as she scooted out along the high branch. She got her feet under her and he could feel his mouth go dry and his pulse pound. He didn't dare call out to her, afraid she might lose her balance if he surprised her. She crouched low and sprang toward his balcony. He leapt forward as well. She caught the balcony at the same time he caught both her wrists.

She looked up at him, shocked, her eyes going wide. He could see the golden flecks in the dark of her eyes had nearly taken over, blotting out all that chocolate. Her female cat was close to the surface, and his leopard scented her again, that beautiful, alluring fragrance that nearly had pushed him over the edge.

He pulled her easily onto the balcony. "Good evening. Nice of you to come calling," he greeted, setting her on her feet.

"You were supposed to be asleep," she accused, sounding annoyed.

"Were you planning on crawling into bed with me, or shooting me?" he asked.

She gave a little sniff. "Shootin' you might just be the best solution. I'm leanin' in that direction."

He reached out, spanning her throat with the palm of his hand, tipping up her chin. "For future reference, Saria, you might remember, I can smell lies."

She blinked. Frowned. "No one can do that."

"Don't bet on it." Every breath he drew into his lungs was all Saria. She was potent, ripe, a woman so seductive she was impossible to resist, yet completely unaware of her allure.

She studied his face, unsure whether to believe him. In the end she capitulated, not taking any chances. "I came to protect you. There's been strange things happenin' around here and everyone is a little on edge. I thought it best to look after you. You're payin' enough money to support me while I try to sell my photographs for a couple of months or more, if I'm careful. I'm not losin' you to some ghost cat."

He released her slowly and stepped back, afraid if he didn't, he might yank her into his room and throw her right down on the bed. He'd had enough dreams about doing just that. The rain had plastered her shirt to her skin and he could see her nipples like two hard pebbles inviting attention. His leopard snarled when he turned away from

130

her. He had to breathe deep to hold the animal at bay.

"Baby, I don't need protecting. Do I look like a city slicker to you?" He was both pleased and outraged at the same time. He liked the idea that she'd wait all night on his balcony to make certain he was safe, but he was appalled that she might think he was unable to defend himself. She'd obviously returned to her home to get more weapons.

"I don' mean to offend you," she said. "There's been . . ." She trailed off.

He swung around to face her again, understanding dawning. "You sent the letter to Jake."

She went very still. Too still. He saw her hands tighten on the rifle. Her face paled. He smelled fear. The tip of her tongue moistened suddenly dry lips. "Who's Jake?"

"I told you, Saria, I can smell lies. You had Father Gallagher deliver a letter to a priest in Texas with instructions to give the letter to Jake Bannaconni. Why didn't you just mail it? And why didn't you sign it?"

"I shouldn't have sent the letter," she said. "It was silly of me. If you came all this way because of that letter, I can only apologize and give you back your money."

"Are you telling me you didn't find dead bodies that looked as if a leopard had killed them? A leopard and a man?"

She shook her head but refused to answer aloud. Her gaze shifted away from his. Drake took the weapon out of her hands and set it carefully just inside the door of his room, against the wall, out of her reach.

"Honey, you don't want to lie to me. Why didn't you just send the letter directly to Jake?"

She pressed her lips together nervously, and glanced at the tree as if she might fling herself back over the balcony.

As a precaution, Drake shackled her wrist with gentle fingers. "Are you afraid of me? Or of someone out there?" He didn't want to interrogate her, he wanted to hold her and comfort her.

At his touch she went very still, a wild animal cornered and looking for a way out. She was both very vulnerable and dangerous. Her cat was close, Drake could tell by the glow in her skin, the gold taking over her eyes and the wild, feral scent she gave off. His leopard prowled and his own body was as hard as a rock. Her leopard would protect her from any danger. And in truth, she could easily leap off the balcony and land without harming herself whether she knew it or not. He had to be careful. A female leopard was unpredictable at best, and close to the Han Vol Dan, she could be terribly edgy and moody, one moment receptive, a seductive kitten, and the next all teeth and claws.

"Saria," he prompted gently. "You needed help. I'm here to help you. Let me."

He didn't think she would answer. She didn't look at him, but out into the night. Rain poured over them, but neither made a move to go indoors.

She sighed and shrugged her shoulders. "I'll take you to Fenton's Marsh. That's where I saw the bodies, but by now, the alligators have them. You're not goin' to find anything to help you one way or the other." Her words tumbled out in a rush, a concession.

"I work for Jake, Saria. If you knew enough to contact him, you know what we're dealing with here." He had to tiptoe around the subject, feel her out, see how much she really knew without scaring her off.

She suddenly raised her head and looked him directly in the eye. Her eyes gleamed gold in the night. His leopard lunged for her, desperate for her. He had to breathe away the change, all the while keeping his gaze locked with hers. She was so close, so still. So very dangerous and she didn't even know it.

"Are you one of them?" Her voice was almost a purr.

"A shifter?" He kept his voice gentle and stayed absolutely still. There was nothing more dangerous than a female leopard close to emerging, but not yet receptive. "Yes." He waited a heartbeat. Two. "As are you."

She frowned, shook her head and stepped back, away from him. He didn't let go of her wrist, but instead moved with her.

"Didn't you know? Surely your family talked to you about it? Isn't the reason you hesitated going to the police because you realized whoever killed those men could be someone you know?"

"I'm not," she denied. She looked confused. Even frightened. "I'm not a shifter."

This was going to be far more complicated than he'd first imagined. She seemed to know little of shifters. He could see the genuine shock and denial when he told her she was a leopard. The idea was frightening to her. He was in uncharted territory. He could handle alpha males in their prime, but a woman on the verge of the Han Vol Dan was altogether a different matter.

"Come inside, Saria, and dry off. It's late and we have to be up early," he coaxed. "At least be comfortable while we talk. I've got a dry T-shirt and you can get under the covers while we talk. I'll stay on the other side of the room if it makes you feel better."

"You could give me back my rifle."

"I think we'll be better off with just the knife you're carrying."

She managed a small smile, shrugged, a small feminine lift of her shoulder that tightened his body to the breaking point, before she stepped inside his room. At once, her scent filled the air, the alluring fragrance of wild, rain, temptress, uniquely Saria. He drew her deep into his lungs, fighting to hold on to sanity. She didn't quite trust him, but she had confidence, he had to give her that.

Saria was afraid, but not for herself. Her very coolness shook him. She was leopard all right, entering a potential enemy's den without batting an eyelash. She'd make a fierce mother, protecting their children, standing with him through every bad time. She was afraid for her family — she had to be. And he liked her all the more for that loyalty as well. He wanted her more than ever.

Drake opened the bathroom door for her and stepped back to allow her entrance, thankful he'd cleaned all evidence of blood from the tiles. "Towels are on the shelf there. I'll grab a T-shirt for you. Throw your clothes over the shower rod and they'll dry by morning."

She nodded, already towel-drying her hair. Drake rummaged through his bag for another clean shirt. He forced himself not to look when she stuck her hand out the door for it. The idea of her stripping with only a thin door between them sent need rocketing through him.

He paced back and forth in front of the French doors, inhaling the fresh rain. He needed to cool down. Already his temperature had soared several degrees and if he was going to convince his woman he was trustworthy, he had to be a gentleman — no — a saint.

She came out with only his T-shirt on. It hit her just above her knee, was far too wide for her, but she managed to look sexy in the damn thing. Her hair was tousled, as if she might have just been made love to. He gave her a faint smile when she lifted an eyebrow at him.

"You're damned beautiful," he said. "This might not be the best idea."

"You could always give me the gun," she pointed out.

"Get under the covers. You've still got your knife."

She hadn't tried to hide the weapon from him. It was in her right hand, but he had the feeling she was adept at using it with either hand — and he was so far gone even that turned him on. He stayed across the room, toeing a chair around to straddle it, just inside the open French doors where he could get away from her potency if his cat became too difficult.

Saria sat on the bed, pulling just the comforter over her legs. They stared at one another. He could see the answering heat in her eyes, which didn't make things easier. She moved her hand absently back and forth, stroking the comforter, but the gesture made him suppress a groan. She was naturally sensual, the way her body moved, the heat in her eyes, her parted lips. She was throwing off so much sex appeal it was all he could do not to step out into the rain again. He had the feeling he'd find the raindrops sensual.

"Tell me about the bodies."

She shook her head slowly. "You tell me about shifters."

"I'm not going to play this cat-and-mouse game with you, Saria," Drake said. "You sent a letter asking for help, and Jake sent me."

"I shouldn't have sent the letter. I was

mistaken."

"Damn it." He leapt to his feet, as restless as his leopard. "Now you're flat out lying to me. What the hell are you doing in my bed if you're going to lie?" Before she could respond to the question, he continued. "There was no mistake. Just spell it out for me and cut the dancing around. I get it that your family is involved and you don't want them taken down. Chances are good it isn't one of them. You would have smelled them all over the body. You'd know their scent anywhere."

She bunched the comforter in her fist. "What will you do if a shifter really is killing people?"

"I investigate with my team. If a shifter has turned killer, we have no choice. It's a death sentence. It's a difficult reality, Saria, but we can't have a serial killer on the loose. Putting aside the victims and their families, we can't be discovered." He damn well wasn't going to lie to her when he was demanding the truth. His eyes blazed fire and he turned away from her, pacing again, trying to still his cat when heat banded across his line of vision and the leopard pushed close to the surface.

Saria's distress level had to be affecting her leopard. It would strive to protect her when her emotions were in chaos. She had no idea why her hormones were throwing her into such a state of edgy desire, or why her body was hot and needy. He wanted to comfort her, to hold her, but he didn't dare get near her.

"I don' know what to do. You're a stranger and you're asking me to put my family's lives in your hands."

He faced her, tall and straight, his eyes antique gold, the eyes of a cat. He didn't attempt to hide it from her. "Honey, no matter what, I'm here now, whether you help me or not. I can't allow a shifter to go around killing people. I doubt that you can either. Wouldn't you much rather be close to the investigation and help me, than to be on the outside and not know what's happening?"

She took a breath and nodded. "Yes. Just remember these are my people."

"You remember if you're with me, you're under my protection. I suspect something happened to scare the hell out of you. Tell me."

Her gaze shifted away from his. "I tried to mail the letter through our local post office. It's very small and everyone meets there to chat and catch up. Jake Bannaconni's name is rather notable. He's written up in all those tatty little gossip rags, as well as making headlines in newspapers. It's possible someone saw his name on the envelope. In any case, the next day, I found my letter taped to the bottom of my pirogue. I'm the only one who uses that boat, not any of my brothers. Whoever put it there clearly was warnin' me to back off. If it wasn't one of my brothers, I was afraid for them."

Drake pushed his hand through his hair, needing something to relieve the sudden buildup of rage. She'd been threatened. He studied her face. And that wasn't all. She hadn't given him the entire story. He took a breath to ease the tension building in the room. "Tell me the rest, Saria. Everything. I need to know everything."

She bit her lip, her gaze jumping to his face and then sliding away. "He attacked me. The night I gave Father Gallagher the letter, on my way back to my pirogue, in the trees, he attacked me."

Drake's heart nearly stopped beating and then began a wild hammering. He heard a roar in his head and for a moment his vision banded with yellow and red stripes. "How?" He could barely get the word out. His leopard was so close his voice was more a growl than human.

Her eyes searched his face. Very slowly

she turned until her back was to him and she lifted the T-shirt.

Drake stared in absolute horror at the four long furrows down Saria's back. For a moment he was paralyzed, unable to move or speak. His leopard went mad, roaring so loud he drowned out every other sound. For a leopard to abuse a female that way was unconscionable. For such an atrocity to be committed against Saria was not to be borne.

He stalked across the floor, looming over her. His fingers ached, knuckles curling. Sweat broke out as he fought off the change. Fur slithered over his skin in a wave and retreated. His leopard growled and hissed, storming at him, raging at the injustice. The need for violence was sharp and powerful.

5

Saria sensed danger immediately. On the wall, she saw the shadow of a man loom over her, although she didn't hear him. His shadow was large and frightening, a tall, broad-shouldered masculine frame that seemed to dwarf her. He smelled wild, feral, *leopard.* She had smelled that particular scent before. Every cell in her body froze. Panic welled up. Her fingers tightened around the hilt of her knife.

What had she been thinking, putting herself in such a position? She knew Drake was leopard, some instinct had warned her, yet she'd felt such a deep compulsion to be with him. She should have been repelled by the killer inside of him, but instead, she was so drawn into his spell she could barely breathe. She couldn't stop the shiver that went down her spine, or the ache between her legs. She felt so on edge, her skin tight, her breasts aching, so sensitive that she swore there was an electrical current between her erect nipples and her vagina — and *him.*

She glanced over her shoulder. Drake's gaze drifted over her, marking her, his eyes heavy-lidded, hot, so sensual she couldn't look away from him. He looked hungry, a predator intent on prey, and her body had come alive after being in a long sleep. She wanted him. Oh, God, she wanted him with every cell in her body. The chemistry between them was intense, much like a strong electrical current. The shock waves raced through her body, settling in every nerve ending until her skin crawled with need.

Drake Donovan made her so aware of herself as a woman when she was near him. And so aware of him as a man. Somehow all that chemistry had drowned out her good sense and she'd walked right into his lair. She could feel heat radiating off of him, infecting her with some wild hunger she couldn't resist, no matter how terrifying it was. She should have been poised to run, but instead she held her breath and waited for him to touch her. She *craved* his touch.

"Did he bite you?"

His voice was a velvet whisper sliding over her skin like the touch of fingers. His breath was warm on her neck. Masculine heat surrounded her. She closed her eyes and remained still. Her mouth was so dry she could barely manage to get out a single word. "Yes." Her heart pounded hard, the blood rushing hot through her veins. Sweat trickled down the valley between her breasts. Moisture dampened her cotton boy shorts.

His fingers skimmed down one of the long furrows in her skin, the lightest of touches, but she felt it burning like a brand through her skin to her very bones. Her breath left her lungs in a single gasp.

"Where?"

His mouth was against the raw wound, his lips brushing lightly, the most sensual thing she'd ever experienced. Lightning forked through her body. He kissed his way up the long wound, the shirt bunched in his fist. Electricity coursed through every fiber of her body as if his lips were connected in some way to her nerves. She could feel his knuckles sliding up her back along with the shirt. Nothing had prepared her for the way her body came alive at his touch. Her mind, her body, every part of her responded to his presence.

It was both frightening and exhilarating to feel as if a part of her was slipping away to join with a part of him. She should stop him, it was hardly decent, but she was already lost under the spell of his mouth. His lips felt soft and whispery against her skin, cool and firm, but at the same time, left behind tiny little flames that burned hot.

She heard his breath catch as he pushed her shirt high enough to reveal the bite mark on her shoulder. His lips drifted over her skin, tasting her, branding her in the most exquisite way. His touch was always feather-light, yet she felt as if his prints sank into her skin and found their way to her bones.

"He marked you on purpose. It was clumsy and very wrong," he said. "Who was he?"

This time there was an edge to that velvet voice, sending a shiver of fear down her spine.

"I don' understand what that means," she admitted, hating that her voice trembled.

He brushed his mouth over each of the puncture wounds on her shoulder and then abruptly dropped her shirt and stood up, backing away from her. The silence stretched to a screaming point. Reluctantly, Saria turned to face him, feeling very alone and lost.

Drake stood just inside the French doors, the rain coming down in silvery sheets behind him, silhouetting him. She tried not to stare, but she couldn't take her eyes off of him. He was physically beautiful to her. The width of his shoulders, the thickness of his chest, the ropes of muscles, so defined he seemed to ripple with power with every movement. His sensual voice and hypnotic eyes mesmerized. The intense sexual desire stamped into every line of his face made her want to give everything to him.

Her pulse pounded in her head — and throbbed between her legs. She felt hot and needy and restless. She didn't know if she wanted to leap on him and ravage him, or claw at him. All she knew was her body crawled with need for him. The other leopard — the one he claimed had marked her — hadn't left such a need behind, but Drake with his soft kisses had infected her with a violent ache that she doubted would ever go away.

"What's happenin' to me?" It was frightening to feel so out of control. Saria had directed her entire life and now she felt as if she couldn't even take command of her own body.

Drake rubbed his hand over his face. "It's called the Han Vol Dan. When a female leopard begins to go into heat in the same cycle with her human, she will emerge for the first time. The two become one. You are both leopard and human."

"In *heat?*" Saria couldn't control the violent blush stealing up her neck into her face. She felt in heat. She wanted him — *craved* him. She . . . *needed.* Drake was in grave danger of being jumped if he stayed there looking like a sex god. "Like an animal? You're sayin' I have a female leopard livin' inside of me and she wants . . ."

"A mate," he finished for her.

She wanted to deny it, but she felt wild, uninhibited. Needy. Hot. Her skin felt too tight and her breasts ached. She hated the feel of clothes on the body and it was all she could do not to pull the T-shirt off — away from her skin. She had a terrible desire to crawl across the floor to Drake and rip his trousers from his body. Her fingers curled in the comforter, holding tight to keep herself in place. She knew she was squirming, but she couldn't sit still, not with the growing fire between her legs. Her breath came in ragged gasps. She didn't know whether to weep — or beg.

"I can't think," she whispered desperately. "My blood is roarin' in my head." The plea in her voice was unintentional, but she heard it and she saw the effect it had on him.

Drake appeared shaken. Her gaze was

drawn to the large, thick bulge in the front of his cotton pants. Her mouth went dry and she shifted her weight before she could stop herself, sliding sensuously out from under the thin comforter.

He held up a hand, palm out and stepped back into the cool rain. "Baby, you have to stop right there. I want you more than you can imagine and I'm no saint. We're going to have to ride this out together."

That was *exactly* what she had in mind. She licked her lips, images rising of sliding all that soft cotton right off his hips. She wasn't certain her shaky legs could support her and she slipped to the floor, arching her back in a long luxurious stretch.

Drake groaned, the sound husky, sexy, a despairing note that sent fingers of arousal teasing up her thighs. Her temperature soared until it felt as if she had a fire burning out of control between her legs. She couldn't stop moving, her body undulating erotically as she stalked him across the floor like the leopard he'd named her.

"Damn it, Saria, you'll hate me in the morning. Breathe through this, it will pass. You have to take control of her. If you touch me, I won't be able to stop myself. You have no idea what happens to a male when his woman is close to the Han Vol Dan. I'm on a thin edge, baby. Try for me. Saria, please, honey, just try for me."

The pleading in his voice was both an aphrodisiac and a red light. She loved that she made his body hard and that he was nearly as out of control as she was. His eyes had gone gold, that shimmering, priceless gold she couldn't resist, but he'd called her his woman. She was *his.* She wanted to be his. She wanted him to bite her shoulder and claim her, not some horrible bastard who cared nothing for her feelings. Drake shook with the effort to hold himself back — for her. She could easily see his concern for her. Few people ever seemed to genuinely worry about her.

She took a deep breath, her head hanging low while her hips pushed up and back, the need so terrible she felt tears running down her face, but she managed to stay right where she was, only feet from him. She could smell his wild scent with every breath she drew into her body. She could taste him in her mouth, an addicting, feral tang she began to crave.

"I want you to claim me." There was sheer seduction in her voice, a husky, desperate pleading that came out more of a wanton purr. "Like he did. Mark me like he did. I don' want his scent on me. I want yours on me . . ." She raised her eyes to his. Her vision seemed strange, banding with colors. "I want yours *in* me."

"Baby, you're killing me," Drake whispered.

His eyes were completely gold, watching her with a heavy-lidded dark sexual intent. Sensuality was stamped in his tough features, on his mouth. Her body inched forward toward him of its own accord and his hand dropped low, to absently stroke that hard bulge. The sight of him, so darkly erotic, sent another wave of fire crashing through her body.

She forced herself to stop again, dragging in air, the sound harsh and ragged. "I'll try if you promise to do it — to mark me as yours."

A sound escaped his throat, half growl, half groan. "Your leopard will settle soon. If you still want me to do it after she retreats, I will. But it has to be your decision when you're not in the midst of a thrall. You have to want *me,* not just any male because your leopard is out of control."

She reveled in the hoarseness of his voice. He was suffering just as she was. She could see his need burning just as deep as her own. Tears clogged her throat. She had to find the strength to resist the need to desperately plead with him to take her. It was humiliating to know he was turning her down and she was shamelessly enticing him, but her body burned and throbbed until she was so edgy with need she couldn't be still.

"Talk to me. Anything. Tell me about the leopards." Anything to take her mind from the clawing hunger.

"We're a species living long past our time," he said. His voice had an edge of hoarseness to it, but he struggled to soothe her. "There are pockets of us all over the world, mostly in the rain forests. I was shocked to learn you have a lair here. I think Fenton leased his company's land to the families to give them a place to run free and live without fear of discovery."

She ran her hand down her aching body, trying hard to concentrate on his words when she was burning from the inside out. She knelt back onto her heels, cupping her aching breasts, her fingers pressing hard against her burning nipples.

Drake swore. There were small beads of sweat on his forehead. "Damn it, Saria. Give me something to work with here."

He took a step toward her and she willed him to continue, to take the decision from her. She eyed him hungrily. His face was carved with sensual lines, his eyes golden and hooded, glittering with stark, raw hunger. She'd driven him beyond endurance. If she touched him, his control would be gone and he would take her just the way she craved, right there on the floor, wild and uninhibited, his body pounding into hers, relieving the terrible ache. He took another step toward her with a groan of despair.

The sound echoed loudly through her mind. Drake Donovan was a man of honor. He was trying to save her from herself. He was trying to save both of them. What the hell was she doing to him? Shocked, she pressed one hand to her mouth and held the other one up to stop him. He'd done everything but pour cold water over her.

"I can do this, Drake." Determination crept into her voice. "Just give me a minute. Tell me how to control her."

He took a deep breath and ran his hands up and down the strong columns of his thighs as if his skin itched, or was too tight — just as hers was.

"She is you, honey," he explained. "You're feeling both of your needs. It doesn't help that I'm in the room with you. If we're mates, as both my cat and I believe, we've known one another in at least one past life, and we're familiar with each other's body.

The addiction is already there. You're fighting all of that."

She swallowed hard. "Step out of the room. Just for a moment. Give me a moment."

She knew he would, although she didn't know why she trusted him so much. Or how she could behave in such a terrible wanton fashion and still look him in the eye. She was unashamed of wanting him — just ashamed of her behavior. If he would be honorable, so could she.

Drake looked at her for a long moment, his gaze hot, revealing he was skating to the very edge of his control before he moved away from her. The tension in him was tangible, as it was in her, a torturous, skin-crawling, belly-clawing need neither could hope to ignore.

"You won't make me dishonor him," she hissed to the entity living inside of her. She took a deep breath and willed the female leopard to retreat. "I need time to get used to you. Give me some breathing room."

Her skin itched and her jaw ached, but the terrible fire eased a little without Drake in such close proximity. She closed her eyes and let lust wash over her, accepting the terrible, almost violent desire rushing through her like a fireball. Her blood ran hot, and she just kept breathing to try to cool down.

It took a few more minutes of deep breathing before she dared look around her. Her vision slowly cleared. Her body trembled uncontrollably. There was no way to get to her feet, but thankfully, reason was creeping in.

Grateful, Saria crawled to the bed and pulled herself up so she could rest her stomach against the edge, lean over and lay her face against the cool comforter. She wept for a few minutes, unable to stop. Nothing in her life had prepared her for such violent need. What would have happened if she'd been with a male other than Drake and her leopard had been so needy? She couldn't just blame it on her leopard. From the moment she'd laid eyes on Drake Donovan, she'd wanted him. She couldn't help it — maybe because he was a handsome stranger with some undefined power clinging to him. Maybe she was just a raw country girl who had no real experience with such a man, but whatever the reason, he'd set her blood rushing hotly and her pulse pounding. That had to have added to the clawing hunger entrenched inside her.

Drake stood at the edge of the doorway, watching Saria as she leaned against the bed and wept. The T-shirt rode up over the curve of her bottom, revealing small pink-striped underwear. The material fit lovingly, showing the smooth undersides of perfectly rounded cheeks. His cock, already pulsing with urgent desire, dripped, the tightness intense. Every nerve ending seemed centered in his groin.

She was everything he'd ever dared to dream of. He wanted a woman of courage. Of passion. One who preferred the outdoors and was unafraid to be his partner. He wanted a lot of sass and a little ferocity. Saria was the embodiment of all those things. He knew she belonged to him, but she was young and inexperienced. The idea of being a shifter was new to her and the intensity of the mating cycle of their species had to be frightening.

"Saria?" Drake kept his voice gentle, tried — without much success — to keep the lust and passion from his tone. The craving for her didn't let up, not for a second, and he knew it never would even if she rejected him.

Saria slowly turned, sliding to the floor to sit with her knees drawn up and her back to the bed. She sent him a tentative smile and his heart did that strange stuttering. He knew what courage that little smile had to have taken.

She didn't flinch away, but looked him straight in the eye. "I think you're safe now. I'm not goin' to jump you."

He gave a soft, self-deprecating laugh. "I'm not certain that's good news. I don't think I've ever wanted anything more in my life than I want you. It's not going to go away." He wanted her to hear the ring of truth in his voice. "I'm afraid we might be in a little trouble here, honey." He pulled a water bottle from his pack, opened it and handed it to her.

Saria took the bottle and patted the floor beside her.

Drake hesitated, afraid of what could happen that close to her, but she didn't drop her gaze from his and he couldn't resist the temptation of her trust. He sank to the floor beside her and drew up his knees. Their hips and shoulders touched. One soft thigh rubbed along his as she shifted a little, taking a long drink and handing him back the bottle.

"This is goin' to happen again?"

"Yes. And next time this will end far differently." He set his mouth over the rim of the bottle, where hers had been. He could taste all that pent-up lust — or maybe it was his.

"How many times have you been through this with a woman?"

He frowned at her. "I've seen a woman go through the Han Vol Dan, and of course my leopard was affected, it sets males on edge, but she wasn't *my* woman. I didn't have to fight like this for control. This is . . . beyond imagining."

"Do you want this to happen again — with me?"

He shook his head over the absurdity of the question, his gaze drifting possessively over her face. "I think of you as mine. Of course I want it to happen and if we're together, Saria, it's inevitable. You have to face that and I meant what I said. The next time you're in that state, I'm going to be inside your body. Once I take you, I'm not going to stand aside, so know what you're getting into before you make a decision."

She reached for the water bottle, took another sip and licked her lips. Her dark eyes met his again. "Kiss me."

He studied her face. "You like playing with fire?"

"I don' understand. It's a kiss."

He took her hand and curled her palm over the large bulge in the front of his thin cotton pants. Heat spread through both of them. An electrical current surged through both of them. "It's not just a kiss, Saria. Don't try to fool yourself."

"I have to know."

He arched an eyebrow at her. "You have no sense of self-preservation. If I were any other kind of man . . ."

"But you're not," she pointed out.

The confidence in her voice shook him. He swore and took another cooling drink. She hadn't removed her hand and damn him to hell, but he didn't want her to.

He curled his fingers around the nape of her neck and tipped her face up to his as he brought his mouth down on hers. He tried to be gentle, but he didn't feel gentle, he felt raw and desperate and she tasted like heaven. "Open your mouth." He growled the demand.

She obeyed, her lips trembling, and his tongue slid against hers, drawing her sweetness deep inside him. The room spun away as he indulged himself. It was all he could do not to devour her. Her mouth seemed to have a direct connection to his every nerve ending. His groin hardened impossibly, an ache he feared would never go away. She melted into him, so that he breathed for her, exchanging something intangible as they devoured one another.

He was the first to pull back, afraid they

would burn out of control again. They stared at one another a long time, gazes locked, breath coming in ragged, harsh gasps, with that strange electrical current sizzling between them.

"Does that answer your question?" If it didn't, Drake wasn't certain they could ever touch one another again. His mouth on hers was like lighting a stick of dynamite.

She nodded, touching her lips with trembling fingers. "I've never liked kissing," she explained. She pressed her lips together, as if holding on to his kiss. "That was definitely not my normal reaction."

"Thank God for that," Drake said, meaning it. The thought of her kissing any other man like that was enough to make him want to commit murder.

"I had to know." Saria looked a little dazed. She looked up at him expectantly. "So, okay then."

Her lashes were incredibly long. He leaned close and brushed the corner of her eye with his mouth. "Okay what?"

"Do it. I want you to do whatever you said that leopard did to me. I don' want him. If I'm goin' to really turn into a female leopard totally out of control, I want you." She stared directly into his eyes. "I'm makin' the choice. I want it to be you, not some other male I don' want to be with."

His cock jerked beneath the warmth of her palm. His fingers shackled her wrist and he gently lifted her hand away before he lost all reason. His mouth went dry and his heart pounded too hard, too loud, too fast. "Honey, you don't know what you're saying. If I put my mark on you and your leopard accepts me, we're making a lifetime commitment. I would never let you go. We'd be married, have children and do all those things you're not so certain you want to do. I'm not a boy to have a crush on. You have to be certain you know what you're getting into."

"I'm tryin' to figure it all out," Saria said, and took the water bottle from him again. She tipped the contents down her throat. "You told me this is goin' to happen again, right?"

He leaned over to lick a lingering drop of water from the edge of her lip before he could stop himself. They stared at one another. He felt a little as if he were falling into that dark expanse of chocolate as he barely managed a nod of assent.

"Then I want you. Whatever happens, you're a man of honor and I can live with that."

She didn't know what she was giving to

him. She was too young and had no idea of the laws of their people. "Once we consummate our relationship, if a man touches you, one of our people, a leopard, he's challenging me to fight to the death for you, Saria. Understand this. I am leopard, born and bred in the rain forests and even as a man I have the law of that world imprinted into my bones. I live by that law. I would fight for you with the last breath in my body."

She swallowed hard, but she didn't look away. "As I would you."

"Why? Why tie yourself to someone unknown?"

"Who then? The male that attacked me?"

"There are others."

"My brothers . . . and that would be eww."

He shook his head, knowing he was killing his chances, but he felt protective toward her and in any case, once she wore his mark — she was his. It mattered little if their relationship was consummated or not. He could wait until she was ready and felt safe merging her life with his, but he wanted her to come to him knowing her options.

He got to his feet and reached down to help her up. "Fenton leased his lands to seven families. I'm betting all seven families are leopard. There must be available males within those families."

She was intelligent and quick. She knew exactly which seven families he was referring to. She knew every family in the swamp and she had to have noticed they stuck together.

"Yes, I know all of the available men."

"They'll all want a chance to see if your leopard will accept them."

"I don' want them." She stood close to him, looking him straight in the eye. "But I don' want you to feel as if this is something you have to do. I don' belong with any of them. I grew up with them. If I was attracted to one of them, wouldn't I already feel it?"

"You think you could fall in love with a man like me? Male leopards are bossy, arrogant, temperamental and jealous as hell."

A smile teased the edges of her mouth. He could see trepidation in her eyes, but she refused to back down. "I figured as much."

A slow smile began somewhere around the edges of his heart. "You're sure, because there's no going back. They'll smell my scent on you."

"You couldn't smell his scent," she pointed out.

"He didn't know what the hell he was doing. No self-respecting leopard would tear your skin like that. He was so busy trying to mark you as property, he neglected to inject his scent into you. Your leopard couldn't have been close to the surface or his leopard would have reacted."

"I don' understand," she said, "but it doesn't matter." Her slender arms slid around his neck and she leaned her body against his, lifting her face to his.

He felt her soft breasts against the wide expanse of his chest and a small groan escaped as he lowered his head. He took her mouth with more of an edge this time, letting some of his hunger spill out, allowing himself the indulgence of feeding on her sweetness, of taking command of her mouth. He moved her more fully into his arms, the ropes of muscle locking her there, his kiss aggressive and demanding.

A part of him still expected resistance, but she melted into him, pliant, all soft skin and heat. She simply opened herself to him and he poured himself inside of her. Whether she could fall in love or not, he knew he could. Whatever strange connection there was between them wasn't all leopard heat.

"Get on the bed, baby. Lie on your stomach."

She shivered, her eyes enormous. This was a huge step in trust. She would be completely vulnerable, but, he realized, she'd been as vulnerable as a woman could be with him earlier and he'd protected her. She looked at him for a long time before she did as he asked. He noticed she was very careful to pull the T-shirt over her thighs. Her silky hair spilled over the pillow, the ragged ends making her look like a pixie princess.

Drake crawled on the bed beside her, stretching out, propping his head up with one hand while he massaged the tension out of her with the other. "I need you to tell me everything about the bodies you remember," Drake murmured, his voice low, almost hypnotic.

Her long lashes flickered. She was tensed, waiting for him to hurt her as the other male had done, but he simply massaged the knots in her shoulders while he waited for her response.

"I didn't know any of them. I found the first one a few months ago. I was out in the swamp taking pictures of a family of owls, the mother feeding the babies, and I saw lights over by Fenton's Marsh. No one goes there. It's kind of an unspoken rule. We all have kept our word to Jake Fenton and we watch that piece of land for him."

"There's undeveloped oil there," Drake said, mostly to see her reaction.

164

"We all figured as much. That's not our way of life. And I don' think the body dumped just off the marsh had anything to do with oil either. There were two boats. I thought drugs or gun runnin' you know. The swamp is isolated and if you know your way around, you could elude law enforcement fairly easily. You can get to the lake, the river or the gulf."

He rolled onto his stomach, settling his chest over her, both hands working on her muscles, his elbows propping him up. He waited until the flare of tension in her receded under his massaging fingers. He wanted her to feel relaxed and unafraid.

"So you see lights in the middle of the night, figure drug smuggling, or possibly gun running, and you jump right in your little boat and head over there *alone*. I got that right, didn't I? You thought that would be a good decision?"

She gave an inelegant snort, half laughter and half derision. "I waited for them to leave, Drake. I wasn't just goin' to stick my head in a noose. I didn't expect to find a dead body."

His fingers gentled, stroked and caressed. No, she hadn't expected a body, but she'd hauled it out of the water and examined it with alligators around in the middle of the night. He sighed. She was definitely going to give him trouble.

"I didn't know him. He looked about forty. He was in good shape, had a tattoo on the back of his hand. I sketched it. Someone had stabbed him in the stomach, but that wasn't what killed him. A leopard had bitten his throat and suffocated him. It was a kill bite."

He bunched the T-shirt at the hem and slowly worked it up over her firm, rounded bottom and those intriguing pink-striped boy shorts. Higher still, over her waist and up the expanse of her back until he had the shirt raised to her neck, exposing all that soft skin.

Saria swallowed hard and started to turn her head to look at him, but he gently stroked his hand down her hair, preventing her. "And because he was both stabbed and bitten, you were afraid it was one of your brothers," he ventured. He began idly tracing circles on her back, between her shoulder blades, occasionally sliding caresses over the long, nearly healed furrows.

It took a few moments before she once again began to relax. "I've lived here all my life. If I hadn't accidently seen my brothers shift, I don' think I would have ever found out about leopards. It seems so far-fetched.

Even now I have a difficult time actually believing the entire thing and look what's happened to me."

"So you didn't tell anyone."

"No. I know that was wrong, but Remy is a homicide detective. What if it was him? And maybe they had no choice."

He blew warm air over her skin and nuzzled her shoulder over the vicious bite the male leopard had put there. "And the second body?" He brushed little kisses back and forth over the puncture wounds.

"That one scared me. It was about two months after the first one and it was a little different. Only one boat and there were beer bottles nearby. I thought maybe they'd come there together, the killer and the victim, friends — and they got into an argument. The first man, I was certain it had something to do with criminal activity, but the second one didn't look that way, although he was stabbed in the stomach and suffocated with a leopard bite."

Drake felt the tremor that ran through her body. "We'll figure it out," he said softly and pressed a kiss into the sweet spot where her shoulder and neck joined. She shivered and he felt the sudden electrical current surge between them. "What happened then?"

"I wrote Jake Bannaconni a letter. I tried to word it so that if he really was aware of shifters or was one himself, he would realize what was happening and come out to Fenton's Marsh and investigate himself. I took the letter to the post office and put it in the outgoing mail. Two days later the letter was pinned with one of my fishin' knives to the bottom of my pirogue."

"A warning."

"I certainly took it that way. I was angry with myself for not being more careful with the letter. Anyone could have seen it."

He took his time exploring that soft expanse of skin, kissing his way along her shoulder, his teeth teasing, scraping back and forth to send shivers down her spine before nipping gently. "And the third body?"

"I couldn't help watching Fenton's Marsh, and about two months to the day after the second killing, the third body was there. This time it was in the water, anchored down. No one I recognized as a friend, but I'd seen him before, maybe in the French Quarter. I couldn't place him, but his face was familiar. I knew I couldn't just let it go, so I took a letter to the priest and asked him to get it to Bannaconni."

"So the bodies have turned up every couple of months. Could there be others?"

"Of course. There's a lot of water out there and alligators tend to eat anything they can find, especially if it's rotting meat."

He tasted her soft skin, his tongue trailing over her shoulder, his lips following. He shifted position, keeping his hands on her shoulder as he partially shifted, allowing his leopard to emerge. He knew she would feel the sudden slide of thick fur against her skin, the hotter breath of the cat, but he was already sinking his teeth deep in the holding bite of the male leopard. He felt the female rise just below Saria's skin.

Saria cried out, throwing her head back, her body writhing beneath his, but his legs trapped her thighs, holding her down. Her breath was shocked, gasping, her body burning under his touch. His male lunged for the female. The moment he felt the female leopard's acceptance, he shifted back, lapping at the punctures and pressing kisses along Saria's shoulder. Breathing deep, he pressed his forehead against the back of her neck.

"It's done, honey. Your female will accept my male." There was no way she couldn't feel the urgent need of his body. He was pressed tightly against her, but he stayed very still, breathing away the lust that had risen sharp and fast and all too raw. He waited for her tears, for the recrimination he was certain would come. He refused to move from her, holding her close, trying to comfort her, when he knew he must have scared the hell out of her.

She lay beneath him, breathing hard, trying to still her hips as she pushed back against him, her breathing ragged. "Why was that so erotic when you did it?"

He closed his eyes and breathed a silent prayer of thanks. Very carefully he eased his body off hers, retaining his hold so he could roll her over against his side, wanting to see her face. She looked up at him with an enormous, wide-eyed stare. Her eyes were nearly all gold, and she looked a little dazed. Her mouth was parted and she was panting a little. She looked as if she'd just been made love to.

"I don' understand what you do to me."

"Whatever it is, Saria," he said softly, leaning down to brush a gentle kiss over her mouth, "I'm grateful. I didn't want to hurt you."

"I felt her. She leapt toward you." There was wonder in her voice.

Drake brushed the silky tendrils of hair falling over her forehead back from her face. "You're really beautiful, do you know that?"

"No, I'm not. My mouth is too wide and

my eyes are too big for my face. But thanks, you actually make me feel beautiful and I've never felt that before."

His heart did that strange stuttering. She was so candid with him. The leopard in him appreciated that she didn't lie about her feelings. She might be struggling to understand, but she wasn't hiding from the intense, almost violent attraction between them. He'd seen intense physical attraction between other leopards and he'd certainly felt his leopard's reaction to women in the throes of the Han Vol Dan, but even he hadn't been prepared for the brutal needs that seemed to consume them both.

"You're amazing in that you're not running as fast as you can from me. I couldn't blame you if you did."

She flashed a smile and sat up. "I think whatever this is that's happenin' to me, I'd be takin' with me. I can't exactly run from myself, now can I? In a way, I feel a little sorry for you. You're sort of stuck with me, aren't you?"

He linked his fingers behind his head. She had no idea — yet — what or who she'd tied herself to, but he was going to make certain she didn't regret her decision. He smiled at her. "I don't think you need to worry about me, honey. I'm a big boy."

"Will the other male leopards be able to scent you on me?"

"Yes. Including your brothers."

She made a face. "Ouch. They'll have a few choice words to say to me — or you." She sent him a tentative smile.

"They can say whatever they want to me, but they'd better be very careful what they say to you." His leopard growled low and mean. He knew his eyes had gone all cat. Possession edged his tone.

She leaned down and brushed a kiss across his forehead. "I'll see you in the morning. I need to give all this a bit of thought." She smiled, shook her head and left his room without another word.

6

Drake knew he should have handled Saria differently. He had no idea exactly what he could have done under the circumstances when he was barely in control, but as he showered, he mentally kicked himself. She was probably crying in her room, terrified to come out and face him. He'd traveled the world; she lived in the swamps of Louisiana. He was older by a good ten years; she was young and inexperienced. He had grown up knowing the way of the leopard; she had no idea of the intense drives or the strict laws of their world.

He swore and threw back his head, allowing the water to wash away his sins. What the hell had gotten into him? He'd taken advantage of her. He couldn't resist her and he'd known she was the one he belonged to. She hadn't known he was her mate though; she thought him the lesser of all the evils. She'd grown up with the men in her neighborhood, the other leopard families, and she thought those men were her only choices. He hadn't told her of all the lairs in the various rain forests. Clearly, even though he'd warned her, she hadn't known she was making a lifetime commitment, yet he'd marked her as his anyway.

He had to get himself in hand. She was too young, innocent and inexperienced for a man like him, yet he knew with every single cell in his body that she was his mate. He turned off the water and toweled off. He told himself he was prepared for tears and recriminating looks. Maybe she'd try to walk off the job. He paused. Suppose she already had? What if she'd run in the early morning hours? If she'd gone home to her five brothers there was going to be hell to pay. They'd smell his scent all over her and they would come looking for a rogue leopard, and they'd be out for blood.

He dressed quickly and hurried down the hall to the room he knew Saria had slept in. He could hear the shower running. Some of the tension in his belly eased and he stood for a moment breathing deeply in the large circular library at the top of the stairs before he made his way down to the main sitting room. If Saria hadn't run from him, he had the chance to court her, to make her see she hadn't made a mistake in choosing him.

In the meantime, he was going to have to conduct a dance with the innkeeper. She had heard the leopard fight the night before, there was no question about that. She'd also removed all evidence. Did she suspect him? He would have scented her had she been close enough to identify him before or after he shifted. Her perfume was distinctive, a blend of several fragrances, predominantly lavender. He found it unusual and pleasing, not sweet and cloying like so many others.

Right now, the aroma of coffee and breakfast drifted through the house, guiding him straight to the formal dining room. Several silver warming trays were centered in the middle of the ornate table and three places were set.

Pauline Lafont looked up from pouring freshly squeezed orange juice into wine glasses. She looked up with a smile when he entered.

"Good morning, Miss Lafont," Drake greeted. "Quite the commotion last night. I have to admit, it felt a little like being in Africa."

The innkeeper frowned. "I should have warned you the alligators get quite loud some nights. I didn't notice they were worse than usual, but I take a sleepin' aid."

Drake's eyebrow shot up at the blatant lie, but he played his part of the city man not quite used to the noises in such a rural setting. "Really? You didn't hear that horrible cat fight last night?"

The older woman shook her head. "We don' have a large feral population here. The gators keep them down."

She gestured for him to sit and turned her back to him, preventing him from seeing her expression, but he was leopard and he could smell a lie — and she was lying. They had a feral population of large cats and she knew it. She was definitely covering up for the leopards. Her sister was married to a Mercier, one of the families he suspected of being leopard. She had a connection all right, and she was protecting them.

"This was something *big*," he insisted, pulling out a high-backed chair.

Saria skipped into the room, hair still damp from the shower, her dark eyes sparkling, skin glowing, looking like sunshine to him. Her faded blue jeans were worn and soft, molding to her curves. She wore hiking boots and a thin tee that hugged her breasts and slimmed her waist. For a moment he couldn't tear his gaze from her. She was so damned sexy and there was no forgetting the vision of her crawling across the floor toward him, her eyes fixed hungrily on his cock. He nearly groaned aloud and felt his body stir at the memory. He hadn't exactly gotten any sleep lying there, as hard as a rock. No cold shower and no amount of relief helped. Saria, damn her, looked as if she'd slept fine and was as fresh as the new morning.

He studied her face, looking for signs of tears and guilt. She sent him a sunny smile, just as though nothing at all had happened between them. In fact, it was if she barely knew him other than as a client. That did a little damage to his ego, he had to admit. He'd almost rather have had her crying her eyes out than ignoring what had happened between them.

It was only the awareness of Pauline scrutinizing him with a knowing grin that brought him out of his near hypnotic state. He sent Pauline a rueful grin and pulled out a chair for Saria.

"Good morning," he greeted her, ignoring the desire to shake her up a little by kissing her perfect mouth. He'd spent a few hours in hell thinking about her mouth.

"It's a beautiful morning," she said and dropped into the chair, seemingly as if she'd forgotten the night's events. "Miss Pauline, breakfast smells so good. I cut my shower short because my tummy kept rumbling." She blew the woman a kiss.

Drake settled into a chair across the table from Saria. She was doing the right thing, but perversely, he wanted her attention. He had a crazy desire to leap over the table and kiss her just for the hell of it. Pauline got kisses, even if they were air kisses, but he went untouched.

He forced himself to be casual as well. If Saria could act like they were client and guide, so could he. "This does look wonderful, Miss Lafont. I didn't expect you to get up so early and fix us something to eat."

"I couldn't let you go out for the day without eatin'," the innkeeper replied. "And please call me Pauline. Everyone else does."

He turned his attention to the amount of food spread out on the table, determined to act as blasé as Saria. Carefully he lifted each lid to look into the heated dish.

"That's breaded, pan-fried trout fillet, poached eggs and hollandaise sauce," Pauline offered, a hint of pride in her voice.

Saria scooted some onto her plate. "And no one makes it quite like Miss Pauline, Drake. You've got to try it. I've worked for years to get this dish right. I'm nearly there, too, but not quite yet. I need a little more time to figure out the right seasonin'."

178

He took a healthy helping, ignoring the drawling, sexy way she pronounced his name. "I can see I'll be gaining weight while I'm here," he said. "I do love to eat."

Pauline beamed. "I love cookin'. Try some of my Creole rice cakes." She took the lid off another warmer.

Both Saria and Drake helped themselves.

"You have to try a *couche-couche*," Saria added. "It's Cajun-style fried corn meal mush, very yummy."

Pauline poured them both coffee and added a large plate of hot beignets within reach of both of them. "The cream is fresh," she said. "You'll want that with your café."

He grinned at her. "I suppose that means the coffee's strong."

Saria nodded. "Café au lait is best with beignets anyway." She took a sip of the rich aromatic liquid and then a bite of the warm doughnut.

He glanced at her and his heart nearly stopped. Her eyes were dark chocolate and laughing, the golden flecks brightly gleaming with mischief. The tempting bow of her mouth had a trace of white powdered sugar on it and he nearly leaned over the table to lick it off. She was so beautiful to him, so filled with life, so damned sexy he could barely breathe with wanting her.

"You're eating dessert before you eat your breakfast." He tried to sound stern, but it was impossible when she was enjoying herself so much. She definitely was tucking into her food, unafraid of ruining her figure.

"It's all about the calories, my friend," she said. "Eat up."

He did lean across the table then, unable to stop himself, and brushed the powdered sugar from her mouth with gentle fingers, lingering a little, mesmerized by the softness of her full bottom lip. Her eyes went dark, desire flaring for a moment, just enough to satisfy him.

Pauline cleared her throat, reminding him he wasn't alone with Saria. The innkeeper managed not to smirk at him. Drake cut her off neatly before she could switch subjects. "I was just telling Pauline about the horrible noises I heard last night. Something large was fighting or killing something else. It sounded like large cats to me."

Saria didn't look up, fussing with her napkin. "That would be strange, Drake. We don' have large cats in the swamp anymore. The last one was shot in sixty-six, wasn't it, Miss Pauline? I remember *mon pere* tellin' us how sad it was."

"There are legends," Pauline pointed out.

180

"My sister's husband and his father were out fishin' when he was young and they claim they saw a panther, but if they did, it was a ghost, cuz there were no tracks left behind."

"You have to get used to the sounds in the swamp," Saria added. "I'm often in the swamp at night workin' and it can be a little scary."

His head went up. "What the hell are you doing in the swamp at night?" He looked to Pauline for confirmation. "She shouldn't do that, should she?"

"No, she shouldn't," Pauline said sternly. "What time did you come in last night? I didn't hear anything."

"Probably your sleeping aid," Drake pointed out helpfully. He helped himself to more trout and eggs. The woman was lying her ass off, but he appreciated how smoothly she did it and there was no sense in passing up a great meal.

Saria leaned toward Drake with a laugh. "It wasn' her sleepin' aid, my man. I'm a ninja. No one ever hears me unless I wan' them to. I watched a lot of martial art movies, so if anythin' goes wrong, just get behind me and you'll be safe in that scary swamp."

"I'll be sure and do that," he agreed. "Can

you catch bullets with your teeth?" He liked her calling him "my man" rather than "my friend." It was probably just her way of speaking, but he'd take whatever he could get. It was rather pathetic to be looking for the smallest of signs that she was just as mesmerized by him as he was with her, but apparently he'd fallen much harder than he expected.

"I haven't actually gotten that technique down yet," Saria admitted, laughing. She turned to Pauline. "I was in the swamp last night, tryin' to get pictures again. I've got a buyer interested in winter wildlife shots. The mood of the swamp is so different at night. I sat up in a blind for hours and got cold, but wasn't happy with most of the shots."

"You were in the swamp last night?" Drake demanded. "Alone?"

Saria shrugged. "I often go into the swamp alone at night."

"Where are your brothers?" Pauline asked. "I bet they weren't home."

Saria laughed. "It wouldn't have mattered if they had been. I do what I want. Remy has some big case he's workin' on. I think Mahieu is smitten with your niece, Charisse — he's been courtin' her recently — and the rest left to go give a hand on the river."

Pauline looked pleased. "I would like that

182

match, although Charisse seems a little frivolous for a man like Mahieu. I love her and she's very intelligent, but she's a little . . ." She trailed off and then laughed. "Kooky."

"Bossy," Saria said at the same time. She laughed too. "Don' worry, Miss Pauline, Mahieu is bossy too. They might make a terrific match. Besides, she's a genius, isn't she? No one makes perfume, the exact right blend, like she does."

Pauline beamed at her. "She does have a gift, doesn't she?"

Exact blends of perfumes didn't interest Drake at all, but Saria's penchant for traipsing around in the swamp alone was of paramount interest. "So your brothers just left you alone?" Drake couldn't get over the fact that she had five brothers and none of them were looking out for her. "And you went out into the swamp to take pictures."

"Well, Lojos might have been around, but I didn't see him," Saria said, obviously unconcerned. "And they aren't just *any* pictures."

Drake had the urge to reach across the table and shake Saria. She didn't understand how much danger she was in with a leopard killing people. The killer was most likely watching her every movement. "You put yourself at risk for *pictures?*"

The marks on her back meant a male leopard was already staking a claim — a male she wasn't interested in. Saria wasn't the type of woman to lead a man on and she was definitely attracted to Drake. He wasn't misreading signals. Her brothers should have been protecting her. They had to know she was close to the Han Vol Dan, yet none of them were guarding her and they just allowed her to run around at night alone where anything could happen to her. He was beginning to form a very low opinion of her brothers.

"I attended this lecture once, a woman who photographs the swamps and gets paid for it. I showed her some of my photographs and she gave me a couple of connections, places to sell my photographs." Saria lifted her chin and gave him a look that basically said he could go to hell if he didn't like it.

He studied her stubborn chin. Yeah. That chin was going to be a problem in the coming years. She lifted it just so and his heart melted. The woman was going to get just about anything she wanted from him if he was ever stupid enough to let her know how much she affected him. He was going to have to work very hard to keep a balance between her wild spirit and his need to protect her.

Saria ignored him and leaned toward Pauline. "When I contacted them, they both said they would pay for my photographs. I've made quite a bit of money. A lot is ridin' on these photographs and I want to get them just right. One of the places wants a year-round pictorial of the swamp and if I can get it the way they want, it means a lot of money for me. I won' have to hunt gators."

Drake groaned and put his head on the table. The thought of her hunting alligators was beyond his imagination. What the hell was wrong with the men in her family?

"Can I see the pictures you took last night?" Pauline asked.

The innkeeper was smooth, Drake decided. He sat up straight and speared another rice cake, looking casual, not letting on that he was considering shaking Saria and accusing the innkeeper of being a blatant liar. Pauline hadn't missed a beat, but she wanted to know if Saria had been taking pictures in the swamp during the leopard fight. He would bet everything he had that Pauline would insist on seeing the photographs and she'd take care to examine the time stamp.

Saria looked pleased. "Really? My brothers never want to see them. I wait for hours to get the right shot and when I do I'm so excited, but it's kind of a letdown with no one wantin' to see them. If you mean it, I'll show them to you when we get back this evenin'."

"I'd love to see them too," Drake said. "Since you grew up on the edge of the swamp, you probably have seen some very unusual things others have never had the privilege of seeing." He leaned toward her. "You're a very fascinating woman, Saria. How did you get into photography?"

The warm admiration in his voice caused Saria to blush and Pauline to look at him again with open speculation, but he didn't care. Everything about Saria fascinated him and he wanted to know more. The fact was, he was feeling very possessive of her and he didn't much care who knew, not when she was managing to be so blasé.

Saria sent him another mischievous smile. "I wasn't exactly the type of child who loved school. I wasn't used to anyone tellin' me what to do and on beautiful days, I wanted to be in the swamp, not in a stuffy school room. Photography was the only thing that kept me there."

"You were a wild child, Saria," Pauline confirmed. "No one knew what to do with you. Your *pere* paid no attention to business after your *mere* died. We all despaired of you comin' to your senses."

Saria laughed. "You know what she means by that, don' you, Drake? Every good Cajun girl should get married and have babies. Lots of babies. And they should cook and clean and do whatever their man tells them."

"What else do you want, Saria?" Pauline asked, genuinely confused. "Gettin' married is a good thing. Your *pere* definitely needed to talk some sense to you."

"Too late now," Saria said with a strained smile. "He didn't have anything to say before he died and he sure doesn't now."

Drake glanced at her. Her lashes were lowered, veiling her eyes. Her tone had been even enough, but there had definitely been an estrangement between Saria and her father.

"He should have tanned your hide every now and then," Pauline stated.

Saria smirked, her good humor instantly restored. "I wouldn' cook for him if he'd done that and he liked to eat every once in a while."

"She was tendin' bar when she was thirteen," Pauline sniffed. "And runnin' the family store. It wasn' right."

"So you all told me — and *mon pere.*"

Saria's laughter spilled out. "Not that it did you much good. Even Father Gallagher was upset about the bar."

"Thirteen." Drake was shocked. "How is that possible? There must be a drinking age."

"Of course, there is," Pauline said. "The bar is out in the swamp. No tourists or police."

"I thought you had brothers." Drake was outraged on Saria's behalf. He couldn't imagine a young girl surrounded by drunk men. Her absent brothers had a lot to answer for. He might just teach them a lesson himself.

Saria shrugged. "They were gone most of the time. And I grew up around the various men who were regulars at the bar. They looked out for me."

Pauline gave a dramatic sniff. "No one looked out for you. You didn' like somethin' you just disappeared into the swamp and no one could get you out."

Drake raised his eyebrow. The accents were getting thicker as the women grew more animated. "You really were a wild child."

"I didn't like anyone tellin' me what to do." Saria made it a statement of fact, without apology.

"Oh, she worked, that one did," Pauline said. "She did all the cookin' and cleanin' in that house. She was a little thing, barely able to stand up to the stove."

"I used a stool," Saria explained.

Pauline gave another sniff. "And she did the fishin' and trappin' as well."

"You make it sound terrible, Pauline. I *loved* my life. It was my house and my swamp, my world. And it still is."

"See?" Pauline appealed to Drake. "She's always been like this. It never mattered what anyone said to her, she did what she wanted. We all got together to try to talk to her *pere,* but he wouldn't listen. Told us to mind our own business."

Saria blew her a kiss. "I appreciated it."

"Is that why every single one of the women who tried to intervene ended up with a baby alligator after they interceded on your behalf?" Pauline demanded. "She snuck into their homes and left them all a present — a very pointed present. I received one as well."

Saria threw back her head and laughed. Drake had the sudden vision of a precocious child with gleaming white-gold hair, mischievous and running wild. He found her more fascinating than ever. His Saria had to have a backbone of steel if she was standing up to an entire community at such an early age.

"Did you really sneak into houses . . ."

"*Eight* houses," Pauline pointed out. "All in one night and no one caught her."

Drake shook his head, unable to keep from laughing. "You broke into eight homes and left each one a baby alligator?"

Pauline nodded, beginning to laugh at the memory. "She's very inventive, this one. She tied a bow around the necks of the alligators with a little rolled-up note, like a scroll, and left one in each bathroom, either in the tub or shower. All women of the church and very proper."

"I'll bet that went over well."

"Mind you," Pauline added, "these were town women. They lived on the river, but they weren't like those of us in the swamp. Can you imagine the ruckus those ladies made findin' gators in their fancy bathrooms? I think everyone heard the screams up and down the Mississippi."

Saria burst out laughing again and Pauline, shaking her head, joined with her.

"What did the note say?" Drake asked.

"Wait, I still have mine," Pauline jumped up so fast the chair wavered for a moment.

Drake steadied the chair while Pauline left the room to retrieve the note.

"Remind me not to get you upset with

me," Drake whispered. "You believe in revenge."

"Good thing to know about me," Saria said. "I don' like people pushin' me into anything, even *ma famille*. I had to be an adult and no one was goin' to come into my home and tell me what I could or couldn't do."

"We were tryin' to give you a childhood," Pauline pointed out as she plunked the note down on the table in front of Drake.

"I know that now, Miss Pauline," Saria said. "That's why I said I appreciated the intervention. Later, when my temper cooled, I sorted it out and realized it was done because you all cared. I left an apology at each house a few weeks later."

Drake glanced down at the note expecting to see a childish, angry scrawl. He was shocked that the note was done in calligraphy. He looked up and met Pauline's eyes.

"Do you see why I kept it? That note was such a work of art. She gave us all a baby to take care of because we had too much time on our hands and she didn't need our concern. She said to pour our lonely feelings out to the new baby." Pauline poured herself another cup of coffee and took a beignet. "Of course it was a baby alligator, but so clever to think of it."

"And what did you do for an apology?" Drake asked, more fascinated than ever. Clearly there was quite a lot to learn of Saria and he wanted to know everything.

"I baked them a rare Cajun bread, a recipe that's been in *ma famille* for years. I wrapped each loaf up with a beautiful tissue paper my mom had kept for years in case something important came up and I snuck into their houses and left it on their tables. That was much easier than putting the alligators in the bathrooms."

Pauline beamed at her. It was obvious they had great affection for one another. Drake could understand why. Pauline had no children and Saria had no parents. Naturally they would gravitate toward one another.

"You have to remember, I had a lot of time on my hands to do anything I wanted, so the subjects that interested me, like cookin' and art and photography, I spent a great deal of time on. Things I didn' like . . ." She trailed off with a rueful shrug.

"Saria has hunted alligators during the season by herself. Most of the men won't do that," Pauline added a little slyly.

Drake knew the woman was baiting him. She had thrown that out to test his reaction. He forced down the first explosive reaction and took a quieting sip of coffee. "Why? Do you have a death wish?"

Saria shrugged. "When I was really young, I went out with *mon pere.* Everyone does it when they need money. You get so many tags and they buy them by the size. I happen to be a good shot and you don' have a big target on an alligator. It's about the size of a quarter. The gator is usually rollin' and fightin' and you have to have good reflexes. *Mon pere* took me when my brothers were in the service or workin' on the river. When he got sick and couldn't go out, there was no one else." She shrugged her shoulders. "I rigged a pulley to help me pull in the gator after I killed it."

Drake closed his eyes briefly, drawing in his breath. Saria was matter-of-factly detailing her childhood. To her, it was a way of life, not a bad thing at all. She did what had to be done and she didn't waste time wishing things were different. More, she was proud of things she had accomplished and he — or anyone else — could go to hell if they didn't like it.

Saria took life head on and refused to be intimidated by it. The more he knew of her, the more he found her courage both terrifying and alluring. A woman like Saria would stand beside her man, fight for her children and for the relationship, no matter how tough it got.

"Of course you rigged a pulley," he said and took another bite of the trout. He had to admit the dish was incredible. "I wouldn't be surprised if you walked on water, Miss Boudreaux."

Pauline burst out laughing. "You aren't the first to say that. The Lanoux boys are intimidated by her. I was talkin' to them at the post office and they said courtin' her is like grabbing a gator by the tail." She leaned her chin into her hand. "And didn' you run off Elie, Amos Jeanmard's boy? He looked like a broken man when he left to join the service."

"I was fifteen, Miss Pauline," Saria said, rolling her eyes. "I hardly broke his heart. I hit him over the head with a flower pot and told him if he tried to put his hand down my shirt again, I'd shoot him with my gun. He was such a dog. He was always feeling up poor Charisse as well."

Pauline looked outraged. "You should have told your brothers."

Saria made a face. "Really? Because they were home so much and paid such attention to me? They sent money home and figured that was enough. They were not goin' to deal with *pere,* no one was." She

194

gave Pauline a mischievous smile. "By that time I'd gotten over childish resentments and fantasies of five brothers dotin' on me, and realized it was far better not to be noticed by them. Otherwise they'd be tryin' to boss me." She wrinkled her nose. "Sort of like they do now."

Pauline nodded her head. "It's true, *cher*, your *pere* was a mean drunk."

Drake suppressed a groan. If her father was such a mean drunk, why did everyone think it was okay for Saria to cope with him alone? What the hell was wrong with everyone?

Saria's gaze met his. "He never laid a hand on me."

There was underlying humor in her tone. She wasn't lying exactly, but she sure wasn't telling the entire truth.

Pauline glanced at her sharply. "He switch you, child?"

"Only when he could catch me, which wasn't often, and then I left for days. He didn' get to eat much. He learned quick not to bother, no matter how mad he was." Saria grinned at her, uncaring that her father had taken a thin branch to her.

"It's a little late to be asking her that now," Drake said, making no apologies for the anger and accusation in his voice. Damn

195

them all, leaving a child alone with a drunken father in the swamp. "Where the hell were the churchgoing women?"

Saria leaned across the table and put a hand over his. "Don' be upset. I'm not. I had a great childhood. *Pere* loved me. He drowned in sorrow after *ma mere* died. I wasn't the easiest child to try to raise."

No, Drake had to agree she probably hadn't been easy to raise, not with her need for independence and her iron will. Saria Boudreaux was one of kind. She hadn't thought to complain to anyone about her father or her workload. Loyalty was a big part of her makeup, even to her absent brothers. She hadn't told on Elie Jeanmard when she could have gotten him in deep trouble. If her father cared as she said he did, and he was leopard, as he had to have been — Elie would have gotten beaten within an inch of his life for touching Saria against her will.

"You should have been protected." Any leopard lair knew that their women were of paramount importance.

"My father taught me to take care of myself," Saria said, "and I'm grateful to him."

"I heard Elie and his sister, Danae, are home for vacation," Pauline said. "My sister told me they came into the post office when she was working. Iris said Elie is very handsome and of course Danae is beautiful." She leaned close and lowered her voice, as if revealing a great secret. "Danae is seeing a boy in college and Amos and Elie are *very* unhappy about it. They think it's serious."

"Poor Danae," Saria sympathized. "I much prefer *mon pere* to hers."

"Saria," Pauline hissed her name.

Saria just laughed as she reached for another beignet. "You have a crush on that man," she accused. "I heard a rumor that Amos has been stoppin' by for dinner, but I didn' believe it until now. Tell me *everything,* Miss Pauline."

Twin flags of color lit Pauline's cheeks. She fanned herself. "Amos Jeanmard was the handsomest boy in school. Well . . . he and Buford Tregre. Iris was so madly in love with Buford. We planned to marry, but their families objected — *strenuously.*" She shrugged her shoulders. "Buford dumped Iris and she was devastated. She sat in her room for days sobbin' and then Bartheleme Mercier began callin'. Bartheleme defied his *pere* and married Iris, but Amos couldn't go against his family. They were big and very devout and his entire world."

She looked so sad, Drake wanted to

197

comfort her. Her love for Amos Jeanmard had obviously never faded.

Pauline managed a rueful smile. "Very Romeo and Juliet. I never married. Amos did and had two children. He was very true to his wife, but he visited me often and we'd sit on the porch and talk. We didn' dare come in the house. After his wife died, he began courtin' me again. I enjoy his visits, but we're both set in our ways. He loves the swamp and I love my home here." She shrugged. "I'm too old to change my ways now. We missed our time together, but I have no regrets."

"I always wondered why you never married," Saria said.

"I loved him. I still do," Pauline said simply. "There was no other man for me."

She wasn't leopard, but she'd been the woman Amos had loved. Could she have been leopard in another life cycle? It was possible. If the families were old and could trace their lineages hundreds of years, they might have intermarried, as Bartheleme Mercier obviously had done — marrying outside the shifter species. It would stand to reason without a large genetic pool available.

Drake sighed. The world was a big place and there were few shifters left. To find one's mate was difficult at best. Pauline could have been Amos Jeanmard's true mate, but her soul was now in the body of a nonshifter and Amos had chosen to put his species before his own needs. Drake didn't know if that was a good thing or not. What about Jeanmard's wife? Leopards scented lies. She very well could have lived a very unhappy existence knowing he didn't really love her.

He looked across the table at Saria. He could see the compassion and empathy for Pauline in her eyes. He wanted to take her into his arms and hold her.

"It's nice to think about growin' old with someone," Saria pointed out. "Maybe he'd be happy sittin' on your porch with you. He could still go out in the swamp anytime he wanted. You might discuss it with him before you make up your mind."

Pauline forced a laugh and looked at Drake. "That from the girl who wants no part of marriage and children."

Drake's eyes met Saria's. She damn well better get used to the idea of marriage and children because as he'd warned her, once he staked his claim, there was no going back. What did she think — that when her leopard was ready they'd have wild sex and he'd just go away? He suppressed a groan.

She probably did think that. Damn it all. He should have been more specific.

Locking her gaze with his, Saria shrugged her shoulders. "In my experience, Pauline — and I do have five brothers — men tend to be very bossy. A few of my friends are married, and believe me, the ones staying home are definitely dictated."

Pauline threw her hands in the air and ranted in Cajun-French for a few minutes. Saria was unfazed. She made a face at the innkeeper. "You just said you were too old to change your ways, which means you're afraid he'll try to dictate you." She glared at Drake. "Men are arrogant and bossy and think they're always right."

Drake flashed her a quick, unrepentant smile, looking more wolf than leopard. "Perhaps the men in your life had no finesse."

"See?" Saria pulled back as though he'd encroached on her space. "That's arrogance. And I notice you don' deny being bossy and arrogant."

"Of course not. I'm not in the habit of lying. I have confidence in my abilities or I'd be a damned poor leader, now wouldn't I?"

"What exactly do you lead?" Pauline asked.

He had to hand it to the woman. She was

not only sharp, but extremely quick. "I have a field team. They'll be meeting me in a couple of days. A few weeks ago a boat hit an abandoned oil well and knocked off the cap. I represent Jake Bannaconni's company. He wants to know the exact damage done to the environment and how best to fix it. Mr. Bannaconni is especially fond of this area and wants it as pristine as possible. Once I determine the extent of the damage, I can formulate a plan and my team will come in and aid me with that. Mr. Bannaconni will implement the plan as soon as we complete the study."

"I knew his great-grandfather," Pauline said. "A good man."

"I never had the privilege, but Mr. Bannaconni speaks highly of him." He stood up when Saria did. "Thank you for the wonderful breakfast, Pauline. It was delicious. Saria, when we go through the swamp, would you mind pointing out the Tregre property?"

There was an instant silence as if he'd dropped a major bomb. The two women exchanged uneasy glances.

"Why?" Saria and Pauline both asked simultaneously.

Drake's shrug was casual, but his radar screamed a warning at him. "A friend of

201

mine had relatives with that name from this area. He doesn't remember them, but he thought I might run across someone with that name."

"You wouldn't want to," Saria said. "We don' want to set foot on their property."

He lifted an eyebrow. "I thought all of you got on with your neighbors."

"We get along with them," Pauline confirmed, "because we don' bother them."

Drake shrugged. "No big deal. I just told him I'd keep an eye out. I'll just grab my pack, Saria, with my test kit in it. Be right back."

"I'll be packin' the boat," she said. "I take food and water and tools just to be on the safe side. Meet you there in ten minutes." She snagged one last beignet and sauntered out of the room.

Drake watched her go. "She sure is beautiful."

"And never forget she has five brothers," Pauline warned.

"I'll keep that in mind," he said with a grin as he started out of the room. He turned back. "One other thing, Pauline, and I'm a little embarrassed about this. Last night I was on my balcony and it started to rain some. I just stripped and left my clothes and shoes on the railing. I didn't want to get the floor wet and I figured I'd get them in the morning, but they were gone. I looked on the lawn, but couldn't find them."

Pauline flashed him a smile that didn't quite reach her eyes. "Darn raccoons will carry off anything. I should have warned you about leavin' things outside."

7

Stepping outside the bed-and-breakfast was like stepping into another world. Everything was gray and eerie. Sound was muffled by the thick ghostly fog hovering over the water and winding through the trees. Drake made his way down to the boat and stowed his gear. Saria looked competent at the helm, a picture in her blue jeans and loose sweatshirt covering her slender arms as she waved him to a seat and took them out into the water.

Drake waited until Saria had maneuvered through the small section of lake and headed back through the canal to the swamp. Cypress trees rose up as if guarding the land on either side of the duckweed-filled water. The early morning fog seemed particularly dense over the water, and he said nothing to distract her as she took the boat through a labyrinth of canals and bayous, crisscrossing over the tall weeds until she seemed to settle into a steady speed.

"Before we head to Fenton's Marsh, I'd like to see some of the swamp Fenton leased to the seven families. It will help me get a better feel for everyone."

Saria glanced at him. "How? Swamp is swamp."

He shook his head. "Each leopard is different and his territory is going to tell me a lot about him."

She shrugged. "No problem, but sooner or later, someone is going to spot us and there may be trouble."

"So eventually we'll have eyes on us."

"Most likely."

"In that case, stop the boat." He put a command into his voice.

She frowned but obeyed, slowing and then stopping the boat. The boat sat in the water with the engine idling while they faced one another. He crooked his finger at her. Her frown deepened, but she made her way to him, easily handling the motion of the water as it gently rocked them back and forth.

Drake curled his fingers in the front of her shirt and tugged, forcing her to bend toward him. She put one hand on his shoulder to steady herself. He didn't let up, applying a steady pressure until her face was a breath away.

"You didn't kiss me this morning." He whispered the words against her lips and before she could reply, he took possession of her mouth.

When he touched Saria, the world dropped away, leaving them the only two people in existence. For a man who was always in control, it was a little terrifying to disappear into her hot mouth, her exotic taste, to lose himself so completely in a woman. He started off thinking he'd take a morning kiss to reaffirm his claim on her, maybe shake her calm just a little, but the kiss turned into something altogether different.

Sunlight burst behind his eyes. He merged with her. Into her. Floated with her across the sky. He forgot where they were. There was only Saria and her soft skin and hot mouth. He kissed her again and again. Exchanged soft breath. Turned to ragged gasps. They were flying. Soaring. He shifted her more closely into his arms, fitting her against him so that she was snugly against the cradle of his hips. The movement rocked the boat, so that he had to balance them both. Ruefully he lifted his head, astonished that he'd been so lost in the haven of her soft mouth.

Saria pressed her forehead to his, both

hands on his shoulders. "So it is real." Her eyes were wide with a kind of dazed shock he found endearing.

"*Very* real," he agreed. "And I don't want you to forget it."

"It's a little scary," she admitted.

He framed her face with his hands. "I know it is, Saria. I know I'm asking a lot from you to trust me with this, but I'll see us through it. I won't let you down."

She studied his face for a long time. Around them, the water lapped gently at the boat and a large bird took flight, the sound of the wings surprisingly loud as the creature lifted into the air. He could read the trepidation on her face — but also the resolve. His woman wasn't going to run, not like the birds taking to the air around them; she would see it through no matter how frightened she was. Each show of courage added another string into his heart.

Drake slipped one hand into all that silky hair, bunching it into his hands. "They won't give you up easily, Saria. You have to know that. This is a small community. Every female is valuable. Amos Jeanmard sacrificed his own happiness for his people. I believe he is their leader, but he isn't holding them together the way he once did. Sooner or later a younger leopard will challenge his right to leadership. If that happens before your leopard emerges, he could potentially change the rules on us. In any case, he will expect you to stay with your lair and mate with one of the males here to preserve the shifter lineage. Should a younger male challenge him, he may set the others on a course to reacquire you."

"And you'll fight them all."

"I have experience they don't. And my team will be joining us. They're all experienced in battle."

"They're my friends and family," Saria pointed out.

He brushed his lips gently over hers. "I'm a leader, Saria. We don't ever sacrifice our own kind needlessly. I will do my best not to allow this to get out of hand, but they won't take you from me."

She licked her bottom lip, betraying her nervousness. "I've never . . ." She trailed off. "You might be very disappointed."

His heart skipped a beat. "Never?"

She shook her head. "Growin' up here, everyone feels like a brother. I don' feel anythin' other than affection for them. No . . . fire." Her gaze met his steadily. "Like with you."

He wanted to wrap her in his arms and comfort her. She was struggling to accept her leopard, the chemistry between them and her loyalty to her lair. She didn't see her lair as her own yet, but he knew that was a huge part of her worry. He was a virtual stranger to her, one she had extraordinary chemistry with, one she instinctively trusted, but he didn't make sense if she thought about it too much. She had accepted they would have sex, but she wasn't allowing herself to think beyond that.

"I won't be disappointed, Saria. Many men have a selfish desire to know his woman is his alone. I'm no different."

She frowned. "And if I'd been experienced?"

"I would have reaped the benefits. Either way, I win." He brushed her mouth again. He loved the feel of her soft, full lips.

"I don' think there will be many benefits as it is. Although I think my leopard is a freakin' hussy."

He laughed. "She'll have no problems, but perhaps we'll take it a little slower so the next time she pushes her way to the surface, you won't be so shocked by her."

"Is there slower? Every time you touch me I feel as if I'm burnin' up."

The honesty in her was astonishing. He found her perfect. Saria wasn't shy or backward, and she would approach sex and passion as she did everything else.

She burst out laughing, her fingers tightening on his shoulder. "You're lookin' at me as if I'm somethin' very special. You have no idea what I'm like."

He flashed a quick grin. She didn't know him either. "Isn't that the fun part? Learning about one another? I already know to look before I step into a shower or bathtub in case you've given me a present."

"Fast learner," she said and made her way back to the front of the boat.

He couldn't help but admire the way she moved in her snug-fitting jeans. She was very fluid. Her leopard had been close most of her life, without her awareness maybe, but her coordination was too good, her reflexes too fast. She'd craved the wildness and freedom of the swamp when most women would have rejected the humid, very dangerous environment. She'd thrived, living off the land and learning to avoid the dangers.

Birds were everywhere, tall egrets walking gracefully along the shallower waters. Other smaller birds flitted from branch to branch. Each called, sang or scolded as they searched for food in the cool gray mist. The sun had begun to rise, turning the entire swamp into shades of gold and red muted by the dense fog.

"This area starts the beginning of the Tregre lease," Saria called to him. "They have nine thousand acres and you can see how wild it is. This is probably the thickest vegetation in the swamp. This section of the swamp was never clear-cut. The growth is original."

"Tell me about them."

She sent him a quick look and then turned her attention to navigating. "They're one of the oldest families. The grandfather, Buford Tregre, was a fierce, cruel man. He drank a lot and beat the crap out of his three sons and wife. It was rumored he abused his daughters-in-law as well, but that was hushed up pretty fast. He died a couple of years ago, but not before he did a lot of damage to that family. There is one girl about my age, but she never leaves the property. Two of his sons still live there, both wives left a long time ago. The grandfather wouldn't allow them to take their children. So the girl and at least two boys live there, but we don' see them often, more since the old man died. One brother was killed. Again, it's an unconfirmed rumor that he died running with his wife and son and that the old man killed him."

Drake was very aware of the depravity a

shifter could sink into if he didn't take firm control of his animal. Temper and lust could easily rule their lives. It sounded as if the leader of the lair had allowed the Tregre clan to live outside the rules of the lair. If the grandfather had been corrupt, certainly his offspring could become killers. Joshua Tregre's mother had brought the boy back to the rain forest and had never said a word to her people about why she'd returned. He suspected it had been Joshua's father who had died helping his family escape the old man.

Drake studied the wild, tangled vines and thick brush through the trees. Two men — brothers — whose father beat them and ran their wives off, lived there with two sons and a daughter. They were virtually isolated in that tangled jungle of plants and trees. Unless a complaint was filed, no one was going to venture into that swamp and take a look at the family.

The lair was far larger than he'd first imagined. Cajuns were all about family, and the shifters who had settled centuries earlier in the region had embraced that philosophy and way of life. He was definitely going to need his team and he'd have to call them in quickly. Once word got out that he'd claimed Saria, the Louisiana lair would be up in arms. If they were as undisciplined and out of control as they appeared, there would be more trouble than he'd first expected.

"Get me close."

She took a slow, careful look around. "We can't set foot on their land. They could decide to shoot us," she cautioned, but she maneuvered the boat as close as she could without getting into the tangle of knobby roots.

Drake used high-powered binoculars to study the land. There were several ominous signs warning of no trespassing. Each sign stated clearly violators would be shot. That took care of human visitors. He studied the trees. Rake marks were visible on most of them. He inhaled and smelled the pungent markings of the leopard male, warning others from his territory. There were clumps of leaves built up every so many feet. The male had been busy, determined to ensure no other male came onto his land.

"Whose lease borders the Tregre family's lease?"

"The Mercier land borders theirs and we have a tiny corner of our lease butting up against theirs. Remy forbade all of my brothers to go near there — and especially me."

"Did you listen?"

"Everyone listens to Remy. He's very much like you, soft-spoken, but you can see the steel underneath." She shrugged, maneuvering the boat around a bend and once again coming in closer to the cypress trees with their knobby roots protruding above the water's surface.

"You went to the corner." Drake stated it as a fact. He studied the profile of her face with hooded eyes. Yeah, she had *definitely* visited that corner where the two properties connected. She was going to lead him in a terrible dance.

Saria laughed. "Of course I did, but I did listen to my brother." For a moment her eyes sparkled with mischief.

"And?" he prompted.

She sent him a veiled look from under her long lashes. "I struck up a friendship with Evangeline, the daughter, and we meet sometimes and just hang out together."

He closed his eyes briefly, trying not to imagine what would have happened if she'd been caught by Evangeline's grandfather. "There on the property?"

"I told you, she doesn't leave it — ever."

"Not even to go to school."

"She's homeschooled. I bring her books sometimes."

"And your brothers don't know."

"Of course not. Remy would be really angry. Evangeline is different and very lonely. I don' see the harm in keepin' our friendship a secret."

"If the old man died a couple of years ago, why does she still have to hide that she knows you?"

Saria shrugged. "Her father and uncle might not like it, that's all. We didn't want to take the chance that they'd forbid our friendship."

He suppressed a groan. Saria's stubborn streak of independence must have made her father crazy. She chose her own way, and few things seemed to deter her — not even danger.

She pointed to a particularly muddy bank. "See that, the way the mud has those skid marks. That's a gator slide. They have territories too. They can get quite large and they're dangerous, Drake. If you're messin' around in the swamp or bayou, you have to be aware of the predators."

He glanced at her sharply. She was telling him she could take care of herself — and she probably could under most circumstances. "Sometimes predators are sitting next to you for years, honey, and you can't see them."

Her gaze flicked to his, caught and held before she looked away. "Amos Jeanmard leases this property," she said. "He loves birds and allows me to photograph here whenever I like."

Drake could see why she would want to take pictures. Jeanmard had a little piece of heaven. Birds of every color flitted through the trees. Others wheeled above in a large colorful flock. He spotted hawks and cranes and just about every kind of bird in between.

"I was here that first night. I had set up a blind to capture a series of photographs on owls," Saria said. She nodded across the water. "The tip of Fenton's Marsh is over there."

The fog was slow to burn off, even with the glow of the orange sun beating down on them. He could barely make out the curve of the land mass she was referring to.

"I could just make out the lights of two boats. Someone screamed. It was really scary."

He sighed. "At least you knew enough to be scared, although that didn't stop you from investigating."

She shrugged, undeterred by his judgment. He turned his attention to the Jeanmard property. There were the telltale piles of leaves and the rake marks. These were quite high and deep, but less frequent, as if the resident leopard had less to prove. He studied the deep furrows for a few moments. On three of the trees, a second leopard had raked deep into the tree over Jeanmard's marks. A challenge then.

Drake wasn't surprised. From just the small observations during the fight the night before and with what Saria had told him, he could see the lair was in desperate need of new leadership. Jeanmard had given everything to his lair and he wanted to retire. He wanted to sit on the front porch with the woman he'd loved for years and end his duties to the shifters.

"What is it?" Saria asked.

He would have to remember she was quick and observant. He passed the binoculars to her. "Take a look at the rake marks in those trees."

"I used to see these on the house and in the trees around our property. *Mon pere* would sand them off the walls. What are they?" Saria handed him back the glasses.

"A male leopard marks his territory. As humans we can go into that territory and it wouldn't be considered a challenge, but should I shift to leopard form and enter, he would have the right to attack me. Did you notice the second set of marks?"

She frowned at him and took the binoculars out of his hand again to study the deep furrows in the trees. "They're a little different, not quite as high."

"Exactly." He couldn't help feeling a surge of admiration and pride in her. Few people would have spotted the second set of rake marks even when pointed out to them. Her years in the swamp had honed her observation skills.

"What does it mean?"

"Every lair has a leader. I believe Jeanmard has been the leader of this lair for some time and when his wife died a few years ago, he wanted to step down. I think he's got a challenger."

Saria sat back in the boat and studied his face. "You think there's trouble here, don' you?"

"Yes. I think the lair has needed strong leadership and no one has stepped forward to take over. Whoever is vying for the position now is tentative. His rake marks are not as deep as they should be, nor do they cover all of Jeanmard's."

"You grew up knowing all of this right from the beginning, didn't you?"

He nodded. "I've seen enough here, let's keep going. I'd like to check a couple of other properties. I might be able to match the marks and tell you who is challenging Jeanmard for leadership. If we know who it is, you can profile them for me."

She frowned at him. "How is this goin' to help us catch whoever is killing people?"

"We'll want the cooperation of the lair. We can only get that through the leader."

"What if . . . ?" She trailed off and bit her lip hard, turning away from him.

"Why do you persist in thinking the killer might be one of your brothers?" Drake asked. "What aren't you telling me, Saria?"

The boat swept along the shoreline, giving him a great view of the plants and birds. The sun slowly burned off the fog, so that the gray veil lifted, revealing the true raw beauty of the wild region. To a man who needed an untamed environment in much the way he needed air to breathe, the swamp was a thing of absolute magnificence.

"I recognized the bottles near the last two bodies," Saria admitted reluctantly as she poured on the speed to take them to the next location. "We make our own alcohol and we use very distinctive bottles. They were ours."

"But you have a bar all of your neighbors go to, right? Do all the seven families who lease from Jake Bannaconni frequent your bar?"

"Yes, even the Tregre family. This is as close as I can get you to the Lanoux land. Their property is a V-shaped wedge. Their property line runs alongside of ours."

Drake's leopard roared a protest. He felt a burst of heat through his body. His jaw ached and he had to turn his head away from Saria. That information disturbed him. It shouldn't have, but the thought of Robert and Dion Lanoux growing up close to Saria sent his leopard into a kind of fury. He felt the raking claws and a terrible need to destroy his enemies. He breathed away the need to hunt and forced himself to study the trees.

Saria slowed the boat to almost a crawl to allow him time to find rake marks in the trees. He fixed the powerful glasses onto one of the taller cypress trees on the edge of the marsh. He instantly recognized that there were two distinct rake marks over the older version — probably their father's — and one had been Jeanmard's challenger.

The hairs on the back of his neck stood up. The wind was blowing away from the land, taking any scent with it, but he knew someone was watching them. More than once he'd had a high-powered rifle trained on him. It felt the same now, that itch in the center of his back. He kept the binoculars trained on the trees.

"Get us out of here, Saria," he ordered.

She shivered, as if a chill had gone down her spine. She picked up speed and the boat swept around the bend and out into the center of the channel. "Someone was watching us."

"I didn't see him, but I sure as hell felt him," Drake said.

"I don' want to do this anymore, Drake. I think I've put you in a terrible position."

"It's almost lunchtime, Saria. Let's find a place to eat and relax." He didn't want her bolting on him now. It was interesting to him that she was more afraid for him than for herself.

"I called Charisse last night and asked her if we could picnic on her property. She has more firm land than anyone else and I know a couple of good spots that are secluded and beautiful," she agreed. "They developed one section just for picnics, with the idea they might bring in tourists someday to visit the gardens, although they don' do it now."

The landscape changed from the trees, shrubs and grasses to fields after fields of colorful flowers and exotic plants. Drake stood up in order to get a better view. Acres of flowers vied for space. The gentle wind sent them in motion, producing hypnotic waves of color, purples and blues giving way to dazzling yellows, oranges and reds.

"The Mercier gardens," Saria said, answering his unspoken question with one word. "They can keep them growing longer than most wildflowers too. I think they use smudge pots like the vineyards do." She laughed as she said it, half serious and half joking. "They've got every kind of flower you could imagine, native to Louisiana as well as exotics."

"I've never seen so many flowers. They must have a huge operation."

Saria nodded a little proudly. "Charisse really is a genius and she has incredible olfactory skills. A client can come into her shop and she can design a perfume for that individual that is so incredible there is no one that can rival her. She's really made something of herself and I'm glad for her. She honestly doesn't have the best social skills, but her brother Armande makes up for it. Everyone likes him. He fronts the store and deals with orders and shipping as a rule and she designs the scents and runs the laboratory. Of course the gardeners tend the plants. They make a great team, although the greenhouse and hybrids are all grown by Charisse for scent."

"With an operation this large, they must

make a good living."

"They ship all over the world," Saria confirmed. "And Charisse is generous with the community. She poured money into the school and kept our little schoolhouse going so the children wouldn't have to commute so far when the state was cutting the smaller schools."

She took the boat in to a small pier, securing it to the wooden structure. Drake wasn't altogether certain the pier would take his weight, but Saria jumped out, dragging a large, rather ornate picnic basket and thick blanket with her.

He followed her, conscious of the wood sagging ominously beneath him as he hurried after her. The ground was spongy, the soil a rich, dark color.

"They must have acres of flowers."

"They have all sorts of plants. Many of them native to Louisiana, like bearded pink orchid, brown-eyed Susan, honeysuckle and blue sage. Others, not native, are carefully controlled, such as lavender, poppies, and of course there's all kinds of plants and grasses, too many to name. Charisse had the gardeners give me a tour once. The schoolchildren come out once a year and tour the gardens and then see how perfume is extracted from the plants and made. It's all quite interesting."

Drake was more interested in the trees rising up out of the lower marshes and the rake marks on them. Saria knew where she was going and followed a narrow trail to a flat spot up above the water line where she spread out the blanket and indicated he could sit.

"You didn't have to provide me with lunch, Saria."

Saria laughed as she opened the picnic basket. "No, I didn't prepare lunch, although Miss Pauline is an incurable romantic and wanted me to tell you I did. She is certain the way to a man's heart is through his stomach. She did all this and wanted me to take credit."

"She should know you better," Drake said, "no way would you take credit if you hadn't done it."

"Not even to impress you?" she teased.

"You know you don't have to impress me. I was impressed the first time you spoke."

Her eyebrow shot up. "Spoke? Not my looks?"

"There are a lot of beautiful women in the world, Saria, and you're certainly one of them, but your courage and honesty is a prize beyond everything. That and your loyalty."

"I don' feel very loyal takin' you out to the marsh," she replied in a low voice as she handed him a bottle of cold water.

"What were you supposed to do, Saria, let him keep killing? Sooner or later he'd kill someone you knew. Someone you love."

"What if it is one of my brothers?" Her hand trembled as she passed him a sandwich.

"I think it's safe to say that if it was one of your brothers, the rest of your brothers would know and they'd stop him. We tend to police our own."

"The reason the male leopard who marked me didn' do it correctly might have been because it was a warning, not his leopard trying to get mine to accept his," she pointed out.

He took the sandwich with a nod of thanks and slipped his arm around her. "Saria, your leopard didn't accept his. She didn't rise to the surface looking for a potential mate. She didn't want him. And that male leopard probably has nothing to do with the note at all. You thought it was a warning, but he would have stopped at raking your back. He must have done that because his leopard was in a fury, but he bit your shoulder hoping your female would override you."

"There's a lot to this leopard business I don' understand," she said, leaning a little into him for comfort.

"Give it time. We're just getting started. Your leopard retreats and stays hidden for long periods of time. You're close to the emergence, but not quite there, and believe me, if any male leopard was to push her, she'd fight back ferociously."

"What are we goin' to do next?"

"I want to see the marsh where you found the bodies and then I think I need to pay a visit to your brothers."

She went ramrod stiff. "I don' think that's a good idea."

"I'm not going to go behind their backs, Saria. I need to talk to them about us."

"I'm a grown woman. It's not their business what I do." She stuck her chin out.

Drake leaned toward her, brushing her chin with a light kiss. "They're going to think differently. I would never respect a man who would try to steal my sister rather than court her properly with the knowledge of her family." He pulled her closer, beneath the protection of his shoulder. "What are you afraid of, Saria? If they object, will you back out?"

"No. No, of course not. Why would you think that? I just don' think it's a great idea talkin' to my brothers. They've been actin' weird lately. Really weird."

Which was another reason she worried the killer might be one of her brothers. Drake knew she wouldn't voice it aloud again, but she was definitely worried.

"Weird how?"

"They never paid any attention to me at all while I was growin' up. Well, Remy sometimes tried to tell me what to do, but he was always in a hurry and he'd leave after he'd give me some stupid order. They've lived their own lives and suddenly they're all back and I can feel them watchin' me. They want me in the house at night. Remy said not to go out into the swamp at night and more than once he's checked up on me."

He had to hide his smile at the disgust in her voice. "Imagine. Your big brother checking up on you," he murmured.

She glared at him for a moment and then began to laugh. "I suppose that does sound silly. I don' think any of them realized I grew up, and suddenly they've noticed and they want to put me back in my toddler suit. I'm *so* not appreciatin' their attention." She took a bite of her sandwich and chewed, thinking it over. "It's strange when you think about it. I spent a good portion of my early years tryin' to get their attention and now that I have it, I definitely resent it."

He rubbed his shoulder against hers, a small feline gesture of affection. "I don't think you were ever into authority figures, Saria. You just wanted to be part of them."

She rubbed her chin on her knee. "I was happy when you told me about my leopard because all these years I've felt as if I didn' belong with my brothers. It scares me, but at least I really have a family."

He stroked a caress down her silky hair, his fingers lingering on the nape of her neck. "Of course you're part of them, whether or not you have a leopard. You would still have all the instincts. I was injured some time back and couldn't shift. I've been shifting since I was a boy. For the first time I experienced what it would be like for some-one of our blood to have all the drives of a leopard without being able to unleash it."

She took a sip of her water. Fascinated, he watched her throat work. The sun bathed her soft skin in a golden glow. He was fast becoming addicted to the sweep of her long lashes and her expressive face. He knew he was intrigued with her, drawn to her by more than the chemistry of their leopards. Her lack of guile appealed to him. The fact that he could occasionally catch glimpses of that sultry, sexy woman hidden beneath her innocent face only added to the appeal.

"What do you mean by that?" She rubbed her mouth with the back of her hand and turned her head to look directly at him.

His heart lurched. Those enormous dark eyes seemed a deep well he was in danger of falling into. Drake would have laughed if someone had told him just a few days earlier how fast and hard he would fall for a woman, but now . . . He was so far under her spell he knew there was no way out. He wanted to be lost in her forever.

"Leopards are moody, cruel, cunning, and passionate. Trap all those intense emotions into a body without an outlet, and you could have a very disturbed individual." His fingers settled on the nape of her neck a little possessively.

She didn't move away from him, rather snuggled closer to him, her thigh sliding against his as she reached for Pauline's famous sweet dough lemon pie. The container was chilled to keep the pie as cold as possible.

"I feel moody sometimes," Saria admitted as she carefully extracted the pie from the container. "Especially when someone tries to tell me what to do."

He laughed. He'd never seen anyone enjoy

food the way she seemed to — she seemed to enjoy life more than anyone he'd been around. She just lived each moment, in the moment.

"It's true," she said and held out the lemon pie to him. "You have to taste this. No one does a sweet dough lemon pie the way Pauline does. She's amazing. When I was little I'd go to her house nearly every day and she'd teach me to cook. She never got annoyed with me, or impatient, and she made the lessons fun. I love to cook because of her."

Drake took note of the unconscious love in her voice. Pauline Lafont was a very special woman in Saria's life whether she knew it or not. He didn't take the pie from her hand but leaned over to take a bite. His gaze remained locked with hers. Her eyes went dark, those golden flecks flaring bright. Her lips parted, an invitation, although she seemed unaware of it. The tangy lemon burst through his mouth and he couldn't help the slightly shocked look. "That is pure heaven."

She used her finger to wipe at the lemon on his lip. He opened his mouth and drew her finger in. Her eyes went even wider, darkened with desire — for him. This was Saria, not her leopard, and he wanted Saria.

He took his time, savoring the lemon flavor over her soft skin.

"I'm going to marry you for your cooking."

She looked more shocked than ever. She pulled back, frowning a little. "Whoa. Back off, my man. Marriage isn't a word you just throw around, not even when you're jokin'."

He took the lemon pie from her hand. "Who said I was joking? If you can make this concoction, believe me, baby, I'd die a happy man."

Her lashes fluttered. He resisted the urge to kiss that look of utter confusion right off her face.

"Maybe you should just marry Pauline."

He laughed. "I'd get certain benefits from marrying you."

Saria took her lemon pie from the storage container and thoughtfully took a bite. They both watched the egrets walking with their long sticklike legs through the marsh as they savored the dessert. The water lapped gently in a soothing rhythm and a light wind rustled the leaves in the trees. Drake felt at peace. He waited for Saria to finish her pie and take another drink of water before shifting her so that she lay curled, her head in his lap. The breeze created a wave through the fields of flowers, a riot of color shimmering in the early afternoon sun. They sat in silence for a long time, with the sun beaming down on them and the wind kissing their faces.

Saria suddenly opened her eyes and caught him staring down at her. She lifted her hand to trace his strong jaw with the pads of her fingers. "I've been thinking about those benefits," she said. "You'd think they would be worth it, but I'd drive you crazy. Or you'd drive me crazy. Marriage seems to give men a license to boss women around."

He captured her fingers and brought them to his mouth to gently bite at her fingertips. "You have a very skewed view of relationships, Saria. I'm certain there are men who boss their woman around, but some men are looking for partnerships. If I'm attracted to you as you are, with your independence and opinions, why would I want to change you?"

"I always wondered that — why men would want to change women."

"I don't," he said firmly, nibbling on her fingers.

"So I was wrong when I thought you were upset this mornin' because I went into the swamp by myself? You didn' think I needed my brother's permission?" There was a challenge in her voice.

"I never thought you needed anyone's permission, honey, but there's a killer running around loose and you know it. The fact that the letter disappeared from the post office and ended up tacked to your boat was a clear warning that the killer knows you found the bodies. And then there's the little matter of a male leopard attacking you. Common sense tells us you're in danger and shouldn't be wandering alone out in the swamp — especially if no one knows where you are."

She stayed quiet a few moments. He tangled his fingers in the silky strands of her hair. Thick, like most leopards, she kept her hair fairly short and rather chopped. On her he thought it looked good.

"I did take that into consideration," she admitted. "Ordinarily I might have stopped goin' into the swamp, although, to be truthful, I'm not certain how long I could stay away."

He understood. Her leopard *needed* the swamp.

"But I have the chance of a lifetime with my photography. If I blow it, I'm back huntin' gators, and believe me, it's difficult work. I need my own money. I don' want my brothers to think they need to support me. I received an advance for this job, more than I've ever made in a year, and if I complete it, there's triple that. I have no real choice."

He wasn't going to argue with her. Of course there was a choice, but she was building a career. Photography was not only her livelihood — but something her nature demanded she do. She'd taken money and made a commitment. She wasn't the type to renege on a commitment — one of the things he particularly found most attractive. No, he wouldn't have tried to forbid her to enter the swamp, but he sure as hell would have protected her.

The wind shifted slightly, carrying just the trace of a scent. Very carefully he caught her shoulders and eased her into a sitting position. He turned his body, placing himself squarely between Saria and certain danger. He could smell the mixture of fury and leopard rising.

8

The man striding toward Drake and Saria was dressed in jeans and a light T-shirt, looking casually handsome as only someone with money could manage. Dark glasses shaded his eyes, but Drake could read the fury in his scent, the movement of his body and the fists clenched tightly against his thigh. He was armed — the gun was in a holdout strapped to his leg, but Drake smelled the gun oil from a recent cleaning.

Drake stood up, an easy fluid motion, and reached behind him to offer his hand to Saria. He pulled her up easily and retained possession of her hand, keeping her tucked slightly behind him. The waves of anger coming off the approaching stranger were personal, rather than anger at them for trespassing.

"Armande Mercier," Saria whispered.

Armande's face darkened. He clearly heard her. If Drake was reading him correctly, his leopard was close, fighting for control.

"What the hell are you doing, Saria?" Armande demanded, striding right up to them, cutting into Drake's personal space, obviously expecting him to step back. The move was practiced, an intimidation that had worked well for him in the past.

Drake held his ground, remaining nearly nose to nose with the man. "Saria is guiding me through the swamp. I'm Drake Donovan, Mr. Bannaconni's representative." He poured authority into his voice. This man had been with the others the night before, but he hadn't been the one to fight Drake. He could see the shock when it registered that he was associated with Jake Bannaconni, the man who owned the properties they all leased.

"That doesn't give you any right . . ."

"I take it you aren't familiar with the lease your father signed?" Drake cut him off. "Step back, Mercier. I don't like anyone getting in my face." When the other man hesitated, Drake stepped into him. "Do it now." He kept his voice low, soft even, but the steel was there — and the threat.

Armande stared him directly in the eyes, but Drake's cat was already leaping to meet the threat. His gaze remained unblinking, the stare of the predator, his eyes nearly completely golden rather than his usual green. Armande gave ground reluctantly.

"I don't know why you would react with such anger and rudeness even if you thought we'd inadvertently trespassed on your land, but now that you know I have every legal right to be here, perhaps we can start over."

"I don' know you have a legal right to anything," Armande snapped.

Behind him, Saria shifted her weight, but she didn't react. Drake appreciated that she stayed quiet, waiting, as he was, to see what Armande intended. One wrong move and the man was certain to erupt into violence. Drake wanted to ease the tension. He needed to find a way to get the lair to accept his claim on Saria without bloodshed.

Armande's furious gaze leapt from Drake to Saria. "Damn right I'm angry. I don't want that little slut usin' my land as her own personal brothel. Do you fuck all your clients, Saria, or just the rich ones?"

Drake backhanded him. Hard. The blow rocked Armande and knocked his glasses sideways. So much for easing the tension. Fur rippled beneath his skin, and his jaw ached as his mouth filled with teeth. He fought the change, breathing deep to keep his furious leopard at bay. Cooler heads had to prevail, and right then the man wanted to beat Armande to a bloody pulp, but the leopard wanted to kill him.

Armande tore his glasses from his face and ripped at his shirt, as though to tear it from his body.

Drake stepped closer to him. "You do that, and I won't be able to control my leopard. He'll tear you apart. You've seen him and what he can do. You're angry, but not because Saria's a slut. You tried to force your leopard on hers and she didn't like it. You're the lowest kind of man, Mercier, thinking you're entitled to whoever you want regardless of their feelings. Saria is off-limits to scum like you."

Armande's fury erupted into a threatening growl, driven by the ferocious need of his cat.

"Armande!" The feminine voice cracked like a whip.

Armande froze. It took great effort, but he hung his head, breathing deeply to steady himself before turning away from Drake and Saria to face the newcomer. Charisse Mercier was breathtaking. She knew she was a beautiful woman and she walked as if everyone was watching her, her hips swaying gently and long dark hair flowing down her back. She wore a long pencil-thin skirt, silk shirt and fitted jacket that suited her figure and showed off her small waist. Her boots were fashionable, but looked out of place even on the edge of the swamp.

"Saria, *cher,* how good to see you," she greeted, with genuine affection in her voice. "Armande, I gave Saria permission to picnic here." She smiled at Drake and offered her hand. "I'm Charisse Mercier and this is my brother Armande."

Drake took her hand. She was trembling, but trying to hide it. There was no lie, she was genuinely happy to see Saria, but she was shaking with fear for her brother. News traveled fast in a lair and the intruder had taken down two of their best fighters. She didn't want him attacking her brother.

"Drake Donovan." He identified himself and moved his body subtly. Saria, bless her, took the cue and moved up beside him, offering Charisse a kiss on both cheeks.

"Thanks for letting us use your land, Charisse. It's so beautiful here."

"*Bien merci.* I think so," Charisse said easily. She put her hand on her brother's arm and looked up at him. "I'm sorry, Armande, I should have let you know Saria would be here today."

He jerked away from her and Charisse looked as if he'd struck her. She turned

239

away from them, but Drake caught the sheen of tears in her eyes. Armande gave Drake a threatening stare, looked at Saria and spit on the ground before turning away from them. Deliberately he stepped on his sunglasses, smashing them before walking away.

Charisse gasped and dropped to her knees, gathering the pieces of the broken glasses into her hands. Drake frowned and looked at Saria. She shrugged, sending him a look that said Charisse was different and no one could predict her strange behavior. She went to the woman and put her arm around her, comforting her.

Drake repacked the picnic basket and folded the blanket, trying to make sense of what had just happened. Charisse seemed under her brother's control, yet she had stopped his leopard from attacking. How? If she wasn't the dominant sibling, how had she managed to stop a male leopard in a fury from an attempted kill? Armande had acted jealous, yet if his leopard had been so enamored with Saria's leopard, no one, not even his sibling, could have stopped him. He'd acted more the petulant child than a jealous lover.

Again, Charisse's tears appeared genuine, almost childlike, when just a few moments earlier, she'd been a self-possessed, very confident woman. Something about the situation made him uneasy. His cat was hyperaware, studying the situation, every bit as tense as Drake. He took a careful look around as he packed the picnic gear into the boat. The two women were whispering together, Saria holding Charisse as she might a child, patting her back and stroking her hair.

Drake inhaled, shifting position, allowing his cat to rise close to the surface to process information. Armande hadn't gone far. He was in the trees, watching, and now he wasn't alone. Robert Lanoux was with him. They were being hunted. Was Charisse a distraction? Did she know? A third man was moving into position on the other side of the trees.

"Saria." He kept his voice low, but the command carried. "We have to go now."

She turned her head and saw him pick up her rifle and check the chambers. She didn't hesitate, but ran to him. "It's loaded." She started the engine. "Armande?"

"And Robert Lanoux. A third man. I think it's the first challenger."

Charisse, looking puzzled, ran down to the dock and waved, blowing kisses at Saria. She appeared to be completely oblivious of anything wrong.

"The first challenger?"

He kept his eyes glued to the island and the butt of the rifle snugly fit to his shoulder, finger on the trigger. He had Armande in his site and the bastard was dead if he made one wrong move.

"They came at me last night. I recognize his scent." He never took his eyes off his target, letting Armande know he was dead if he moved. "Get us out of here, Saria."

"Did Charisse set us up?"

Yeah, that was his woman, quick on the uptake, but there was hurt in her voice, and that tugged at his heart. "I don't know, baby, maybe. Or maybe they used her."

She took them out into the channel fast, speeding around the bend and away from the beautiful, but treacherous Mercier land. Drake slipped the rifle back into her custom-built case and sank down. He had to bring in his team. Things were going to hell fast and he hadn't even gotten to Fenton's Marsh yet.

"Take me out to the marsh now," he said. "I need to get a look at it before they do anything else."

"I think we need to go to my brothers," Saria said. "They might not like us bein' together, Drake, but they won't allow any harm to come to you."

Her brothers' first loyalty should be to her, but after some of the things he'd heard, he wasn't certain it would be and did he dare risk being anywhere near Saria when the lair launched a full assault on him? He needed to choose his own battleground. The locals would have the advantage in the swamp. They'd grown up there and knew every inch of it.

"Is this my fault?" Saria asked. "Because I chose you instead of one of them?" She turned her head to look into his eyes. "Tell me the truth."

"I don't know what it's about, Saria. And the bottom line always with a shifter, is whether your leopard will accept your choice as a mate. Female leopards can be extremely difficult."

"She seems like a freakin' hussy to me," Saria muttered. "She would have been all over you if she could have."

"Don't remind me," he flashed her a small rueful grin, hoping to ease the tension. "I must have been out of my mind trying to be gallant."

"I like that in you. Of course, at the time, I wasn't appreciating that trait so much."

Her smile was a wide flash of her small white teeth, but it somehow didn't reach her eyes. She glanced toward the land on either side of them and then back at him. "In order to follow us, they'll have to use a boat to get to the marsh or it will take hours. We'll hear them comin' if they use a boat."

Drake was glad she didn't bring up her brothers again. He didn't want to hurt her with his misgivings, but he had enough complications without adding her family to the mix. He simply nodded. He was armed with guns and knives. His leopard was close to the surface and his woman had a rifle and at least one knife. He wasn't altogether certain she'd shoot one of her friends if she had to, but if they were attacked, she wouldn't panic.

"Do you think Armande really was the one who clawed my back and bit me?"

"Yes."

Saria shook her head. "I don'. I know him. I would have recognized his scent."

That was true. But his own leopard had reacted with a fierce, abiding hatred, as if *he* had recognized the scent. As certain as Saria was that Armande had not been her attacker, Drake was certain that he was. But why? The claiming hadn't been successful. Armande was not a young teen, he'd certainly been around and he held himself with great confidence. He should have known how to claim a female leopard. What in the hell was wrong with this lair?

Drake rubbed his jaw, wishing he'd told Jake to send his team. He was certain he could protect Saria, even if they came at him in a group, but he'd have to kill some of them, and he wasn't sure she'd forgive him. Damn it all, they were fucked any way he looked at.

"Drake." Saria's voice was soft but compelling.

He looked up at her, meeting those enormous dark eyes. She looked so young and innocent, so out of his league he wanted to groan. She stood, one hand resting lightly on the helm, the wind ruffling her thick white-gold hair, her gaze meeting his without flinching. He was struck by the joy that flooded him, an emotion he'd only experienced in leopard form, running free in the rain forest. Now, looking at her, he knew his world was made up of one woman.

"Aside from the leopard factor, and my choosin' you, I want you to know that if you're in any kind of danger, I would stand for you. I took your money and that put you, like any other client, under my protection. That means something to me and anyone who knows me knows I would protect my client with my life against any danger in the swamp — and that includes humans or shifters. That's just one reason. I did choose you. Whether my leopard accepted you or not, or whether it's a permanent thing, I wanted you to be the man to see me through my leopard emergin'. That's for me to decide, not anyone else, man or woman, lair or not. I stand with you. I give you my word."

God. He couldn't look at her, not with that lump in his throat and his heart expanding. Damn her. She was so far, so deep inside of him he couldn't begin to think past her "whether it's permanent or not." He wanted to lay her down right there in the boat and ensure she'd never think of going to any other man to fulfill her needs.

He also had a need to comfort her. She was standing there, running them fast through the water, her legs absorbing the hard slap of the water beneath the boat, her body moving easily, with familiarity, her expression determined, but in her eyes there was confusion and fear — even hurt. His leopard leapt to protect her, reaching for her, just as the man wanted to do.

"This could get ugly fast, honey," he warned.

She nodded. "I know. I just thought it was

important that you knew I wouldn't run —
or betray you."

"You didn't have to tell me." He still
wasn't certain she could pull the trigger
against a friend or neighbor, but it was on
him to protect her from having to make that
choice. "But I appreciate it, Saria. Let's just
hope no one gets stupid here."

"The tip of Fenton's Marsh is comin' up
on our left," she said, slowing the boat just
a little. "Around the next bend there's a
small dilapidated dock. It's mostly rotted,
but we can tie up there and go in that way.
It's a little dangerous, but we're at the
furthermost point from where the others
can get to us by land. I think you can take a
look around and we can get out before they
arrive, unless they follow by boat."

"I'm game," Drake said. "Let's get it
done. Take me to the dump sites. I'll need
to mark this territory fast though first. Stay
in the boat and keep that rifle handy."

She frowned at him. "Mark the territory?"

"If they come at me as a leopard and
they're in my territory, by law they'll have
to come one at a time."

"It isn't safe, Drake, and you know it."

She knew if three had banded together as
men hunting him, it was logical to think
they would do the same as leopards. Of

course, he'd thought of that, but he was going to be in the right, so if things went badly, Jake and his team would have the law on their side. He didn't argue, he simply got out of the boat. The water was up to his knees. It was an eerie feeling wading through heavy reeds knowing an alligator could be near.

Saria stood in the boat, rifle in hand, gaze on the water. She was very still, all but her eyes, moving restlessly, quartering the area around him. He saluted her when he made it to drier land. The earth felt spongy beneath his feet and his leopard reached for the change in an effort to protect him. He breathed deeply to keep the change at bay. Pain streaked down his leg as he quickened his pace, reminding him of his wounds from the night before.

He made it into the comparative shelter of the first stand of trees not out in the water, knowing he wasn't completely out of Saria's sight, but his leopard was impatient to be allowed his freedom. There was a certain urgency the animal was exhibiting and over the years Drake had learned to rely on the instincts of his leopard. He tossed his clothes aside, uncaring that Saria would see him with all the scars and wounds on his body. The change was already on him, his leopard rising as he reached to embrace the transformation.

Power poured through him. Roped muscles stretched and he was running, the leopard raking trees and dragging leaves into piles to mark them as he raced against time to claim as much territory as possible to warn the other males away. It took longer than he wanted, as the leopard reveled in his freedom and untouched wilderness stretching out before him.

He forced his leopard to become aware their mate was unprotected, the one means he knew would deter the animal from continuing. Once he had him circling back, Drake processed the information the leopard had collected on the marsh itself. A beautiful place, it seemed relatively untouched by human or leopard and that struck him as peculiar. If a leopard was killing here, he would mark his territory. There was no scent trace, no markings, and no tree had been touched until Drake had raked it.

What leopard would do that? This lair was confusing. A leopard had a certain nature throughout the world. Instincts were ingrained. It mattered little what region the leopard was from, whether shifter or animal, most of the instincts were the same. Shifters generally mated for life, unlike their animal brethren, but there were very little differences in the nature. Lairs, regions where shifters lived in harmony, had specific rules that were enforced for the good of everyone. They lived by rigid rules to keep the aggressive and dominant males from harming others. Without those rules, no lair would survive. Was this one on the brink of chaos?

He returned to the tree where he'd left his clothes, only to find Saria sitting in it, waiting for him, the rifle across her lap.

"Wait," she called to him. "Don' shift yet. Is it safe for me to come down?"

Drake looked up at her, his leopard staring, curling his lip, wrinkling his nose and grimacing with an open mouth, indicating he found Saria's leopard very attractive and close to her heat. Only Saria would chance sitting in the crotch of a tree bough with a rifle in her lap and casually ask afterward if she was safe. The leopard nodded.

She didn't hesitate, skimming down the tree recklessly, although he noticed she faced the leopard the entire time and never lost her grip on the rifle. He could have told her his leopard would be on her in a second, far too fast for her to protect herself had she been an enemy, but he couldn't help admiring the way she attacked life head-on.

She was leopard and she chose not to fear it, but to take an opportunity to examine a leopard up close.

The measure of her trust in him humbled him. He hadn't earned it. Her instincts had to come from a life together neither fully remembered, but their leopards did. Whatever the reason, he wasn't about to let her down. He took a firm grip on his leopard, who all but knocked her over, rubbing himself all over her skin. He used his large head to rub and mark his scent glands over her.

She sank her fingers into the thick fur, her expression one of pure joy. Drake could tell she didn't know the male leopard wanted his female leopard's counterpart to absorb his scent throughout her body to warn any rivals away. He waited patiently, although he was aware of every minute ticking by, allowing Saria a chance to stroke and caress the leopard as much as she wanted.

"Can you shift with me touching your shoulder? I want to see it up close and feel it." She looked the leopard right in the eye, unafraid of that piercing, intelligent stare.

He was going to be stark naked when he emerged, but if that was what his lady wanted, he could accommodate her. He was a big man, with a deep chest and the heavy, defined muscles of his kind. His thighs were twin columns of muscle, his waist trim and his hips narrow. Even for a shifter, he had an impressive cock, and as he shifted, with the same, quick transition, the sight of her gaze jumping to his groin sent a rush of hot blood filling him. She raised her eyes slowly to his face.

"No doubt about it, honey, my body definitely belongs to you," he said and snagged his jeans. He drew them up carefully over his rather painful erection, willing himself to relax. She hadn't run, although for the first time, she looked a little shaken.

"You're very fast at going from human to leopard."

"I have to be. I run a team that rescues hostages and protects people in dangerous situations. We have to have certain skills to be able to do that without getting killed."

Her gaze moved over the injuries on his body, the old scars and newer raw wounds made by the leopard fight. She had to have seen the terrible scar running down his leg — unless — her gaze had jumped to his groin again. The instant rush was hot and urgent. She licked her lips and his cock jerked, straining against the material of his jeans.

"What if I can't take . . . I mean, Drake,

you're bigger than I imagined."

"You grew up with men."

"*Brothers.* I didn' look at them. I'm tellin' you, they were rarely there and when they were, inevitably I went into the swamp."

He drew on his shirt and reached for her, catching her shirt and pulling her to him until her body was pressed tight against his. He transferred his hold to the nape of her neck. "You can take me. You were made for me, Saria. And I'll make certain you're ready. Keep trusting me, honey. I promised you I'd get you through this."

Her dark gaze searched his face with a mixture of trepidation, confusion and serious speculation. That was his Saria, refusing to retreat. He kissed her. Hard. Deep. There was heat rushing like a firestorm through his system. She belonged just where she was, against his body, his mouth on hers. He could stay there forever. His hand slipped over her back, down to her bottom, to press her tightly against him. He kissed her until neither could breathe. When he lifted his head, she had that dazed look of desire he'd come to relish in her eyes.

"We've got to get this done," he murmured, against her lips.

"Get what done?"

He laughed softly and kissed her again.

"Take me to the dump site, honey. We're going to have company soon and I'd rather we're back at the bed-and-breakfast."

"Oh. Yeah." Saria blinked up at him.

He kissed her because he had to. He could live on her kisses. He'd kissed other women, but there hadn't been — fireworks. Soaring. Lust crawling through his body mixing with something he feared was fast becoming love. Could it really happen that fast? Falling into her eyes? Addicted to her taste? Needing her until the clawing ache consumed him? He had seen a few of his friends fall, and he'd thought they'd gone a little over the edge. Had it been like this?

One moment he'd recognized her as his leopard's choice, but the next, his leopard hadn't mattered all that much because she was *his* choice. He could barely take his eyes from her. He loved that little stubborn chin. Those enormous dark eyes with all those beautiful golden flecks and sweeping long lashes. Her mouth, so soft, so hot and perfect. Her straight little nose. Her matter-of-fact way of approaching life head-on.

"You have to let go of me if we're going to find the sites again," Saria pointed out.

She stayed still, her arms around his neck, her face turned up to his, her body pressed close. Drake could feel her soft breasts against the heavy muscles of his chest. There was something so steady about Saria, like the rain forest he loved. The flow of the river, the wind blowing through the trees. The air he breathed. She was everything wrapped into one woman. He might be losing his mind, his thoughts so damned poetic he wanted to laugh at himself. What was it about her?

"Drake?" Her lashes drifted down over those dark, dark eyes.

"Yes, baby?"

"Kiss me again."

"If I do, we might not get out of here."

"Does it matter?" Her lashes fanned her cheek. Her lips parted in invitation, her face turned up to his.

He heard the soft groan escape his throat. This wasn't her wanton leopard, this was Saria, her body moving restlessly against his, an innocent awakening, a giving of herself to him. There was no way to resist and he didn't try. He lowered his head and took possession of that soft, amazing mouth. One hand slid beneath her T-shirt, fingers seeking the expanse of warm skin. She had a velvety, rose-petal feel to her skin accompanied by the faint scent of peaches.

He stroked her flat belly with the pads of his fingers, absorbing the feel of her, committing her to memory. Saria's tongue danced and dueled with his, stroking and caressing, drawing him deeper under her spell. His hand closed over her breast, taking the slight weight of her into his palm. There was always something exquisite about a woman's form, but Saria, he found, was different to him. The moment his hand claimed her breast, lightning jolted through him, a white-hot electrical surge that went straight to his cock. He felt full, bursting, yet at the same time, his heart seemed to leap right out of his chest. The mixture of such intense lust with such tender love was both shocking and exhilarating, an aphrodisiac he hadn't expected. He hadn't expected his heart to be involved so fast, but he'd long ago learned journeys took their own turns, and with this one, he was in one hundred percent.

"You're such a miracle, Saria," he murmured, his mouth wandering over her face. He kissed her eyes, her nose, the corners of her mouth and that sweet, stubborn chin.

"I'm just me, Drake," she sounded bemused.

He smiled down at her. "And that, honey, is the miracle." He trailed kisses down her throat, his teeth nibbling along her neck, down to her breasts as he bunched her shirt in one fist. His mouth closed over one breast, suckling strong right through the thin lace of her bra. She cried out and arched against him, pressing more deeply into him. His hand came up to roughly massage the soft mound.

A bird called loudly, answered by another one. Drake's leopard leapt and was answered by Saria's female. Drake actually felt the rush of fur sliding under her skin, the scorching heat, and he inhaled the wild, exotic scent. His tongue lapped gently at her nipple once more before reluctantly lifting his head.

"Damn it, honey. We're out of time."

She let out a little gasp of shock, as if she was coming back from a great distance. He dragged down her shirt, and steadied her, as he lifted his head, scenting the air. "They're coming at us as men, rather than leopards. That's not good, Saria. Get back to the boat."

She looked around her for the rifle. She'd set it against the trunk of a tree without realizing it. She shook her head. "Seriously, Drake, I don' know what I'm doin' when you're kissin' me."

Drake put his arm around her and drew her beneath his shoulder, holding her close for a moment. "I should have known they'd come after us as fast as they could. They don't want the other members of their lair to know what they're up to. Will Charisse tell on her brother?"

"You saw her. No way. He covers for her all the time."

He nodded. "I'm armed, honey. I'll stay here. You take the boat and head . . ."

She shook her head. "It's not goin' to happen, so stop right there. We're not splittin' up, although I appreciate the gesture. No sense in arguin' with me, Drake. I won't change my mind."

He took her at her word. "They're going to use bullets. We need a place to defend. I'm not willing to risk the open water with me in the boat with you."

"Neither am I." She sent him a rueful smile as she immediately signaled him to follow her. She moved with confidence through the tangled vegetation. "I'm guessin' they're goin' to shoot you on sight and hope I'm not in the way, unless they don' want a witness."

He'd thought of that. He also was a little worried about what three leopard-driven, lust-filled, out-of-control men would do to Saria if they caught her alone. He was certain Armande had attacked her once. Where the hell was the leadership?

"I might have to kill them." He said it straight, with no apologies. "They're hunting us and I can't take any chances with your life."

"I'm well aware of the position they're puttin' us in." She shot him an emotion-laden look over her shoulder. She kept moving, winding her way through the heavier reeds and tangles of brush. "Don' step there, not even on the edge. The crust is thin here and you'll fall through."

He didn't bother attempting to hide their tracks. These men had grown up in the swamp and were hunters. They were also leopards with all the instincts and advantages of their cats. He stepped exactly in Saria's footsteps as she made her way through a narrow strip of land that was barely thick enough to support them. The reeds began to thin and brush took its place. Rather than cypress trees with the knobby-kneed root systems, evergreen and pine appeared, the grove growing thicker as they went deeper into it.

"You've been here — a lot. I thought no one came here."

She sent him a small grin, not breaking stride. "It was the one place no one thought to look for me. I've been comin' here since I was a child. It's my private refuge. No one else comes here, so I found a place around the other side to pull my boat onto shore and hide it."

"You're taking us through every pitfall you know of, aren't you?" The terrain had gone wet and soft again. He skirted around the areas she did. His leopard shifted inside him, stepping far from the spots that looked as if they might be quicksand. The Spanish-moss-covered cypress trees were back, growing in the thin soil. Around them palmettos, irises and marsh grass vied for space with tangled vines.

Turtles rested on logs and one sat on the bank. Birds were everywhere. Saria didn't worry about disturbing them. The buzz of insects was constant, becoming a kind of music in his ears. He found he was becoming accustomed to the sounds of the swamp. He knew the rain forest in the way she did her environment and he followed her without question.

She suddenly tugged at his arm to avoid stepping near a tree concealing a water moccasin.

"Should have seen that," he admitted.

"You were looking at my butt," she accused.

"So true." And damn it all, it was true. He figured he had a little time off while he followed her. "The view is spectacular."

She shook her head with a little snicker and picked up speed, rushing through a cypress grove that gave way to reeds. He stopped in his tracks. As far as he could see were blue heron and snowy-white egrets. They walked gracefully in the shallow water, dipping beaks into the waters, fishing.

"I've never seen anything like that."

She looked pleased. "I knew you'd think it was cool. You should see them when they take to the air."

"Have you photographed this?"

"Yes. But the money shot is as they're actually risin' to fly, with their wings outstretched, barely skimmin' the water."

"You're really very good, aren't you?"

"Yep. And I'm goin' to make a name for myself with *National Geographic*. I want my own book someday." She began walking rapidly again.

"How would you feel about photographing the rain forests of the world?"

The ground went solid again and the cypress trees gave way to another tangled grove. Saria ducked her head to go underneath a low-hanging branch. Something spit splinters at them both and the sound of a shot reverberated through the swamp. The air groaned under the sudden migration of birds as they rose in fright. An alligator slid into the water with an ominous plop. Drake took Saria down, his body covering hers.

They lay very still for a moment, hearts racing, Drake swearing silently.

"They shouldn't have been able to follow so fast," she whispered.

"They're using both animal and human form, which is against every law we have." His voice was grim. "Slide out from under me, Saria. Reach for your leopard. She'll rise to the surface to protect you. Don't be afraid of her. Her senses will be sharper than yours."

"What are you goin' to do?" she asked. For the first time he could hear fear in her voice and it tore at his heart. Damn them all, they were going to die today for this.

"You don' want her hurt, come out by yourself," Armande challenged.

Saria caught his arm. "Don' even think about it. They know I would never stay silent if they killed you."

"They'll get their chance at me. You start crawling forward and when you get to that heavier brush, break to your right. There's plenty of the cover unless they get crazy and spray the area with bullets. Give me a minute before you decide to shoot anyone. I'm going to shift and go after them."

"They'll kill you, Drake, and you know it. That's what they want. They can explain the killing of a leopard, but not a human being. They're goading you into shifting."

His leopard roared with fury, determined to remove the threat to his mate, uncaring about human life. The three men had dared to fire a weapon near Saria — they deserved death. He felt the familiar ache in his bones, the convulsing of muscles.

"No." Saria turned under him, onto her back, throwing both arms around him, holding on tightly, as if she could somehow hold off the fur slithering beneath his skin and the teeth filling his mouth. His shirt ripped with the ropes of muscles banding over his body. She refused to let go, even when hot breath blasted her throat. She closed her eyes, refusing to look at his face changing, but she never once let go.

There was a moment when he wasn't certain he could stop his leopard. Stiletto-sharp claws burst through his fingers and it was all he could do to bury them into the soft earth on either side of her head while he breathed his leopard into submission.

Her hands framed his face. There were tears swimming in her eyes when she opened them. He knew she was staring into eyes pure leopard.

"Please, Drake," she whispered. "Don' do what they want. Stay with me. We can fight them off."

He had no choice. Not if she was going to cry. The real knife to a man's heart was his woman's tears. He bent his head and kissed them away gently. "Let's go then. Crawl out of here, stay low and don't move brush."

They were both soaked from the wet ground and she shivered a little, still holding him tightly.

Behind them was an explosion of sound, a wild roaring growl and the sound of a man's high-pitched scream of terror.

9

Saria went still, lying beneath Drake in inches of water and mud, looking up at him with terrified eyes. The noises emanating from the groves of trees around them were horrifying. It sounded as if a thousand leopards were fighting over prey. The birds took to the air again, the sounds of their cries mingling with the ferocious growls and snarls rising in volume. Branches cracked and the brush trembled as heavy bodies slammed into them.

Drake rolled off Saria and reached to help her up. She took a better grip on her rifle, dropping behind him as he took the lead, working his way back toward the sounds of the battle. He opened his shirt in preparation for the change. Soaked and covered in mud, they ran through the brush, batting at spider webs as they wound their way along a narrow trail, avoiding sink holes and quicksand until they came to the grove of evergreen trees.

Five men, all heavily armed, surrounded two golden leopards and a huge black one. Drake drew his weapon, but Saria pushed the gun down.

"Don' shoot. That's Elie Jeanmard and four of my brothers," she whispered, her voice trembling a little. "The black leopard is my oldest brother, Remy. I saw him once like that."

Drake rocked back on his heels. He had expected to have to take on her brothers, but not all together.

Clothing was strewn around the ground, ripped and shredded. From the scent, Drake knew the two golden leopards had to be Armande and Robert. They had shed their clothes quickly, to keep from being attacked in human form by the ferocious black leopard. Remy had burst out of the trees and rushed them, giving them little time to shift before he hit Armande, driving him backward into the dark reed-choked water. He had whirled in midair, slashed Robert's muzzle as he dropped to earth and then drove viciously into him, cracking ribs as they tumbled over and over, ripping and clawing.

Fur rained down and blood splashed across the reeds. As fast as the two golden leopards rose, out of sheer desperation for survival, the black leopard relentlessly knocked them down again, his movements fast, twisting in midair, using his flexible, accordionlike spine, and savagely raking the sides and bellies of both cats.

The two leopards had no chance to coordinate their defense against him. Remy attacked them with such ferocity that Drake suspected the bloodlust of his leopard was out of control. If he wasn't careful, he was going to kill them both. The injuries both golden leopards had already sustained would take a long time to heal — and Remy was far from finished.

A black leopard was rare in the wild and even rarer among shifters. In shifters, as a general rule, they were bigger and stronger and in this case, faster. Remy moved with lightning speed, punishing the other two leopards, refusing to accept any sign of submission, forcing them to have to rise to protect themselves even when it was clear they wanted to call a halt to the punishment.

More than once each leopard signaled its submission to the enraged male, but he was having none of it, walking away, prowling back and forth, kicking leaves and dirt toward the two fallen leopards with a furious swipe of his paw and then leaping on them again and again, raking and clawing mercilessly.

No one made a move to help the two hapless leopards. Drake knew it was more than punishment. Remy Boudreaux was furious. Drake understood, even if no one else did. Personally, he would have killed both the bastards. They dared to shoot a gun at Saria Boudreaux. Remy and his brothers had been in pursuit and they heard the shot Armande fired toward Drake and Saria.

Saria's oldest brother was a hell of a fighter, one of the best he'd seen, and for a man to be that experienced, he had to have traveled as a shifter outside the Louisiana bayou. Drake wouldn't have been surprised to learn Remy had served on his own teams in the rain forest. Remy Boudreaux should be the leader of the lair, not Amos Jeanmard, Drake decided. He struck the right note of terror into the hearts of those watching. It was impossible to tell if he would stop before it was too late, but the others didn't seem terribly concerned.

Drake studied Elie Jeanmard, standing passively as he watched the leopards fight. Scent told Drake the man had been Drake's first challenger the night before and the third man pursuing him on the Mercier property. He watched the severe beating with a grim face, but made no move to stop it. This was Amos Jeanmard's son and if Drake was right and Jeanmard was the leader of the Louisiana lair, Elie didn't want any part of leadership. It was understandable. Elie had seen his father do his duty to the lair, but he'd been unhappy, and most likely his mother had been as well. Still, when he realized Armande and Robert were hunting Drake and Saria, he hadn't looked the other way, he sent for Saria's brothers.

"Uh oh," Saria whispered softly. "Maybe you'd better get behind me, instead of the other way around." She made a move to sidle around him, to protect him.

Drake caught her arm in a steel grip, holding her in place. His body partially blocked hers from the battlefield. One by one her brothers shifted their gazes from Remy and the torn and bloody leopards to Drake. He could feel the tension stretching out like a thin wire, until even the black leopard noticed and slowly turned his head. Red eyes fixed on Drake. The black leopard went low to the ground in the freeze-frame stalk of his kind.

"You won't find me easy prey like those two," Drake said, calmly peeling off his shirt. He flexed his shoulders to loosen his muscles as he kicked off his shoes. "Wouldn't be a fair fight, Boudreaux. You're tired and I'm still fresh. I could kick your ass anyway, but if you insist on making a fool of yourself in front of those two dirt bags, I'll oblige."

He kept his voice low, amused, a little taunting and it carried to the black leopard. The animal snarled, ears flat, teeth showing in a grimace. The killing rage was still on him and this time he had a target — a stranger — one who had dared to claim his sister. He knew he shouldn't throw the challenge back in Saria's brother's teeth, but damn it all, he was tired of this lair's out-of-control, strike-first-and-ask-questions-later policies. Someone needed to teach them a lesson.

He was still hanging on to his intellect enough to know his own leopard was driving him a bit, enraged over the attack on Saria, but he'd had it. He *wanted* to give in to his leopard's savage nature. His hands dropped to his jeans, slipping the buttons open quickly.

"What are you doin'?" Saria demanded, putting a restraining hand on his wrist. "Are you insane? That's my *brother*."

It was too late for Saria to stop anything. Her other brothers were flinging shirts off and stepping out of shoes. This wasn't going to be a one-on-one fight with Remy. Saria was their sister and as far as each of them was concerned, she'd been stolen — kidnapped — forced to accept a man they didn't know as a mate. They could smell his scent all over her and it maddened them. Remy continued forward in that slow stalk preceding an all-out attack.

The shotgun blast filled the air. Simultaneously, an automatic weapon sprayed bullets just a few feet from Saria's brothers, throwing dirt and twigs into the air. More bullets were fired in front of the black leopard. Elie swung around, his rifle at his shoulder, but there was no target. Everyone froze.

"Stand down. The next one who moves is dead."

Drake recognized Joshua Tregre's voice. He sounded deadly and no one, least of all Drake, was foolish enough to move.

"Drake, move back into cover," Joshua instructed. "Everyone else just stay right where you are and don't make the mistake of thinking we won't kill you. You don't mean a damn thing to any of us. Fucking bastards, turning on your own kind." He spat the words in disgust.

Two of Saria's brothers flinched, faces

darkening. One glanced at the gun he'd put on the ground near his shirt.

"Don't," Drake warned. "You'll be dead your first step. They don't miss."

The black leopard contorted, fur rippling, joints and bones cracking as the man emerged from the beast. Saria gasped and pushed her face into the back of Drake's shirt to prevent herself from seeing her oldest brother naked.

Remy was covered in blood and rake marks, but he straightened without wincing, his glacier-blue eyes sweeping the surrounding trees. "Don' move. Any of you," he commanded his brothers. He glanced at Drake. "I take it your boys have joined us."

It was a measure of Remy's strength that he'd fought back his leopard's killing rage and sounded matter-of-fact, casual even. He also was drawing attention to himself. It wouldn't work. Drake's team members were too well-trained. Each had a target, or in this case, a couple of them. Remy's brothers had been caught grouped too close together.

Drake gave him a curt nod. "I run a couple of teams in the rain forest." It was a shrewd guess, but Remy was no home-grown boy. He'd been around. A leopard sought out the wilds. If Remy had traveled, he would have run across a lair, and at least a few of the men who worked hostage and rescue.

"Mahieu, throw me my jeans before Saria has a stroke."

Saria's brother was as big as Drake, with the same heavy muscles, but his hair was very dark and he wore it long and shaggy and loose. His eyes were a striking cobalt blue. His face was tough, strong, the lines carved deep. A scar on the side of his neck indicated a knife had nearly ended his life at some point.

"And hurry," Saria added. "I do *not* want to see Remy in all his glory. I'll be scarred for life." Her voice trembled a little, but Saria wouldn't crumble, even under the tense situation.

"Let him," Drake told his team. They were concealed in the brush, impossible to spot, although the Boudreaux brothers had to have scented them by now.

Mahieu, using careful movements, retrieved his brother's jeans and threw them.

Remy caught them in one hand and dragged them up over his hips.

"Remy, the boys need medical attention," Elie Jeanmard pointed out, worry edging his voice. "It may already be too late."

"Too damn bad," Remy snapped. "I don' particularly care if they live." He looked at

273

Drake. Those piercing blue eyes never wavered. "I want to see my sister out in the open. I need to know she's all right. Saria, step out where we can see you. Don' be afraid. If this man is holding you hostage . . ."

Drake kept his hold on Saria. "A little late to play the concerned big brother. Where the hell were you when she was attacked?"

Saria dragged in her breath audibly. The two torn and bloody leopards, sides heaving, tongues lolling, both jerked in reaction, and began trying to drag themselves into the brush. Remy turned to eye them and both ceased all movement. He turned slowly back to regard Drake with a puzzled frown.

"What the hell are you talking about?"

"My point. A couple of weeks ago a member of your lair decided to force his leopard on Saria. I don't see that she had any protection. Not from the lair and not from her family."

"You don' pull your punches." Remy made it a statement.

"You might want to remember that the next time you challenge me to a fight."

A brief smile touched Remy's mouth. "You're also a hard-ass bastard."

"Bet your life I am," Drake agreed without remorse. "You didn't take care of her." He all but spat the accusation.

Saria straightened her shoulders. "I am standing here," she said to both of them. "And I'm not a hostage. I'm with him of my own free will."

"You all right, Saria?" Remy asked. "Come here, *cher.*"

Before she could comply, Drake stepped directly in front of her, cutting her off from her brothers. "I don't think so. You're not going to lay a hand on her."

Remy's penetrating eyes bored into him, the irises almost completely gone. His leopard was still close — still furious. "They dared to fire a gun at my sister," he hissed. "I don't much give a damn whether either of them is dead or alive. I don't think it's too much to ask to get a look at her to make certain she's unharmed. Saria, get the hell over here before I walk right over Romeo." The voice was pitched low, a velvet sheath over a steel dagger. "And don' stand behind your guns. Choose, man or leopard," he challenged.

His brothers stirred, as if to protest.

Armande and Robert, with great effort, shifted back into human form, groaning, weeping, trying to stop the blood from pooling on the ground around them.

Drake's eyes glowed amber. He could feel

the surge of heat and the wild call of his leopard leaping toward the open challenge.

"We shot to scare her," Armande clarified in a weak, placating voice. He'd shifted back into human form so his wounds could be seen to. "I was careful not to hit her."

"Shut the fuck up," Remy snapped, his voice glacier-cold. "I still may kill you." He meant it too, it was obvious in the sudden pacing he couldn't control, in spite of the guns trained on him. He glared at Drake. "Send my sister to me now."

The situation grew even tenser, inching its way to an explosive conflagration as the two male leopards leapt and roared for supremacy, pushing their human counterparts. Drake tried breathing his way through his rage. As a rule, he was the level-headed, calm leopard. His confidence and strength of will controlling his animal was the reason he was the chosen team leader, yet now he was shaking with the need to attack.

"What's wrong?" Saria whispered. "Do you think my brother would hurt me?"

Did he? It was a good question. What the hell was wrong with him? Remy might have reason to believe Drake had taken Saria against his will, but Drake had no reason to believe the man would harm his sister. So what the hell was his leopard reacting to?

Drake rubbed the bridge of his nose, studying the other man. He felt as if someone had rubbed his fur the wrong way. Every cell was alert and ready for combat. His leopard raged.

"Drake?" Saria's voice trembled.

The sound of that one note of fear steadied the man. His leopard continued to claw at him to be free, but Drake immediately turned to Saria. Her face was pale, her eyes enormous. She was trying to be brave, but with her brothers so close to losing control and Drake adding to the chaotic situation, she was frightened. To her credit, she'd kept her word and stood with him, her grip on the rifle never faltering, nor had she run to her brothers — but she wanted to reassure them. What sister wouldn't?

"Do you believe Remy would ever hurt me?" She glanced from Armande and Robert lying in pools of blood to her brother.

"No. He would defend you with his life," Drake said and forced himself to step aside. This was the telling moment. If her brothers could persuade her that she'd acted in haste, he was lost.

Remy held out his hand to his sister, crooking a finger at her. Drake moved a little closer, into a better position to defend her if it was necessary, but he made no move to stop her from going to her eldest brother.

"Let me help the two on the ground," Elie called out, cautiously moving toward the two fallen shifters.

"Go ahead," Drake signaled for his team to allow Jeanmard to give the two downed fighters medical aid.

Saria self-consciously raised her hand to wipe the streaks of mud from her face. Drake caught her wrist and gently put her hand back to her side. "You look beautiful, Saria, and you've done nothing wrong. You protected your client and if they don't see your courage and that you were right to do what you did, fuck 'em."

She blinked, swallowed whatever she'd been about to say and nodded. Saria made her way across the soft ground to her eldest brother. Remy put both hands on her shoulders and inspected her carefully for injury.

"I'm fine, Remy, just a little scared. I've never had anyone shoot at me before." She sounded a little shocked that her brothers had come after her.

Remy wrapped his arm around Saria, and pulled her close to him in a tight, fierce hug. "You scared the hell out of us, *cher.* When Elie contacted us that you were bein' pursued in the swamp by Armande and Robert with guns . . ." He trailed off, that hot blue gaze leaping murderously to Armande again.

Saria looked up at her brother. "I'm sorry. I had no idea they'd react like that. What's wrong with everyone?"

Remy inhaled deeply, taking the combined scent of his sister and Drake deep into his lungs. The piercing gaze swung back to Drake. "I think, *ma soeur,* that man who has his scent all over you is what's wrong."

At the accusation in his voice, Saria's color rose.

"Did this man force himself on you?" Remy demanded.

At the question, Saria's other brothers closed in, forming a tighter circle. Instantly a barrage of bullets kicked up water at their feet. Saria gasped and whirled toward the shooters. Drake shook his head, holding up his hand to stay fire. He held his ground. His shirt was unbuttoned, and like most shifters, he could lose his shoes fast, but his jeans would be a problem. Still . . . He waited, just as they all did. Every man there was looking at Saria, not at him, and he wouldn't have blamed her if she'd caved to the pressure.

She lifted her chin, looked Remy straight in the eye and shook her head. "I *asked* him to mark me. Someone else attacked me, rakin' my back and bitin' me. Scared me to death and it hurt like hell. I asked him to tell me what the Han Vol Dan was, to talk to me about shifters, because no one else had." This time the accusation was quite clear, aimed directly back at her brothers.

The two youngest brothers looked at each other and then at the ground.

"Did he coerce you in any way, Saria?" Remy ignored her pointed charge. "A female cat emergin' can be very amorous. He would know that."

"I coerced him, if you must know the truth, Remy. He was a gentleman the entire time, even though I did my best to seduce him. Is that what you wanted to know?" Now there was defiance and a hint of tears in her voice.

"Saria," Drake said gently. "You don't have to say another word. Come here, honey."

Remy kept his arm around his sister when she turned toward Drake. "He should have come to us."

"It happened too fast, Remy. I didn' know what was happenin' to me. And then I asked him not to go to you."

"That doesn't matter, he should have." This time the cobalt eyes pierced right through Drake.

Drake shrugged. "If you're implying I was afraid of you, you're wrong. I would have come this evening. I had important business that couldn't wait and Saria was safe with me."

"She was so damned safe someone shot at her."

Drake shrugged his shoulders. "I would have killed them before they got to her." His tone was matter-of-fact and absolutely confident.

Remy studied him. "Where are you from?"

"Originally, the rain forests of Borneo. I work for Jake Bannaconni." Drake glanced at the two men, torn and bloody on the ground. "I've never seen a lair like this one. No one that I know of would harm a female and if there was such a male, he'd be killed and burned, his remains buried deep." He poured disgust into his voice, disgust for the entire damned lair.

Remy didn't flinch. "We'll take care of this matter." He lifted Saria's chin so she was forced to look him in the eye. "Do you know what his claim on you means? Did he explain that to you? You don' have to accept him, Saria, even if your leopard does."

"I'm aware of that. I chose him. I still choose him."

Remy sighed. "If he's your choice, Saria, then we'll stand with you. In the meantime, I need to know who attacked you."

"I don' know. I really don'. I couldn't get a scent. Just leopard. I was so scared."

"You should have come to me."

She swallowed hard, ducked her head and nodded. "I know I should have, but I couldn't, Remy, not then. I have reasons."

His eyebrow shot up. "Are you goin' to enlighten us?"

She lowered her voice. "At home. When we're alone, Remy."

He studied her face, his jaw set. He gave a small nod. "You are comin' home then."

"We have to get this done and then we'll come right away," she assured.

"What done?" Remy demanded. His eyes narrowed on his sister, that deep cobalt blue that seemed to pierce through every cover.

"Jake gave me a job," Drake answered, bailing out Saria. She didn't want to answer in front of the other members of the lair, but she didn't want to lie. He took the matter out of her hands.

Remy sent him an irritated look. "Call your team in. No one's goin' to attack you." He managed to make it sound like Drake was a little kid and his mama bear was in the woods ready to protect him should there be need.

Drake stared at him coolly. "You don't have to like me, Boudreaux, any more than I have to like you. You let this happen and you can blame me if you can't stomach shouldering the responsibility, but don't think for one minute your intimidation tactics are going to work on me. I'm not a girl wishing her brothers loved her."

Saria gasped, whirling around to face Drake. "What are you doin'? You're pushin' him to fight you."

Maybe he was. He couldn't get his leopard to calm down. The animal ripped and clawed, wanting to get at Saria's brother. Remy appeared to have the same problem, and if the tension emanating from the rest of her brothers was anything to go by — they were fighting for control as well.

Drake frowned, shaking his head, trying to clear away the red haze. He glanced over at the two fallen leopards, torn beyond belief, Elie crouched low, trying to aid them. His mind felt heavy, leaden, thick and dense, as though the red haze had penetrated his brain, making it impossible to think clearly. For one brief moment, his eyes met Armande's.

Armande Mercier and Robert Lanoux lay in puddles of blood, their bodies shredded, ribs broken, both fighting for each breath. The Boudreaux brothers looked at them with deadly intent, still not satisfied with the punishment Remy had inflicted, yet there was something off. An alarm bell shrieked at Drake, yet he couldn't quite put his finger on what was wrong.

"Something isn't right here," he said aloud to Remy. The man was a homicide detective, obviously a leader. Surely he could feel it too.

Remy opened his mouth, closed it again and looked around. Yeah. He was feeling it too. He signaled to his brothers to finish dressing. Drake sent the signal to Joshua to call them in, but he was uneasy.

Joshua Tregre stepped out of the brush, automatic weapon ready, although he looked relaxed. He skirted around the brothers to close in to one side of Drake, about twenty feet out. Joshua's sun-bleached hair, worn shaggy, made him appear more of a surfer than a leopard, until you looked into his piercing blue-green eyes. His gaze held a stormy, turbulent sea, rather than a calm one, belying the laugh lines around his eyes. He had the deep chest and upper body strength of most of his kind. The weapon he held so comfortably appeared part of him.

A second man emerged from Remy's

right, only thirty feet from the fallen leopards. Drake sent a small salute. Jerico Masters nodded. He was head of security at the Bannaconni ranch when Drake was gone, which was a good deal of the time. A quiet man, he was dark-haired with green, watchful eyes. Drake was a little worried to see him there. With Jerico gone, who was watching over Jake, his wife Emma, and their children?

The last man surprised Drake. Evan Mitchelson was a very quiet man, big and muscular, a former prizefighter with a major speech impediment. He rarely spoke, but used sign language. He never shifted in front of others and Drake had often wondered if he could. He held a gun as if he were born with one.

"Nice to see you boys," Drake greeted quietly. "We have a little situation here. I need to know if your leopards are acting strange. Enraged. Pushing for supremacy, goading you to pick a fight or fire your weapon."

Remy sent him a shocked look. He looked at the three newcomers. Joshua nodded. "Almost from the moment we came into the marsh. We all discussed how edgy we were. We put it down to you being in danger. We just double-timed here."

Evan signed frantically. His leopard was rarely let loose because he was a killer, very difficult to control under the best of circumstances and Evan was fighting just for survival right now. He wanted to leave the marsh.

Jerico nodded his own confirmation. "How did you know where to look?"

"We followed your scent — well," Joshua looked guilty. "*Her* scent. Her leopard is putting off some major pheromones."

Saria rolled her eyes. "Great. You can smell me throughout the swamp. Just what I wanted to know." She moved a little closer to Drake as if for protection. He could see the subtle movement was subconscious.

"Sorry, ma'am," Joshua apologized. "Your leopard is rather alluring."

Drake's leopard clawed so hard, his muscles contorted and his jaw hurt. He felt the change sliding over him almost too fast to comprehend. His vision banded and he just happened to glance toward the two injured men. Armande's eyes met his. The man stared back at him with despair and something else — something indefinable. The strange look steadied Drake as nothing else could have. It was if the two fallen shifters knew something the rest of them didn't and were waiting for a catastrophe to happen.

He risked a glance at Remy and saw he was battling as well. "I think it's this marsh." He spoke loud enough for his voice to carry to the wounded shifters, watching them from the corner of his eye. Both looked uneasy, but they were as troubled as the rest of them.

Remy frowned but signaled to his brothers to work at controlling their leopards. "Perhaps we should all leave this place immediately."

Drake glanced at Saria. "What about you, honey? Is she quiet, or giving you fits?"

"She's extremely quiet. In fact, if it wasn't for all of you talking about pheromones, I might not even know she exists." Her gaze slid away from his, and for the first time, he knew she lied to him. Her leopard was reacting, but she didn't want to admit it.

"Remy, I want my men out of here. Evan is having great difficulty with his leopard."

"I am as well," Lojos admitted.

"Same here, Remy," Gage said. "If I don' shift soon, he's goin' to tear me up inside."

Remy looked to his other two brothers. Mahieu and Dash both nodded their agreement. "Elie, the boys are goin' to help you move those two. If you have a painkiller, give it to them." He glared down at the two wounded shifters. "We're goin' to pack you out of here, but all of us are havin' trouble with our leopards. Shut the hell up and stay that way. Neither of you had better give a reason to kill you, because it isn't too late dump your sorry asses in the swamp."

Gage and Lojos immediately went to help Elie get the wounded men on their feet. There was a lot of hushed cursing, but neither of the punished shifters was stupid enough to protest. They began walking back toward the dock where the Boudreaux brothers had left their high-powered boat, picking their way carefully around all the hazards.

Remy and Mahieu remained behind. They waited until the others were completely swallowed up by the brush before they approached Drake and his team members.

"Boss, do you need us here?" Evan signed.

Drake shook his head. "I'll meet you all back at the inn."

Joshua sent a hard look toward Remy and Mahieu, but he followed Jerico and Evan after the others.

"I'm Remy Boudreaux, Saria's oldest brother. This is Mahieu," Remy held out his hand.

Drake took it. "Drake Donovan. Jake Bannaconni sent me to check into some things for him. I hired Saria to guide me in the swamp and things just got out of hand fast."

Remy nodded slowly. "I can see how it could happen, and if you're her choice, we'll stand with you. We need new blood here. Our lair has dwindled down to nothing. Most of us have no choice."

"You might consider heading into the rain forest and seeing if you can find a mate," Drake said. "Although I'm fairly certain you've already done that."

Remy shrugged his shoulders. "I tried. I'm sendin' my brothers as soon as things settle down here. We didn' believe Saria had a leopard."

Drake opened his mouth to snap a reply. As far as he was concerned, that was no reason to neglect their little sister, but he didn't know all the circumstances and he honestly couldn't be certain if his leopard was driving his wrath at Saria's brothers.

"I do have one," Saria said unexpectedly, her eyes shining.

Drake wanted to smile. He slipped his arm around her shoulders and brought her close to him. "Yes you do."

"She's a little tough to control in this place," she added, again avoiding his eyes.

"You've been here before," Drake said. "What's different?"

Saria frowned and looked around her. "I don' know. It's beautiful, but it always was. More flowers and plants than I remember, but it changes all the time dependin' on the weather and the storm surges. You can see all the water. Sometimes it washes away the top soil and other times the water deposits rich soil here. This marsh is very wild and natural. Of all the places, this land has the most diversity of life and even terrain. All of this is marshland, but, although we call it Fenton's Marsh, it's a huge piece of property. The land firms up the more you go inland."

"Are you goin' to explain what's goin' on, Saria? All hell's broken loose in the lair. If Elie hadn't contacted us, I'd be in jail right now for killin' those two," Remy said.

"I don't think anyone expected me," Drake said. "Saria needed help and I was there. Our leopards definitely recognized one another. When the other one attacked her, her leopard hid from him."

Remy's eyes went ice-cold. "Who was it, Saria, and don' tell me you didn' recognize him. You had to have smelled him. And when he marked you . . ."

Drake felt a surge of anger at the words. He turned Saria around and raised the hem of her shirt, revealing the long marks, still red, although scarred over.

Remy and Mahieu both snarled, almost simultaneously, their leopards reacting to the sight of Saria's wounds. It mattered little that the furrows were nearly healed and had happened some time ago.

Remy moved closer, inhaling deeply in an effort to detect a scent. Saria shook her head and yanked down her shirt, glaring at Drake.

"I couldn't tell who it was. I don' know why I couldn' smell him, Remy. Maybe I was too scared. I thought he was going to kill me. I never had a leopard attack me before. I'd never been that close to one."

"You should have come to me immediately."

"And say a leopard attacked me? The only leopards I knew about were my five brothers." She made the statement staring him steadily in the eye.

"You knew?" Remy asked.

She nodded. "I saw all of you when I was a kid. At the time, *Pere* was still alive and I watched him carefully after that. I watched all of you. It was excitin' and scary. There were rake marks in the house some times and I saw all the signs. I'm good at trackin'."

Remy shook his head, clearly shocked at his younger sister. "If you'd come to us, we would have talked to you about it."

She pressed her lips together for a moment, but Drake could see she was distressed, although she quickly hid it with a casual shrug. "I thought maybe you didn't come around me much because I wasn't one of you."

She tried to hide the pain in her simple, honest statement, but Drake felt it — and so did his leopard. The big cat leapt so hard against Drake, his entire body shifted position, his muscles rippling and contorting. He had to breathe deeply to keep the animal at bay. Evan had said he kept his leopard under strict control, rarely letting it loose, and only then when they were completely alone because his animal was so violent. Drake was beginning to think his cat was following suit — at least around Saria's family.

Remy stepped back, drawing Mahieu with him. "Do you generally have problems with your leopard?" he asked in a low voice.

Had Remy sounded taunting or snide, Drake was fairly certain nothing could have stopped his leopard, but there was a note of worry there and Remy was once again looking around with wary, assessing eyes.

"No. Never. My leopard is always calm, otherwise I could never lead the teams into combat situations."

Remy nodded his agreement. "Somethin's not right. I can still feel it and it isn't Saria's leopard," Remy said. "I don' think it's safe here for either of you."

"It's important, or I wouldn't keep her here," Drake said. "I might be able to make it back on my own if you . . ."

"That's out of the question." Saria raised her stubborn chin, her large dark eyes gathering flecks of gold in warning. "I'm your guide and I stay with you. I know how to shoot. Let's just get this done and go home."

Drake sent Remy a rueful grin. "She's hard to argue with."

"She's always been like that. I'll expect the two of you back at the house." Remy gave his sister a stern look. "And talkin', Saria. I want to know everythin' goin' on, you hear me?"

"I hear you," Saria said, then muttered under her breath, "I think the world heard you."

"What was that?" her brother snapped.

Drake could see the amusement in his eyes belying his tone. "We'll be there." His palm slid down Saria's arm to her hand, his fingers tangling with hers. He gave a little tug. He wanted away from Fenton's Marsh as quickly as possible.

Saria looked up at Remy, still a little shocked that her brothers had come to rescue her. "*Bien merci,* I had no idea you'd come."

Mahieu stepped close to hug her tight. "Of course we'd come for you, Saria."

"Don' make me cry, Mahieu. I didn't know."

"We're *famille.*" He leaned close. "*J'aime beaucoup, ma soeur.* How did you not know that? If you're in trouble, Saria, we all come."

10

Drake nodded to Saria's two brothers as he took her with him back down the narrow path leading away from the water, but he walked carefully, keeping them in sight until they had put foliage between them. Saria lifted her hand toward her brothers in a brief wave, but she didn't say anything more, although they shifted positions, Saria taking the lead.

Drake frowned. His leopard was still prowling, pacing back and forth, fighting him occasionally to get out. "You're certain your female isn't giving you trouble?" He watched her closely, searching her dark eyes for signs of trouble.

Saria shook her head, glancing back at him. "She's quieter now."

Drake looked around them. Fenton's Marsh smelled like death to him. "Let's get going. I want to do this before nightfall."

Truthfully, he wanted Saria away from the

area, although he couldn't say the marsh wasn't beautiful. He could see why Fenton's pristine acreage was the habitat to so many wildlife species as he followed Saria into the interior.

Flowers grew among the darker greens of the plants, tall stalks strangely striped a dark and light green. The blossoms resembled a golden lily with dark splotches in the soft coned petals. Scattered among the taller flowers was another species he didn't recognize, each one of them growing about halfway up the striped stalk of the strange lily. Just as the vines tangled in the branches of the trees and wove them together, the smaller bright-colored flowers did the same on the ground.

Moss hung in long veils from tree branches, and every kind of plant possible seemed to vie for space in the thick brush. As they moved deeper, away from the water's edge, the foliage was even thicker, resembling a dark jungle. Mushrooms and fungus grew in abundance. Here, the flowers were thick carpets covering the ground beneath the trees.

"This is like a rain forest in here. The soil must be incredible."

She sent him a smile over her shoulder, immediately capturing his attention. "I've photographed every inch of this land through here. I'm slowly working my way south. I can't find the names of some of these plants and flowers anywhere. Like I said, no one comes here, they haven't for years. I'm hopin' there's somethin' important to *National Geographic* or one of the other science mags."

"Get some plant named after you?" He watched her walk, the easy sexy sway of her hips. She walked with straight shoulders, and that gentle sway emphasized her narrow waist. She wasn't fashionably thin, but rather had curves where a man like him most appreciated them.

"No, that's more Charisse's style. I just want to have my photographs paid attention to and somethin' like that would make me famous. I could really make my livin' that way." She flashed him another look over her shoulder and he forgot everything about his surroundings. It was a beautiful place, but there was nothing there more beautiful to him than she was.

"Stop it." She laughed softly. "Sometimes I don' know what to do with you."

"I can give you advice," he said.

The ground was growing spongy beneath his feet again, indicating they were crossing back toward the water on the other side of the long finger of land. Saria laughed softly again, but she didn't reply.

Drake was silent for a moment, trying to figure out a subtle way to broach the subject of her brothers. He kept his voice very gentle. "You know we have to tell your brothers someone is killing using both a leopard suffocation bite and a knife," Drake said, wishing he didn't have to bring them back to the purpose of their visit to the marsh.

For a few moments, it had been just the two of them again, but she had to come to terms with disclosing the information to her family. He wanted them both on the same page. They needed allies to figure out what was going on inside the lair. No one would talk to him, his team or probably Saria. They needed her brothers.

"I found those bodies some time ago and there won't be any evidence left," Saria pointed out.

"We don't have a choice, Saria. They know something is wrong."

Saria kept her gaze fixed on the trail as they walked. The path was becoming thinner, the surrounding area more hazardous, but Saria knew exactly where she going. "It won' be easy," she ventured. "Remy is a homicide detective and he won' like that I was afraid of them."

"Saria," Drake said softly. He stopped her by gently shackling her wrist and forcing her to turn back to him. "Whatever led up to your fears was real. One time coming to your rescue doesn't erase years of neglect. You had a reason to suspect them."

"Maybe, Drake, and maybe it was pride. They seemed so close to one another and I was so alone and not a part of them. Maybe I wanted to punish them in some way."

Drake leaned into her and brushed the top of her dirt-streaked face with a kiss. "It's always easy to second-guess yourself with new information, but at the time, honey, you did the best you could. You were trying to protect them."

She squared her shoulders and nodded. "Thank you for not making that worse back there with my brothers. I know you were angry."

He raised an eyebrow.

She smiled and shrugged. "Your eyes start glowin'. Really, Drake. They go gold and then shimmer. I think every once in a while I'll be tempted to get you angry just so I can see all that shimmering fire."

He bunched her hair in his fist and brought his mouth to hers. When he lifted his head, his eyes were every bit as golden as she'd claimed. Saria laughed and the tension in his belly dissipated. She was back, sure and confident. She'd been shaken for a moment, but she'd been true to her word, and she stood with him.

"I wasn't angry so much as my leopard was behaving badly."

"*All* of you were behaving badly. I thought my brothers were going to kill you. And Remy nearly killed Armande and Robert. It was very tense there for a while." She gave a little sniff. "I was the only one with a lick of sense.

"I'm takin' you the safe way around and stayin' out of the marsh as much as possible. This way is longer, but less hazardous, although we're comin' back into the reeds, so look sharp if we go through water. What are you hopin' to see?" she asked. "The bodies are long gone."

"My leopard will be able to scent them. I want to know if there were others. It's possible your killer has been using the island for a dump site for a while."

"I don' know why, but I still think the first time was different than the others. There were two boats, and I suspected they were up to some illegal activity."

"Two different killers?"

She frowned, shaking her head as she

wove her way through the reeds. "No. More like that time it wasn't planned and the other times deliberate."

He noticed she kept her rifle cradled carefully in her arms and she was very alert, watching for alligators as they neared the reeds. She stopped at one point and then gave an area a wide berth.

They walked for perhaps another mile. His leopard began to settle, allowing him to breathe easier. The terrible need to explode into rage subsided gradually, and with it the tension drained from his body, allowing him to drop his guard enough to enjoy their surroundings.

The foliage had fewer wildflowers tangled among the dense shrubbery and more trees and large brush spaced farther apart. There was evidence of small animals everywhere. Birds had settled back into the branches and when they neared the outer edges of the curved property, he could see egrets and herons wading in the shallow reeds.

Saria took them to a sheltered cove, one where the ground was solid and trees lined the water's edge, shading the edge of the marsh and the reeds jutting out into the water.

She spread out her arms and turned in a circle. "This is where I found the second body. It was half in and half out of the water over there." She pointed a distance away to a long path where the brush was flattened leading to the edge of the reeds and deeper water — obviously an alligator slide. "And over there." She pointed to a spot a good deal away from the slide where someone might choose to picnic, thinking themselves safe from the gator. "There were bottles from our bar lyin' on the ground."

He took her hand and led her back to the interior, away from alligators and dead bodies. The ground was solid and the trees had thick branches. If need be, she could easily climb up one, although there was no evidence of alligators this far inland.

"I'm going to shift and take a look around, Saria. It may take a while."

"I want to take some photographs of you. Is that all right? In your leopard form."

"You know that's not a good idea." Drake hated to deny her anything. "Even for your own use, it's just not a good idea."

"How could anyone tell the difference between a shifter and a leopard?"

He handed her his shirt, shrugging out of it easily. "They'll know the picture was taken here in the marsh, honey. How will you explain a leopard in Fenton's Marsh?"

Saria seemed fascinated by the muscles

on his chest. She stared while she folded his shirt. Drake kicked off his shoes and dropped his hands to the front of his jeans. Her gaze dropped with his hands as he parted the material and peeled them from his body. He liked that she was fascinated. She was going to have to get used to seeing him naked and she didn't seem to mind, although she appeared a little intimidated.

"Your brother Remy is a tough man." He tried distracting her.

She blinked, trying to focus on his face. "All of them are."

"This lair needs a strong leader. And he fought circles around their appointed fighter. He'd take any of them down in seconds."

"My brothers stay to themselves."

"Isn't Mahieu seeing Charisse?" He handed her the jeans, desperately trying to think of anything but sex. Suddenly sex was on his mind in a big way, and being a man, he found his thoughts physically impossible to hide. She was already intimidated enough by the thought of having sex with him.

"Well, with any of my brothers you just never know. Lojos and Gage have been givin' him a really bad time about her, teasin', you know. Mahieu doesn't say much, but he's been hittin' the jazz clubs with her."

She made no attempt to pull her gaze away from his body. Her eyes grew big and she raised her eyebrows. "I don' know, Drake, you're just a little bigger than I expected."

The woman could make the devil blush. Instead of stepping back from him, she stepped closer to him and reached toward him hesitantly, as if afraid he'd bat her hand away. He went still. So did his leopard. Both held their breath. Her gaze jumped to his face, burning into his, then dropped again to his heavy erection. Tentatively, her fingers brushed over his cock, a soft slide of just the pads of her fingers, as if he might burn her skin — instead, she burned his.

The breath slammed from his lungs. Hot blood rushed through his veins to pool into a wicked, urgent need. Every nerve ending seemed centered in his groin. Her fingers stroked over the length of him, tracing him, shaping him, sliding lower to cup his sac. A low growl escaped, his throat closing on the sound so it came out strangled.

"So hot," she murmured as if to herself. "Alive."

"Very alive," he admitted, gritting his teeth. He didn't want her to stop, but it was torture, pure and simple.

Saria looked up again at Drake's face.

Lines of desire were etched deep. His eyes had gone fiery gold — like the blazing sun. She moistened her lips. Everything about him was beautiful to her. She loved the idea that his body was so hot and hard just for her. There was something powerful and freeing about taking control. Her fingers played over his body as if it was a musical instrument, sliding and stroking and shaping while she committed the feel of him to her memory. A single pearly drop of his essence leaked from the smooth, velvet head.

Saria stared down at the drop and licked her lips a second time. Her mouth watered. Deep inside, she felt her leopard stir, and then stretch with languid interest. The amorous cat had been driving her crazy earlier in the swamp — something she didn't want to admit to Drake in front of her brothers, but now she didn't want her leopard's response. She wanted this exploration to be all her. Looking up, she thought that Drake's face could have been carved from stone. His eyes were hooded, heavy-lidded, his expression one of pure power and passion. His eyes had gone completely golden with lust and unbridled need — for her. She drank in the sight of him, her heart pounding with daring.

"Drake." She stared down at his erection.

"Show me."

He didn't ask questions, or protest. He took her hand and wrapped it around him like a fist. He showed her how to pump him. He felt like velvet over steel, a fascinating combination. She wanted to spend a long time learning all about his body, what made him gasp with pleasure and what brought him to his knees. What put that sexy, heated glitter in his gold eyes.

She'd read about sex, and she'd certainly fantasized, but she hadn't considered being with any of the men she'd grown up with. This man with his rock hard body, the blazing heat in his eyes and passionate nature was everything she'd imagined. Her body felt hot and needy, her skin so sensitive that the thin shirt hurt. She felt hungry for him, starved to know the taste and feel of him. She wanted to make her own claim on him.

She hadn't thought of herself as a jealous woman, but the thought of another woman touching him made her want to claw with lethal intent. She wanted to be the one to please him, to be the one he craved with the same intensity she craved him. The need came in waves, a hot rush through her veins pulsing through her feminine core. The deep urgent desire was not entirely brought on by her leopard, although she understood the feline much better than she had.

Drake Donovan was the sexiest man she'd ever encountered and the chemistry between them was off the charts. There was no resisting the terrible urgency in her body. Without thinking, she bent her head to taste that silky drop, her tongue curling around the broad head. He jerked in her fist, swelled more. A growl rumbled in his chest and she licked with small delicate strokes, smiling when she was rewarded with hot pulses.

"I'm not a damned saint, Saria," he hissed, his voice nearly demonic.

She looked up at him, a chill sliding down her spine at the desperate tone in his voice. His eyes blazed with a dark lust that only intensified her ravenous hunger for his taste. His hand moved hers to the base, wrapping her fingers tightly around his thick erection. She let the hand bunched in her hair guide her to her knees in the thick grass. The impressive amount of flesh in her fist held her fascinated gaze.

"Draw it into your mouth, nice and slow," he instructed. "Just like that. Easy now, get used to the size and feel." He threw back his head and groaned when she obeyed. "Use your tongue, baby."

She pulled back and licked him, much like

a cat licking at a bowl of cream. When he pulsed against her tongue, she enclosed him in her mouth. All that silken steel. The taste of him was feral, hot, all male. His hips jerked and she blinked up at him again, seeing the amazing gold of his eyes shimmering with heat.

His hips jerked again in a desperate, shallow rhythm she immediately caught onto. She drew him deeper, and allowed her mouth to glide back. He drew a ragged, harsh breath in response. She heard her own moan as he filled her mouth again, as she felt power surge through her, a dark passion that fed the lust driving her. She needed him like this, groaning, at the very edge of his control, while her untutored mouth drove him wild.

"Saria." He said her name. That was all, a single word, but his voice was rough and demanding, a harsh plea for mercy, a command to continue.

He was thick, stretching her lips, filling her mouth, hot and pulsing with life. He tasted so male, so much dark passion, hot and delicious. She licked at the underside of the broad, sensitive head, enjoying the sensation and his reaction. He groaned when she took him deeper. His hand suddenly fisted in her hair, holding her still while his hips jerked in a series of shallow thrusts.

"Relax, honey. Just relax and breathe. Take a breath and hold it when I slide a little deeper. I won't let anything happen to you."

She did as he said, taking a breath, feeling him slide deeper until she was afraid she might choke, but he went no further and the sensation of feeling his heart beat in her mouth gave her an answering pulse deep inside her core. She felt white lightning arc through her body, as if every nerve ending was connected to her mouth.

"Flatten your tongue."

Even as the words left his mouth he groaned as she complied, rubbing that sweet spot under the broad head as he slid out. He held her head still as he slid back inside. Again she had to fight her own reflexes not to panic, but he was careful. He began a rhythm, pulling her closer, letting her take a breath and pulling her head down onto him as he thrust.

"Suck harder, honey. Yeah. Like that. That's so fucking good. More, honey, give me harder. I need it."

She listened to his harsh instructions, following them carefully, giving herself up to him, wanting only his pleasure, loving the sounds of his groans and the helpless thrusting of his hips. She dug her fingers into his hip, holding him closer, using her tongue and the heat of her mouth to bring him closer to release. She felt him grow larger, felt the heat and fire of him. He pulsed with life, with such erotic passion she couldn't have stopped herself if she'd wanted to.

His hand pushed her head down just a little farther as she took a breath, jerking in short spurts, and then she felt his hot release pouring into her. He moaned low and long, the sound as arousing as the hard flesh jerking in the heat of her mouth. His fingernails sank into her scalp and one shoulder as he breathed hard.

"Use your tongue, baby," he urged. "That feels so damned good."

She lapped at him, a gentle ministry to calm them both. She was breathing nearly as hard as he was. She felt achy everywhere, almost desperate to rip off her clothes and impale herself on that thick, velvet-over-steel spike.

Drake drew her up, holding her close to him. "That was unbelievable, Saria."

"I'm sure I'll get better," she said, her gaze suddenly worried.

"Better might kill me." He brushed a kiss over her temple. "We'll finish this at the inn in a comfortable room with a bed. Your first time should be special, honey."

She wasn't certain she could hold out for special, but he had a point. The swamp was no place to try to have sex. She nodded, unable to get past her own desire. She needed breathing space from him.

Drake could tell Saria was struggling and he cursed himself for allowing her to service him when he couldn't show her what making love was. He could see she wanted to be alone and he hated that he had to comply, to just leave her after she'd given him so much pleasure.

"Will you be all right?"

"I practically live in the swamp," she said, studying the edge of the trees. "I can take pictures while you do whatever it is leopards do."

Uneasy, he shifted, staying close to her for a moment to rub his fur all over her, in his own way trying to reassure her before he set off. Drake searched the entire area, crisscrossing the wild terrain, using every means available to search out evidence of a leopard making a kill. He had never been so frustrated — or alarmed — in his life. There were numerous places where he scented blood and death, six to be exact, and he'd uncovered more empty bottles from the Boudreaux bar, but nowhere did he find evidence of a leopard. Not a single track. Not a scent mark. No fur.

His leopard at times was very settled and then suddenly would become so agitated Drake feared he might not be able to control him. There seemed no pattern to the sudden surge of temper as Drake picked his way through several acres. Saria was at the center of the ever-widening circle he used to hunt for evidence and he made certain he could scent her at all times.

He knew Saria couldn't have imagined a leopard bite. It was fairly distinctive. She'd agonized over writing the letter to Jake, so there had to be truth in what she'd seen. Leopards left trails. They marked everything. Where they'd been. Territories they moved through. It was natural behavior and, although he was extremely strong and controlled, he doubted if he could stop his leopard from marking. Especially after a kill.

He retraced every step, aware time was slipping away. He didn't trust the marsh at night. The lair of leopards was so out of control, it was impossible to know what they might do next. Before anything else, he had to keep Saria safe. He needed to get back to the inn, shower, collect his team and meet Saria's brothers. There was nothing here to indicate leopard, but there was no doubt in his mind that Fenton's Marsh was a killing ground.

He made his way back to Saria as the sun was setting. Layers of crimson red, burnt orange and antique gold filled the sky, turning the reflecting waters surrounding the tip of Fenton's Marsh into shades of color. An alligator, so still it appeared to be a log, sat on the bank, just above the reeds. A slight breeze created a ripple through the field of reeds, so that waves appeared to be lapping at the alligator's feet. The gator was large, at least eighteen feet or more, a majestic, prehistoric creature from another age.

Bats wheeled and dipped over the water, feasting on insects, small dark bodies against the colorful sky. The birds walking like stick figures in the reeds seemed no more than cardboard silhouettes against the brilliant colors of the sunset. The tree trunks reflected in the water made it look like a painting, shimmering colors of gold and red.

The swamp was breathtaking as the sun came down. Saria crouched low, eye to her camera, capturing the beauty of the coming evening in a frozen image. Her clothes were streaked with dirt and her hair was wild, but she belonged there in the midst of all that beauty. She took his breath away. He could see the outline of her breast pushing against her T-shirt, that soft inviting curve, her narrow rib cage and tucked-in waist. As she shifted position, he admired the curve of her butt and hips.

Saria moved with confidence in spite of the sun going down. She was unafraid, even though she was well aware of the dangers of the swamp. She took several pictures, snapping quickly, and he waited patiently so as not to disturb her. She was leopard. She would know he was there.

When she slowly straightened, stretching to loosen tight muscles, he shifted, emerging naked, going for his clothes. She turned to watch him, raising the camera to her eye again and snapping as he pulled on his jeans.

"You didn't?"

"Just your face." She laughed. "You had such a shocked look I couldn't resist. You're not the only perv here, you know."

He loved that she was unapologetic about enjoying his body. He found it strange that he'd only just met her. It seemed a lifetime ago, as if he'd known her forever, and yet each encounter was perfect and new. He had often imagined falling in love as a slow process. Learning about one another, the incredible chemistry that came with that first rush of desire and then a slow, smoldering growth that was calm and sure and steady. His experience with Saria was all of that and nothing like that. He fell like a ton of brick, dropped right into her fathomless dark eyes and kept falling.

He knew he couldn't live without her, when only a few days ago he didn't know of her existence. He'd been half alive, walking through the world without seeing or appreciating the beauty of it. Saria gave him the gift of sight. The sound of her laughter was like music on the wind, elusive and impossible to catch, yet she'd given him that gift as well. The trust in her eyes when she looked at him humbled him. The way she freely gave herself to him, uninhibited, willing for him to instruct her just so she could please was a gift beyond all measure.

"Take us home, Saria. We'll get cleaned up, pick up my team and go meet your brothers."

She blinked, looked away from him and spent an inordinate amount of time putting her camera away while he dressed.

Drake moved up behind her and slipped his arms around her waist, resting his chin on her shoulder. "Tell me, honey. If you're worried, talk to me. I don't want you ever to worry needlessly. We can figure it out."

She moved against him, fitting her body

315

into his as if for reassurance. "Are you expectin' trouble with my brothers? Is that why you're bringin' your team?"

"Is that what you thought?" He nibbled on her neck, finding the sweet spot where her neck and shoulder joined. He could tell he found it by the way her breathing changed. He kissed her there several times. "I want your brothers to get to know them as human beings. We need allies in the lair. We can't be fighting them all the time and your brothers are a force to be reckoned with. Remy is strong and intelligent, a natural leader. The lair will listen to him."

She turned in his arms, linking her hands behind his neck. "*Merci.* I don' want you fightin' with my brothers."

"I doubt there's need. Unless, of course," he bit gently on her shoulder and nibbled his way up her throat to the corner of her mouth, "they try to take you from me."

"I think they're glad to get rid of me, at least until my little hussy emerges."

He pulled back to look down at her. "Saria, you don't think we're going to have a one-night stand do you?"

She frowned. "I was hopin' we'd practice a little before she emerges," she admitted, color sweeping into her face. "I know I can please you if you just give me the chance."

He framed her face with his hands. "Baby, you have this all wrong. A claiming isn't just for one night. It's not just my leopard claiming yours. We're a mated pair. We stay together."

She looked startled. "Leopards don' mate for life. I mean, I know you mentioned that once but I thought you were . . ."

"Shifters do. *We* do. Saria and Drake. We mate for life." He stared down at her frown. At her stubborn chin. "Are you saying you planned on using me for sex and then you were just going to send me on my way?" He couldn't help feeling a little outraged. He was experienced. Older by several years. Worldly. And she was going to use him and send him away. Damn it all to hell. "We mate for *life,* Saria."

She dropped her arms and stepped back. "I didn' understand that part."

"Clearly." He gentled his voice. Maybe he'd scared her. "Did you think I was taking advantage of your leopard?"

Her gaze jumped to his. "Drake, I didn't know. I'm sorry, I just have to get this clear in my head. I thought you'd be with me and then have to leave. You don't live here. I guess it just made sense you'd be goin' away — after."

He pushed down anger. What kind of man

317

did she take him for? On the other hand, there'd been warning signs she'd thought that way and it did make some sense. He'd ignored it because he wanted her feeling the same deep feelings he'd already developed for her.

"Look, Saria, I know I was selfish earlier. I should have stopped us and waited until we were in a room with a bed so I could make love to you properly. I'm not going to make excuses, but I won't be a selfish lover. I'll put you first and make sex great for you. More than great."

Saria looked more confused than ever. "You don' even know me, Drake, not really. I'm not a city girl and I don' ever want to be. This is my home and I love it. My life is simple for a reason. I had choices. This is my choice."

"I know that, baby. I see you. Every part of you. Of course I know you have choices. I want me to be one of those choices."

She bit her lip. "I'm not like other people, Drake. I'm just not. I can't breathe sometimes away from here. I do what I want. I don' like hurtin' others and I know if we were together, you'd eventually try to tell me what to do and I know I would never do it." She shook her head. "I don' want to end up with children, an unhappy husband

and a divorce."

"The female leopard is not submissive to the male, Saria," Drake said. "She's wild and moody and he has to be in tune with her in order to be a successful mate. I didn't choose you because I thought you'd be submissive to me. Am I a dominant male? Yes. There's no probably, but I want a woman to stand by my side, to think for herself, to argue with me if she believes she's right. I want you. It's up to you to decide if you want me the way I am." He glared at her. "But you're not using me for sex and throwing me away after."

A slow smile crept into her eyes. "You drive a hard bargain. I was lookin' forward to usin' you for sex. You're very yummy."

He gave her his darkest scowl, not giving in to his inclination to laugh at the absurdity of the situation. "Just remember the next time you want sex, you'd better mean it."

She rolled her eyes, not impressed with his ultimatum. "We'd better get out of here. You don' want to be traipsin' through the swamp at night. Not even with me."

Drake hid a smile. Yeah. He liked that little stubborn streak and the challenge she was always going to present. She had a passion for life and that same passion would spill over into the bedroom. He followed her back through the swamp as they retraced their steps, careful to step where the ground was solid.

Halfway back to the boat, he felt the snarling awakening of his leopard. The beast clawed and raked at him, an urgent demand to be let free. He found his amusement fading to be replaced by anger. Anger grew into rage with every step he took as they wound their way quickly through the rapidly darkening swamp. Who the hell did Saria think she was, treating him like that? Use him and walk away? She was a control freak. She needed a real man to teach her a lesson. His leopard roared at him, fighting to set free, to . . .

Drake pulled himself up short. What the hell was he thinking? Saria was young and inexperienced. And afraid. He couldn't blame her. She was only trying to sort out an unfamiliar situation. He never would harm a woman or even consider doing such a thing. He stopped and looked around them. He had wrestled internally for some time as they made their way back to where she'd docked their boat, almost as if he'd lost track of time. His leopard subsided, giving him some breathing room as he followed Saria into the boat.

What the hell was going on? He needed to

talk to his team. To her brothers. To really investigate Fenton's Marsh and figure out what was wrong with the place. It felt — evil.

The Boudreaux house was somewhat small, but very well built. Mahieu escorted them inside and Drake's team immediately deployed close to the windows. Remy kept the lights off, other than a few candles, and they sat down to discuss the situation. Drake sensed Saria's nervousness. They'd showered — in separate rooms — and she'd been quiet since they left the swamp. He couldn't blame her, he was fairly quiet himself, wondering just what had happened between them. She did sit next to him on the couch, which he was grateful for. She fit beneath his shoulder, his thigh touching hers, and that seemed to give her confidence to launch into her story.

Remy and the others listened patiently to Saria without once interrupting her. When she finished, there was dead silence. Drake looked around the room. Her brothers looked shocked. His team was more prepared. Jake had briefed them before they had come to help.

"You thought one of us had done this." Remy made it a statement. "Become a serial killer?"

Saria slipped her hand into Drake's, her fingers tangling tight with his. "I didn' know there were any other shifters, Remy. I didn' want to betray any of you, but when I found the second body, I knew I couldn't just let the killin' continue."

"So you tried to mail a letter but found it the next day pinned to the pirogue. None of us use that, only you, so you knew the warnin' was for you, and all of us had access to your boat." Remy's voice was thoughtful more than critical.

Drake stayed silent, shifting on the worn couch to bring Saria a little closer to him in an effort to comfort her. His team remained silent, deployed by the open windows, using leopard senses to ensure their privacy.

Saria nodded. "I was very scared."

"For God's sake, Saria," Remy snapped suddenly, "I'm a fuckin' homicide detective. You couldn't have thought it was me."

"I didn' want to think it was any of you. I was afraid, Remy." Her voice trembled.

Drake cleared his throat to rid himself of the snarl building. At least his leopard had subsided, giving him some breathing room. The sound was loud in the silence of the room, bringing immediate attention to him. All five of Saria's brothers stared at him.

"You knew about this?" Remy asked.

Drake nodded. "Jake received her letter. It wasn't signed, and it was worded very carefully. It implied someone was using Fenton's Marsh to permit a large cat to kill humans by first stabbing the victim and then allowing the animal to administer a suffocating bite to finish the job. Naturally he was intrigued and he sent me to investigate. At the time, of course, I had no idea Saria had sent the letter. I asked for a guide into the swamp and she came highly recommended."

Remy nodded. "That makes sense. She is considered one of the best guides around. Even with our leopards, she's difficult to find if she doesn't want to be found."

Saria smiled and Remy glared at her. "That was no compliment."

Drake brought her hand to his mouth and brushed a kiss across her knuckles. As long as he wasn't the one trying to find her, he thought Remy's observation was a great compliment. She sent him a quick smile.

"What did you find out there?" Remy asked.

"No bodies, but the scent of large pools of blood in the ground told me a number of males have been killed out there."

Remy pressed two fingers to his eyes. He looked at his sister. "Where are they, Saria?"

he demanded.

Saria blinked. She pressed her lips together. "Where is what?"

"The photographs. You took pictures of the dead bodies and the wounds on them. I know you did, so cut the crap and let me see them," Remy snapped.

Of course she had. Drake should have thought of that. It was exactly what Saria would have done. She would have recorded the entire scene and the surrounding area. She would have done exactly as her brother said. Face, wounds, everything. She was a photographer and a damned good one. She would have needed proof to show Jake Bannaconni. And she'd probably seen enough crime scenes to photograph them correctly.

"Give them to him, Saria," Drake said. "Remy's the investigator."

She bit down on her lower lip. "Remy, at two of the scenes, there were bottles from our bar. The kind we use exclusively. And Drake found evidence of other dump sites. There were no bodies, but he found where someone had lost a lot of blood and the same bottles were there."

"You went lookin' for more bodies?" Remy asked.

Drake nodded. "I wanted to confirm what Saria had told us. The bodies were long gone. The alligators took care of that, but my leopard found several more kill spots."

There was a brief silence. The brothers exchanged long looks. Remy sighed. "Did you catch the scent of a leopard, somethin' strong enough you might be able to recognize if you came across it again?"

Drake shook his head. "Nothing. Not a rake mark. No pile of leaves. No scent marking and nothing near where the victims were killed. Just blood and death. No leopard."

"That's a good thing, isn't it, Remy?" Lojos, the youngest brother asked. "It isn't a shifter."

"Could you be wrong about the bite, Saria?" Remy asked. "Maybe Fenton's Marsh is a body dump, but there is no leopard involved."

Saria made a face at him. "You think I don' know a leopard bite when I see one?" She jumped up and rushed from the room to get the proof.

Remy flicked his gaze at his younger brother Lojos, who silently followed his sister. Drake realized Remy was uneasy and worried for Saria's safety even there in their home with all of his brothers and Drake's team to protect her.

"What is it you're not telling us?" Drake asked.

Remy sighed and glanced at Mahieu, who shrugged. "The dead bodies in Fenton's Marsh aren't the only ones. There have been five women that we know of murdered in similar fashion to what Saria says is goin' on in the marsh. All stabbed with a strange bite mark to their throats — a leopard bite. The first killin' was several years ago. We think there are more. It's easy to go missin' in New Orleans. We've had unsolved murders of women and people disappearin' for years, but the bodies found were very distinctive."

"Are you saying these killings have been going on for years — that they're connected?"

"We believe so. And if a serial killer is on the loose and no one has come close to him before now, then Saria is in real danger. She's alone all the time in the swamp. Everyone knows her and knows she photographs everythin'. If she found his current dumpin' ground, and she sent a letter which he managed to intercept, she's on his radar."

Every muscle in Drake's body tensed. The thought of Saria in danger was more than disturbing — everything male — in both leopard and human — protested.

"You've been watching all the females in your lair closely to protect them," he guessed shrewdly.

Remy nodded. "The leopard bite bothers me. I doubt it's real, but suppose someone knows about us and is tryin' to cast blame on us — to bring us out into the open. We've married into families incapable of shiftin' over the years. It's possible someone born with the traits of a leopard but unable to shift could do this."

Drake nodded. "Our species is capable of great cruelties. Without the ability to shift and allow the leopard freedom, yes, it could happen easily."

"Saria bein' so close to the Han Vol Dan complicates matters," Mahieu added. "Every male for a hundred miles is crazy. Armande and Robert have both lost their minds."

"It's a lot more complicated than a female being close to emerging," Drake contradicted. "This lair is in trouble and I think you all know that. You need strong leadership to keep leopards in check, especially around an actual city. This lair lacks that. You weren't there the other night when they sent a fighter to challenge me. Robert Lanoux broke one of the most important rules in any lair and he went unpunished."

"He was punished today," Remy said grimly.

"Yes, but you're not the leader of the lair, Jeanmard is. Or was. You know this situation will only grow worse if something isn't done."

"Are you advocatin' one of us become the leader of this lair?" Remy sounded incredulous.

"Not one of you. You," Drake said. "Because if you don't, you're going to have murders all over the place. If you think the attack on Saria was a one-time thing, you're sadly mistaken. I've seen this happen before. Leopards have intense drives. You have to meet those drives or your leopard goes rogue. You all know that."

"I have a serial killer to catch. Puttin' this lair back together again is a full-time job."

Drake nodded. "You're going to have to send your males out to find females away from this place so you don't risk the bloodlines becoming contaminated. More than anything, that gets dangerous. There are all kinds of problems here, Remy, and someone has to fix them."

"Boss," Joshua interrupted. "We've got company out there and they don't look friendly."

11

Drake leapt to his feet, the jump taking him across the room to the hallway where Saria had disappeared. He landed in a half crouch. Mouth set in grim lines, face a death mask, he turned already glowing eyes on Remy. "Where is Saria?" It was a clear demand, his voice a growl.

Joshua and Evan immediately moved position, a covert shift to cover their leader while Jerico remained at the windows, his weapon cradled comfortably in his arms.

Mahieu and Gabe blew out the candles, plunging the room into utter darkness, but with leopard vision, they had no problem seeing.

"The darkroom is a small shed behind the house," Remy said. "Lojos went with her." There was worry in his voice.

"Remy Boudreaux!" Amos Jeanmard's voice called from outside. "We have Saria. She is a member of this lair and it has been decided that she is not allowed to leave our lair. We need her here. It is her duty to mate with one of our males. She will be given the chance for her leopard to choose. As lair leader I demand you and your family comply for the good of the lair."

A roar of fury erupted from Drake. He began ripping his shirt away, claws forming, leaving thin traces of blood along his chest. "You'd better choose where your loyalty lies, Boudreaux," he spat out. "Your sister or this poor excuse of a lair."

Jerico yanked open the door as Drake kicked aside shoes and began peeling off his jeans.

"I challenge for leadership," Drake snarled, "as is the right of every leopard." He shifted on the run, leaping from the living room straight through the door and landing twenty feet from Amos Jeanmard.

The leader of the Louisiana lair ripped hastily at his clothing, stumbling back from the snarling, hissing interloper. He couldn't refuse the challenge — no leader could — but it was obvious he hadn't expected a challenge to happen so quickly.

Drake's vision was all banded heat. He located Saria, who looked disheveled. There was a bruise coming up on her cheek, her hair was wild, and her mouth set in grim lines. She stood very close to a tall stranger, a man he'd never seen — or scented — before, but he inhaled deeply, knowing he would never forget that scent now. The man stood so still he could have been carved from stone, and he wore a strange, almost desperate expression on his face. A few yards from them, Drake could see Lojos on the ground, unmoving.

The scent of blood reached him and he grimaced, prowling back and forth, roaring his challenge. The other lair members shifted back away from him each time he approached them. Twice he rushed Amos, stopping the charge only inches from the man as he finally stripped, his body contorting and cracking as he shifted.

Scents mingled and merged. Fear. Sweat. The swamp itself. Saria. Drake's leopard took them all in, adding to the feral, wild need welling up. As old as time, the instinct was on him to protect his mate and drive away every hated rival. There would be no turning back and no remorse if a rival died.

The moment Amos was fully leopard, his teeth exposed, his old, wise eyes red with fury, Drake whirled around and slashed that snarling face. How dare he try to separate Drake from his chosen mate? How dare this old leopard rip Saria from him by force, al-

331

lowing a male to put his hands on her, to mistreat her? Drake followed the first humiliating slap with a series of powerful, raking blows, driving the older leopard back, spilling blood down the face as he tore fur and carved deep furrows into flesh.

The old leopard rose onto powerful back legs, driving forward in an effort to gain supremacy. Drake met him with a violent charge, hitting him low. There was an audible crack as ribs broke. He fell onto his side and Drake was on him, closing his mouth around that vulnerable throat. His teeth sank deep and satisfaction well up. He snarled. The old leopard's eyes blazed with a golden fury of hatred, an old warrior refusing for a moment to relinquish power. Almost immediately, his human took back control. Staring down, with blood and the thrill of victory filling his mouth, Drake watched those golden eyes slip to a human grayish-green as the leopard submitted.

There was an eerie silence in the swamp, as if even insects were shocked by the swift change of leadership. A roar of protest went up. Behind him, a gun went off and Drake released Jeanmard and whirled to face the new threat.

Joshua stood grim-faced, his eyes flat and cold. "You want leadership, you challenge him in the way of our people or I shoot you dead right here and now." Disgust and loathing filled his tone. He aimed his weapon at a man who was armed and obviously thought of shooting him.

Drake inhaled and pulled the scent of his enemy deep into his lungs. It was nearly the same as that of the man who had struck Saria. Drake welcomed the fight, roaring his challenge, signaling he was ready for any threat. He prowled back and forth, swiping a large paw over the ground to kick up dirt and leaves, sending them flying in the direction of his enemy.

"Gaston," Remy spoke very quietly, but his voice carried easily. "You'd better shift now before I shoot you myself."

This, then, was one of the families Drake hadn't heard much about as of yet. He charged and pulled back, kicking more dirt at the man, snarling his disgust. Gaston Mouton slowly handed his weapon to Robert Lanoux. Robert was covered in bandages and favoring his right side. He winced as he reached for the gun. Gaston unbuttoned his shirt with one hand, all the while studying his opponent. As the edges of the shirt parted, his chest was revealed. He was a big man with the heavy, roped muscles of his kind. Not an ounce of fat. A washboard stomach. Narrow hips and thick muscular thighs. A male in his prime — one no doubt believing he would mate with Saria.

Drake saw a red haze of fury as Gaston shifted, his speed only a hair slower than Remy's had been. He was far more confident than Drake expected, when he would have resorted to a weapon. Gaston and Drake paced back and forth, snarling and hissing at each other, each sizing up the enemy.

Without warning, the two leopards blasted into action, hurling themselves into the air at one another, bodies crashing hard as they met in midair, both going for the head and neck in an effort to inflict the most damage quickly. Blood spurted, ran down matted fur on both animals. They broke apart and slammed back together, a fierce, violent ballet of claws, teeth and sheer power.

The night echoed with roars of rage as the leopards broke apart, sides heaving, blood dripping, a brutal, primitive battle with neither male giving an inch. They exploded toward one another again, leaping into the sky, slamming together in an effort to get to a vital organ. Gaston fell back, claws ripping and tearing at Drake's underbelly, trying to gut him. Using his flexible spine, Drake twisted as he came down on all fours, rushing the other leopard to take advantage of the awkward landing. Gaston rolled, came up fast and met the charge head-to-head.

Drake didn't want to kill the bastard and that knowledge only made him angrier. He shared the leopard's fury on several levels, not the least was that they'd struck Saria. He was already thinking like a leader, trying to do what was best for his lair. He didn't want leadership, he only wanted Saria.

This fighter was fast and deadly and it required every ounce of his skills to keep from getting killed while he held his leopard back, waiting for his moment. His leg was on fire, but the steel was there, the muscle and power. He had every confidence he would win, but he wasn't so confident that he could keep from doing permanent damage.

The two leopards dove into the air again, came together and crashed to the ground locked in a deadly embrace of claws and teeth, raking and biting at each other. Drake saw his opening, twisted and sank his teeth into the vulnerable throat. Beneath him, he felt the wild heart, the taste of hot blood, excitement of the kill, and triumph of the win all mingled together.

They stared into one another's eyes. There

was no fear in Gaston and in a way, Drake admired him. He was a man he'd want on his team, yet there might be no other choice but to kill him.

"Submit, Gaston," Remy ordered. "Are you stupid?"

As the shifter's body grew still under his mouth, and the tension in Drake's leopard eased a little, Drake heard a warning shout and he was hit from behind, driven off his feet with no chance to whirl around and defend himself. He went down hard, shaken by the ferocity of the hit, his insides jarred and bruised. As if in a distance he heard Saria scream and a man grunt as if in pain. Nothing mattered but rolling, getting to his feet and finding his attacker.

"Damn it, Drake, stop holding back your leopard. Kill them both. They don't fight fair and the entire lot of them can go to hell," Joshua shouted. "If you don't take this one out, I swear I'm shooting every damned one of them."

Joshua's fury was mixed with a deep loathing and disgust. They lived by rules, firm, unbendable rules for survival in the forests of the world. Without those rules, leopards would be out-of-control killing machines. There had to be order and the Louisiana lair didn't seem to have any rules of fairness or honor.

Joshua's words penetrated the lair and the smiles of hope faded into worried frowns. If Drake had been holding back against one of their best fighters, what was he really capable of?

"Anyone else makes a move toward Drake and tries ambushin' him," Remy said, "will be going through me."

On some level, everything around Drake penetrated, but he was in another realm, one from long ago when the main rule of the jungle was kill or be killed. Blood thundered in his ears, roaring like a massive waterfall drowning out generations of civilization. He leapt high, springing off powerful back legs, meeting the other's charge in midair. His opponent missed his throathold and got a mouthful of loose, baggy fur-covered skin while Drake's leopard sank his teeth viciously into the muzzle and bit down, shaking his head.

He drove his opponent over backward, claws tearing wide strips from the belly. The leopard nearly convulsed with pain, raking and tearing in desperation. Drake let go of the muzzle and drove in for the exposed throat. His attack was skilled, vicious and precise. His strength was enormous, fueled by rage and the need to dominate. In that moment, he was nearly all leopard, a primitive, perfect killing machine.

He lost track of time, shaking his enemy, punishing with claws and teeth, driving in again and again for the kill. The leopard had no chance to recover his feet, only to fend off the inevitable with increasingly feeble — yet desperate — claws and teeth. Drake's leopard didn't feel any of the bites and rakes, only the need to vanquish his enemy.

"Drake," Jerico called to him. "Enough. Back off."

He heard the voice, muffled and distant, unable to clearly make out the words. The sound penetrated the red haze of his mind but made no sense. No one approached him, as he roared his defiance and slammed into the fallen leopard again and again.

"Drake, please." It was Saria. She didn't yell.

The man beside Saria touched her arm. The leopard saw that. He instantly dropped his fallen enemy and whirled to face the new threat, growls rumbling deep in his chest. His gaze locked on her attacker. Drake's leopard charged, stopping a few feet from the man who didn't move a muscle, sweat pouring down his face. The leopard swiped at the earth with his massive paw before turning back to once again grip his prey in a suffocating bite.

"Drake, come back to me," Saria said softly.

Drake tried to breathe away the rage. He forced his leopard away from the body. It took a lot of strength. Twice his leopard slipped out of control, rushed back and raked the fallen cat before he could get the beast inside him to use all the pent-up energy prowling back and forth, scaring the crap out of the rest of the lair.

It had been a fast, vicious fight, meant to intimidate, and it had. The men fell back each time the leopard approached them, roaring his challenge. Remy dropped to his knee first. His brothers followed suit. One by one the remaining members of the lair slowly complied until there were only the three fallen leopards who had already submitted and the man standing with Saria. As Drake approached, the scent of fear nearing terror permeated the yard.

"What the hell's wrong with you, Jules?" Remy demanded of the man who had taken Saria.

Jules cleared his throat. "I can' move. Tell him I can' move." He looked down between his legs.

Drake could easily see the razor-sharp

blade of a knife lined up tight across Jules's balls. Saria held the knife rock steady. Her eyes met Drake's. She grinned at him and shrugged her shoulders. Blood trickled down the inside of Jules's thigh.

"He royally pissed me off."

Drake inhaled deeply, calming the leopard so he could shift. Shifting hurt like a son-of-bitch, a hot, bright fire rushing through his entire body, but he ignored it and caught his jeans when Evan threw them to him. He forced his tired muscles to work when all he wanted to do was collapse on the ground like the other leopards. He would not show weakness to these poor excuses of shifters, not when they'd forced him to nearly kill someone. He wasn't altogether certain he hadn't.

"I see that, honey," Drake managed, his breath a little ragged. "Hang on one more minute for me." He took several steadying breaths and crossed what felt like a football field, although it was only a few steps. Without any warning, he slammed his fist hard into Jules's jaw, sending the man staggering back away from Saria's blade.

Drake reached out to pull Saria close to him. "I guess I should have waited a minute or two to see if you actually needed rescuing."

Her smile widened. "It was very sweet of you to make yourself leader of the lair just for me. I'm not quite certain what you're goin' to do now, but all the same, I appreciate the effort."

He sighed and glanced at her brothers. They all wore huge grins, even Lojos. He gave them his best scowl. "Get these three medical attention. I want the word to go out to all families, those not already here. They have twenty-four hours to swear their allegiance or leave." He lifted his head and looked around him, eyes like steel. "Things are going to change around here whether you like it or not. You'll live by the rules of the lair or get out. I don't much care at this point who stays or who goes, but if you stay, you'll start behaving with honor. I will clean up this lair and you won't like how I do it if you don't comply."

Not waiting for a reaction, afraid his rubber legs might give out, he wrapped his arm around Saria's shoulders. She seemed to sense how weak he really was because she slipped her arm around his waist and walked with him to the house. Jerico and Evan dropped in behind them, walking backward, facing the members of the lair as they guarded Drake and Saria.

Remy slowly stood up, frowning at the

others. "What the hell were you all thinking? If you had killed that man, I would arrest you, leopard or not. Idiots."

"Maybe their problem is bad blood," Joshua taunted. He stood in the shadows, his weapon ready, his eyes hard. "I haven't seen much worth saving here, Remy. Cowards. Fucking cowards." His gaze settled on the two older men who were in the back, both holding shotguns.

The two men looked at each other. One spoke. "Who are you?"

"The name is Tregre. Joshua Tregre. I believe you're my uncles." Joshua spat on the ground. "Although it leaves a bad taste in my mouth to admit it."

The older of the two men sucked in his breath. "You're Renard's boy." The two men exchanged another look. The older one pushed past Elie Jeanmard and stood in front of Joshua, clearly not intimidated. His face was lined and worn, his once blue eyes faded to gray. He studied Joshua carefully, almost suspiciously before letting out his breath and nodding his head as if he approved of him. "You look like your father."

"You think I don't remember you, Uncle Beau?" There was bitterness in his voice. "Mom never once talked of that night, and she only said good of you and Gilbert, but I remember. My leopard remembers. You betrayed us and that monster of a grandfather killed his own son. I saw it and every night when I go to bed, I still see it. So don't think for one moment I've forgotten because I was little."

"Leopards don' forget, boy," Beau answered wearily. "None of us have forgotten that night. The old devil took our wives. He would have killed them too. Neither Gilbert nor I ever considered that he might kill Renard. Your mother was at risk, but not you or Renard, at least that's what we believed, and we figured Renard would just come back. Renard refused to allow his wife to bring you back. He sent her runnin' with you while he fought the old man. It was worse after that for all of us. My wife killed herself and Gilbert's run off."

"Why didn't you just kill the bastard?"

Beau shook his head. "You don' know what it's like livin' with a monster."

Joshua shook his head. "Your sons?"

Beau gestured toward two grown men just rising after swearing allegiance to their new leader.

"And your daughter? One of you has a daughter. There have been rumors."

"Rumors the old man could never prove. We told him she died at birth."

"What a waste, hiding your daughter, living like rats. You need to meet a man named Jake Bannaconni." There was bitterness in his voice.

"Joshua."

Drake's quiet voice penetrated the anger and disgust. Joshua sucked in his breath and turned toward the man who always had provided calm when rage got to be too much. Turning his back on his uncles, he strode toward the house, his shoulders stiff with outrage.

Drake watched him come, judging his mood. "I'm sorry, Joshua, for putting you in such a bad position. I recognized the surname, but didn't investigate. I should have asked you before putting you . . ."

"I would never have let you come here without backup. The minute Jake told me where you'd gone, I was already packing." Joshua looked him straight in the eye. "And as long as you're staying here, I will be too. No one lifted a hand to help my mom, least of all that family." He looked Drake over and suddenly grinned. "I think you should get back inside before you make a fool of yourself, boss."

Drake smiled back, swaying slightly. Joshua Tregre had always been a puzzle to him. On one hand he was quiet but confident. There was little arrogance in Joshua, and, unlike some leopards, he rarely was in an altercation. But, there was something very lethal about him. A good man to have at your back, Drake had always felt he would make a bitter, relentless and merciless enemy. They'd worked together for several years and never once had Joshua said anything about his past to him — or to any of the others on the team.

Drake stumbled and nearly went down, shocking himself. Joshua caught him as Remy shut the door on any audience.

"Put the stubborn son of a bitch down on the couch," Remy ordered. "Our fearless leader has dripped blood all over the floor."

"I'm not your damned leader," Drake denied, groaning as Joshua helped lower him to the couch. "I think your sister is a pain right now."

"Hey!" Saria protested. "It's not my fault you think you're a white knight."

"For future reference," Lojos said helpfully, holding a bag of ice to the back of his head. "Everyone thinks Saria is a pain. And for your information, poor Jules didn' hit my sister. He would never hit a girl, let alone Saria. Neither Gaston nor Jules would harm a woman."

"No one here would dare hit my sister,"

Remy said. "Any one of us would kill them. Their body would be buried so deep in the swamp no one would ever find them."

There was an edge in Remy's voice that had Drake turning his head to study the set features. Yeah, he could believe the brothers were capable of getting rid of anyone hurting their sister and Remy was letting him know.

"So what did happen to your face, Saria?" Drake asked, although he could barely see anymore. Blood dripped steadily from the wounds on his face and burned in his eyes.

She knelt beside the couch, handed him a cool cloth for his chest while she went to work on his face. "They hit Lojos as we were going inside . . ."

"Yeah," Lojos interjected. "Jules and Gaston had no problem hittin' me." He glared at his brothers. "It's evident none of you had a problem with them hittin' *me.*"

Remy feigned indifference. "Our new exalted leader took care of that."

Drake jerked Saria's wrist down, removing the cloth so he could send Remy his darkest, most intimidating scowl. "Shut the hell up, you Cajun jackass. I'm *not* your leader."

Saria laughed softly. "Maybe you really do need me after all. You certainly get yourself into messes. Don' worry, I'll take care of you."

Joshua and Jerico snickered. Evan turned back to the window hastily, but not before Drake caught the big grin.

"I hope all of you are enjoying yourselves," he snapped and laid his head back, closing his eyes, more because he had to than because he was dismissing them. "Tell me what happened to your face, honey."

Saria wasn't a dabber. She washed the blood from the deep lacerations and then, before he knew what was happening, doused him with disinfectant. He nearly fell off the couch, howling. Saria rolled her eyes and pushed him back down.

"We're just gettin' started," she pointed out. "You really are a baby, aren't you?"

"You're certainly not one of those women who believes in making a fuss over a man, are you?" His voice dripped acid.

"You mean mollycoddle him?" she sniped right back.

One of her brothers snorted. The argument wasn't getting him anywhere. Why had he thought her young and sweet and innocent? He had a damned tiger by the tail and he hadn't even realized it. So much for Drake Donovan, the man whose instincts never failed him. He caught her wrist again.

This time she was scrubbing the hell out of his chest. Their eyes met and he felt himself falling like a ton of brick. Dark, enormous eyes locked with his. All those golden flecks intrigued him, all that dark chocolate enticed him.

"You're a very scary woman, Saria Boudreaux." He touched the bruise on her face with gentle fingers. "How did this happen?"

She rolled her eyes. "You're not distracted easily and never give up when you want something, do you?"

"You might want to remember that in the future."

She sighed. "I hit my face on the side of the building. Jules is strong and I knew he'd freak if I got hurt. I couldn't get out of his hold so I jerked toward the building. I didn' expect to hit quite so hard, but it worked. He let loose to catch me around the waist so I wouldn't fall. He was all worried, so much so that it never occurred to him that I managed to pull my knife and lock it where it counted until I said somethin' to him."

"Poor man," Gage muttered. "He shoulda been expectin' you to pull somethin' on him. I'm a little disappointed in him."

"Take a look at my head before you go and feel sorry for that ass," Lojos suggested indignantly. "He nearly killed me."

"It's a bump," Mahieu corrected, but he once again checked his brother's head.

"Pour a little of Saria's disinfectant over it," Drake suggested. "It'll fix him right up."

"Go to hell," Lojos grumped.

"This disinfectant is good stuff," Saria said. "In any case, I need to take a look at your back, Drake. Roll over."

He groaned. "I don't want to move."

"You should have thought about that before you got in the fight."

Drake opened one eye and looked at her. Her eyes had gone liquid as she looked at the injuries. His heart began to pound. "Baby," he said softly, uncaring that her brothers — or anyone else heard him. "You can't cry. Not now. You'll break my heart."

"You did this because of me."

"I did this for me," he corrected. "My leopard and I are one and the same. Fuckin' idiots think they can intimidate the world. They shoved and I shoved back harder. That's all. It will happen again." He studied her slightly averted face. "Did I scare you?"

She shook her head, but Saria didn't want to lie to him. She lifted her chin and looked him directly in the eyes. "Maybe. A little. I've never seen anything like that before."

He wrapped his palm around the nape of

her neck. "I was careful for the most part. I didn't want to really hurt anyone, just more like teach them a lesson." He pressed his forehead against hers. "I'm not a violent man."

Joshua, Jerico and Evan choked dramatically and began coughing.

Remy snorted. "And if you believe that, Saria, I've got a sinkhole I can sell you for farmland."

"You're not helping my cause," Drake complained.

"Ignore them. I always do," Saria advised. She swallowed, leaned closer and brushed her lips over his. The lightest of touches, but his body stirred — and damn it all — it hurt.

He swore there was a snicker coming from somewhere, but when he glared around the room, everyone was looking away. He rolled over very carefully, his breath hissing out of his lungs, his body on fire. "Fucking jackasses. I should have done a lot more damage."

"Oh, I think they got the point," Remy said. "When you stop fussin' over that man, Saria, you can tell me where the photographs are. This time, I'll get them."

"I put them in the left top drawer in a case and hid the negatives away from here, just in case somethin' happened."

"Like someone killed you?" Remy demanded.

"Yeah. Like that," Saria admitted, shrugging.

He swore under his breath, something about stubborn women who needed a man to take them in hand, as he stalked out. Drake turned his head and flicked a look at Joshua, who immediately trailed after him. Drake wasn't about to take the chance that someone from the lair — or a killer — might try another sneak attack, not when his body needed time to recover.

Gage and Mahieu exchanged a long look. "No one would try to jump Remy," Gage said. "He's got a rep around here."

"Maybe, but a bullet doesn't care much about reputation and I've seen several of your neighbors all too ready to use a gun." Drake didn't bother to lift his head up again. His belly burned with every movement. He was getting too old to fight three or four challengers. Foolish males feeling their leopard's drive did that sort of thing — or someone insane enough to crave leadership — which was *not* him.

He had to smile when he heard Remy's voice. "What the hell are you doin' tailin' after me? You think I need a damn baby-sitter?"

Remy stalked back into the house, Joshua trailing behind him. Joshua hadn't replied, nor would he, Drake knew. He'd been given an order to keep Remy safe and he wasn't about to be intimidated by the Cajun snarling at him. Joshua simply sent the affronted homicide detective one level look from eyes that said it all. He moved on past the man and stood to the side of the window facing into the swamp.

"Your men are downright hostile."

Drake snorted. Remy had the photographs and he had to see them. Gritting his teeth, he righted himself. The lacerations along his ribs and across his belly burned like hell, but he'd sustained far worse injuries. No broken bones this time, only minor gashes and rips that would heal fast. His leopard blood would see to that.

"Yours aren't?" Jerico demanded, turning to face the detective. "I've never seen a lair like this one, not in all my travels. Drake could have killed all three of those men and maybe he should have. In the rain forest, men act without honor, there are consequences."

Joshua stiffened. "This lair has been without honor for a long time."

The Boudreaux brothers bristled, coming to their feet.

Drake swung his feet to the floor, holding up his hand for silence as he waited for the room to quit spinning. "A lair needs strong leadership to control the leopards, all of us know that. And something else is going on here. I don't know what, but I intend to get to the bottom of it. We all felt it out there in Fenton's Marsh. We're not turning on each other. The only people we can count on right now are the ones in this room."

"Sadly I have to agree with that," Remy told his brothers. "Although I'd put my life on Gaston and Jules. Right now, however, I can't risk it." He handed the photographs to Drake.

Saria had carefully catalogued each body, the wounds and the surrounding scene. The stab wound was the same each time, a straight puncture to the abdomen the victim had never seen coming. The knife hadn't killed him. He'd been awake to see his attacker shift and probably look right into his eyes as he delivered the suffocating bite. The victim had to have been terrified.

Drake looked up at Remy and saw the same understanding in his eyes. Whoever was killing these men had done so cruelly and deliberately, needing to see the life leave their bodies. A serial killer then. A shifter who enjoyed killing for the pleasure of it.

"The crime scene almost looks as if two people went there together, had a couple of drinks and one killed the other." Remy frowned as he studied one of the photographs. "You say you couldn't find a hint of another male? A leopard or human?"

"I picked up Saria's scent, but nothing else," Drake confirmed. "There was a strong scent of blood in the ground in several other places. I don't think Saria found all the bodies. If I had to guess, maybe six."

Remy shook his head, his teeth snapping together as if he wanted to bite down hard on something. "This makes no sense. The wounds are almost exactly alike every time. The stab wound is very precise. It enables the killer to take the fight out of his victim fast and yet keep them alive to spend as much time as he wants terrorizing him — or her."

"This is the work of a leopard — a shifter," Drake said heavily.

Remy scrubbed his hand down his face as if removing something oily and thick. "I was so certain it was someone who couldn't shift tryin' to put blame on us."

"You didn't want it to be a friend or neighbor."

Remy shook his head. "No, I didn't, although I checked up on everyone. My brothers first." He shot Saria a small smile. "You can stop feelin' guilty for thinkin' it might be one of us. I will admit, I doubted it, but I checked all the same."

"Great, bro," Lojos said. "You didn' tell me that."

"I didn't think it was necessary. I'm a detective, Lojos, and I take my job seriously. The first thing I do is clear my family and then move on to a pool of suspects. Because I thought the women were killed by some-one with shifter blood that couldn't actually shift, the suspect pool was large. This nar-rows it down."

"Off the top of your head, Remy," Drake said, "who would be your first suspect?"

Remy's gaze shifted just for a moment to Joshua and then he shook his head. "You know it doesn' work that way."

"Sure it does," Joshua said. "My grand-father was a monster. Why your leader didn't take him down years ago, I have no idea, but he beat my grandmother continu-ally and then started on his sons. You know why my mother left, right?" He dared Remy to state the reasons out loud.

Remy frowned and shook his head. "I was gone for years. Most of us were. We only started hearing rumors about a daughter recently, and Saria met her in the swamp a time or two. Her name is Evangeline. We thought her mother had died in childbirth, not committed suicide. No one goes on the Tregre land. It borders Mercier land and even Charisse and Armande don't go there."

"And no one thought to check? Teachers? Anyone?" Joshua demanded.

"Check what?" Remy snapped back. "The boys went to school and no one thought they had any other children. They kept to themselves and had a reputation for scaring off trespassers. They had the right to live the way they wanted."

"Not like that," Joshua snapped. "He abused those women."

"And the men," Remy said. "Yes, he should have been stopped, but no one knew it was goin' on until after he was dead. Your father's death was reported as a huntin' accident. Here in the swamp, accidents happen all the time. No one liked the old man, and we made up stories about him, but he rarely came out of the swamp and none of his sons did. All *pere* ever said was to stay away from them. Mercier told his children the same thing."

"So when Saria came home telling you there was a female child, a young woman

356

no one knew about, you didn't think it was worth investigating?" Joshua demanded.

Remy's gaze was steady. "I did go see her. She's twenty, and she told me she was homeschooled and that her brothers, father and uncle have watched over her. Yes, at times she's lonely, but she said she had Charisse as a friend and that more and more they're takin' her out of the swamp. She's nervous, but after meetin' Saria, she thinks she'll be fine. What more could I do? She claims no one has ever laid a hand on her. She saw the old Buford a time or two, but he never saw her. It was drilled in her to stay hidden from him."

"And you believed her?" Drake asked quietly when Joshua made a derisive noise. "Old man Tregre was leopard. How the hell would they hide the scent of a leopard . . . ?" He trailed off, his eyes meeting Remy's.

"How *would* they hide the scent?" Remy asked thoughtfully. "That's a damn good question."

"Could the Tregre brothers have found a way to hide the scent of a leopard from everyone? And what about DNA? Surely there had to be some saliva in the bites of the victims you found, something on the body to indicate a leopard attack," Drake said.

Remy shook his head. "That was why I thought it was a simulated attack. How could a leopard deliver a suffocating bite without leaving either scent or saliva behind?"

"No one could do that, could they?" Lojos asked. "We have a tremendous sense of smell."

"I think someone *did* do just that," Remy said, "but how it's possible, I have no idea."

Saria shuddered and slipped onto the couch beside Drake. "Then it's possible it wasn't Armande who attacked me after all. It could have been anyone — the killer. Maybe that's why my leopard didn't accept him. She was confused with no scent or other identifying markers."

Drake slipped his arm around her, making a determined effort not to wince at the movement. "Maybe the Tregre land should be our next visit."

"I'll take you," Remy said. "We can go tomorrow. My brothers will come along with your team, just to make certain we have enough men to look thoroughly around."

"I will take him," Saria sent her brother a steady look. "He hired me and I do my job."

"I don' want you in the middle of this," Remy growled.

"She's already in the middle of this, Remy," Drake said. Weariness crept in. All he wanted to do was get back to the inn and crash in a bed. "The killer knows she's onto his dump site and half the men here have lost all good sense. She can stay right where I can keep an eye on her."

"I don' need protection," Saria protested.

Drake laughed softly and brushed a kiss into the thick sun-bleached hair. "You can't have it both ways, honey. Either you're guiding me to the Tregre swamp or you're staying home."

"Of course I'm goin'," Saria said.

"I'm keepin' these pictures, Saria," Remy said. "You did a good job on photographin' the scene. I'll get the bottles collected for prints if any are left."

"Most of the places were in the marsh, with the ground impossible to walk on, but there's tracts of land that are rich in soil and very solid," Saria said. "I think the two men went there, shared a drink and then one killed the other and moved the body to the marsh."

Drake shook his head. "The leopard dragged his victim to the marsh. There was a trail of blood from one site to the place where Saria found the body. I'm heading back to the inn. Let's do this tomorrow."

Remy nodded. "Don' go gettin' in any more fights or I'll have to arrest you."

Drake heard the faint humor in his voice. "You can always try."

12

Drake made his way to the entrance of the inn, his team sweeping tirelessly behind him. Joshua circled the inn while Evan went ahead and Jerico trailed him. It was quite frankly annoying. He knew how Jake and Emma Bannaconni felt when they left their home surrounded by bodyguards, but damn it all, he *was* the bodyguard. He headed up his own teams for hostage rescue both for Bannaconni and in the rain forest. He glared at Evan. It didn't help that he was certain Evan hid a grin.

He swore under his breath and Saria glanced up sharply at him.

"Are you all right?" She sounded anxious. "I could ask one of the men to help me get you upstairs."

Great. She thought he was about to fall down. Suppressing the groan, somewhere between annoyed and amused, Drake dropped a kiss on top of her head. "Just don't like our escort. Fucking idiots thinking they have to guard me."

She coughed. He searched her averted face suspiciously. "You'd think my own woman might have a little sympathy for my situation. These men are never going to let me live this down."

Pauline Lafont stood at the front door, her hands on her hips, a stern look on her face as he came limping up. "I hear you went chargin' to Saria's rescue and got yourself in a bit of trouble," she greeted.

Drake sighed. "News travels fast around here."

Pauline stepped aside to allow him entrance. Evan, already in the room, stood just to the right of the large living area, gun loose but ready in his hands. His gaze met Drake's over the top of Pauline's head and flicked to his left, toward the corner Drake didn't have a visual on. His hand signed subtly. Pauline was not alone. Drake forced his body to straighten and he stepped just a little ahead of Saria, sweeping her back with one arm, signaling Jerico with another subtle hand movement as he did so.

Saria didn't protest, nor make a big deal out of it. He loved that about her. She had a measure of trust in him he wasn't altogether certain he deserved yet, but he was determined to live up to it.

"He definitely has heroic tendencies, Miss Pauline," Saria chattered, as if Drake just hadn't signaled possible danger.

She'd read him, he knew she had, but she didn't miss a beat. His heart swelled with pride. The more he was around her, the more he knew absolutely that she was the *one*. She would stand with him, no matter the danger, or the hard times. Saria Boudreaux was the kind of woman a man kept forever.

He stepped past Pauline, already turning to face whoever was hidden behind the corner. The scent of blood and sweat hit him immediately, providing identification. Amos Jeanmard lay on the sofa, an ice pack pressed to one cheek, his chest heavily bandaged. He didn't bother to try to get up, obviously very conscious of Evan's weapon. The barrel was down, but still pointed in his direction.

Joshua came in through the kitchen, gun ready, his gaze on Jeanmard. He signaled all clear to Drake.

"Jeanmard," Drake greeted.

"Lickin' my wounds and lettin' my woman fuss over me a bit," Jeanmard said. "You hit like a freight train."

Drake nudged Saria. "See that? His

woman fusses over him. She doesn't call him a big baby," he whispered, overly loud.

Jeanmard snorted. "You won' be gettin' sympathy from me. I tried to get you out of it, but you went all Rambo on me. Now you're stuck with her." He grinned, self-satisfied. "Me? I'm retirin' on the front porch and rockin' with my woman."

Pauline pushed past Drake and sank down in a chair opposite Amos. "I put supper out after I tended to Amos, so please feel free to eat. I'm sure you're all hungry."

Joshua nodded. "Thanks, ma'am."

"Don't think for one moment I believe your crap, Jeanmard," Drake said, towering over him, hands on hips. "You knew *exactly* how I'd react. You played me. You and Remy."

Jeanmard grinned at him. "Not Remy. I knew either you or Remy would come at me. I wasn't expectin' such a violent attack and thought I could put on a bit of a show before handin' over the reins. Instead, I think you broke all my ribs."

Drake glanced at Jerico and then to Joshua. Both shook their heads. The house and grounds were clear of any enemy. Jeanmard was alone. Drake signed his crew they could stand down and eat. They sent him a small, taunting grin, knowing he had gotten

364

himself in over his head here in the Louisiana swamp — for a woman. He wouldn't be living it down any time soon.

"Take a seat before you fall down," Jeanmard suggested. "There's no need to play the tough guy around me. I've felt you hit and I'm already suitably impressed."

Drake might have believed him if he hadn't caught the note of laughter and knew he'd been played for a sucker. The old man had wanted out and he'd found a sure way to do it. "I might have killed you," he pointed out, sinking down into one of Pauline's comfortable chairs. It felt a little like heaven to him.

"I'll get you some food," Saria offered.

He caught her hand and pressed a kiss to her knuckles. She was worth it, although a little sympathy might have added to the deal. He felt Jeanmard's scrutiny and let her hand slide away. "You've got a few problems here, Jeanmard."

The older man gave a small derisive laugh. "Actually, there are a *lot* of problems, but they're all yours now, not mine. The broken ribs are worth it. And call me Amos."

Drake glanced at Pauline. She hadn't said a word, but she obviously knew Drake and Jeanmard had fought.

"She knows everythin'," Jeanmard said. "I

never lied to her, not once in all the years she waited for me." There was genuine love in his voice. "I knew she was my mate — my leopard recognized her — but she had no leopard and I was afraid our lair would eventually disappear. It was a mistake. *My* mistake. I wanted to keep all the shifters here instead of sendin' them out as I should have." He groaned as he moved to try to ease his position a little. "I did my duty and I never cheated on Adrienne. My loyalty was the only thing I could give her. She was a good woman and good mother. I loved her in my way, but she deserved more." He looked at Pauline. "You deserved more."

Drake felt the older man's sorrow. The look between the innkeeper and the old leopard was so intimate, he had to look away. To love like that and yet sacrifice for the good of a species. What a wasted effort.

"Every choice in my life I've made," Pauline said quietly, "I made each one, knowin' what I was doin'." Her voice was firm. She stood up. "I'll get you a plate of food if you think you can eat now, Amos."

Saria was like Pauline Lafont — a woman who would stand by a man in spite of his mistakes. Drake waited until Pauline had slipped into the dining room.

"That woman is humbling. She's magnificent."

Amos forced himself into a sitting position, his face going gray. He clenched his teeth to keep from moaning and Drake didn't add to his indignity by offering to help. Amos breathed shallow for a few moments before forcing a small rueful grin. "Yes, she is. Saria is quite a bit like her."

"I was just thinking the same thing."

"I hope you do better by her than I did Pauline."

Drake stretched out his legs. His bum leg was one big ache, and he wouldn't be surprised if he found he was black and blue from thigh to ankle. His very bones hurt. "I think I'm too damned old for this fighting crap."

"I know I am." Amos glanced toward the dining room and lowered his voice. "Tell me about the Tregre boy. What's he like?"

"He's a good man. Rock solid. I put my life in his hands on a daily basis and I know he's going to be there for me, no matter how bad it gets. That's the kind of man he is," Drake answered without hesitation. "So you answer me this — what the hell happened in that family and why didn't you stop it?"

Amos sighed. "I went to school with Buford Tregre. He was a bully then. Mean as a snake. All the girls were terrified of him. Even the teachers were careful of him. His father was a mean drunk and no one ever saw his mother. They were part of the lair — we knew they were leopards, but they stayed to themselves. Mostly they lived off the land, huntin' and fishin'. He dallied with Iris Lafont, Pauline's sister, promised marriage, but in the end he kicked her out to marry a shifter, and then kept her tied to him by continuin' to lie and saying he'd leave his wife for her. He was a no good son of a bitch and treated women like shit. As for his wife, once she set foot on Tregre land, no one ever saw her again."

"And no one checked on her? I thought families here were close."

"No one is close with the Tregre family. No one."

"And his sons?" Drake prompted. Someone was killing in the swamps and it had to be stopped. There was no question whoever was doing it was a shifter. He still hadn't checked out Amos Jeanmard or his son. He was not disclosing information to the man and as long as he was staying at the inn where Saria was, she would either be in his room, or one of his men would be sitting outside her door in the building, and another outside.

Amos frowned. "I don' know what to think about those boys." He rubbed at his chin, his frown deepening to a scowl. "Like their daddy, we didn' see much of them. Like I said, Buford was a mean drunk and he ruled with his fists. I don' think they had much of a childhood and they didn' go to school much. The three of them were close though. You fought one Tregre, you fought them all. Renard was the oldest and he had it the worst. He looked out for his mother and the other two boys. When he went away for a while, it shocked everyone. I think that's when the old man got worse."

"But then he came back with a wife. A shifter," Drake prompted when the older man went silent.

Amos shrugged. "Yes, he brought back a beautiful wife and I knew I had mismanaged everything. I had thrown away my life with Pauline and doomed our lair to extinction. I was born and raised in the swamp. Worked most of my life here. Never left, never thought of leavin'. I thought this was all there were until Renard brought her home with him."

"The other brothers married someone from the outside, not a shifter, didn't they?" Drake guessed.

"Buford despised anyone who wasn't a

369

shifter. He even grew to hate his wife and children — all but Renard — his other two sons because they married non-shifters, and his wife because she wasn't his true mate."

"You knew that and you didn't stop him?"

"I didn't know it until Renard came to me and told me all the boys were gettin' out. He said his father was insane. He told me he was certain the old man had killed his mother and that he had attacked his wife one night when he was workin' out in the swamp. The other women admitted to their husbands that Buford had been doin' the same thing to them and threatened to kill them if they told."

"My God. What the hell did you do when everything went to hell and Renard died?" Drake couldn't keep the accusation out of his voice. He wanted to jump across the room and smash the man. Renard's wife and son had made it out, but his brothers and their wives hadn't.

"He did do something," Pauline said. She handed Amos his plate and set his drink on the coffee table. "He ended up with nearly every bone in his body broken and he was in a coma for three months."

Drake let out his breath. The mire in the swamp just seemed to deepen. The more explanation, the more the questions. "And

Tregre wasn't arrested?"

"At the time, his brother was chief of police." Amos sighed. "You're drudgin' up a lot of shit, Donovan. It was many years ago. I was trespassin' on their property. They said I attacked him. There was an investigation and Buford was cleared of all charges. There was even an implication that I might have killed Renard. In the end, they didn' go that far, but I had no other recourse but to back off. Hell, I didn' remember much for months after. I had physical therapy and my leopard took a long while to emerge again. I told the lair Tregre's land was off-limits and left it at that."

Saria slipped into the chair next to Drake, handing him a plate of food. His stomach growled, reminding him he hadn't eaten in a long while. His mind was foggy, trying to take in everything Amos had told him, and still read between the lines. There was no doubt Buford's sons might be as cruel and depraved as their father. Buford Tregre was certainly capable of being a serial killer. Hating was what he seemed to do best. And Joshua's uncles had sons of their own, both old enough to be suspects as well. He shook his head. It was all complicated and he felt like shit.

Saria smelled like heaven, that scent he'd

come to know as exclusively Saria. She'd obviously showered, which explained why Pauline had managed to get Amos his food first. He didn't mind not getting his food immediately, Saria had to be exhausted. She'd been streaked with dirt and probably blood and sweat from him. He'd been thinking about the mess he'd gotten himself into, allowing her to take care of him instead of the other way around.

"Are you all right?" he asked.

She sent him a dazzling smile. "I wasn't the one who got all chewed up in a fight. I'm fine. And Miss Pauline outdid herself. The food's fantastic."

The tension coiled so tight in his gut unraveled. There was something so amazing in the way she enjoyed her food. Maybe it was just the entire package — the way she enjoyed her life. When she ate, she ate, enjoying every single morsel. If she had to protect herself, she did so with the same intensity she did everything else. She made him feel alive — and happy.

He let himself grin back at her like a foolish idiot. "She is a good cook," he admitted and watched with admiration as she tucked into the food on her plate with gusto.

She frowned at him. "Eat. What are you doin'?"

"I like watching you eat."

Amos laughed. "You're a goner, Donovan. When a hungry man spends more time lookin' at his woman than eatin', he's in trouble."

Pauline joined in his laughter. "Eat, Drake. When Amos told me what happened, I knew you'd need to eat something to rebuild your strength. You'll have all the time in the world to look at Saria."

Beside him, Saria stirred a little uncomfortably. He knew she wasn't yet convinced they'd be spending their lives together. She was willing to entertain the idea, but she'd been so dead set against marriage and she obviously had her life plans that didn't include a permanent man — and he was damned permanent.

"Remy get out his shotgun yet?" Amos asked.

"Not yet, but I wish he would," Drake said.

Saria choked. He helpfully patted her back. "Something wrong, Saria?"

She glared at him and took a sip of water. "You won' be feelin' so full of yourself if Remy does show up with a shotgun. He'll be meanin' business."

"I'll look forward to it. It may be the only way I can make an honorable woman out of you." He looked up at Pauline. "She's dragging her feet."

"You got second thoughts, Saria?" Pauline asked.

Saria chewed thoughtfully, taking her time answering. She didn't think to lie, or even hedge. "I want to be with him, it's just the whole permanent thing, you know? I don' know if I can actually live with someone all the time. I'm used to doin' my own thing."

"But you *want* to be with him," Pauline asked. "No one's forcin' you, or coercin' you in any way?" She didn't look at Drake, but he had the uncomfortable feeling that if Saria answered in the affirmative, she'd pull out a gun and shoot him on the spot. He was coming to believe Louisiana women were a little on the dangerous side.

Saria made a little moue with her lips and he leaned down to brush a kiss there. He couldn't have stopped himself even if Pauline had a gun pointed straight at his heart. He kissed her again when her eyes went wide.

"You shouldn't tempt me," he pointed out.

"Is that called coercion?" Saria asked, her fingers touching her lips as if holding his kiss to her.

Pauline sighed. "Just marry him and put you both out of your misery," she counseled.

Saria laughed. "I can see I'm in the minority here."

Satisfied, Drake concentrated on his dinner. It was late. He was tired, and his body hurt, but Saria sat close and the room felt comfortable. His men were close and would take over the watch so he could get rest.

"Miss Pauline," he said. "I have to say, you're a magnificent cook."

"Thank you, Drake. I do love to see people eat."

"I intend to do a lot of eating and I can guarantee my boys will be perpetually hungry."

She laughed, nodding her head as if satisfied.

"We're heading upstairs. I think I'll soak in a hot bath to get the kinks out," Drake announced. "I'll see you first thing in the morning."

Pauline nodded and Amos lifted a hand. Drake forced his body into a standing position. His bum leg didn't want to work, burning all the way into his buttocks. He stood for a moment, letting the pain consume him, accepting it, before he took that first step. He was used to battle and the results after his leopard had gotten into a vicious encounter with another male, but it always took him by surprise, that sweeping pain roaring through every muscle.

Saria took their plates into the kitchen, giving him just a couple of minutes with Joshua. The man was waiting by the stairs.

"I haven't had the chance to tell you, we've got two men out in the swamp. Jake sent for reinforcements and as soon as they heard you might be in trouble, they came running. Conner Vega and his woman are staying with Jake to cover there. Elijah is spending the night out in a blind. We figured if Saria saw lights near Fenton's Marsh more than once, it's possible whoever is using it as a dump site will still continue to do so."

"How'd you get a couple men in the swamp without a guide? In fact, how'd you find me?"

"Followed your woman's scent. The woman is putting out some pretty potent pheromones. Her leopard is close."

Drake let out his breath. Another complication. There was no question the Han Vol Dan was close. Saria was a virgin and would need an introduction to sex before her leopard took her over and went ballistic on them. He had to get her away from all the other males before her leopard decided to show itself again. He couldn't chance killing a friend.

"Who's with Elijah?"

"New kid goes by the name of Jeremiah Wheating. Don't know much about him, but he listens and Elijah and Conner vouched for him."

"Elijah has a bad reputation. Could get him killed here."

"Comes in handy," Joshua said with a shrug. "It could help us depending on what's going on around here. I've set up shifts for the guards. We all need sleep, so we'll only have one man on. Hopefully you can get Saria to sleep in your room, or you sleep in hers."

Drake nodded, and watched her come toward him. He loved the way she moved, flowing across the floor, all soft curves and fluid grace. Her skin was extraordinary — beautiful. He couldn't resist running the pad of his finger over the curve of her cheek just to feel how soft she was. "Come on, let's go upstairs."

She didn't even blush, but took his hand and went with him. Saria's honesty was humbling. She didn't care what the others thought — not even her brothers. She'd made her choice, and if she wrestled with the thought of permanency, at least she gave him everything she had while she did it.

His fingers closed around hers and he

brought her hand to his chest while they went up the stairs. "I need you to stay with me tonight, Saria."

He heard her swift intake of breath. She glanced sideways at him from under her long lashes. Her small tongue came out to lick at her full bottom lip. His cock jerked. He tried to keep from letting his mind wander in that direction. She didn't protest, but he made her nervous.

"I know I was very bold today in the swamp," she said. "I enjoyed it too, but I'm not . . ."

"Honey, look at me. I'm just about as banged up as I can get without broken bones. I can guarantee you going to sleep with no problem." He hesitated, wanting to be completely honest. "Waking up might be different."

"If I'm in your room, somethin's goin' to happen and you know it," she said. "I might even be the one to start it. I dream about you."

"Do you think I'm afraid?" He winked at her as he pulled open the door to his room. "You can have your wicked way with me anytime you want. And a man likes to know his woman dreams about him."

"What if I don' meet your expectations. Men have them. Don't tell me they don't. I imagine you must be fairly experienced and the thought of tryin' to live up to that is rather dauntin'." Her accent was thicker — and more sensual.

Drake dragged her into his room, kicked the door closed and wrapped his arms around her, ignoring the protests of his body. His mouth descended on hers. He indulged himself for several long minutes, showing her just what he thought of that kind of drivel. When he lifted his head, they were both breathing raggedly.

"If I don't get it right the first time, Saria, I promise to spend hours, months, years, practicing until I do. You won't have any complaints and if you don't, believe me, babe, I won't either. A man likes to know his woman is satisfied. In any case, I've noticed you tend to follow instructions beautifully when you want to."

Saria laughed. "Okay then. If you're sure. Take your bath and I'll get a few things. Will we be goin' out tomorrow?"

He nodded. "I want to get my bearings and talk some more to Remy as well as some of the others in the lair. But" — he planted another kiss on her mouth — "not so early this time."

"I guess you do need to sleep in."

"I wasn't intending to sleep," he admitted.

Saria shook her head, and left him. The tub was deep and wide. He made a mental note to himself that it was large enough for two. One thing about Pauline's inn, it had plenty of hot water and he sank gratefully into the deep tub. Lacerations stung, but the water was soothing and he closed his eyes and let himself drift.

He was exhausted. It had been a long while since he'd had to fight leopards, and for a test of whether his leg would hold up or not, this had been a baptism by fire. He laughed softly to himself. His doctor had been very specific. Shift — but take his time. Go slowly. Feel the leg out. Make certain it held up before using it strenuously. Somehow he didn't think he was following the doctor's orders too closely. Yeah. He was fine. His leopard was fine. The world was right again — well, almost. When he considered there was a psycho serial killer leopard on the loose and an entire out-of-control lair to deal with — maybe things weren't quite so right. But for now, for tonight, knowing Saria would lie beside him, he'd take whatever peace he could and be damned happy about it.

"Are you plannin' on stayin' in the bath

all night?"

Saria's soft voice pulled him out of his revelry. He'd drifted off, floating in hot water that had gone warm on him. He ducked his head under the water to rinse out his hair and came up looking for her. She stood in the doorway, dressed in a short tank top and small pair of boy shorts that clung to her hips and buttocks lovingly.

"You sleeping in that?"

She tugged at the hem of the shirt that didn't quite cover her belly. "What's wrong with it?"

"I'll just have to take it off you in a couple of hours."

"You want me to go to bed with you *naked?*"

He stood up, stark naked himself, allowing the water to pour off of his body. "Yes. I want to feel your skin against my skin."

Saria didn't avert her eyes. She reached for a towel and instead of handing it to him, when he stepped from the tub, she began to dry him off, her hands gentle as she skimmed the soft material over the lacerations on his chest and belly. When she lingered, he pretended not to notice, standing patiently, waiting for her to claim his body in her own way.

She seemed fascinated and not at all shy.

Nervous, yes, but not shy. She stroked the towel down his back and over his buttocks, removing the water drops as she continued down his legs.

"You're really quite beautiful," she said. "Very symmetrical."

He was struck by the tone of her voice. It was factual, observant, almost scientific. He found himself smiling. "Symmetrical?"

She touched his muscles. "Each side is amazingly perfect when the human body isn't really that way at all."

"You do know I'm real, don't you?" He tried not to laugh.

"You'd be perfect to photograph, Drake."

"It isn't going to happen, Saria." He looked down at the expression on her upturned face and he did laugh. Dragging the towel from her hands, he tossed it aside, wrapped his arms around her and walked her backward into the bedroom. "No matter how much you pout, how cute you are, no matter if you're the sexiest woman alive, the answer is *no.*"

"Consider that you should do it for art. For science."

He lifted her easily and tossed her on the bed. "Absolutely, unequivocally, *no.*" He plunged the room into darkness.

"We'll see. You have to open the French doors."

"Are you too warm? And the answer will always be no."

"I have to sleep with the windows or door open or I can't breathe."

He opened the double doors. The night breeze slid into the room and Saria smiled at him. He couldn't help just standing there by the door admiring her with the moonlight spilling into the room. Her hair was tousled, her skin gleaming like porcelain and her body soft and curvy and inviting.

She patted the bed next to her. "Come and lie down."

"You don't have a camera hidden somewhere, do you?" He put suspicion in his voice.

"I might," she teased.

"I'll have to search you." She was studying him just as thoroughly as he was looking at her. He liked the feel of her gaze on him. He might be exhausted and hurting, but she made him feel more alive and exhilarated than he'd ever felt in his life.

He approached the bed slowly, watching her eyes, watching the heat flare there. Her eyes darkened, but the amber flecks grew brighter, becoming like tiny pieces of gold, now molten and spreading through the dark chocolate. His groin tightened and he knelt over her, catching her ankles in his hands and dragging her body down to him.

She moistened her lips, but her dark gaze never left his. His palm slid up the curve of her leg, tracing her form. Her long lashes swept down and then up, so that she watched him through half-closed eyes. He stroked his hands up her legs and over her hips, hooking her thin boy shorts and slowly lowering them from her body, all the while holding her gaze. The gold spread through the irises of her eyes until the color formed perfect circles. He read fear there, but the desire outweighed the fear.

He stretched out beside her, one hand splayed on her stomach, feeling her muscles bunch beneath his palm. She trembled, her eyes going wide, but she didn't try to pull away from him. He wanted her with every cell in his body. He brushed a kiss along her temple, down to the corner of her eye and along her cheek. He heard her breath turn a little ragged and he drew lazy circles on her bare skin just under her breasts as he nudged her top up a little.

He found he was trembling as well. He needed her. She had brought life to him when he had long ago given up on it. He worked a job where life expectancy just wasn't that long. The adrenaline rush had gotten him through, but now — now there was sunlight and laughter. There was all this golden skin and her honesty. There was need as he'd never known it before.

Drake caught the back of her head, holding her still while he took possession of her mouth, catching her breathy sigh. Kissing her made him a little drunk. There was the odd sensation of soaring when he wasn't a fanciful person. Once started, it was impossible to stop. He slid his tongue along the seam of her mouth, more than willing to sink further under her spell.

Her mouth was soft warm velvet, her tongue tangling tentatively with his. Her hands went to his shoulders as he shifted just a little to ease his body partially over hers. The tips of her breasts brushed his bare chest through the thin material of her tank top. He pulled the shirt from her in one swift movement and as she gasped, he covered her mouth with his again, swallowing her little shocked cry.

He was a little shocked at the need burning in him, the almost desperate fire raging in his bloodstream. He wanted to go slow and be careful with her. He couldn't even blame his leopard for the primitive desire to devour her whole. Lust mingled with an almost overwhelming love, making his hands shake as he brought his palm up to cup her full breasts.

He kissed his way down her neck, his teeth biting gently at her scented skin as he followed the line of her throat to the swell of her breasts. For just a moment he looked at her, drinking in the confused, nearly dazed expression, her little moan of pleasure and half-closed eyes. "You're beautiful," he whispered. "So damn beautiful you break my heart."

Her breathing had become agitated, her breasts rising and falling, so tempting with her hard nipples thrusting up at him in invitation. He lowered his head and lapped gently. Her entire body jerked. She had sensitive nipples and beneath his hand he felt her body shudder with pleasure. He closed his mouth around her right nipple and suckled. Her back arched, pushing her more deeply into the heat of his mouth. Her cry was soft, her hips bucking. Both hands settled in his hair, but she didn't push him away. Her cries were like music, a beautiful melody that sent him spiraling deeper into a fever of need. His tongue played over her nipple, stroking and flicking, before his mouth pulled at her strongly again, sending her writhing beneath him.

"Drake?" There was a soft note of fear in the midst of her drenching desire.

"You're all right, honey. I've got you," he whispered, meaning it. He would never allow anything — least of all him — to harm her in any way. "You'll love this."

She swallowed, subsiding on the pillow, nodding, her eyes large and brimming with gold.

Holding her gaze, he moved his attention to her left breast, tugging her nipple gently, watching the heat flare in her eyes before he lowered his mouth and lapped, just before the need to feast overtook him and he suckled like a starving man — suckled until she was writhing again and moaning almost continuously — until her fists tugged at his hair.

One hand smoothed over her belly, stroked her hip and slid briefly over her mound to feel the damp welcoming heat there. She threw her head from side to side and lifted her hips into his palm, gasping for breath. He slid one finger into all that hot honey, that sweetness he craved.

"Oh God," she whispered, her eyes going completely gold and feral.

He bent his head and licked at her breast, watching her closely as he added a second finger in her tight channel, stretching her as gently as he could.

"Drake," she called his name, eyes slightly shocked at the sensations pouring through her. "I need . . ." She couldn't articulate the rest.

"Take it easy," he soothed her. "I don't want you hurt. We have to go slow this time. You need slow, trust me, Saria. Slow is good."

He stroked again and, as if he'd somehow lit a torch, a flash fire raced through him like a fireball. He groaned. He wasn't certain he could go slow, not with such a craving clawing at his belly.

"I need to taste you, Saria." His voice was nearly a growl. Hunger was edging out sanity. He had to have her now, had to mark every inch of her with his scent. He'd never been so rock-hard in his life. He kissed his way down her body until he could kneel between her legs. She looked at him with dark, golden eyes, so wide, glazed with heat and need.

He took a breath and looked down at her body, allowing his gaze to drift slowly over her. *"Mine."* He exhaled on the word and looped her legs over his arms, pulling her closer as he lowered his head.

She smelled wild, and his own primitive nature leapt at the challenge. Saria equaled untamed, she went her own way and didn't make apologies for it. He heard her breath hitch and he tightened his grip on her hips in warning. She'd had her way with him and he had allowed it; he wanted the same. She was all his and he intended to indulge himself. He nuzzled her inner thighs and drank in her scent. Part cat, he needed to rub along her skin with his, to bite gently and taste, to use every tactile sense he had to stake his claim on her.

He swiped his tongue over all that heat and she bucked in his arms. "Ssh, it's all right," he whispered. "Relax for me." His eyes met hers again. There was trust there. She swallowed hard but she nodded her assent.

He kissed his way back up her inner thighs, nipping gently with his teeth, letting her get used to the feel of him between her legs. Very slowly, with great tenderness, he ran his tongue over her heated center, an artist painting the gentle waves of an ocean lapping at the shore. He took his time, enjoying the tremors running through her body. Her temperature went up so that skin to skin, she radiated heat right through him.

13

Saria knew she was drowning in desire. She felt consumed with need, with arousal. Looking at Drake, at his face, every line stamped with pure sensuality, the set of his mouth, his eyes, all carved deep with dark hunger. His eyes were all cat, staring at her as if she was prey, his gaze focused completely on her, as his hands gripped her hips tightly.

Fear skittered down her spine, yet excitement welled up like a fountain. He looked all man, a tough, scarred man at the edge of his control and knowing he was that way because of her — *for* her — was exhilarating. She wanted him to look at her like that — all hungry leopard, a man craving — *needing* her body. *Her* body. *Her* skin. *Her.*

His eyes locked with hers. Fierce. Intent. Her heart beat so hard she was afraid it would come through her chest. He licked his lips. Her heart jumped. Heavy-lidded eyes were dark gold, glittering with a harsh need.

"Give yourself to me." Instead of harsh, his voice was oddly tender, completely at odds with the stark sensuality. "Completely to me. No one will ever need you more."

An alarm bell went off somewhere in the back of her mind, but she was too far gone. She needed him — needed this. She couldn't stop her body from moving suggestively, invitingly, or the soft moaning whimper that escaped her throat as she nodded. She couldn't speak, couldn't form a coherent word.

His hands tightened on her hips. With her legs draped over his forearms, she was completely open to him. He kept watching her face even as he slowly lowered his head toward her burning center. She felt tears stinging. How could she ever survive? Her body was on fire, tension building until she wanted to beg him to stop it, to do something — anything.

She felt his tongue lap at her, a dark rasp that sent a million electrical currents racing through her body. He groaned and shifted just a little, pressing more deeply into her. She heard herself cry out, a strangled sound lost in her own ragged breathing. She clenched the comforter with both fists, trying to hang on to something solid, to anchor herself as he began to eat her — to devour her. He took his time, licking, sucking, painting circles and letters with his tongue until she realized he was actually writing his name inside of her.

Each stab of his tongue, the gentle scrape of his teeth, the hard strokes and gentle licks sent flames racing through her body. The fire only leapt higher and higher, raging out of control, building and building with no let up. Her head thrashed wildly and if he hadn't been holding her hips in a ruthless grip, she might have flown off the bed. He didn't stop that slow, sensual torment or the flat broad strokes of his tongue. She heard her own keening cry, begging him for something . . . What, she wasn't certain. Then she was fragmenting, coming apart in a rolling explosion that sent waves rippling through her body.

He rose over her, shifting her legs back even farther, using his arms as he positioned himself at her entrance. She felt his heavy erection stroke across her entrance and she shuddered with need. He pushed gently into her, just a scant inch, but he was large and the stretching, burning feeling was instantly intense. She stiffened and caught at his shoulders, her nails digging deep.

"Relax. Just relax. You're ready for me, honey. I'll go slow."

She swallowed hard. She wanted this, wanted him deep inside of her, filling her, but maybe it was happening far too soon. She felt trapped beneath him, out of control, a fire raging inside of her that was already building again, hot and powerful. More than Drake, she was afraid of herself, of the strong connection to him. She had never dreamt she would have such a physical response to anyone. She stilled as he pushed deeper, stretching her further.

It felt — good — scary — shocking and oh so right. Streaks of fire raced from between her thighs to her belly, even up to her breasts as he invaded, sliding deeper and deeper until he met resistance. She gasped, arching her hips, needing to ease the burning feeling, yet wanting more.

"Easy, baby, this might hurt for a moment. Let me do this. Just stay relaxed." His voice was husky, edgy, barely controlled.

Saria's gaze locked with his. Her body was no longer hers, but belonged entirely to Drake. She was on fire with such need she could only nod her head, begging and pleading with her eyes for him to fill her. Oh, God, he was so thick, so hard, like a steel spike, hot and searing. She could feel the pulse of his heart along the thick veins. It seemed impossible for her body to be able to accept any more of the long length. He was very still, holding himself pressed tight against her barrier, so that same pulse beat inside of her.

The world seemed to stand still while she drowned in sensation. The heat. The fire. The desperate need. She wanted to push herself onto him, yet at the same time she wanted to fling herself off the bed. Because once he did this, she would want him always. He would be a craving that never stopped. Already her body betrayed her, giving him everything he wanted, demanding he give the same to her.

She made a single sound. Protest? Or assent? She didn't know. Her heart stuttered as she saw the gold in his eyes flame with tenderness — with something close to love even while his mouth curved into pure lust. The look on his face was wildly exciting, only adding to the arousal spiraling out of control in her body.

He opened his hands and she instinctively threaded her fingers through his. He slammed her hands to the mattress, surging forward over the top of her. A searing pain burned through her body, but he went still again and she lay with her heart pounding and her fingers wound tightly in his, breathing long shuddering breaths.

"You're so tight, Saria. So damned tight." His voice sounded ragged and harsh.

Saria loved his voice, almost desperate for her. There was a dark hunger in his eyes, an implacable resolve she found thrilling. Her body needed more and she moved, a little experiment, lifting her hips against him. His breath hissed out and his eyes glittered dangerously.

"I want you in me, Drake. Every inch of you filling me," she whispered.

Saria's erotic demand sent a fireball careening through Drake's body. He surged a little deeper and the scorching constriction of her sheath added to the firestorm racing through him. He could count her heartbeats right through the tight walls of her velvet channel. He took a breath, willing his body to go slow, to be gentle. He eased a little further into her and felt her muscles grip and milk.

"Baby, be still, you can't do that."

Saria's eyes were glazed and hot, her body thrashing beneath him, hips bucking, trying to force him deeper. He leaned close to nuzzle her shoulder, teeth biting down to hold her still. He could feel her leopard rising, and his leaping to meet her.

"Fight her off, Saria. You're not ready for that kind of rough sex," he pleaded.

Her gaze met his and she took a breath, her fingers tightening around his. He surged forward, burying himself deep. She writhed under him, her hips rising to meet that deep thrust. Liquid heat surrounded him, and her muscles clamped down. He withdrew and plunged deep again, watching her face for signs of discomfort. The searing heat was consuming him and soon he wouldn't be able to hold back. He'd never been out of control with a woman before, but he could feel his control slipping fast.

Whether it was her leopard so close, or Saria's natural sensuality, she couldn't — or wouldn't listen to him, her body tightening rhythmically around his until he thought he'd go insane with pleasure. He heard his own groan, his surrender to the inevitable as he gathered her closer, the stroking caress of his cock causing her to cry out, her tone desperate.

He pulled back slowly in preparation, waited a heartbeat and then plunged deep and hard, setting a ferocious, almost brutal pace. He could hear his blood roaring in his ears. Her moans and pleas added to the frenzy of need driving him into her again and again, impaling her with a hard, frantic rhythm, every cell in his body alive with a growing ferocity, his cock a steel spike impaling her again and again.

Her head tossed on the pillow and her breath came in sobbing, gasping pleas. Her body coiled tighter and tighter around his, a strangling, scorching heat that sent streaks of pleasure racing through him as the tension built and he pushed her higher and higher. Her hips rose to meet his thrusts, even as she fought him a little, trying to writhe out from under him, the winding tension building too fast, too hot.

He could feel her body pulse around his, tightening until she felt like a scorching vise clamped around him, drawing his essence from his body. He jerked her legs over his shoulders, knowing he couldn't hold on, determined that she would soar with him. He thrust hard, over and over, long, hard, deep strokes, driving her into a frenzy of lust and need. He could feel the sensations increasing in strength through the tight walls of her sheath, see the intensity of need threading through the passion in her eyes.

"When I say, baby, just let go. Don't fight me. Just let go, but wait, honey, it will be worth it. Just wait." He licked along her shoulder once in a small caress even as he repeatedly slammed his cock deep into her, filling and stretching her, creating a friction over the sensitive bundle of nerves.

He waited until he could feel the raging flames threaten to consume her before he jerked her legs higher, positioning his body to apply pressure to her most erotic, responsive spot. "Now, baby. Let go now." He bit out the command through clenched teeth, and felt her instant response.

She didn't hesitate, but let herself go, her gaze locking with him. There was fear and trust mixed in the depths of her enormous eyes. Saria's body clamped down on his like a strangling vise. He stroked over the spot one more time and she gasped, her gaze going glittering gold as her body exploded in powerful waves that milked his own release. Her cries echoed his hoarse shout and he collapsed over the top of her, while his cock jerked and pulsed in her scorching hot sheath.

He fought to regain the ability to breathe, his hair damp and his body covered in a fine sheen. Moonlight from the open doors spilled across her face. Her hair was damp as well and she looked dazed, even a little frightened. He kept his fingers tight in hers, allowing his body to slowly come down from such an amazing high. Her muscles continued to rock them both, little aftershocks that kept sending electrical currents rushing through him. Her soft breasts felt perfect against his chest, his body still entwined tightly with hers.

Nuzzling her neck, he kissed his way up to her mouth, easing his weight just a little from her, although he kept his hips tight against the cradle of hers. Kissing her was a forever pastime. It was easy to lose himself in the heated velvet of her mouth, that dark, enticing erotic taste that was Saria. He levered himself up onto his elbows and framed her face with his hands, kissing her over and over. He loved kissing her. She gave herself to him, as she had when he made love to her. Totally. Holding nothing back.

"I can't live without you, Saria," he admitted softly, searching her eyes for an answering sign that she might feel the same way. "I've been alone too damned long. No one will ever need you or want you the way I do. Don't run from me."

She moistened her lips. "I'm scared."

The admission turned his heart over. "I know you are, baby. I swear I don't want to take over your life. I want to be a part of it. Say yes. I don't want to make love to you once or twice and then have you disappear out of my life."

"It's a big commitment. I'm not easy, Drake. Nothin' about me is easy. Ask my brothers. Ask Pauline. I don' know if it's my leopard, but since I was a child, I've gone my own way and I don' know any other way."

"Has it occurred to you that your independence is one of the things that attracts me most? I don't want to change you. I like you a little wild, honey."

"I don' want you to tell me it was all a terrible mistake a few weeks from now, Drake. I think it's your leopard and my leopard makin' you so crazy about me. You belong with someone like Charisse or Danae. You told me yourself every leopard for miles would be crazy for me. Look what happened the other night."

He kissed the tip of her nose. "Is that what you think? That I don't know the difference between a woman I want and one my leopard wants? We're shifters, Saria, not separate entities. I am my leopard, just as you are yours. We *both* are the same and we *both* choose you. Your leopard would never allow you to choose anyone incompatible. Mates can repeat for many life cycles. You're the one I want. Just as you are."

She blinked, but held his gaze. "I know I want to be with you, Drake. I'm not afraid of commitment, just of myself. I know how I am. I don' want to disappoint you. What if you want to live somewhere else and I go with you and can't stay? That could happen. When I was away at school, I couldn't breathe."

"Then we'll come back."

"But you'd resent me."

He laughed softly and leaned down to kiss her again. He did it thoroughly, until he almost lost track of what had been said. "Silly woman. I don't give a damn where we live. Besides, someone has to clean up this lair. And you'd probably run up thousands of dollars in phone bills calling Pauline."

A slow smile started at the curve of her mouth and warmed her eyes. She raised her head to capture his mouth with hers, her kiss not quite so tentative this time.

"So the answer is yes." He made it a statement.

"Yes."

"So are you Catholic? Do we get married in a church?"

She blinked at him again. He nearly laughed at the shock on her face. "Love. Commitment. Marriage. Babies. That's what that yes was all about, Saria. You said it and I know a woman like you won't go back on your word."

"Commitment. I was agreeing to commitment. I thought I was findin' my way to lovin' you until you mentioned that baby part. I wouldn't know what to do with a baby. Sheesh, Donovan. You don' want much do you?"

"No, just everything."

She shook her head, but her eyes told him she was already his. He kissed her again before she could form any more protests. This time when he lifted his head he laughed softly. "Fine, we'll put the baby idea on hold for a little while, but not too long. Miss Pauline wants grandchildren."

"That's such a low blow."

"Because you'd do anything for Pauline," he said.

Drake eased his body off of hers and rolled onto his side, taking his weight from her. Saria's gaze drifted over his face.

"It's hard to let go of that physical connection with you. I feel a little empty." She took his hand and put it over her heart. "Do you feel my heart pounding? I swear there's buzzin' in my head instead of brains. I think you managed to short-circuit something."

He wrapped his arm around her waist and pulled her tight against his body, not wanting to let go of the physical connection between them either. "I think this is the only way I'll be able to keep you, Saria — a little dazed and bemused from sex. When it wears off, let me know and we'll start again. That way, you won't see the marriage and baby part sneaking up on you."

Saria yawned. "I'm watchin' you."

"You're trying to go to sleep. Not yet, baby. Let me run a quick bath for you. You'll be sore tomorrow and I've got more plans when we wake up." He dropped another kiss on her temple and slid from the bed.

Saria made a halfhearted attempt to catch his hand, then turned away to snuggle back under the comforter. Drake laughed again and padded barefoot to his bathroom. The clawfoot tub was old-fashioned, deep and inviting. He'd soaked away the bruises and painful aches and he was determined that Saria do the same. He wanted her experience to be only pleasurablc. When the tub was nearly filled, he went back to the bedroom to get her.

She lay on her side, her thick, wild hair partially covering her face. The ragged ends on top were a little spiky and he found himself smiling as he watched her. Her lashes lay like two thick crescents on her cheeks, she breathed lightly and softly, drawing his attention to her curved mouth.

She looked young in her sleep, soft and beautiful and way out of his league. His heart did that strange little stutter that had warned him from their first meeting that he was in trouble.

How had his life become so intertwined with hers so fast? How did one fall for a woman and know he couldn't live without her in a matter of days? For him, their time together was forever — he was that certain. He knew Saria was meant for him and that no matter what happened in the future, it would be Saria he always wanted.

He scooped her into his arms, ignoring her sleepy protest. She might not need a man to protect or take care of her, but she had one that wanted — no — needed to do just that. He laughed softly at her squirming and cradled her tight against his chest as he took her through to the bathroom. She was solid in his arms, all soft curves and satin skin. He couldn't help kissing her upturned mouth for a long, languid indulgent few moments before trailing more kisses to the tip of her left breast.

She didn't flinch or pull away as he half expected her to do. She had to be a little sore. There was blood and semen on her thighs, evidence of her first time, and she'd been incredibly tight. He was a large man and he'd felt the stretching of her body.

"I'm sorry if I hurt you, Saria, I tried to be gentle." He had been so close to the edge of his control, a shocking first for him.

"Silly man. You didn't hurt me." She glanced down at the steaming water. "You aren't plannin' on throwin' me in there, are you?"

"Not this time," he admitted. He lowered her feet first until she was standing. "It's going to feel good, honey."

"So would sleep. And while I'm sittin' in here, you can entertain me. You aren't sleepin' while I'm takin' a bath." Saria sank down into the hot water and sighed with pleasure. "You're right, it does feel good. You really are incredible, you know."

"I wish, honey, but the sad truth is, I'm selfish. I want to wake you up tomorrow morning or maybe an hour or two from now." Drake laughed and nudged her legs over. "I'm coming in with you."

She leaned her head back against the porcelain. "I'll probably drown, or we'll soak the floor, but I'm fine with that. This is very relaxin'. Maybe I can sleep right here."

He placed her feet in his lap and began a slow massage under water. "Go ahead, Saria, I'll carry you back to bed."

"Tell me where you grew up," she encouraged, opening her eyes to look at him through her long lashes. "I think you would have made an interestin' child."

"I come from a lair in the Borneo rain forest. Children there are pretty much taken care of by everyone. We run free and have no idea we're learning skills that will come in handy later on in life. Survival, hunting, basically, all the things you learned here."

"School?" she asked.

"Mandatory. We have teachers in our villages and then later we are required to go to outside schools. We're encouraged to travel to other lairs in search of true mates. That keeps our lair strong as well as the others."

She frowned, sitting up a little straighter. Her breasts floated temptingly and Drake stroked one creamy swell to the darkened tip. Her nipple hardened under his touch.

"Is that what we should have done? All of the children when they grow up, search out other lairs?"

"Of course. Bloodlines get weak or they marry outside the lair and produce children with leopards who are unable to shift."

Drake knew he sounded distracted, but she had beautiful breasts. He leaned forward, cupping the slight weight on one palm and drew her nipple into his mouth. His cock jerked, and a warm, pleasant feeling of exquisite happiness filled him. This, then, was how it should be. He knew the terrible craving for her would rise, an urgent, almost brutal need, but there was this — comfortable — right — relaxed contentment.

She ran her fingers through his hair. "I love the way you look at me, Drake."

"Good, because I love looking at you."

"You make me feel beautiful."

"You are beautiful."

She made a small derisive sound in the back of her throat. "My mouth and eyes are too big for my face. And I'm sort of . . ." She looked down at her body and made a face. "Curvy."

His thumbs slid over her nipples, sending a shiver through her body. "You're so responsive — and I love your curves."

She wiggled her toes. "I rather like that foot massage you had goin'. If you're gettin' all hot and bothered again, I'm sleepin' through it this time."

"Clearly I'm going to have to improve my skills." He took her foot back in his hands. She looked exhausted — happy — but exhausted.

"I don't think improvin' your skills is a good idea. You'll kill us both." She closed her eyes, a small smile tugging at her mouth.

He didn't want her to fall asleep in the

tub, but the water was still hot and he wanted her to soak a few more minutes. "Would you mind filling me in on some of the families? The shifters, those who are part of the lair. I need to know what they're like."

She opened her eyes enough to peek at him. "Like who? I didn't know anyone other than my brothers were shifters. I didn't even know the Lafont family had shifter blood in them. As secrets go, they've all been good at keepin' them."

"There's one family that leases from Jake and no one has mentioned them," Drake said. "Can you tell me a little about them? The last name is Pinet. No one has mentioned them at all and that makes me wonder. I need a complete list of suspects."

Saria made a derisive sound in her throat. "You can cross them off your list of suspects. They have a big family, very close and lots of fun. Good people. Mr. Pinet was there when you fought Amos for leadership."

"I didn't fight him for leadership, I fought him for you."

She shrugged with a little smirk on her face. "Whatever. Mr. Pinet was there, but not his children. The three older boys, Charles, Leon and Philippe, are serving in the military, so they're not even around here at the moment and they just aren't like that. Mr. and Mrs. Pinet have a daughter, Sabine, who went off to college this year. And the two younger boys are still in high school."

"I see." Weariness was overcoming him fast. Drake picked up her other foot. "You know most of these people. Who would you suspect? And who do you suppose Remy suspects? Because I got the feeling he was holding something back."

"You're probably right about Remy. He plays things close to his chest." Saria yawned and covered her mouth. "I need to go to sleep, Drake."

He took her hand to look at her nails, devoid of color. She'd probably never had a manicure in her life. His fingers stroked over hers. "Okay, honey, let's get you into bed. But at least think about it. Whoever is doing this didn't just start. Maybe they were cruel to animals. A bully in the play yard."

He stood up, allowing the water to cascade off him, tugging at her hand so she stood as well. He released the plug to let the water out and lifted her onto the bathmat.

Saria reached for a towel, but he took it from her hands. "My turn." He dried every inch of her as gently as he could, and then himself, before lifting her into his arms.

"I could get used to this."

"You're going to get used to a lot of things," he predicted.

Her smile was drowsy. "You're so sure of yourself."

"I know when I'm good at things."

She burst out laughing, a soft musical sound that tightened his groin. He drew back the comforter and placed her in the middle of the bed. Before she could scoot over, he stretched out beside her. It had begun to rain and the sound through the open French doors created an intimate rhythm on the balcony.

"Don't you love the sound of rain?" she asked.

"Yes." But it was her laughter he loved. He wrapped his arm around her waist and scooted her tight against him. "Where's your knife?"

"My knife?" She echoed the word, her tone dripping with innocence.

He bit her shoulder gently. "I know you have it here somewhere. You sleep with the damn thing."

Her laughter was taunting. It slid inside him and wrapped around his heart. "Does that scare you?"

"Hell yeah," he said. "One of these nights you'll get angry with me and . . ."

"Wait!"

Saria started to sit up and then retreated when he refused to move his arm. He pinned her with one leg draped over her thigh.

"What is it?"

"Lojos and Gage came home one day very angry, about two years ago. They'd been off trappin', and I'd never seen them in such foul moods. They aren't like that, you know? They laugh a lot and tease the way men often do, but Gage actually punched the wall outside and Lojos was like a bear with a sore tooth. At first I thought they got in a fight, but then I heard them talkin' to Dash. Someone had gone along their trap lines and tortured the animals. Most were still alive, and the boys killed them to put them out of their misery."

"What were they trapping?"

"You know nutria isn't native to Louisiana. They came here from South America to fur farms and were released. No one knows if it was accidental or on purpose, but they're impacting our wetlands adversely. A huge study was done to put in place a plan to control the population and we participate. But we don't torture animals, Drake. There's a huntin' season, just like with alligators. We want the swamp to

411

flourish. With oil spills and hurricanes and everythin' else we have to contend with, almost all of us here conform to the regulations. And no one that we know would ever torture an animal for fun."

"Did they find out who did it?"

She frowned. "That was the strange thing. There were no tracks."

"And no scent," he guessed.

"At the time, they weren't admittin' to me they were shifters, so if there wasn't any scent, they didn't mention it, but they didn't want me goin' out in the swamp by myself."

Drake listened to the sound of her voice closely there in the dark, with the rain providing a musical background. There was an underlying hurt in her tone when she spoke of her brothers. The boys in her family had been close, but it was as if they hadn't really noticed her until she got older. By the time they wanted to exert authority over her, she had taken firm control of her own life and resented their interference.

He rubbed his chin over the top of her head. "Would they have told Remy if there was evidence of a leopard as well as a human attack?"

"Of course. Remy's the acknowledged head of the family and he'd beat the crap out of one of them if they held somethin' like that back."

"He didn't try to beat you," Drake felt compelled to point out.

"Remy would never hit me. None of my brothers would." She was silent a moment and then half turned toward him to look at him, her eyes wide. "I had forgotten, but now that you say that, I remember Remy takin' the switch from *Pere* and breakin' it in half. I got in trouble for sneakin' off at night."

She talked so rarely about her childhood that he wanted to hear more. "Why'd you sneak off like that?"

A half smile touched her mouth. "I was angry with *mon pere* for gettin' so drunk. He made a terrible mess on my floor and even the sofa. Pauline had made me the most beautiful cover. Our sofa was old and fallin' apart and he ruined the cover. I knew I'd never get the stain out, so I threw a bucket of water on him where he was layin' in the mess and stormed out. He was too drunk to catch me that night, but I went back a couple of nights later and he went to switch the tar out of me."

"How old were you?"

"About nine." She turned back, snuggling into her pillow. "I haven't thought about that in years. Remy had come home and he came barrelin' out of his room and yanked the switch out of *mon pere's* hands and told him if he ever touched me like that again, he'd get the switchin' of his life. Funny that I didn't remember that until now. That's probably how I always knew Remy wouldn't ever hit me in anger. He was furious with *mon pere.*"

"I would have been too."

She laughed. "You say that now. You haven't lived with me. Pauline says I could try the patience of a saint. As I recall you said you were no saint."

"I did say that, didn't I?" He spread his fingers over the slight roundness of her stomach. He loved the way she felt so soft. "I'm definitely not, as much as I'd like to be for you."

"I rather like that you're no saint. I couldn't live up to one."

A sudden blast of wind sent a barrage of rain into the room and the curtains flying. Saria yelped and put the covers over her head as the drops of water poured over them. Laughing, Drake leapt out of bed and caught the doors to close them.

"Miss Pauline is goin' to kill me," Saria wailed, her voice muffled. "She loves those curtains."

Drake pulled the first door closed, but

stopped, looking out over the water in the distance. Rain swept down in silvery sheets, dotting the surface of the lake. Something moved just inside the tree line, where the hammocks were slung in the trees.

"What is it?" Saria peeked out from under the blankets.

When she went to move, he held up his hand as he would have for one of his team members. It didn't occur to him she wouldn't obey. Saria was intelligent and she knew the danger of what he'd done — challenging the leader of the lair. Already the two of them had been hunted. Armande and Robert swore they were only trying to scare off Drake, but Robert had made his try twice with a weapon.

Drake didn't move, but stayed very still, allowing his leopard to come close to the surface, improving his night vision. The heavy rain made it difficult to see into the heavy foliage. The water behind the trees had allowed him to see a shadow he couldn't identify merging with the darker interior of the grove.

They had one guard, the others needed sleep, and Pauline Lafont owned one very large piece of property. He silently cursed himself for provoking the male members of the lair. He should have taken care of hunt-

shoulder.

"Of course I am," Pauline assured her. "You're my girl. My child."

"I thought I'd lost you. I can't, Miss Pauline. I need you."

"You won't lose me. Amos and I have always loved each other, Saria, but you're my daughter. No matter . . ."

Saria shook her head, knowing Pauline didn't understand her, didn't know how close to death she actually had been. Pauline peeled Saria's arms from her neck and led her to a small, ornate sofa. She sank down, drawing Saria with her.

"You don' understand," Saria tried to explain. "He was here, in the house. I thought he might have killed you and Amos. No one heard him. He slides in and out of places and there's nothing of him left behind. No trace."

Pauline frowned as Drake held out the small glass of brandy. Saria didn't take it, so Pauline did, holding it up to Saria's mouth. Saria gulped the fiery liquid. It burned all the way down. She coughed and blinked back tears.

"Feeling better?" Pauline asked gently.

Saria pressed her lips together firmly and nodded. She glanced at Drake to see if he was horrified by her momentary madness.

ing the killer and then worry about everything else.

A deer nosed its way out of the trees onto the edge of the inn's rolling lawn. Drake didn't move. He watched the animal step cautiously, almost delicately onto the expanse of green. He looked warily around and moved to a line of shrubs guarding roses. Every third step the animal stopped and waited. Twice he looked toward the trees where Drake had thought he had seen a shadow move.

Drake shifted his gaze to follow the line of the deer. The trees were close together, some of the trunks quite thick. The rain pounded the leaves, turning the night into a thick gray veil. Every now and then a gust of wind blew straight toward the house. He inhaled, trying to catch an elusive scent. Nothing. The deer continued to make his way toward the roses, leery, but determined.

The brush near the trees moved and a skinny dog emerged, nearly crawling on its belly, away from the deer toward a garbage can. Drake gave a sigh of relief and closed both doors, and as a precaution, added the floor lock.

"Nothing?" Saria asked.

"Nothing, honey. You can put the knife away." He crawled into bed and gathered her close again. "You won't be needing it."

"What a shame." She brushed his mouth with hers and closed her eyes.

Drake lay awake for a long while, holding her close, marveling at how a woman's skin could be so soft and yet house a backbone of steel. God, but he'd fallen hard. He didn't even know how it happened, but every moment in her company just made him fall deeper in love. He drifted off to sleep, inhaling the fragrance of her hair.

Drake's eyes snapped open and he lay in the gathering dawn, listening to the rain, listening for a sound that might have awakened him. He'd been exhausted and he knew he'd slept heavily. He touched his leopard. The animal had woken along with him, but was settling down once again, as if he, too, had no idea what had woken him.

Saria was cuddled up beside him, warm and soft, on her side, unmoving, not restless at all. That surprised him. He expected it would difficult for her to sleep beside someone, just as it had always been impossible for him, yet both of them had slept easily together.

He lifted the corner of her pillow where her hand was hidden. He wasn't at all surprised to see her knife inches from her fingers. He moved it back a little more, not wanting to take any chances when he woke her. Smiling, he cupped her breast, his thumb stroking back and forth over her nipple. She felt like rose petals, soft and velvety and so warm.

"Turn over, baby," he whispered in her ear, taking time to tug at her earlobe with his teeth.

Saria murmured sleepily, but obediently turned toward him where he could nuzzle at her warm breasts. She sighed drowsily and one hand landed in his hair, stroking small caresses there. He lapped at her nipples for a moment and then drew one into the heat of his mouth. She made a small appreciative sound and cradled his head to her.

"Mmm, nice way to wake up."

He took his time, lavishing attention on every square inch of her body, learning every sensitive spot that sent her writhing and tossing against him. He indulged his every whim, loving her with his mouth and hands, getting to know her body as intimately as he knew her strength of character.

A thump on the door brought Drake's head up alertly, and Saria yanked up the covers. She moistened her lips, her eyes holding a mixture of disappointment, amusement and alarm. "I can't think anymore, you've destroyed my brain."

"Good," he whispered unrepentant, leaning down to give her another kiss.

The thudding came again, this time more imperious.

Saria laughed softly. "The children are calling."

He growled a swear word in her ear and then bit down on her lobe, making her squeal. "What is it?" he called, his voice gruff.

"Sorry to disturb you, boss, but you need to see this — now," Joshua's voice called out.

14

Joshua Tregre. Saria had made a point of studying him for signs of depravity and cruelty, once she'd heard his last name. His surname carried a terrible stigma in the swamp and yet Joshua seemed to be a decent man. Certainly Drake and the others trusted him.

"Just a minute," Drake said and slid out of bed.

"I'm goin' with you," Saria informed him, leaping out of bed just as fast. "Give me a minute." She raced for the bathroom, snagging her jeans and a top as she rushed on through. He'd better not leave her behind.

She caught a brief glimpse of herself in the mirror as she attended to her morning rituals and hastily yanked on her clothes. She was a little surprised to see she looked the same. She didn't feel the same. She felt — beautiful. Loved. Part of someone.

"Let's go," Drake called.

She smiled to herself. He sounded so commanding. So like someone who expected instant obedience — and he probably did — when it counted. He didn't treat her at all the way he sounded in a crisis. She trusted his judgment, which made it easier to follow his dictates in a dangerous situation. She also loved that he waited.

She ran out to join him, laughing when she saw him pulling on his shirt. "I'm so much faster than you, and I'm the girl."

He grinned at her, that cocky, arrogant grin that tugged at her heartstrings, and he took her hand before opening the door. Joshua looked grim and Drake's smile faded.

"What is it?"

Joshua shook his head. "Sorry, boss. We had a visitor. Had to be a couple of hours ago. The kill's fresh on the lawn. A deer and a small dog. He tore them to shreds. He wasn't looking for food either, just the fun of ripping something up."

"Leopard?"

"Both had classic kill bites." He glanced uneasily at Saria. "And he used a knife on them as well. He had to have slipped in when we were at the other side of the house and he must have made the kills when he left. I noticed the deer earlier chowing down on some roses."

"You mean he was in the house?" Drake demanded.

Joshua's gaze again shifted briefly to Saria and back to Drake. She felt her stomach muscles tighten into knots.

"In her room, Drake."

Drake took the lead, signaling Saria to stay behind him. Joshua fell in behind her. She became aware of the silence. Neither man made a sound. She could hear her own breathing, but not their footsteps. The rain on the roof lent an eerie feel to walking down the darkened hallway to her bedroom.

Drake pushed open the door and stood just inside, surveying the damage. Saria peeked under his arm and her breath caught in her throat. She slipped her hand into Drake's, her heart pounding. Someone — *something* — had ripped every single item of her clothing into tatters. The bedding and mattress were in shreds. She could hear her heart pounding in her chest, the blood roaring in her ears.

"He hates me. I've never had anyone hate me," she whispered.

Drake slipped his arm around her and pulled her into the heat of his body. She hadn't realized until that moment that she was shivering. "He's demented, Saria."

"He's fixated on her," Joshua said.

Saria swallowed the protest. It would have been silly to object anyway. The evidence was right in front of her. Without question, whoever was killing and dumping bodies was the same person who had shredded everything in the room belonging to her.

"It's creepy to think someone is out there watchin' me. He must know what room I'm in."

"He's leopard," Drake said. "He can find you by scent."

She pressed her fingers against her trembling mouth, willing herself not to shake in front of Drake or Joshua.

"Did you see him?" Drake asked Joshua.

"I saw where he went into the swamp, but I couldn't follow him. He left tracks for about a mile and then he was gone. No scent trail at all. None, Drake. And there's nothing in the room. His scent should be everywhere. The doors were closed and he was in there a few minutes, enough that the room should reek of him. He's like a damned ghost."

"He was too close to her, Joshua," Drake said.

She caught the look that passed between the two men. Drake was angry. Outwardly he appeared calm, but Joshua flushed and nodded his head as if guilty of something.

"It isn't his job to guard me, Drake," she said. "I don' even like the idea of it. This is my home and I'm capable of protectin' myself, even against this killer." She had to fight to keep her voice from swinging out of control. "I may be afraid, but I can handle this."

"No one is saying you can't," Drake answered. "He got too close. He came into a building where we were sleeping and we didn't hear him."

Saria felt herself turn white. If the killer had gotten into the inn with all of them sleeping, *everyone* had been vulnerable. "Pauline," she whispered aloud. She jerked her hand out of Drake's and turned and ran, fear sweeping through her body, threatening to choke her. As her fear rose, so did her leopard, she could feel the power and energy of the cat as it fed her strength.

Her birth mother had slipped away long before Saria had a chance to know her and her father had slowly but surely followed. He'd taught her the ways of the swamp and how to take care of herself, but it had been Pauline she'd run to all of her life. Pauline had soothed her when she cried, explained life's mysteries, had bandaged every scrape and taught her how to cook and sew and cope with life. Pauline had been her surrogate mother and she loved her fiercely and protectively.

Behind her, she was vaguely aware of Drake racing after her down the long hall, calling her name, telling her to stop, to wait, but she couldn't. Her heart pounded and there was a strange roaring in her head. Her lungs burned as she grasped the railing and leapt over it to the first floor below. She landed on her feet in a crouch and took off running again through the entryway to the living room and down the hall toward the back of the house where Pauline's small apartment, basically the entire southern wing of the house, was located.

Drake was on her before she reached the door, his arms catching her around the waist, pinning her arms so she had no chance to fight. "Be still," he hissed in her ear. "Let me see first."

She shook her head mutely. Pauline was her mother whether there was a blood relationship or not. She'd always known it, but not like this — this terrible fear of losing her forever. Drake signaled Joshua and he stepped to one side of the door. Jerico had joined them and apparently Evan was circling around outside. It was all too late. She should have thought to protect Pauline above all else.

Drake stood to the right of the door and knocked. "Miss Pauline? Amos? Are you all right in there?"

For a heart-stopping moment his call was met with silence. Saria jammed her fist in her mouth. Her legs suddenly felt like rubber. Something stirred behind the closed door. There was a soft rustle, footsteps and Pauline opened her door, blinking sleepily at them. No one had thought to turn on a light, but Saria caught the flare of cat in her eyes. She might not have a leopard, but she had leopard blood flowing in her veins and had excellent night vision.

Saria flung herself into Pauline's arms and to her horror, began to weep almost hysterically. The relief at seeing her alive was so overwhelming after such fear of what she might find, that she couldn't stop herself, not even knowing she was making a complete fool of herself in front of Drake's men.

She nearly bowled Pauline over, but the woman closed her arms around her firmly and held her close, murmuring soothingly as she looked over Saria's shoulder to Drake for an explanation.

Jerico and Joshua immediately left, giving Saria some privacy. She noticed, but was too distraught to acknowledge their gentlemanly behavior.

"Saria, honey, tell me what's wrong," Pauline coaxed.

"I'm sorry, I can't stop," Saria admitted. "Hit me or something."

"What did you do?" Amos demanded, glaring at Drake.

"Not *him*," Saria hastened to explain, hiccupping. "The killer."

"Killer?" Pauline echoed and glanced at Amos, mystified. "Saria, you aren't makin' sense. Come into the parlor." She stepped back to allow them into her private wing of the house. The room they entered was a small sitting room. "Drake, pour a small glass of brandy."

"I hate brandy," Saria sniffed.

"Yes, I know," Pauline soothed, "but it will help. Amos, stop glarin' at the boy and bring that comforter. I think Saria's in shock."

Saria clung to Pauline. "You know I only went to school because you wanted me to. You know that don' you? I did everythin' you asked me to do. I didn' listen to *mon pere,* to the church ladies or my brothers, only you. You know that, don' you?"

"Of course I know that."

"You're *ma mere,* you always have been." Saria tightened her arms around Pauline's neck, burying her face on the older woman's

He looked relieved, but not about to run.

"I'm sorry," she whispered to him.

Drake reached for her hand and brought it to his mouth. "Don't be. You're entitled. You've had a hell of a time now for weeks, for months. You've been through a lot."

She wanted to protest. She'd met him because of all the terrible things and he had made every minute so worthwhile. Making love to him had been wonderful, but she wasn't going to bring that up in front of Pauline and Amos. They were waiting for an explanation for her breakdown. The brandy burned like a fireball in her belly. She glanced up at Drake again for direction. She'd blurted out important, confidential information. Maybe too much information. Her brothers knew what was going on, but they couldn't let the lair know, not before they'd had time to investigate everyone.

Drake nodded slightly, giving her permission to disclose the truth. Her face burned with embarrassment. She'd never been so out of control. The fear of losing Pauline had struck her like a ton of bricks and she'd panicked. She'd never felt that kind of fear before, that terrifying moment when one could lose that important person who meant the world to them.

"I was afraid for you, Miss Pauline," she whispered. Even her throat was sore after the storm of weeping. "Someone broke into the inn tonight. Into my room." She blushed, but met Pauline's gaze steadily. "I was in Drake's room, but Joshua discovered the intruder and chased him into the swamp."

Amos frowned. "He's leopard. He had to have his scent. We can . . ."

Drake shook his head. "That's the problem. There is no scent."

"That's impossible. Everything leaves scent behind," Amos protested.

"Let Saria tell us," Pauline advised gently. "There's much more to this story, isn't there, *cher?*"

Saria nodded. She started from the beginning, when she'd first seen the lights around Fenton's Marsh and she'd found the first body. Pauline and Amos remained silent while she grimly told them everything. She didn't leave out the attack on her, or the fact that the leopard had left no scent. Drake took up where she left off, revealing that Remy had been investigating a series of murders where bodies of women had been dumped on the edges of the city, along the river and in the bayou.

"And you think this killer was here in the

inn?" Pauline asked.

Saria bit her lip as she nodded. "He was in my room, and he destroyed all my things." For some insane reason her eyes brimmed with tears again.

Pauline patted her knee. "Then it was a good thing you were in Drake's room, now wasn't it, *cher?* Do you have any ideas who this killer could be, Amos? You know most of the families well."

Amos shook his head. "Every one of us has secrets, but I can't imagine anyone other than old man Tregre being a straight-up killer — and he's dead."

"One of his sons? Or his grandsons?" Drake prompted.

Amos sighed and rubbed the bridge of his nose, shaking his head. "I doubt it. They don' have much backbone. I can't imagine any of them pullin' off a homicide let alone as many as you claim."

"And Elie?" It had to be asked. Elie Jeanmard had called Saria's brothers when Robert Lanoux and Armande Mercier had hunted them in the swamps. It sounded out of character for him to be a serial killer, but one never knew.

Amos opened his mouth to protest and then closed it, in an obvious attempt to give the idea thought. "I don' think Elie is capable of murder. I really don'. He was always a gentle boy, loved animals and I suspect someone capable of the kind of thing you're describin' would have shown tendencies in childhood towards killin'. Elie didn't ever hunt gators."

Saria nodded. "That's true, Drake. Elie has always been one of the sweetest boys around."

Drake paced across the room more to hide the sudden flare of jealousy than the need for restless movement. The sudden surge of dark emotion caught him off guard. He had confidence in himself, and more, he had trust in Saria. It made no sense that her innocent statement would make jealousy claw at his gut. He didn't want to own Saria, he wanted to love her, be her partner, and share his life with her. He wanted the free spirit, that indomitable will that fascinated and intrigued him. He liked that she was open and friendly with everyone — even other men, yet he hadn't been able to squash that flare of jealousy. It was an ugly feeling and one he didn't want.

"Drake?"

Her voice was pitched low. Almost intimate. The sound washed through him, as clean and fresh as spring water, driving away his demons. He flicked her a quick look

432

from where he stood in the shadows. He had gone still once again, holding himself apart until he could figure out what was wrong with him.

He glanced at Amos. The man wore a dark scowl, watching Drake's every move closely with a suspicious expression. Drake glanced away, looking around the small parlor. This was a small room, the furniture more Victorian rather than modern. A small fireplace was the focal point of the room. A table with a lacy cloth covered the older wood. His gaze rested for a minute on the detailed, ornate vase on the floor beside the hearth. The vase was two feet high and sat on clawed feet. A large floral arrangement consisted of the same strange flowers he'd noticed in Fenton's Marsh as well as ferns and other greenery.

He frowned and crossed the room to the study the arrangement. The flowers smelled wonderful, the petals looking dewy soft. Golden, with dark rosettes, they reminded him of a leopard's pelt. "Where did you get these flowers?"

There was a long silence. He turned to look at Pauline, silently demanding an answer. Pauline frowned, the question obviously unexpected.

"They're called Leopard's Lover," she said.

"Don' answer that," Amos snarled belligerently. "Are you accusing Pauline of somethin'? First my boy and now Pauline." He half stood, his fists clenched.

Saria jumped to her feet as did Pauline. Pauline rushed to Amos's side, taking his arm to soothe him.

"He didn' mean that, Amos. What's wrong?"

"Drake?" Saria asked.

Drake held up his hand. "It's happening here in this room — the same thing that happened out in the marsh." He raised his voice. "Joshua, Jerico, come on in here."

Amos subsided back into the chair, but he still wore a frown. Pauline sank down beside him, one hand still resting on his arm as if she could stop him from attacking as he so clearly wanted to do.

"What happened in the marsh?" Amos demanded.

Joshua and Jerico came from different sides of the house, entering through different doors. Drake beckoned them to come all the way in.

"Do you feel anything? Do your leopards feel anything?"

Joshua was the first to nod. "He's agitated.

I feel hostile and aggressive and it's coming from him."

"Mine too, boss," Jerico agreed.

"Mine as well," Drake said. He looked at the older man. "And clearly your leopard is reacting too. But neither of the women feels it. Why is that?"

Drake approached the vase. His leopard clawed and raked at him as he inhaled. "Joshua, smell them up close."

Joshua handed his gun to Jerico and cautiously crossed to the large vase. Leaning down, he took a deep breath, allowing the fragrant scent of the flower into his lungs. He gasped and stepped back. "My leopard went crazy, Drake. This flower is dangerous to us."

Pauline and Saria both pulled a long-stemmed flower from the vase and held it to their nose. Drake could see it was actually two flowers, with one winding around the long stalk of the other. The leopard petals were larger and shaped like a champagne flute where the smaller flowers climbing the stark stalk were all dark chocolate, a beautiful, but obviously deadly flower.

"I don' feel anything at all," Pauline said. "Well, maybe . . ." She trailed off.

Saria shook her head. "My leopard's not angry."

Amos stood up and came to take a whiff of the flowers. He leapt back and continued backtracking until he was as far from the flowers as he could get. "My leopard went crazy, raging at me. He's always calm, but he wanted to kill."

"You said they were called *Leopard's Lover?*" Saria asked, puzzled. "I've photographed them in Fenton's Marsh, growin' wild there. I've only seen them one other place. When I go to meet Evangeline Tregre on the edge of her property, where the Mercier corner is as well, those flowers are everywhere there. How did you know their name? I thought they were a new, undiscovered species."

"My sister brought me the flowers last night when she came for dinner. I've always loved them. The Merciers grow hybrids all the time, looking for certain fragrances," Pauline explained. She glanced at Drake's frowning face. "Iris was married to Bartheleme Mercier. He died a few years ago, but it was really Charisse and Armande that built the perfume business up. They're worldwide now. Iris is very proud of them and when I visit I go to the greenhouse where they develop new hybrids. *Leopard's Lover* has been in development for years. Charisse was tryin' to perfect the scent. She actually started the project before she was even in high school and she's been workin' on it ever since."

Drake's leopard raked and clawed at him, making it difficult to think straight. "We've got to get out of this room."

The other men nodded in relief, pushing through the doors to get away from the subtle fragrance their leopards were reacting to. Pauline led them back into the inn's largest sitting room across from her wing of the house. The distance provided instant relief and Drake waited until he felt his leopard settle before he tried to put the pieces together.

"Charisse Mercier, your niece, Pauline, started growing hybrid flowers before she was even in high school, so years ago. Am I getting this right?"

Pauline nodded. "I can't remember the exact year, but she documents everything. These flowers were inspired by shifters, of course. She was very excited about them and she's worked for years to get not only the fragrance she wants, but the look."

"They're beautiful," Saria said.

"And deadly to our males," Drake pointed out. "How did they get out of the greenhouse and into the marsh? She can't just plant flowers that she knows nothing about and not expect an impact on the environment."

"I don' know. She keeps all hybrids in the greenhouse and it's completely enclosed. Charisse is very careful. She actually has a special room where the air blows all contact from your clothes and shoes so nothing gets transferred to the outside swamp."

"I know I saw the flowers scattered along the property lines on the Mercier land and quite a bit on the Tregre side. The soil is very rich there, almost black, and Fenton's Marsh has spots very much like that," Saria said. "The marsh, of course has a high water table, but there are acres of great soil. That's mostly where I've seen the flowers."

"Anywhere else?" Drake asked.

Saria shook her head. "I'm all over the swamps and bayous. Most everyone has given me permission to take photographs. I don' go on the Tregre's property and I always ask Charisse before I go onto Mercier land because I don' want to disturb their work and I never know when they're harvestin' somethin'. I've only seen those flowers in two places. I photographed them and had intended to ask Charisse about them. It's possible she doesn't know they somehow got out of her greenhouse."

"They couldn't have walked out," Drake

said. "Did she know the reaction the smell has on the male leopards?"

Pauline's frown turned into a scowl. "Of course not. The fragrance is beautiful, almost heavenly. I love it, that's why I asked my sister for an arrangement for my house. Saria said her leopard doesn't stir . . ."

Saria made a small sound in the back of her throat, drawing attention to her. Her face flushed with color. "That's not strictly true, Pauline. My leopard stirs . . ."

"You said she didn't react," Drake said.

"I know I said that. She didn't react with aggression or hostility so I didn' connect her reaction to the flowers and I was embarrassed to say anything." Her gaze met his steadily. "She gets amorous."

Immediately the memory of Saria on her knees in the swamp, her mouth on his cock, flooded his mind. He hadn't thought about flowers. He hadn't thought about anything but that fantasy mouth and the pleasure surging through his body. The place could have been overrun with flowers for all he knew.

"It could be that you're close to the emerging," Drake said, holding her gaze, letting her know silently he was proud of her courage for telling him in front of the others.

"It isn't the same," she said. "At first I thought it was too, but in the parlor, well, let's just say it was a good thing we were surrounded by company."

She was painfully honest and once again, Drake felt a surge of pride in her. It couldn't be easy confessing she wanted to jump him in front of the woman she considered a mother — or the other men for that matter.

Pauline glanced at Amos and then cleared her throat. "I did have that reaction as well. Now that I think about it, when I'm near the flowers I definitely feel more amorous, for want of a better word."

"This is crazy," Joshua said. "Flowers? You're telling me that a flower makes women want sex and men want to fight?"

"The leopards," Drake said. "And in a way it makes sense. When a woman is close to the Han Vol Dan, every male within miles becomes belligerent and aggressive. The male leopard responds both aggressively and sexually to her scent. If Charisse managed to reproduce the scent of the female leopard during the emerging, the flowers would drive every male shifter crazy and enhance the female's sex drive."

"I can't believe a flower would do all that," Amos said. "It's just a flower."

"It's a scent," Drake pointed out. "Leopards are all about scent."

"I'm going with Mr. Jeanmard on this, Drake," Joshua said. "It's a flower."

"And that's why we're not leaders of the lair," Amos said. "What other explanation is there? It seems ludicrous, but all of us felt our leopard's reaction. If it happened out in Fenton's Marsh as well . . ."

Jerico nodded. "We all felt it. There was something out there, something making our leopards belligerent and aggressive."

"So what does it mean?" Saria asked. "Charisse can't know how the males react, or she would have destroyed the flower. I know her. If she's been slowly perfecting this plant, she's looking for a fragrance to manufacture — probably a signature fragrance worth millions."

"How long have the flowers been growing on Tregre land?" Drake tapped his finger on his thigh, his mind racing. If Charisse had been experimenting for years, then the flowers could have been subtly influencing the lair.

He had traveled extensively and had seen many lairs. None had the degree of inner destruction this one had. Something was terribly wrong, but, like Joshua, it was difficult to imagine that a flower's scent would be responsible for the slow disintegration of

441

an entire lair.

"I only went there for the first time a couple years ago," Saria said. "The old man was scary and *mon pere* would have switched me had I gone near him. When he died, I braved it, and met Evangeline. I honestly can't remember when I saw them for the first time, but I always take photographs and I'll have those in an album somewhere. I always record dates and places and time of year when I put them in my albums. Seriously, though, I doubt more than two years."

"Talk to Charisse. She should be able to tell you," Pauline encouraged. "She always writes everything down, she has to."

Drake shook his head. "I don't want you telling your sister or Charisse." He gave Amos a hard look. "Or Elie. Nothing that's been said here can leave this house, not until we complete our investigation. We've got a serial killer on the loose and he's one of us. Finding him has to be our first priority. I'll talk to Charisse myself. Agreed?" He wasn't asking. Technically, Pauline wasn't a member of the lair, but Amos was and he had sworn his allegiance.

Amos immediately nodded, but Pauline bit her lip, looking upset. "I don' understand. You don' suspect Charisse of any wrongdoin', do you?"

"I don't want news of this to get out during an investigation of a serial killer. We've got to be careful. I don't want to put Charisse or anyone else in danger by shining a spotlight on them." Drake chose his words carefully.

Saria glanced at him sharply as if she might protest, but subsided when he lifted his hand in a subtle gesture to stop her. She pressed her lips together and swallowed as if choking on her obvious need to defend Charisse. She knew he hadn't exactly answered Pauline and truthfully, he couldn't answer her, not right at that moment.

Pauline seemed to accept his explanation at face value. "Okay. I won' say anything, but Drake, you get to the bottom of this fast."

"Yes, ma'am," he agreed.

"I'm goin' up to see the damage in Saria's room. Do you really think whoever was here is the serial killer?" Pauline asked.

"Yes," Drake said. It was the stark, raw truth. He knew the killer had been in the house — that he'd come for Saria. The evidence in the room showed rage — a very personal rage. The killer knew Saria, or at least he fantasized that he knew Saria. Whatever the circumstances, her being with

Drake was some kind of betrayal in the killer's mind.

"I'd rather not go back up there if you don' mind," Saria said.

"Drake can come with me," Pauline decreed. "Amos, you stay here. Your ribs are cracked and climbin' all those stairs won' be good for you."

"Joshua, Jerico, stay with Saria," Drake ordered.

Her eyes glittered at him a little dangerously, but she didn't argue, which was good, because as far as he was concerned, she was getting protection. He wanted to warn her brothers as well. If the killer planned on making this personal, anyone she loved could be at risk.

Pauline led the way up the sweeping staircase, stopping at the top in the circular library to turn back toward him. She rested one hand on the stone fireplace and looked him in the eye. He waited, knowing she'd maneuvered the situation to get him alone.

"Do you think this man came here to kill Saria?"

Her stare was direct and for the first time, Drake could see the leopard in her. She was as fiercely protective of her chosen daughter as any birth mother could possibly be. She might not be able to shift, but her leopard was strong.

"Yes I do," he said, respecting her with the truth.

It wasn't what she wanted to hear and he could see her take the blow, but she took a breath and nodded, still studying his face.

"You look at her the way my Amos always has looked at me. You won' let anything happen to her." She made it a statement.

"No, ma'am, I won't."

She stared at his face for a few more long moments and then, apparently satisfied, she led the way to Saria's room. "She's a good girl, you know. Smart and funny and filled with courage. She won' ever be happy away from her swamp for too long. It's always been her refuge."

"Tell me why her family didn't pay attention to her."

"You mean Remy and the boys? Saria was a mixed blessin' for her parents. They had five sons and then Aimee got sick. Her health had never been good, you understand, but LeRoy he wanted lots of children. He was very old school, a very hard man. Don' get me wrong, he loved his wife and his children, but he ruled and he just never saw that Aimee was weak. She became pregnant with Saria and she just sort of slipped away. She retreated from reality. The boys knew and loved her and it was a tryin' time for them, losin' her that way. She stopped talkin' and just took to her bed."

"Saria's father didn't mistreat his wife?"

Pauline shook her head, one hand on the doorknob to the room. "No, he wasn' like that at all. Stern, but he would never have laid a hand on Aimee, he adored her. When she died, he took to drink. He withdrew just as Aimee did. In a different way, but he was determined to drink himself to death and he did."

Pauline pushed open the door and stepped back, one hand to her throat, staring at the damage. Saria's clothing was in shreds, much like his had been the first night he'd arrived. There was no doubt a leopard had been in the room and had thrown a temper tantrum.

"How could he do so much damage and no one hear him?"

"This would have taken minutes," Drake said. "An angry leopard can do a tremendous amount of damage in a confined space in seconds. He was in and out of here right under our noses. There was only one guard awake at a time and this is a big property to patrol."

Pauline closed the door and leaned against it. "Saria is an unusual girl. She didn' have a mother and barely had a father. Her brothers were consumed with grief and far older, leavin' the house to get away from all the death there. Saria took care of her father. It wasn' all bad. He took her into the swamp, huntin' and fishin', treatin' her like a son. I was never sure he noticed she was a girl. She just took over runnin' things while he drank himself to death. She would come here, this little girl with a mop of blonde hair and eyes too big for her face. I never had children and she wormed her way into my heart."

Pauline looked at his face and read his reaction. He couldn't help it. Saria should have been looked after as a child — cherished, not left to take care of a drunken parent.

"Saria knew no other way of life. I tried to get her father to let me take her — and he agreed — but she refused to go. Every night she went out the window and went back to her house. I gave up. Maybe it was wrong of me, but there is no arguin' with Saria. She doesn't argue, she's stays quiet, says no once, and then does what she wants. She was determined to take care of her father and she did."

"Saria deserved a childhood."

"She had one, Drake, just not one the

447

world would approve of. She went everywhere with her father as a toddler, and young child. She learned to shoot so she could help him hunt alligators. She knows how to track game, trap, fish and hunt. She can take care of herself and for all his failin's, LeRoy gave her that. She's a strong woman and when the boys came back and actually noticed they had a younger siblin', it was too late to take control of her. She did what she always did, she goes her own way quietly. There's no drama with Saria and she's as honest as day. The only thing I can take credit for is convincin' her that school was important."

Drake smiled at her. "I doubt that was the only thing you did for her. It's obvious you're her mother, Pauline. She loves you with everything in her."

Pauline's eyes brimmed with tears. "Why would this killer single her out?"

"I have no idea. Maybe because she figured it out that he was leopard and she sent for help. Sometimes, a very sick person can fixate on someone. She's entering the Han Vol Dan. She's very close and every male leopard in the lair is well aware of it. It's possible he believed he would claim her and then she betrayed him by choosing me. There's no way of saying what triggers a

448

sick mind to do terrible things, but clearly, he's angry with her."

"She won't let you protect her."

Drake looked her straight in the eye. "I'll take care of her, Pauline. Nothing will happen to her, I give you my word. She can do whatever she wants, and I'll be right beside her. Where I go, my men will go and they won't make the mistake again of letting him get close. The killer pissed them off royally."

Pauline started down the stairs and then stopped again, resting her hand on his wrist. "You won' take her too far from me will you?"

"I don't think Saria will ever go far from you for long, Pauline," he said. "I want to show her the rain forest, but I know this is her home. This is the place she loves, and she is not going to be happy if she's away from you or the swamp."

Pauline beamed at him. "I knew you'd understand."

"I've lived my life all over the world," he said. "I've never had a home until I found Saria. She *is* home to me. It won't matter to me where I live, as long as I have her with me. I travel for work and will have to continue to do that for a while, but this will be our home base." He sighed. "After all, that man of yours tricked me into challenging for leadership."

"It was a win-win situation for him. If you hadn't challenged, Remy would have, or one of Saria's other brothers."

"He talked it over with you first. That old wily coot."

"Of course he did. We both wanted to ensure Saria's best interests. If you hadn't challenged, you weren't in love with her and she shouldn't be with you."

"I can't believe that old man skunked me."

Pauline laughed. "That old man has a lot of tricks up his sleeve."

Drake shook his head. Now that he'd had a brief glimpse at Amos Jeanmard, he could understand how he had achieved a leadership role. Now it was up to Drake to find out how much damage Charisse Mercier's hybrid flower, bad decisions and poor bloodlines had done to the lair and who among them was a serial killer.

15

Elijah Lospostos was a steely-eyed, extremely handsome man in a tough, scary way. He had a wealth of gleaming black hair spilling down into eyes the color of mercury one moment and as dark as night the next. Saria stood at the helm of her boat, winding her way through the choppy water, trying not to think about how dangerous he looked or why he would take orders from Drake Donovan. Elijah and his partner, Jeremiah Wheating, two more members of Drake's team, had spent the night in the swamp and they waited for nightfall for the entire team to return.

The rain poured down in thick silvery bands, making it difficult to see as she tried to keep the boat in open water as much as possible on the way to the strip of land facing Fenton's Marsh. She had five men in her boat, all silent, all grim-faced and all knowing something she didn't. On the other hand, Drake hadn't hesitated in asking her to take them into the swamp. She had the feeling none of them needed her as much as she thought they did.

She sent another quick look at the five men who took orders from Drake. They were all dangerous men. The lair had no idea how very dangerous these men were, and yet — they all took orders from Drake. A small frisson of fear slid down her spine. She didn't know Drake quite as well as she thought she did, not if he commanded men like these.

She turned her face up to the skies. Dark clouds rolled and churned, driven by a vicious wind. Her legs absorbed the pounding of the boat as it skimmed over the rough water. She noted none of the men seemed adversely affected by either the foul weather or the bumpy ride. She wasn't certain why they were going out on such a night, but they were all armed. Whatever Elijah had told Drake earlier in the day, he had emerged from the meeting grim-faced, his eyes, usually so warm, were flat and cold and frankly quite scary.

She hadn't asked questions as she normally would have, because he had told his men she was coming with them and his tone said not to question his judgment. She saw the shock on their faces, although they tried to hide it.

"You warm enough?" Drake asked.

He stood close to her, close enough for her to feel his body heat right through her windbreaker. He rested one hand lightly — possessively — on the small of her back. She felt her stomach do a slow tumble. It didn't matter that her brain was trying to warn her that she was in over her head with him, her heart — and all the rest of her body — reached for him.

She nodded. "I'm used to the weather. Your friends?" She nodded toward the men in inquiry.

He grinned at her, looking a little wild with his hair wet and dripping and his face a carved bronze. "They're used to it as well." He bent to put his lips against her ear. "I love storms. I find them invigorating."

She felt the blush start somewhere in her toes and rush through her body like a heat wave. It was the way he said it more than the words. "Aren't they all leopards?" she hissed. "Because if they are, their hearing is excellent."

His teeth closed gently on her earlobe. Someone coughed and someone else made a little snickering sound. Yeah, they were all leopards.

She punched Drake in his rock-hard gut. "Back off, playboy. I've got a job to do and you're tryin' to distract me. I'm responsible for the safety of these men." She nodded toward the banks on either side of them. "Shine your light into the water and the banks on either side."

Joshua and Jerico did so. Eyes stared back at them. Alligators hunted in the water and in the reeds.

She smirked at Drake. "All those logs in the water are not logs."

He laughed. "Is that supposed to scare me, honey?"

"No," she admitted, because it was absurd to think he was afraid. She smirked again. "But I'm at the helm, and *that* should scare you." It was a clear warning and the boat suddenly zigzagged. Not enough to pitch him over the side, but enough that he grabbed her to steady himself.

Joshua burst out laughing and Elijah hid a smile.

"Having trouble with your woman, boss?" Jerico asked.

"I can't very well pitch her out of the boat," Drake replied, "but I won't say the same for you."

This time all the men laughed.

"I don't know exactly what we're doin' out here," Saria said, "but if it involves stealth, sound carries on the water."

"We've got a little time until we expect company," Drake said.

She arched her eyebrow at him, locking her gaze with his. "What aren't you tellin' me?"

"I didn't want to talk about this around Pauline," Drake admitted. "I'm sorry, Saria. You've been very patient not asking questions in front of her."

She shrugged, hugging his apology to herself. He *had* wanted to tell her, he just hadn't found a safe opportunity.

"Elijah and Jeremiah spent the night in your blind last night."

She blinked, glanced at the two men and swiftly turned back to guiding their boat. "By the owl's nest? How did they find it? I don't tell anyone about it. I brought it piece by piece and built it myself."

"It was very sturdy," Elijah said. "And I thank you for that. There was a lot of activity on the ground and I was appreciative of being up high."

"You're welcome. But how did you find it?"

Elijah looked a little uncomfortable. Drake came to his rescue. "You're a female

455

leopard in the midst of the Han Vol Dan."

"I stink?"

He laughed. "You smell good, sweetheart. Good enough to . . ."

She showed him her fist and he subsided.

"So you spent the night in the blind and you were lookin' for what? The killer to come back?"

"Not exactly," Elijah said. "I took a look at the water route and realized a boat could come in and rendezvous easily with another without being seen, unless someone happened to be spending the night in a blind in the swamp and what were the odds of that happening?"

"I don' understand. What does that have to do with the killer?"

"Nothing, and maybe everything. I happen to have a very odd expertise," Elijah admitted. "I inherited one of the most successful drug cartels in the world today. I know a drug running operation when I see one and this one is sweet."

Saria whipped her head around, staggered and nearly fell. Drake's hands landed on her hips as she steadied herself. "You're crazy. No one I know is runnin' drugs here."

Elijah shrugged. "I don't know who happens to be doing the drug running, but it's definitely going on and that's what you saw that first time you found a body. You were damned lucky they didn't see you. This is a huge operation and if you, someone who knows this swamp inside and out, hasn't figured it out, probably no one has. Probably you saw a killing provoked by a drug deal gone sour. That's why it looked different to you."

So he was up to date on everything she'd said about the bodies. Of course he had to be. And he was so certain someone was running drugs. Absolutely certain. He'd *inherited* a successful drug cartel? What did that mean? What was he doing in the middle of the swamp in a fierce storm at night? What did she really know about any of them?

Drake put a hand on her shoulder. She tried to shrug it off. He would feel her tremble and would know she was suddenly afraid.

"He's not with the cartel, honey. He's with us."

She didn't know what or who "us" was. She suddenly wished she'd told someone, her brothers or at least Pauline, what she was doing. Of course they deliberately hadn't told her until they were on the water. Drake's fingers tightened on her shoulder. He stepped closer, crowding her. She slowed the boat to slide around a bend into the more treacherous water.

"I need to concentrate."

"I didn't mean to frighten you," Elijah said. "I wanted you to know I was telling the truth. The minute I saw the setup and took a look at the surrounding land . . ."

"What surroundin' land?" She tried not to sound belligerent, daring him to accuse one of her brothers or any of her friends. *They'd smelled her fear. All of them.* She swallowed hard and blinked her eyes rapidly to clear her sight.

"You see all those flowers we're passing? Fields of them. Hundreds, maybe thousands of them."

"For perfume. In case no one told you, there's a worldwide very successful business here. They don't need to run drugs."

"Did you take a look at the amount of poppies they're growing? They have fields of poppies mixed in with the other flowers, probably more than an acre's worth."

"The Mercier family has a license to grow all kinds of plants others can't. Don't you think they're watched closely? The property is inspected on a regular basis. They have hundreds of plants, many poisonous."

"And I'll bet at certain times of the year, they don't welcome anyone on their property," Elijah persisted.

Saria hesitated. That much was the truth. "When they're harvestin' and Charisse is in the laboratory, they're workin'. Visitors are a distraction."

"I'll just bet they are," Joshua murmured.

Saria skirted the barrel roots of a large cypress grove as she maneuvered through a narrow passage. She didn't like where the conversation was going at all. She'd known Charisse all of her life. The woman was a little strange at times, but always, always a friend. There had been few girls in their area and they all were close friends, counting on one another. Saria couldn't remember a time that Charisse hadn't been in her laboratory, studying scents. She was considered brilliant in her field and mildly obsessive. That obsession had turned the Mercier family perfume business into a multimillion-dollar proposition.

"I'm tellin' you, they sell perfume, lotions and soaps all over the world. They have no need to take a chance on sellin' something illegal." Saria tried to keep from being belligerent but it came out that way.

"And they sell their perfume and all those little soaps packaged so nice in fancy boxes, don't they?" Elijah challenged.

"Elijah." Drake said the name in a low voice. Nothing more, but there was silence.

Only the wind and rain could be heard.

"Let him tell me," Saria said. "If I'm wrong, I need to know. What do you think is in those boxes? Of course they sell them all over the world, perfumed soaps are part of their business."

"And they have several wholesalers who take huge orders, don't they?" Elijah continued.

"The boxes go through customs," Saria defended, lifting her face to the sky so that the rain washed away her anger. She liked Charisse and Armande. They donated money to schools, to the church and were huge in the community, more than most other members of the lair. They were odd, but Charisse in particular had always been a friend to Saria.

"Fancy soaps and perfume. Customs stamps them and off they go, with that nice little ball of opium right in the center of the soap."

Saria shook her head. "They have drug-sniffin' d—" She broke off, her heart jumping suddenly. *If a leopard couldn't find the scent of another leopard, then maybe whoever was creating scents could find a way to mask a scent.*

Her breath hitched in her lungs. She shook her head, her eyes suddenly burning with tears. The world was shifting out from under her. Of course all the evidence would point directly to Charisse. She was the genius behind the scents. But Saria knew Charisse. She was very childlike in some ways. Saria could almost believe that Armande might be that greedy, his mother had certainly indulged him, but Charisse . . . Saria shook her head.

Although, Armande didn't have the talent Charisse had with scents. Nor did he have ambition or drive. Yet he was devoted to Charisse. He protected her from the bullies at school. She'd been the smart one, advancing to higher grades too fast to catch up emotionally. She just wasn't capable of running drugs on an international level. It wasn't in her makeup and Saria didn't care how much proof Drake and his team gathered against her.

On the other hand, if somcone was harvesting opium from Charisse's poppies, how could she not know? Saria stared straight ahead, aware of the silence in the boat. They'd all come to the same conclusion as she had. If a leopard couldn't be scented, then someone had developed a way to prevent dogs from sniffing out drugs — and that someone had to be Charisse.

"You're wrong, Drake," she said in a low

voice. "I know everythin' points to her, but she isn't capable of what you suspect. You're way off base."

"I hope you're right, honey," he said gently.

She hated the compassion in his voice. She glanced over her shoulder at his set face. "Charisse is incapable of drug runnin'."

Drake slipped his arm around her waist. "And her brother?"

Armande. He was a spoiled sulky boy who had grown into a spoiled sulky man. The only one he seemed to love was his sister. He could look past himself long enough to see her and for a few minutes get out of his very self-centered world. Saria honestly doubted if he was intelligent enough to pull off such an operation. Charisse had the brains, but she was too childlike in a lot of ways. Armande . . . She sighed. Armande was a selfish brat, but everyone liked him. He had charm when he wanted.

"How do you plan on findin' out?"

"We're going to follow them through the swamp to see where our drug smugglers go. Whoever is supplying is supplying to a local," Elijah said.

"The swamp?" Saria echoed faintly. "Are you crazy? The swamp isn't like your rain forest. Scent isn't goin' to do you much good if you sink into a marsh. Snakes, alligators, you name it, the hazards are everywhere." She brought the boat around to the edge of the reeds. "Even gettin' onto land at night is extremely dangerous."

"That's why we have a secret weapon," Drake said.

She jumped onto the land, splashing a little in the reeds to tie up her boat. "What's that?" She poured sarcasm into her voice.

"You. You're going to guide us."

"Now I know you're crazy."

"They'll hear a boat, but you know how to move from one strip of land to the next and you probably know shortcuts."

"You want to *run* through the swamps at night?" Saria looked around for a place to sit down. She was feeling a little faint. They had no idea what it was like to travel in the swamp. "The land is a bog. There are pockets of quicksand. There's actually water under us with a thin layer of dirt and growth. You just don' understand." In agitation she ran her fingers through her hair, making it spiky and disheveled, but she didn't care. She felt like yanking it out by the roots. They were all crazy.

"We're well aware of that."

"You can step through in places and just

sink down. And have you ever heard of water moccasins? Because we have those too."

"You hunt and trap and fish all through here. And you take photographs. You've been running wild in the swamp since you were a little girl, Saria," Drake pointed out. "You can do this and you know it."

"*I* can do it, but not guidin' all of you. Drake, you can't ask me to be responsible for six people. There are at least three places we'll have to wade in reed-choked water where alligators are huntin'."

"We have guns," Joshua pointed out.

"Do you know *where* on an alligator you have to actually shoot to kill him? Do you have any idea how small the actual target on a gator is? It's about the size of a quarter and you'd better not miss. All of you may be a big deal out in your own environments, but you're amateurs here. Just the fact that you came up with this hare-brained scheme without first askin' someone who knows the swamp shows you're amateurs."

All six men remained silent, watching her with steady, unblinking eyes. Cat's eyes. Hunter's eyes. They were unimpressed with her arguments. She sighed, giving up. She just shook her head, caught the rifle Drake threw to her and turned her back on them.

Idiots. Even the youngest child in the swamp knew more than they did.

Shaking off her thoughts, she concentrated on listening. Insects hummed. Bullfrogs called back and forth. The rain kept falling steadily. She hunched her shoulders and blocked out everything but the rustles in the thick foliage. She knew exactly where to step, but she often crossed paths alligators used to slide into the water.

"Where to?"

"We need a clear view of Fenton's Marsh and the best path to follow a boat heading toward the Mercier land," Drake said. "The leaves are off the poppies and they'll have harvested the opium. They'll be destroying the evidence now."

She wasn't going to argue with him. But if by some miracle he was right, what did that mean? Because if dogs couldn't sniff out the drugs, that would mean the killer would have access to whatever kept him from having a scent. It was virtually impossible for Charisse to be a killer. She didn't have a mean bone in her body. She was clingy, and she drove everyone a little crazy with her eccentricities, but no one would ever say she wasn't one of the most compassionate people around.

She pushed all thoughts of Charisse out

of her head. She had to just stay focused on the safety of the men she was guiding. She should have told Drake to shove it. In the swamp, she was the leader — not him. She bit her lip and led the way. They were eerily silent, but she refused to glance over her shoulder to make sure they were keeping up. She set a brutal pace, skirting around poisonous brush, making certain to place each foot carefully on ground she knew was sound. As it was, the rain had soaked in, making the surface far spongier than normal.

Drake touched her shoulder and she stopped moving automatically. He moved in front of her, and held up his hand, his fingers spread wide. His men appeared to melt into the darkness. One moment she could see them and then they seemed to disappear. There was no sound, no rustling of leaves, no snapping of twigs, they simply were gone.

She hadn't heard the sound of a boat nor had she seen lights, but her heart began to pound, and deep inside, she felt her leopard unsheathe her claws. Saria tasted fear in her mouth. The fact that she knew her leopard had actually gone on alert scared her more than the men disappearing around her. She was so out of her depth with these people.

She needed time to assimilate the fact that she was leopard too. After all those years of envying her brothers and feeling so alone, she had the very thing she'd wanted, yet she was afraid of it. Now that she was a part of it all, she wanted to curl up somewhere quiet and just be still.

Drake touched her shoulder and she crouched, wondering how she knew what he wanted. He pointed to his left and something moved in the brush, but she could only hear the rain. There was a long moment of silence. She could count her heartbeats as the tension stretched out. The relentless rain slackened in intensity, slowing to a slow drizzle, a heavier mist that blanketed the swamp and hung in thick drapes over the water.

Drake crouched beside her. "We have company. North of us, two boats in the water, side by side. They have the lights covered. Can you get us to a trail taking us toward Mercier property without putting us in the open?" He whispered the words against her ear, his lips tight against her skin and a slow burn — a very inappropriate reaction — started in her very core. Her leopard rose to meet his. She closed her eyes, shocked that her leopard would add such complications to an already impossible night.

Drake's palm curved around her nape. "Don't let her escape yet. Keep in control."

"Are you kiddin'," she hissed back, furious at him, knowing it was her leopard, but not really caring. "How am I supposed to be in control when I don't even know what to expect?"

"You're strong, Saria. If you let her too close to the surface and give her free rein, if there are leopards in either of those boats, the moment the wind shifts, they'll know you're out in the swamp tonight."

She hissed at him, suppressing an unfamiliar urge to swipe at him with her fingernails. Her cat was out in force and in a bad mood. The rain, the proximity of too many males and the tightness of her skin all made her feel edgy and trapped.

"Baby, listen to me," he said. "I know it's hard. She comes close and retreats . . ."

"Tell me somethin' I don't know," she snapped. "I'm in the damned rain, soaked through, surrounded by madmen with a leopard inside of me who goes from being a hussy to a psychotic bitch in seconds. I've got so many hormones runnin' through my system I don't know what I'm doin'."

"Breathe her away. Shove her back and be

forceful. She has to realize you're intelligent and you refuse to allow her runaway emotions to control you."

Saria took a slow look around, knowing her eyes were changing as her vision banded in waves of heat. She knew where every single member of Drake's team was with her leopard's heightened awareness. Her leopard suddenly switched from being angry to preening. "Funny how she suddenly likes all these men around."

The moment she said it she knew she had made a terrible mistake. A low warning snarl rumbled in Drake's chest and he turned glowing golden eyes on her. Saria shivered. His leopard was closer than hers, and he was enraged at the scent of the males surrounding her. She bit back the *very* bitchy urge to ask where all his control was, and forced air through her lungs. One of them had to be sane in this tense situation and clearly, when it came to her hussy of a leopard, it wasn't going to be Drake or his leopard.

She felt her leopard respond to the aggression in his, a slinky stretch and languorous yawn. Crouched down as she was, she had to fight to keep from arching her back and rubbing along Drake's leg. She refused to give in to her leopard's urge to look enticingly at the men behind her. She could already feel the heightened tension.

Saria took another deep breath and turned her displeasure on her leopard. The little hussy had a tendency to choose the worst possible moment to show herself and she loved the attention of the men surrounding her. Saria, however, did not. And finding Drake practically on top of her didn't help her foul mood.

"Are you kidding me, Drake? Don't you dare add to the complications right now. I cannot put up with a man actin' like a crazed jealous lover when I don' even know how to handle being leopard. I'm responsible for all these lives and you think I'm wantin' to seduce a bunch of strangers? Get ahold of yourself. I certainly don' want any other man and right now, you aren't lookin' all that good to me either."

She glared at Drake while she mentally kicked her leopard. *Go back to sleep you useless sex kitten. If you want to play, wait until we're in a bedroom.*

Drake dropped his hand on the top of her head, rubbing the silky strands of hair between his fingers. "I'm sorry, honey. Leopards are very territorial when it comes to their females, especially when she's in . . ."

"*Don't* say it. If you say I'm in heat one more time I swear I'm goin' to stab you right through the heart," Saria bit out between clenched teeth. It was bad enough to know she was putting out enough scent to call in every male for miles let alone have him say it aloud. She sent him a look that should have withered him on the spot.

Her leopard was turning grumpy with her, wanting the spotlight and annoyed that Saria wasn't giving in to her demands. Saria had a will of iron when she was aggravated. She'd never let a whipping, or the women of the church or anything else move her when she'd had enough, and she turned that iron will on her leopard. *Back off. You aren't helpin' me right now. Go back to sleep and just stay there until I get us out of this mess.*

Her leopard subsided sulkily. Saria sent Drake another quick glare from under her lashes. "It would be nice to deal with you so easily."

"I said I was sorry."

"Jealousy is *not* an attractive trait," she said in a low tone. "And we need to get movin'. I don't think that boat is goin' to wait for your silly leopard to behave."

"If we have to shift into leopards to make this run . . ."

She stopped him with a look. "I'm goin'

471

to be running on two legs, they can too." She was not going to give her sex kitten of a leopard any excuse for coming out and rubbing herself against a bunch of naked men.

"I got it," he said.

Straight behind her, she heard a quiet snicker and saw Drake's golden eyes flick in that direction. His jaw tightened, but he didn't say anything and no one was stupid enough to make any more disparaging sounds.

"Get us moving, Saria."

She ignored the hard edge to his voice, knowing his leopard was riding him pretty hard with the other males in such close proximity to her. It wasn't Drake, she repeated to herself, he wasn't a man who would ever mistrust her.

He put a hand on her shoulder, moving up close behind her, placing his feet exactly where hers had been. Behind them, the men fell into a single file line, doing the same.

"I know it's hard not to look for an excuse to run from me, especially when everything is so new and volatile. I really appreciate that you choose to hang in there with me."

She sent him a small smile over her shoulder, glad that he knew it was a struggle. "We're goin' to have to pick up the pace. Let them know they can't set a foot off this path. It gets very narrow up ahead and we're goin' to be crossin' a couple of gator slides. A couple of miles into the interior we'll be hittin' very thin ground. There're only a few spots thick enough to hold weight, so stay close and know where to put your feet. Forget the boat. I know exactly the locations we can spot it."

She forced confidence into her voice when she didn't feel it at all. She'd explored the swamps, it was true, and often at night. But she was relatively light in comparison to them and she'd been vigilantly watching for signs of alligators. Contrary to popular belief, alligators could not run fast on land, but they could lunge with lightning speed and in short bursts could move quickly enough.

She set a fast pace to begin with. The land along this first stretch was stable and if anyone misstepped, they would be safe. A mile or so ahead, the land thinned to a narrow strip. Either side of it one could easily fall through. Nevertheless, she refused to go any faster than she deemed was safe. She could feel their urgency, but she had no doubt she could beat the boat around the larger land masses by moving through the interior. Once away from the water's edge, cypress groves and reeds, they would likely be away from the threat of alligators as well.

It was strange running in formation. She heard the pounding of her own heart as well as her breathing, and the only footsteps she heard were hers. The men picked up her exact rhythm, running in single file, feet hitting the ground in exact unison with each other and with her. After a while it made her want to vary her rhythm just to see if they would somehow anticipate her change-up.

Chiding herself for thinking childish thoughts, she scanned the ground ahead of her, using the strange night vision her leopard provided. She knew this area of the swamp inside and out, she'd practically spent her childhood here, searching for nests to photograph and often hiding from any adult who was silly enough to try to find her. She'd perfected her tracking skills all through this particular strip of land. She knew every hazard and where the gators liked to hang out. She knew the sounds and the warnings.

She picked up speed and swept through the thickest grove of trees, knowing the gators didn't inhabit this particular area. It was too far from the water and their mud slides. Tangles of vines and roots were their biggest hazard, so they could move quite a bit faster. Once outside the heavy growth, she should be able to catch a glimpse of the boat lights and determine which direction they were going. She hoped the boat would veer away from Mercier land, but she had a sinking feeling she wasn't going to get that lucky.

As the thick grove of trees gave way to brush, she slowed her pace just a little, signaling they were moving into a hazardous area. She kept her footsteps very precise as she jogged over the ground, wincing with every footfall. Water pooled, turning the surface to a mixture of mud and floating debris. The rain wasn't helping, raising the water table as inevitably as the tides did. Praying the men were as precise in their steps, she led them through a very narrow strip of hazards where one wrong step would take them under the thin crust to the water below.

The men followed, slowly as she did, stepping one after another in the exact spot as the man in front of him. They watched the ground, trusting her to guide them through safely. In a way, it was somewhat exhilarating, even as the weight of the responsibility for their lives was crushing. This section of the swamp was honeycombed with thin spots and holes covered with tangles of vines where an unwary person could easily fall through. She'd mapped the way in her mind, but the chance of the ground eroding was always there.

She breathed a sigh of relief as they came up on the edge of the cypress grove. She held up her hand and everyone stopped instantly. She waited a heartbeat, her eyes straining to see the small open space through the trees where in the distance a boat would sweep around the bend and could be seen for no more than a moment. She had timed the pace in her head, slowing down when needed to ensure the lives of the men in her care, but setting a fast enough tempo that they would be able to catch a glimpse of the boat and the direction it went.

One second later, a blurring light blinked in the waterway, holding to her left. She knew, with a sinking heart, that the boat was traveling into the canal that led to the Tregre-Mercier swamps.

"We're heading into the reeds," she whispered to Drake, knowing with their hearing the others would be able to heed her warning. "Stay close, but keep an eye out for gators. They'll be in the water. We're goin' to move fast through here."

Her heart was pounding. She had a very

healthy respect for alligators. She gripped her rifle and took the first step into the reed-choked water. The water went up to her thigh. She took a deep breath and kept moving steadily through the murky water, not fast, not slow, feeling her way with each step. Her night vision allowed her to see the dark loglike shapes lying in wait in the reeds and near the barrel roots from the cypress trees sticking out of the water.

The tension stretched, and the men remained absolutely silent as they moved in unison through the treacherous water. She tasted fear in her mouth, but she refused to show it. These men were her responsibility and she wasn't about to put them in danger by having a panic attack. She had failed to mention to Drake that stepping at night into murky water known to be filled with hungry, aggressive alligators terrified her. She made a note to herself to have that conversation with him at a later date.

Saria felt a small branch roll under her foot and shifted her weight to catch herself from slipping. Drake steadied her, his fingers curling hard around her upper arm. She licked at her suddenly dry lips. The branch felt, for a moment, like a small alligator and set her pulse going through the roof. They were close to the shore again, which didn't make her any happier. Alligators liked to hang out under the bank in the reeds.

Swallowing her fear, she forced herself forward. Drake kept his hand on her arm, probably because he could feel her trembling. The moment she was on solid ground, she felt relief flooding her body. Her knees went weak, legs like rubber, but she took a couple of deep breaths and began to pick up the pace. They had an easy run and could make up speed once they got away from the bank.

She set as fast a pace as she dared, running instead of jogging. They had to hit the other side of the swamp nearest the southern bank before the boat got around the land mass. The boat had to travel miles around the land while she and Drake's team could cut through the swamp. They made up a lot of time. The vegetation was thick, but mostly tangled vines, trees and brush. The ground was solid until she reached the outer banks. She was shorter than the men and had to duck a few times, but they had to constantly avoid low-hanging branches, veils of moss and vines to keep from getting clothes-lined. Not one of them broke stride. She was beginning to realize these were men who saw a lot of action in many different environments and were afraid of very little.

She ran fast in the rain, her footsteps kicking up mud and water as she raced along a narrow deer trail. She'd spent a lot of time in this part of the swamp capturing nests on film. She hadn't worried about predators here other than an occasional bobcat and they always avoided her. This was the one section where they could make up time before they hit the second reed-choked water hazard where she knew for certain a large bull alligator made his home. He'd been known to kill and eat his own kind. He took bait from hooks and actually bent the largest, strongest hooks most of the hunters used trying to snag him.

They had to make it through the water onto the shore of the next strip of land and race to the tip of land on the other side of the finger of land to catch another glimpse of the boat, to know for certain where it was heading.

She moistened her dry mouth and took the plunge into the reed-choked waters. There were cypress trees knee-deep in the murky water, an entire grove of them, with many rotted trunks pitting the bottom along with the ever-spreading barrel roots. The alligators had many places to hide. She was tired, her body feeling leaden, with so many

miles of running, being so vigilant throughout.

To her horror, halfway to the next bank,
she saw a water moccasin bearing down on
her fast. She had her rifle cradled in her
arms, determined to keep her weapon dry
and there was nowhere to run. The creature's head was inches from her hip when
Drake struck with blurring speed. He
snagged the snake just behind its head,
yanked it from the water and threw it a
distance away. She heard it hit a tree off to
their right.

Saria opened her mouth to thank him, but
nothing came out, so she just kept moving.
If the large gator that occupied this territory was near, he didn't show himself and
they made it to the bank and began the next
run.

It seemed to take forever to cross the
swamp. The smallest distance between the
two canals was pitted with holes and under
at least an inch of water, making it difficult
to find the tiny strip of stable land. Several
times they had to leap on small rocks to
prevent themselves from sinking into the
mire.

As they reached the bank, the boat came
into view, slowing as it approached the dock
to the Mercier property. A man stood wait-

ing on the wooden deck overlooking the river. The boat definitely was Mercier, but the two men in it were the Tregre brothers.

Saria let out her breath slowly and would have sat if there was a place to do so, but they still had a long way to go.

16

Drake wrapped his arm around Saria as morning light crept through the soft rain, tucking her beneath his shoulder. She was exhausted. They all were. After running through the swamp most of the night and making their way to the Mercier property, they had discovered that all the flowers had been cut back in preparation for winter. If there was evidence, it had been destroyed. The greenhouse was under heavy security, which they bypassed without a problem, but there were no poppies inside, nor evidence of opium. They did find the room where Leopard's Lover grew, and as Pauline had stated, numerous precautions had been taken to keep the flower's seeds from leaving the greenhouse.

The laboratory was situated on the property behind the residence almost on the very foundations of the original plantation, and a long way from the acres where gardens were located. The entire area around the newer estate was landscaped, the grounds well manicured and maintained. The Mercier house was clearly a mansion, two stories, at least six to seven thousand square feet with an upper and lower wraparound deck. As homes went, it was impressive.

Drake decided they'd already left scent throughout the acres of gardens and the greenhouse, so he left the laboratory and home for a different line of attack. He wanted to consult with Remy and share information with him. It was possible they could inspect a shipment going out of the country or intercept the local delivery.

They made it back to the Lafont inn by nine. Pauline had breakfast waiting for them, as well as for early morning visitors. They could smell the mouthwatering food from outside the house and all of them inhaled the aroma of coffee gratefully.

Saria stopped the moment she saw the car. "That's the Mercier car. Charisse and Armande must be here. I can't have them seein' me lookin' like this. We're all a mess. They'll know we were runnin' the swamp last night."

"We'll go in through the balconies and shower. That way we can come down looking fresh." He brought her hand to his mouth. She was trembling. Exhausted. He shouldn't have involved her, but he hadn't wanted to chance leaving her behind in case the killer came back. Nor could they have ever made it so quickly through the swamp. They'd managed to find out the Tregre family was involved without a single shot being fired.

She looked up at the balcony. "I'm not certain I have enough strength left to climb, Drake."

He knew what that admission cost her in pride. "Come on, baby, I'll get you up to our room." He tugged at her hand, taking her around to the side of the inn where the tree was close enough to use the bough as a bridge. "It's going to be slippery, but you can make it." He took the rifle from her.

His team had scattered, entering the house silently, making their way to their rooms, where they showered and changed to warm, dry clothes. He stayed close to Saria, knowing she was exhausted. It had been a long, rigorous night. She hadn't complained once about being soaked and cold when he knew she had to be chilled all the way to the bone.

Saria went up the tree like a small monkey. Drake was right behind her, just in case of a misstep, but she eased her way across the thick limb and then jumped onto the balcony. "You locked it last night," she said and sank down into the corner, uncaring of the rain. Her hair was plastered to her face and she shivered constantly.

Drake stepped up to the door and quietly picked the lock, pushing the door open before turning back to her and extending her hand.

She smiled up at him without taking his help. "I think I'll just sleep right here."

Drake simply lifted her into his arms. "I can't let you do that, honey. You're shivering nonstop. Let's get you into a hot shower."

He cradled her close to his chest, nuzzling the top of her head. "If you prefer, I can go down without you. You can stay upstairs and go to sleep after we get you warm."

"I'm not sure it's possible to ever be warm again." Saria rubbed her face against his soaked shirt. "But if you're goin' downstairs to face the firin' squad, I'll be there with you."

"They can't possibly know we were investigating them," Drake said. "Not this fast."

"What are you goin' to tell them? They'll know we were out in the swamp."

"It's always better to stick as close to the truth as possible," he told her, setting her

485

down in the bathroom. "They're leopard. They'll know we just came in. It was just easier to get warm before facing them. We're going to tell them we spent the night in the swamp. I'm the new leader. My men are here with me and we're familiarizing ourselves with the area, as well as taking care of the business Jake Bannaconni sent us to do in the first place."

She regarded him shrewdly. "You like to use his name because he's leasing most of the properties they use and they're a little afraid to lose their lands."

He smirked just before kissing her. His woman was smart and he liked that. He peeled the soaked shirt from her body while she stood there shivering almost uncontrollably. He had to crouch down to unlace her boots. He doubted if she could have done it, her fingers were like ice. Steam from the hot water filled the bathroom, helping to heat the room as he stripped off her wet jeans and underwear and helped her into the shower.

Only when he was certain she was leaning against the wall with the water pouring over her, warming her, did he strip off his own clothes and join her. The hot water felt like heaven. Drake just let it seep into their bodies, driving out the terrible cold. When

Saria's teeth quit chattering, he shampooed her hair. She was unusually quiet and that worried him a little.

"Are you afraid of Armande or Charisse?" he asked, hoping she was just chilled.

"Of course not. Now their mother is an entirely different proposition. Why do you think they're so close? A woman like Iris *Lafont*-Mercier — and believe me that is a hyphenated last name — is never happy unless she's tellin' everyone else what to do. You can imagine what she thinks of me."

Her voice changed to a very strident imitation of what he could only assume was Iris's voice. "That child is runnin' wild and we have a civic duty to do somethin' about it. I've called the truant officer on her repeatedly and if she doesn't show up for school it will be child services."

"That bad, huh?"

"You have no idea. I think she drove her husband to an early grave. He left everything to Armande and Charisse. Iris wouldn't have cared if it had only been Armande, the darlin' of her world, but she had no use for Charisse."

"Why? I thought you said her daughter was brilliant."

"Oh yeah. She is, but she's strange. A little off. Different. And all that ability garnered her a tremendous amount of attention in school and from her father. That sort of took the spotlight away from Armande, who is extremely handsome and charming, but without her brilliance. Mama leopard did not like that one bit."

Drake whistled softly. "She's nothing like Pauline."

"No. She's a force to be reckoned with. She'll like you, though. She's very partial to males. Don't be surprised if she flirts."

"Flirts?" he echoed faintly.

"She's quite beautiful and she knows it."

"And she works at the post office?"

"You get all the local gossip at the post office. She knows everyone's business and she could really keep an ear out on what her children were up to. All the other women couldn't wait to tell her if Charisse or Armande did one wrong thing. My brothers always have felt sorry for Armande because they think he has to baby Charisse and his mother is always on him."

"But you feel sorry for Charisse."

For the first time in hours, Saria smiled. "I can totally identify with her. I hide from Iris Lafont hyphenated Mercier every chance I get. I get the same lectures Charisse does."

"What would that be now?" Drake carefully rinsed her hair clean. "You're out of school."

"Aw, true, but I'm not a lady. Apparently ladies do *not* go into the swamp and they fold their hands in their laps, wear skirts and cross their legs at the ankles properly."

"Does Charisse have to do all that?"

"Of course. She is *always* proper." Saria shoved the wet strands of hair from her face and leaned against Drake tiredly. "Don't worry, I won't leave you alone with her. Neither will Miss Pauline. We're all used to gettin' told how improper we are."

"Not in front of me," Drake said.

She smiled at him. This time the smile reached her eyes. "It's just her way, Drake. I did grow up wild. She never lied about anything. I did skip school when I couldn't take it anymore. *Mon pere* was a drunk — that was true as well. I don't cross my ankles and I never wear dresses. And that's all right with Miss Pauline and it's always been all right with me. Charisse is my friend. She doesn't seem to mind either."

"Neither do I. Do you have any idea how much a dress would have gotten in the way last night?" he asked.

She flung her arms around his neck and pressed her body tight against him. "You're insane, but you're my kind of man."

"I'd better be. You really got us through last night, Saria. I had no idea just how treacherous the land could be."

"I know you didn't," she agreed, sounding a little smug.

Her face was hidden so he couldn't see her expression but a small shudder went through her body. It could have gone bad in a heartbeat.

"I'm sorry I put you in such a terrible position, Saria. It was thoughtless of me."

"At least we found out the Tregres are involved. This may have nothing to do with opium or the Merciers," Saria said.

"When Elijah and Jeremiah followed the boat, they recovered several soaps with a small ball of opium in the center. The soaps were Mercier soaps, Saria," Drake said.

Her head snapped up. She stepped away from him and turned off the shower, yanking at a towel. "Just when had you planned on tellin' me that?"

She was angry. For one moment her eyes had blazed fire at him. He felt the quick jerk of his cock in reaction. She turned away, toweling the moisture from her body, but he could feel the heat from her body, and the rise of aggression in his body in direct proportion to the passion in hers. She made him feel so alive. He wanted to kiss her, but Saria Boudreaux was close to being fully leopard and she was every bit as dangerous as a female cat enticing a male. Her claws and teeth could be lethal.

"When we knew for certain the Merciers had to be involved. We were all over the swamp last night. The Tregres have two shacks on their land besides their home. The roads in and out are rarely traveled. No one is making soaps there or inserting drugs into the middle of them, Saria. You saw the property."

She straightened up, looked him right in the eye and threw the towel on the floor. "Charisse is not capable of doin' what you're accusin' her of, and in spite of the fact that Armande Mercier is a selfish bastard a lot of the time, he isn't either. You don't know them the way I do." She stomped into the bedroom, caught up her only other pair of jeans and yanked them on. "I'm runnin' out of clothes and need to go home."

His heart stuttered. She was angry. Magnificent in her loyalty, but angry with him. Thinking about retreating. He stayed silent and picked up his jeans rather than picking her up and tossing her onto the bed. His leopard roared for supremacy, eager for the chase, but Drake was much more cautious.

Saria was a woman who went her own way. *He* had to be her choice, first and always. Her fierce loyalty had to be to him. She didn't give loyalty or trust easily and yet she gave it to Charisse. There was something more going on here than he had first realized and he needed to dig a little deeper.

He watched her out of the corner of his eye as he dressed. She was pacing, all pent up restless energy, her anger driving her in spite of the exhaustion he could see on her face. When she crashed, she was going to crash hard. He took a deep breath to still his prowling leopard.

"Clearly I need to get to know Charisse better. If you stand for her, Saria, there must be a lot more to her than I know. Everything points to her. The scent expertise, the disturbing flower, the lack of scent at crime scenes, the opium, all of it, and yet in the face of all the evidence, you persist in believing in her innocence. I trust you and your judgment. If you think she's innocent . . ."

"I *know* she is," Saria defended staunchly. "Someone is setting her up to take the fall. Charisse wouldn't know a setup anymore than she would be capable of being a drug dealer. She's childlike in a lot of ways."

Drake nodded his head, trying to put *child-*

like with the woman who had approached them on their picnic in her pencil-thin skirt, high-heeled boots and silk blouse that clung to and accented every curve. Charisse had appeared poised and confident, polished even. Her nails were perfect, her slender legs encased in silk, and her makeup impeccable . . . until her brother had snapped at her. She'd cried like a child and Saria had comforted her. That had seemed affected and out of character to Drake. Which was the real Charisse?

"I'll keep an open mind," he promised. He had no idea how he was going to accomplish that, but he would try — for Saria — he would try. He knew if she was wrong it was going to be a terrible blow to her, and he had a terrible feeling in the pit of his belly that Saria didn't have very many people in her world that she loved as much as she obviously did Pauline and Charisse.

Saria dragged a comb through her hair. "I would appreciate that. I know you feel the evidence is damnin', Drake, but it really is all circumstantial."

He refrained from pointing out that Charisse was the brilliant chemist and clearly the brains in the Mercier family. Arguing would only cause Saria to dig her heels in. He didn't want the hole to be so deep that if she was proved wrong, she couldn't get out of it.

Saria walked down the stairs with him, but she didn't hold his hand. She even walked a step behind him. His leopard roared at him, angry with the small separation between them and Drake couldn't help but agree. He'd been damned diplomatic. The tension pouring off Saria didn't help soothe his leopard either. His female's care was paramount at all times and dissention just didn't work between leopards. It made the shifter edgy, moody, difficult to deal with — not a good circumstance for him when he was about to sit down with what probably was a criminal mastermind.

At the bottom stair he turned abruptly, blocking Saria from stepping down. His hands settled on her waist. "Kiss me." It was an order, not a request, and he frankly didn't care how it came out.

She pulled back subtly. "Here? There are people in the next room. The door's open."

"Right here. Right now. I need to know you're with me. Kiss me. Kisses don't lie, Saria. I need this."

Saria's enormous eyes widened. Darkened. Her long lashes fluttered. Her fingers linked behind his neck and she leaned her body into his. "Kisses don't lie? All right then. If you're certain you need this."

She didn't wait for him. She took his mouth, her lips brushing gently across his, her tongue teasing the seam of his so that he opened his mouth immediately to her. The world dropped away. The anger. The tension. There was only the pouring of love from her mouth to his. He took her passion — her unspoken commitment to him — straight to his heart and locked it up tight.

"Saria! How very unseemly of you." The female voice hissed with displeasure.

Saria didn't startle or pull away from him. She finished kissing him as though no one had interrupted them, her mouth loving his. When she lifted her head, she looked only at him — straight into his eyes. "Better?"

"Much. Thank you." He took her hand and kissed her knuckles before turning to face the woman who had spoken.

Drake thought he was beyond all shock. He had traveled the world and seen a lot of sights, but Iris Lafont-Mercier was one of the most beautiful women he'd ever laid eyes on. It was the last thing he expected. She looked young enough to be Charisse's sister. He knew leopard women often aged gracefully and even if Charisse was in her early twenties, Iris had to be fifty or more. Her skin was perfection, without a single wrinkle. Her hair was a thick mass of spun gold and if there was gray, it looked like threads of silver among the gold. She had a beautiful figure, looking as if she'd never had a child in her life.

She was waiting for his reaction. She was used to the admiration of men and counted him as no exception. There was no doubt in his mind that Iris manipulated every single man in her life without mercy. Drake kept his expression absolutely blank, nor did he allow his eyes to flick over her with any interest.

"You must be Mrs. Mercier," he said deliberately.

Saria's fingers dug into his palm, but he only brought her hand to his chest, pressing it right over his heart in reassurance. Had she trembled? Could Saria be a little afraid of Iris Mercier's sharp tongue?

"It's Iris *Lafont*-Mercier, actually," Iris replied in a slightly superior tone. "Pauline is my sister. Our family can be traced back hundreds of years."

"Drake Donovan, ma'am," he said. "Miss Pauline has mentioned you."

"I came to see you," Iris stated firmly. "We can go into the parlor and speak in private."

"Saria and I are engaged, Mrs. Mercier . . . Lafont-Mercier. You know as well as I do, leopards don't have secrets from their mates. Privacy is unnecessary."

For a moment those cool blue eyes blazed a deep turquoise, but Iris's perfectly painted mouth curved into a bright smile. "If you insist. This is lair business and I understand you defeated old Amos."

She made it sound as if Amos Jeanmard had been well past his prime and Drake had taken undue advantage. He pressed Saria's hand to keep her from defending him.

"If it is lair business, all the more reason for Saria to be there."

Iris's eyes narrowed. Clearly it hadn't occurred to her that if Drake married Saria, she would be the alpha female.

"That's just preposterous. Saria Boudreaux is little more than a child. She's certainly not equipped to help you run a lair." The bite to Iris's voice was well-practiced and effective.

Drake tightened his hold on Saria's hand when he felt her tremble. He bared his teeth at Iris, his look anything but a smile.

"Fortunately for everyone, Saria is wise beyond her years and knows more about the people and the swamp itself than most in the lair. I am very lucky she is my mate." He gestured toward the living room where he knew her children and Pauline waited.

"We'll talk in there. My men are tired and need to eat before they retire. I don't want to disturb them."

Iris went ramrod stiff and turned her back to him, sweeping from the room, her hips an enticement in spite of her obvious anger. She used her sexuality without even being aware of it anymore, it came so natural to her.

Charisse's beauty seemed to pale in comparison to her mother's. She looked washed out in the vibrant colors she wore and her hair was pulled back in too severe of a style. Drake hadn't remembered her that way, but she sat quietly subdued, hands folded in her lap, looking straight ahead. She glanced up at Saria and sent a small smile of welcome, glanced at her mother's set face and quickly looked down again.

"Where are you manners, Charisse?" Iris demanded. "Is it too much to ask that you greet the leader of the lair when he walks into the room? Or are you deliberately trying to make me look as if I haven't taught you anything?"

Charisse's face flamed red. She moistened her lips, looked helplessly at her brother and swallowed hard. When she lifted her face, tears swam in her eyes. "I'm sorry, Mr. Donovan. It's nice to see you again. Saria, good morning."

Drake noticed Armande was not taken to task. He had a choice of greeting them and adding to his sister's misery, or simply nodding his head in their direction. He nodded and shifted subtly, turning his body a bit protectively toward Charisse. Drake liked him better for it, and could see why Saria forgave him quite a lot.

Drake took the small sofa across from Charisse and Armande, settling Saria beside him. "Where's Pauline this morning?"

"Makin' herself a slave to her guests," Iris said caustically. "Why she turned our family home into a bed-and-breakfast when she didn't need the money, I'll never know."

"She enjoys the company," Saria answered, her voice deceptively low. "And cookin' for her guests is a good deal of her fun. I'm surprised you don't know that about her."

Iris pressed her lips together tightly, her blue eyes narrowing. "I see your manners haven't improved any, Saria, but I expect nothing less of you."

"I suppose you think it's perfectly okay to be rude because you're so much older," Drake said very softly. His voice carried a low menace.

Charisse went white, moving closer to her

brother for protection. Her breath hitched audibly. Armande put his arm across the back of the sofa, around her shoulders. Iris went very still and her blue eyes glittered dangerously. Two high spots of color appeared in her cheeks.

Before the woman could retort, Drake sighed. "I know you must have come over this early for something important, so let's get to it. I've been up all night acquainting myself with the area and I'm hungry and need to sleep. How can I help you?"

Iris pressed her lips together hard in a gesture of complete displeasure before she relaxed and nodded her head. "Yes. You're right. This is a lair matter and must be dealt with. My son was viciously attacked by Remy Boudreaux and I demand justice."

Drake stared at her a long time without expression, deliberately allowing the silence to stretch until the room was taut with tension. He slowly turned his head toward Armande. His vision banded and he knew his eyes had gone cat. To have a man dare to hunt Saria with a gun, *fire* it at her, hunt him and then hide behind his mother. It took every ounce of discipline to keep from leaping across the room and slashing a claw across the coward's throat.

"Is this true?" His voice came out as a growl.

Armande flushed a deep red. He glanced at his mother and shook his head. "No, sir. It is not."

"Then I believe we are done here."

Iris hissed out a breath. "No we are not. Look at him. He can barely walk. His chest is black and blue. He's tryin' to protect the very man who nearly killed him."

"In a lair, Mrs. Mercier, the male leopards settle things in their own way. We can't go to the police and if someone commits a crime against another member of the lair — particularly a female — he can be ostracized — driven from the lair — or killed. That is our system of justice and has been for hundreds of years."

"My son has never committed a crime," Iris snapped. "You're protectin' Remy Boudreaux because of Saria. And I have told you *repeatedly,* it's Lafont-Mercier, *not* Mercier."

Drake turned a predator's stare on Iris. "We're done here, Mrs. Lafont-Mercier. And if you're not willing to abide by my decisions, you are welcome to leave the lair. In fact, you have no choice but to leave the lair."

"This is my home, not yours." Iris leapt to

her feet, clutching her handbag like a weapon. She glared at Armande, clearly expecting him to come to her aid.

"Not if you don't accept the leadership. Of course you could always push your son to challenge me. I would kill him, but maybe that's what you want. You don't seem to listen to him even when he gives you the truth."

Iris's eyes brimmed with tears. She sank back down and looked helplessly for a tissue. "That's a horrible thing to say to me. I love my son — my children. He came home so broken. He's not a fighter. He wasn't raised to be so — so *crass*. He has a good position in our company and works hard. Remy Boudreaux is a bully. Everyone is afraid of him. All the Boudreaux boys grew up rough. You don't know because you've just arrived here. Saria will tell you that I'm tellin' the truth. Everyone is afraid of her brothers."

Saria leaned toward Iris, open sympathy on her face. "My brothers are rough, Iris, that's true, but you know they're just. Remy would never touch anyone, least of all Armande, who we count as a friend, unless he was provoked."

Iris scowled at her son. "What did you do?" Her lower lip trembled.

Armande looked down at the ground.

"This matter has been resolved to everyone's satisfaction, Mrs. Lafont-Mercier," Drake said. "Your son took his punishment like a man and earned the respect of the lair. I understand why a mother would be distraught seeing her son broken and bruised, but some things are better left alone. Armande is a grown man and shouldn't have to talk about certain things with his mother — especially if he's paid the price for a mistake and everyone else has let it go."

"But I'm responsible . . ." Iris trailed off when Drake shook his head.

"No, ma'am, you're not. Armande is a grown man and subject to all the laws of the lair. You've done your part in raising him. He's a good man by all accounts and you should be proud of yourself — but he has to stand on his own two feet now. No man within the lair is going to respect him if they believe he's hiding behind his mother's skirts."

Iris's frown was more of a beautiful pout. "I suppose you're right, but I do believe Remy used excessive force." She glared at Saria. "And I'll always believe that. Remy despises my son because he's so charmin'."

"Mother." Armande rubbed his hand over

his face, clearly mortified.

"I'm sorry if that embarrasses you, Armande. You, at least, took after me with your looks. Women chase after you the way men chase after me. Poor Charisse managed to get brains, and for that we're eternally grateful."

Beside him, Saria sucked in her breath. "How lucky you are that both of your children are beautiful, Mrs. Lafont-Mercier."

Iris didn't answer. Pauline entered the room and filled the sudden silence. "I know you and your men are tired, Drake. And you have to be hungry. Breakfast is on the table and Amos and I will be gone all afternoon shoppin' in town. The place will be quiet so you all can rest. I'll come back before supper and fix plenty of food."

"Thank you, Miss Pauline," Drake said. "I'll admit we're all worn out. It was a lot of country to explore." He smiled at Iris, searching to find the right note to connect with the difficult, beautiful, if somewhat childish woman. "You have a beautiful home."

She sniffed. "Not quite the way I wanted it, but it will do until I can remodel. My husband had such garish taste and *someone* insisted on indulgin' him."

"Mother, Charisse has provided a good livin' for all of us and dad was dyin'. She naturally wanted to give him whatever made him happy," Armande defended.

Drake noticed Charisse immediately closed her fingers over Armande's arm in an obvious signal to stop. It was too late. The mere fact that Armande would take his sister's side over his mother's made the woman furious.

Iris sniffed indignantly. "Charisse was spoiled rotten by that man and now I have to undo all the damage he did. She has a lot to learn before she'll be much good to anyone. And if she continues to date that horrible man she's seein', I may have to disown her. I will not have that man comin' to our house. He's as rude and as obnoxious as that drunken father of his. He owns a *bar,* Charisse. Whatever were you thinkin', goin' out with him?"

Clearly disgusted, the woman rose. "Pauline, I must leave. The thought of Charisse embarrassin' our family *again* with her poor taste in men is leavin' me faint." She glared at her daughter. "What are you waitin' for? You're already drivin' me to an early grave actin' the harlot like you do with that man."

"Iris," Pauline said sharply. "You will not

talk to my niece like that in my house."

Iris turned her glare on her sister. "Of course you would side with her. You always have." She swung around abruptly and marched out of the house. Even as angry as she was, she still managed to look beautiful.

Armande rose slowly, his body stiff and sore. He held his hand out to his sister. "Come on, Charisse. Let's get her home. If we're lucky she'll start drinkin' early and take to her bed in one of her 'spells.' "

Saria stood as well. "I'm glad you're datin' Mahieu, Charisse."

Charisse shook her head as she allowed her brother to pull her to her feet. "She'll run him off or seduce him. One way or the other, she'll get rid of him. I knew better than to say yes, but he was so persistent. Please tell him I'm sorry."

"Mahieu is tough, Charisse," Saria assured. "He won't run — and he certainly won't be seduced."

"Then he'll be the first," Charisse said. She walked out, her head high, Armande's arm around her shoulders.

Drake stared after them. "I don't even know what to say."

"I'm so sorry, Drake," Pauline said. "I had no way of warnin' you. My sister can be difficult, although not always that bad."

"What the hell would make a woman that beautiful so bitter? She definitely doesn't like other women, not even her own daughter."

Pauline shrugged. "She married the wrong man. Bartheleme wanted her because she's beautiful, but he didn't love her, not like he should. He was jealous and possessive, but he wasn't her true mate. Her life was horrible — intolerable for a woman like Iris who needed attention. Bartheleme lavished attention on Charisse and treated Armande as if he didn't exist. He treated Iris the same way. Worse, the man Iris had fallen in love with before Bartheleme came along, rejected her because she can't shift. He wanted his children to be leopard. Obviously both Charisse and Armande can shift, so in the end she didn't accept his reasons. She believed she wasn't good enough for either man and she's become the bitter woman you see."

Drake shook his head. "All of you should have traveled away from the area to find other lairs. Marrying someone for the sake of producing shifters and not loving them, not finding your true mate, eventually destroys a lair."

"Amos and I found that out the hard way," Pauline agreed. "He was good to his woman, but I think in the end she knew he loved me. We tried hard never to see one another, but sometimes, we just couldn't stop ourselves. Amos stayed true to his wife. Iris met Buford Tregre while she was still in high school. He was already married but she fell madly in love with him, believed his promises that he would leave his wife and marry her. But of course he didn't. She was crazy about the man, but he was ugly to her when she never could shift. He said she was worthless after stealin' her virtue. She was pregnant and she lost his baby. No one knew. In those days good girls didn't ever get pregnant, and certainly not by a married man."

"I think she had a very narrow escape," Saria said. "That man was cruel to his wife, his sons and their wives."

"When you're young and terribly in love, it doesn't feel like an escape, Saria," Pauline pointed out gently. "Iris is beautiful, but men only seemed to want her to show her off. There was never a true, steady love for her, like Amos has for me. She's agin', although she doesn't want to admit it, and she's frightened. Charisse just reminds her every day that she's growin' old and the men are lookin' to someone younger now."

"Perhaps if she learned not to be so mean

to everyone, a man would give her a chance," Drake pointed out. "As it is, no one is going to chance being with her."

Pauline laughed. "Do you think she's dumb enough to show that side of herself to a man she's settin' out to seduce?"

"I suppose not." He cleared his throat. "This baby she lost, Buford's baby. You're certain she lost it and didn't pass off Armande as Bartheleme Mercier's child?"

Pauline gasped. "No. No, Drake. She lost Buford's baby. She was so distraught and miserable. And Armande is quite handsome."

"I could have sworn you once told me Buford was handsome," Drake pointed out, keeping his tone strictly neutral.

Pauline took a breath. "I guess he was, in the early days before I knew what a monster he was. Somehow he didn't seem quite so good-lookin' when I knew his character. Armande is Bartheleme's son," she added decisively.

Drake nodded his head, turning his attention to Saria, taking her hand. "You're nearly falling asleep right here, honey. Can you eat something and then we'll head for bed."

Saria nodded and followed him to the dining room. Most of the team had already finished and were headed up to bed. Joshua paused by Drake's chair.

"I'm wiped out, man. Do you want a guard posted?"

"I doubt it's necessary with all of us in the house. Let's sleep armed. We'll activate the security system and let Pauline know it's on so she won't set it off when she comes back. We'll sleep light enough and no self-respecting shifter is going to run around as a leopard in broad daylight out in the open. There are too many of us for the killer to show up."

Joshua nodded. "Thanks, boss. For some reason, I can't keep my eyes open. I must be getting old and can't hang with the young crowd anymore."

Drake laughed and pointed at Jeremiah, the youngest of all of them. He was desperately trying to cover a huge yawn. Joshua clapped the kid on the back and his team went upstairs to their rooms, leaving him alone with Pauline and Saria.

Pauline took Saria's face in her hands and kissed her forehead. "I hope Iris didn't hurt you with her snide comments."

"No. I always hope she won't come at me that way, but then I see what she does to Charisse and I know she does it because I'm friends with Charisse. Charisse is an amazing woman, Miss Pauline, and her mother doesn't even see it. I went with her once to the hospital. She visited the children's ward and she brought them all kinds of things and spent hours talking to the kids on the cancer floor. They all knew her by name. She goes there often. Her mother found out because we were late getting back and she was furious with Charisse and told her she'd better not bring some horrible disease home."

"Iris has a terrible fear of illness," Pauline said. "She always has." Pauline patted Saria's hand. "Get some sleep, *cher*, I'll be back this evening."

Saria blew her a kiss and sank down into a chair at the table. She was too tired to eat, but Drake was eating, so she drank a cup of coffee, hoping it would keep her awake long enough to get up the stairs to bed.

In the end, Drake carried her up the stairs and tucked blankets around her. The coffee definitely hadn't worked — she nearly fell asleep sitting at the table. The moment her head hit the pillow she was asleep, barely aware of Drake's body pressed tightly up against hers.

She dreamt of her leopard running in the swamp, feeling the freedom of her animal form for the first time. She'd never realized how easy it was to travel in the body of a cat, flowing over every obstacle, sensing where the ground was thin, hearing the very heartbeat of the swamp. A whiff of drifting smoke through the swamp had her cat wrinkling her nose. Her heart accelerated as adrenaline poured in. All wild things despised the smell of smoke, that heralding of imminent disaster. Her leopard coughed — lungs burning. She coughed.

Her cat clawed at her, raked and snarled in warning. "Bad dream," Saria murmured, trying to pry her eyes open to bring an end to the beginnings of a nightmare. She coughed again and opened her eyes. It was impossible to see anything with the room filled with smoke.

"Drake!" She shook him, rolling from the bed onto the floor where she could breathe a little easier. She dragged his body down after hers. He landed heavily, just beginning to stir. Something wasn't right. Drake always — *always* — came awake completely alert. "Drake! Fire. The inn is on fire and the smoke alarms aren't goin' off. Wake up now!"

17

Drake heard Saria's voice from a great distance, as if he was in a long tunnel and the fog was so thick, it muffled not only sound but vision as well. He opened his mouth to call to her, but instantly his lungs burned for air. He coughed, realizing he was on the floor and Saria was trying to wake him. What the hell was wrong? His leopard roared at him, clawing and raking in alarm. Smoke in the room was so thick he could barely make out Saria, who knelt over him.

"The smoke alarms aren't workin'." Saria pressed her mouth against his ear. "I think we've all been drugged. If we can't wake up, neither can the others."

Drake fought the layers of fog, pushing himself up onto his hands and knees. His stomach lurched and his lungs burned. "Get to the balcony, Saria. I'll go warn the others."

She crawled along the floor to the French

doors and reached up to the doorknob. Drake paused at the door to the hall to watch her. He couldn't feel any heat coming off the door, but he was cautious as he reached for the handle, still watching Saria. She should have already been on the balcony.

"What's wrong?" It was impossible to ignore his stomach, the terrible churning, and he knew he was going to be sick very soon.

"It won't open. Somethin's blockin' it." She tried her shoulder, but the door wouldn't budge. Saria pressed her hand to her mouth, suppressing a cough. "I feel sick, Drake."

"Me, too, baby. We'll get out of this." Drake crawled back to her. Smoke was coming in under the hallway door, which meant the fire was probably in the hallway, although the sprinkler system hadn't come on and the door wasn't hot at all. Puzzled, he tried the balcony door. Something was holding it closed from the outside. "Get back, honey," he ordered and made his way to the chair.

He had to stand to get a good swing at the thick glass, but he called on his leopard's strength and smashed the glass. Fresh air poured in. He was careful to break off the jagged pieces before allowing Saria through the broken glass.

She staggered to the railing, coughing, turning back to look at the other balconies. "All of them are blocked, Drake. We'll have to open them for the others. They might not be awake, or they're tryin' to crawl through the hallway like you would have done to warn everyone." She bent her head and vomited, over and over.

Drake did the same, emptying the contents of his stomach. Strangely, it made him feel a little better. "I'll go left. You go right, but Saria, don't you go back into the inn."

She sent him a wan smile, wiping at her mouth with the back of her hand. "I'll be careful."

Drake leapt up, caught the edge of the roof and somersaulted up to run along the outer edge to the next balcony. Sure enough, the door had been barred from the outside. He glanced down to the lower story, expecting to see flames or smoke, but it didn't look as if the fire was burning on the first story at all.

"Evan." He yanked the board from under the knob and opened the door. Thick black smoke billowed out of the room. "Evan!"

He waved his arms to try to dispel the smoke before running into the room. Evan was sprawled half on, half off the bed as if maybe he roused himself enough to know there was a problem, but couldn't quite wake up. His leopard was probably roaring at him, desperate to break through the drug in his system. Lifting the man in a fireman's carry over his shoulder, Drake took him out of the room and dumped him on the floor of the balcony.

Evan coughed a couple of times, enough that Drake could see he was waking.

"I have to get to the others, Evan. As soon as you can, help Saria. She's working her way down the balconies on the right side. Understand?"

Evan nodded, drawing in a deep lungful of clean air. He signed that he was sick, bent over and expelled the contents of his stomach.

Drake glanced over to the balcony where Saria should have been. The French doors were wide open with smoke pouring through them, and Saria was nowhere to be seen. He cursed aloud, knowing she'd gone inside despite his orders to stay out. He hesitated between going to the next team member, or going after Saria. As he turned toward the right, stepping up onto the railing in preparation for a leap to the roof, she appeared in the doorway, dragging Jeremiah behind her.

Drake didn't wait. He went up onto the roof, but ran to his left, to the next room where, once again, he found the door barred. Anger was slowly building, now that he was fully awake and the drug was wearing off in the clean air. He ripped open the door. Elijah crawled toward him, dragging a chair behind him. The smoke was particularly thick in the room, thick and black, as if he were much closer to the source than Drake's room had been. Drake could see that Elijah had been violently ill in the room, which had probably allowed him to rid himself of the drug in his system and wake up enough to know they were in trouble.

The moment Drake flung open the doors, Elijah clawed his way onto the balcony, coughing and gasping, and mad as hell. "Someone tried to kill us, Drake. This was no fucking accident."

Drake nodded his head. He'd already come to that conclusion. "You all right? I have to get to Joshua."

Joshua was in the last room at the end of the hall, nearest the circular library at the top of the stairs. If the smoke was coming from there, that would make Joshua closest to the source and most likely to be in trouble. Drake remembered that he'd been particularly tired.

Elijah nodded and waved him away, even as he tried desperately to drag fresh air into his lungs.

Drake glanced to his right, looking for Saria. Evan and Saria were helping Jerico from his room. Jerico was on his feet, staggering between the two, but he was alive and well. Drake once more took to the roof. He was exhausted, but feeling better now that he could breathe and the drug was mostly gone from his system. He could feel the aftereffects — a pounding headache and his stomach still churning, but his strength was coming back and with it — rage. Pure rage.

Someone had gone into the house, someone who knew the security system and code. So a family member? Pauline? Amos? One of the Merciers? As he ran across the roof, he caught sight of two men in the trees, running toward the inn. He recognized Joshua Tregre's uncles. The two men were streaked with black just as he and all of his men were from the smoke. He called out to Elijah, alerting him, as he dropped down to Joshua's balcony. Through the French doors he could see black smoke had filled the room. His heart dropped. How could Joshua be alive when he couldn't even see into the room?

He yanked away the bar of wood and, gulping air, rushed in. Joshua wasn't on the bed or the floor. The door leading to the hall was open and he could see that the hall itself was black with thick smoke, yet there were no flames licking along the floor, ceiling or walls. Drake rushed back outside, took another lungful of fresh air and ran through Joshua's bedroom out into the hall. Joshua's room was nearest the large, circular library at the top of the stairs. Drake could see the stone fireplace had low flames burning around smoldering logs. Wet wood had been set on fire.

Coughing, he hurried to the fireplace. He could see that Joshua had been there before him, probably opening the vent someone had closed when they set the fire with wet wood. Drake looked over the railing. The fire in the sitting room had the same wet wood smoldering in it. Joshua had crawled down the stairs in order to try to open that vent as well. He had the front door open and was lying half in, half out of the house.

Drake leapt over the railing and ran to Joshua, his lungs burning for air. Dragging him the rest of the way out, he turned the man onto his back to make certain he was breathing. Joshua's lashes fluttered and he looked up at Drake and gave him a weak thumbs-up.

"You're insane," Drake said. "You should have gotten out immediately."

Joshua's teeth looked very white against his black-smeared face. "Figured it was best to get the smoke out." He coughed and tried to sit. "I think I puked my way through the house. Miss Pauline isn't going to be happy with me."

"You're a damn fool," Drake said, sitting next to him. "You ever scare me like that again and I'll kick your punk ass."

"Got it, boss," Joshua said, staring up at the overcast sky. "I wouldn't mind if it rained right now. Did everyone get out?"

"Yeah. They're all fine. They look like hell, same as you."

Joshua tried to laugh and ended up coughing. "I think someone is really mad at you, boss. You kicked the wrong person's ass."

"I'd like the opportunity to kick it again and maybe do it right this time," Drake said. He shoved his hand through his hair. His fingers were streaked with smoke. "I have to go back in there and open that vent. Smoke can damage a house pretty bad. I'll get the doors and windows open and hopefully get it moving out of there."

"Someone turned off the security system."

"Figured that out, did you? Probably one of your ex-girlfriends," Drake said.

Joshua shoved at him with his foot. "Go away. You've given me a headache."

"I think the drug you ingested and the smoke did that."

Joshua rubbed the bridge of his nose, smearing the black streaks. "It had to be the coffee. Damn it, Drake. I feel like shit."

"Think about that the next time you play hero."

"Fuck you."

Drake laughed and pushed himself up. "You aren't going to have a voice for a week or so. Makes me deliriously happy. I'm going to open all the doors and windows and get that vent open. Don't you move. I'd better find you in the same exact spot when I come back." The relief he felt that Joshua was alive was tremendous. They'd been lucky. Really lucky.

Every one of the doors on the ground floor were locked from the inside, but hadn't been tampered with as the balcony doors had been. Someone had waited for the drug to take effect, barred the balcony doors and closed the vents in the fireplaces before lighting the wet wood, creating the smoke. All they had to do was sit back and wait for it to fill the inn and hopefully kill off the team — and Saria.

It took quite a few trips into the house to open it fully to allow the fresh air in. Drake opened the fireplace vents and put out both fires. He had to make several trips outside to breathe, and Elijah and Evan both joined in to help. The upstairs windows were next. They turned on the overhead fans and located several standing fans in closets to rid the house of the smoke.

Saria brought a jug of clean fresh water to the front of the house where Elijah, Evan and Drake sat on the grass beside Joshua.

"Jerico and Jeremiah have a couple of prisoners. The Tregre brothers claim they dropped by hopin' to talk to Joshua and found the downstairs filled with smoke. They couldn't get in because all the doors were locked so they went down to the edge of the lake away from the trees hopin' to get a cell phone connection to call the fire department. Trouble with that is, go down the road a piece and you can call easily and both would know that." She handed Joshua a glass of water and poured another for Drake. "They're lyin'."

"Big surprise there." Drake downed the entire glass of water and held it out to her.

She ignored him and handed a glass to Elijah and another to Evan. "Miss Pauline is goin' to be so upset. I'll call Amos and tell him what happened. Remy and my brothers are on the way," she added.

Drake leveled a look at her. "We could have handled this ourselves."

"I wasn't certain just how you were goin' to handle it, Drake." She took the glass from him and poured water into it. "I don't want you killin' anyone."

"Now why would you think I'd do something like that?" he asked softly. She should have been far more shaken up than she appeared.

"I think your woman has ice in her veins," Joshua stated.

Drake shot him a hard look. It was possible all of his men were thinking the same thing, but they were polite enough not to say it out loud.

Saria laughed. "Did you think I was going to faint?"

"Naw," Elijah said, "Joshua did that for you."

The men laughed. Saria sent Drake a small smile. "I will admit it probably wasn't a good idea sendin' for Remy. He sounded angry."

"Baby, he beat the shit out of Armande

and Robert for discharging a weapon around you. I can't imagine what he'll do if he thinks the Tregre brothers had anything to do with trying to kill us all." Drake couldn't help smirking a little. "Your brother is far worse than I am."

"I doubt that," Saria disagreed.

"Smart woman," Elijah said. "Don't let him fool you with that calm civilized act of his."

"It did occur to me, when I saw the rest of you, that maybe he was hidin' somethin' from me," Saria replied with that small secret grin that always made Drake's heart stutter.

His men had accepted her. She'd led them through the swamp, never once complaining of the rain and muck. She'd risked her life helping to get the members of his team out of the smoke-filled inn and immediately had thought to bring them all water. She didn't panic — something all of his men would admire. Including her in their teasing signaled their acceptance and camaraderie.

"You realize, Saria, these two men were the ones in the Mercier boat, the one delivering the opium to the other boat." Drake kept his voice low and even. His eyes met Elijah's. Drake had to look away from the compassion there.

Did Saria realize the implication? No shifter could go to jail. They wouldn't survive in captivity and they couldn't die in jail where a doctor would autopsy their body. He was leader of the lair. It would be up to him to pass sentence and carry it out. Remy might be a problem. If his first loyalty was to the human law rather than lair law, Drake would have to find a way to handle the situation without any harm coming to Saria's family. The shifter code had to be placed above all else. He sighed. Things were going to hell fast. The possibility that one or both of the Tregre brothers were serial killers was growing by the moment. Certainly depravity ran in their family. Their father had been cruel and if the rumors were true, he'd murdered his own son.

"Drake," Saria said quietly.

His gaze locked with hers.

"Don't worry about me. Do what you have to do."

He would have kissed her, despite her black-streaked face, if all his men hadn't been grinning like monkeys.

They had arrived at the inn through the waterway, so it was rather startling to have cars driving up to the house, reminding him they weren't on an island. Remy leapt out, rushed across the lawn to his sister, yanking her up off the ground and into his arms in one move.

"You all right, Saria?"

"I'm fine. All of us got out."

"This is bullshit."

"I thought so too," Saria agreed with a small smile. She carefully extracted herself from her brother, brushing at the smears of black on his shirt.

"I'm sendin' you out of the country if this keeps up," he threatened, turning to glare at Drake. "You keep puttin' her in harm's way and the two of us just may end up dancin'."

"Any time, Remy," Drake spat out, disgusted. He was damn tired, angry and ready to kick the ass of every member of the lair. "How the hell did you allow things to get to this point? You had to have known what was going on right under your nose. I suppose you looked the other way because it was convenient, just as you did when Saria was growing up."

Behind Remy, his brothers spread out and behind Drake, his men did the same. Saria made a move as if to get between them, but Drake snagged her wrist and pulled her behind him. He raised glittering eyes to the Boudreaux brothers, his leopard clawing for supremacy. His chest was already bare, as were his feet, so hands dropped to the buttons of his jeans, ready to strip.

"Any of you want to challenge for leadership, do it now or stand down. I'm damn tired of this entire community." Fury pushed adrenaline through his veins, and his skin rippled as he breathed deep to try to keep his leopard at bay. He'd had enough of all of them.

Remy bowed his head and his brothers followed suit. "I was not challengin' leadership," he qualified, "only takin' offense at you makin' it all personal. My sister is years younger than me. Maybe you're right and we should have looked out for her better. Those years were difficult on all of us and she always seemed as if she was happy. Maybe it's guilt and the need to make it all up to her that makes me edgy. Bottom line is, she's my sister and I don't like anyone threatenin' her or puttin' her in danger."

"Then let's find this bastard and put him in the ground," Drake said.

Saria slipped her fingers into the back pocket of his jeans. He felt the connection between them immediately. Felt his leopard calm instantly and hers rise to the surface to stroke along his cat. The knots of tension in his belly unraveled.

"I've got a couple of men that need interrogating. Care to join me?" Drake asked Remy.

"They won't like seein' me with you," Remy warned. "I have a reputation. Undeserved, but there it is." He offered up a small smile, just a flash of his white teeth, but it was a conciliatory gesture.

Drake reached behind him for Saria's hand. It was strange to think he hadn't known her just a week or so earlier. She'd fast become his world. There was something soothing about her presence even when his entire body was aware of her at all times. Her fingers threaded through his and instant satisfaction flooded him. Relief. She was always there. Steady. Constant. No matter what happened. No matter how bad.

"Maybe you should go with your brothers back to your house, shower and get clean clothes. I'll send Elijah and Joshua with you. They're both tough as nails and between them and your family, you'll be safe."

"You want to get rid of me."

"There's that too." He smiled down at her. She wasn't a woman he had to soft-soap the truth for. "I'd rather you weren't here when we question these men." His gaze flicked to Joshua. Hers followed and she barely nodded her head, understanding his silent plea. He didn't want Joshua there either. If his uncles were every bit as sick as his grandfather had been, Joshua might take it pretty hard. It was always a difficult thing to face knowing one's bloodline could carry insanity. Drake had been with Jake Banna-conni for some time and had seen firsthand when leopards went wrong. Jake's parents had been two of the cruelest, sickest indi-viduals Drake had ever come across.

Saria nodded. "A shower sounds good."

Drake retained possession of her hand. "You won't take off on your own, right?"

"Are you sayin' you think I can slip away right out from under the noses of your men and my brothers?" she teased.

"Probably. I sure wouldn't bet against it. But you won't."

"I won't. I know someone really danger-ous is runnin' around out there and . . ."

"They're looking right at you," he finished for her.

She nodded, her expression serious. "I'll be safe."

Satisfied, Drake looked to his men — not her brothers. Joshua and Elijah were men he would trust with his life — with Saria's life. They both nodded their understanding.

Remy looked at his brothers. "Take them home. Don't let her out of your sight. In fact, when she takes a shower, one of you guard outside that window. If these two aren't doin' the killin', he might make another try for Saria."

Mahieu nodded and stepped back to allow his sister to precede him to the car.

"Give us a minute," Elijah said. They needed weapons and the weapons were in their rooms. "I'll get your things, Joshua."

Joshua didn't protest, but remained stretched out in the grass. He regarded Drake with open suspicion. "You getting rid of me, Drake?"

Drake scowled at him. "I'm entrusting you with the life of my mate, Joshua. Tell me who's better for the job and I'll send them."

Joshua grinned at him. "Just wanted to make you say it, boss."

Drake flipped him off, ignoring the laughter of the Boudreaux brothers. Elijah came out with a bag filled with weapons. Remy rolled his eyes.

"You goin' to war?"

"Damn straight," Elijah answered.

Drake extended his hand and pulled Joshua from the ground. "I'm counting on the two of you. Don't let anything happen to my woman."

Elijah nodded and he and Joshua followed the Boudreaux brothers and Saria to the car. Drake and Remy went around the house to find the two prisoners.

Drake crossed his arms over his chest and regarded the Tregre brothers as they sat on the ground beneath the trees, a small distance from the inn. Jerico had left them untied, but Remy immediately snapped cuffs on both of them, and he wasn't gentle about it.

"I'm going to give you a chance to tell me the truth," Drake said and held up his hand to forestall either of the brothers from speaking. "Before you decide to be stupid, you might consider that some leopards can smell a lie. Remy has quite the reputation in the police department and moved up the ladder fast. He's actually a detective now. A homicide detective. Now why do you suppose that is?"

"You notice there's been a lot of dead bodies' turnin' up around here?" Remy added. "Cuz I've been noticin' that."

"Would have been a few more, Remy," Drake said, "if Saria hadn't woken up when she did. Seems to me that your sister's been in harm's way quite a bit lately, like maybe someone's targeting her."

"You think someone's targeting my sister, Drake? Your fiancée?" Remy asked, beginning to pace. He was a big man and he seemed to flow, all muscle and sinew as he paced back and forth in front of the Tregre brothers.

"That's what I think," Drake said.

"You find someone stupid enough to be tryin' to kill my sister and your fiancée, what do you suppose we should do about it?"

"I guess we'd have no choice, Remy. They'd have to disappear." Drake stared at the two brothers with no expression. "So which one of you is Beau and which is Gilbert?"

"I'm Beau," the man on the left identified himself.

"So you're the mastermind behind all of this," Drake said. "The drugs, the killings, the attempt to kill off my team — and my woman." He made it a statement. His voice was pitched very low, very soft, and his stare was all leopard — all predator.

Remy shot him a quick look, no doubt wondering about the drugs, but Drake never broke eye contact with Beau. Either he was the greatest actor in the world, or something Drake had said shocked him. His mouth fell open, his face turned red and he shook his head violently, his gaze shifting to his brother, who looked equally as shocked.

"Killin's? I don't know what you're talkin' about. I never killed anyone. *Never.* And I wouldn't. If I was gonna kill someone, it

would have been the old man," Beau denied.
"I don't know anything about any killin'.""

Gilbert shook his head. "Remy, you know
us. We never killed anyone."

"What the hell were you doing here if you
didn't intend to kill us?" Drake demanded.
"You think intending to kill but not finish-
ing the job is going to get you off the hook?"

"You got it all wrong," Beau said. "I knew
this was goin' to happen. I told you, Gilbert.
I knew we should have just laid low."

"You knew what was going to happen?"
Remy asked.

Gilbert sighed. "We were set up to take
the fall. We were set up, Remy."

Drake toed the man's boot. "How many
times have you heard that, Remy?"

Remy smirked. "Oh, that one's new to me,
cuz I'm wet behind the ears." He glared at
the Tregre brothers. "Is that what you think?
I'm wet behind the ears? You think you're
smarter than me?" He bared his teeth in a
semblance of a smile. "You hear that, Drake.
Gilbert thinks he's smarter than I am."

"You're twistin' my meanin', Remy,"
Gilbert said. "We came to talk to the boy —
Renard's boy. We figured he was blood kin
and might help us."

"Help you kill off his team? His friends?
The only family he's ever known?" Drake

scoffed. "If you think that, you don't know the meaning of loyalty and you sure don't know Joshua."

Both men shook their heads. "We didn't come here to kill anyone," Gilbert insisted. "We knew you'd been out in the swamp last night. You were at the Merciers and also our property, lookin' around. The scent was everywhere."

Beau looked at Drake with something close to respect. "You cut through the swamps followin' our boat, didn't you? I didn't think anyone could do somethin' like that and I've lived in the swamp my whole life."

Remy held up one finger. "You cut through the swamp followin' a boat?"

"All of them," Beau said. "All his men, and Saria led the way. They must have run."

"And waded through the reeds in a couple of spots," Gilbert contributed. "There was no other way."

"My *sister* was runnin' the swamp at night? Wadin' through the reeds with gators?"

Remy's voice had gone very quiet. Drake had hoped he wouldn't go all commando on him, but now that he knew how insane he'd been to even try it, let alone have Saria with him, he couldn't really blame the man.

"We knew they were running dope, Remy," he said. "Although we're familiar with the rain forests and the danger in them, we had no idea how truly dangerous what we asked Saria to do last night really was. She was amazing and we were damned stupid to risk it."

That was as much as he was conceding to Remy. The man could take it or leave it.

"So you were runnin' dope, Beau? Right under my nose?"

"There's a big difference between takin' a boat out to deliver soap to a buyer and killin' someone, Remy," Beau pointed out. "We didn't kill anyone."

"So how did you get into the drug business, Beau?" Drake asked.

"Delivery," Gilbert emphasized. "That's what we were comin' to talk to the boy about."

"First of all, let's get something straight," Drake said in disgust. "Joshua is a man. He does a man's work and he takes a man's responsibility."

Beau sighed and looked at his brother, shaking his head. He looked down at the ground, defeated. Gilbert scowled. "You don't want to hear the truth."

"Sure we do, Gil," Remy said. "Spit it out and don't try sugarcoatin' it, because I think our leader has an itchy trigger finger right about now."

"You may have heard the rumors about our father," Gilbert muttered. "Every one of them was true. He raped women and beat them. He beat our mother, beat us. He killed Renard. We couldn't prove it, but he did. And he gambled. Mostly he lost."

Drake raised his eyebrow.

Gilbert flushed. "I'm not whinin' about my life. I'm tellin' you the truth. He began workin' for the Merciers, runnin' their gardens for them. Mostly, he told everyone what to do. And he made deliveries to special customers. Eventually we took over makin' the deliveries. The money was good and we didn't think much about it until we started makin' those deliveries in the middle of the night to boats comin' in from all over."

"So you're saying you didn't know about the opium when you first started working for the Merciers?"

Gilbert shook his head. "When the old man got sick, he told us to take over the night deliveries. That was when we knew. So about three years ago, we get a call and we go. We should have stopped as soon as we figured it out, but the money was good and we didn't want to keep huntin' gators."

"And there was Evangeline," Beau added. "We both felt we had to protect her."

"Did someone threaten her?" Remy asked.

Beau looked at his brother. "Not outright. One night we came home and Evangeline's room was wrecked. There was a knife stuck in the middle of her mattress. We'd hesitated about makin' the delivery, hedgin' a little when the call came in. We didn't do that anymore. We figured whoever made those calls was tellin' us we play ball with them or Evangeline dies."

"Who made the calls?"

The two men looked at one another. Gilbert shrugged. "I don't know. They used something, a device, to change their voice to a mechanical sound."

"So after all this time working for the Merciers, you want us to believe you don't have a clue who gives the orders?" Drake demanded.

Beau shook his head. "We didn't want to know. We thought it was safer that way. They have a master gardener and crew tending the flowers. We just make the deliveries. To the dock, to the local shops and the special ones."

"So what were you coming here to tell Joshua?" Drake asked. They were telling the truth. They'd closed their eyes to everything but the money for a lot of reasons, but their voices resonated with the truth.

"We thought if we told him what was goin' on he'd think of a way to get us out without puttin' Evangeline in danger," Gilbert admitted. "We argued about it. Beau didn't think you'd believe us. In the end we didn't really have a choice. We knew you had to have seen us. That girl — Saria — she's good in the swamp. She got you to the point in time to see the boat dockin'. She just doesn't know how to quit."

"She got us there," Drake said. "In plenty of time to identify both of you."

"Well, we finally quit arguin' and came up through the canal and swamp in our boat. It's docked down there at the lake. When we got close to the inn, we could see smoke. We tried the doors downstairs, but they were all locked," Gilbert explained.

"Gilbert was goin' to break in, but then we heard glass shatter on the second-story balcony. We ran, afraid if you saw us, you'd think we started the fire. But when we got down to the lake, both of us couldn't just leave, knowin' there were people maybe burnin' in the inn, so we ran back."

Again, there was that ring of truth in Beau's voice that Drake couldn't ignore. He glanced at Remy, who nodded. He thought they were telling the truth as well. They were guilty of taking drug money, but neither man was a killer — certainly not a serial killer. And Drake doubted if either possessed the brains to mastermind placing opiates in perfumed soaps.

"Your old man never told you who came up with the idea to put opium bricks in the soaps?" Drake asked, already knowing the answer.

"I didn't even know that was what was in the boxes," Beau said. "I didn't want to know."

"Where do they manufacture the soaps, lotions and perfumes?" Drake asked.

Beau frowned and looked at his brother. "The factory is in town, not out in the swamp. The laboratory where Charisse works is on their property, but everything is made in town. We pick up our deliveries there."

"And your special ones?" Remy prompted.

"They're waitin' at the Mercier dock for us, already loaded in the boat."

"Beau, how dumb can you be," Remy burst out in disgust. "Runnin' drugs, for God's sake. What the hell's wrong with you?"

Beau hung his head. "We were losin' everythin', Remy. The house, the boat, everythin' and we've always done what pa told us to do. We got good money for makin' the deliveries and workin' for the Merciers gave us great benefits. They're fair employers."

"Other than you have to run drugs for them," Drake said.

Beau didn't reply.

"What are you goin' to do with us?" Gilbert asked.

"I haven't decided yet," Drake said. "For now, go home and keep your mouths shut. If you get another call, you'd better let us know immediately. And then take Evangeline to the Boudreaux home. You understand me? Don't make me come looking for you."

Remy bent down and unlocked the cuffs on both men. "You were damned stupid to get into this mess," he repeated. "And you're lucky Drake is leader."

"Oh, they'll be punished," Drake said. "I have to give it some thought."

"Tell the boy . . ." At Drake's scowl, Beau cleared his throat, "Renard's son, we'd still like to talk with him. If he'd like."

"I'll tell him." Drake pinned him with his predator's stare. "Don't make the mistake of running away or going to the Merciers. I'd hunt you down and I'd never stop until I found you and I killed you. You don't want me for an enemy."

Beau nodded. "This is my home. I was born here and I'll die here. I got nowhere else to go. Gilbert's the same. And we've got Evangeline and the boys to see to. We're not goin' to be lookin' over our shoulders the rest of our lives."

Drake watched the two men walk heavily toward the boat before he turned to Remy. "We didn't get much on our killer."

"Drugs? You didn't think maybe that might be important to tell me?" Remy demanded.

"Sorry. We were going to talk to you first thing after we rested. Someone drugged us and tried to kill us all with smoke. I have to talk to Pauline. She set the security alarm and someone turned it off and disabled the smoke alarms. They blocked all the balcony doors from the outside."

"And you think it was the killer?"

"It has to be someone familiar with the inn's security system. The Merciers were here and all of them heard Pauline say she was leaving for the day. Any of them could have done it."

"Charisse or Armande. Damn it all, Drake, it always comes back to them. Mahieu is taken with that girl."

"So is Saria." Drake shook his head. "But she's got the brains, knows chemistry and certainly is always around when something goes wrong."

"Just damn it," Remy said.

18

"Hurry, Drake, hurry," Saria chanted in a whisper. She repeated his name over and over, a mantra to save her.

The bathroom was quite small, much smaller than her room, but it was at the farthest point of the house away from the sitting room where Elijah and Joshua and her brothers were gathered. She bit down hard on her thumbnail as she paced the few feet across the tiled floor.

"You have to get here fast."

She'd promised him she wouldn't leave the safety of her brothers or his men, and she knew she couldn't, but she was fast losing control of the situation and she *needed* him. Right. Now.

Her back arched and she muffled a cry as she dropped to the cool tiles on her hands and knees, dragging air into her lungs, to breathe away the burning fire consuming her. Her breasts felt swollen and achy. Her skin was hot. Molten lava seemed to be in her veins. Something alive raced under her skin, so that she itched, and if she looked, she could see it moving. The pushing up of her skin made her feel slightly sick to her stomach. Between her legs, she was on fire. There was no other word for it, a fierce conflagration burning out of control.

"This can't be happening. Not now. Not in front of my *brothers.*" Her face flamed bright red. She had to stifle a sob.

Deep inside, her female leopard stretched and preened, pushing her rump into the air, until Saria found herself sliding sensuously across the floor. Her jaw ached, her teeth felt too full for her mouth. She could hear the conversation in the front of the house, although the men spoke in low murmurs. There was no way to concentrate on what they were saying, even when she tried to distract herself. Her joints ached and popped with every movement and she couldn't stay still, her body undulating nearly out of control.

For a time she breathed deep, in and out, a form of meditation, trying to relieve the burning need that built and built, coiling tighter and tighter inside of her until she was afraid she'd go insane. Her fingers curled into claws and the tips of her fingers hurt, pinpoints of pain that only were relieved when she dug them into the cool tiles. The scratch marks horrified her. She had to get out of the house before she destroyed it.

Her clothes hurt her skin and her skin was too tight, stretched over her bones until it was thin and threatening to tear. A low sob escaped. She glanced at the window, her only escape. Her vision blurred, strange bands of color streaking across her vision. The scent of male leopards inundated her and she groaned in despair.

"Drake." She whispered his name again, aloud, to give her strength. She'd promised him she'd stay in the protection of her family and his men, but like this, she was a danger to everyone.

She staggered to her feet, her hands cupping her aching breasts. They felt too heavy for her frame. Inflamed. In need. She could barely breathe with such desperate need. Somehow she made it to the window. Her hands fumbled at the windowsill, nearly useless, her fingers bent and curved, so painful that anything she came into contact with only added to her misery. She wouldn't leave — not yet. She'd hold out to the last possible second, waiting for Drake to come back, but she had to have fresh air.

It was late afternoon. He must have waited to talk with Pauline and help arrange for cleaners to come in. That would be like him. He would take responsibility for everyone around him. She clenched her teeth and pain exploded in her mouth. Drake needed to get to her fast and help her figure out what to do, where to go, and how to get her leopard out.

She shoved the window open and stuck her head out, gulping in the fresh air. Her beloved swamp was only a few feet away. She could just crawl out the window and find her favorite tree and wait outside for Drake. If anything happened, she wouldn't be stripping in front of her brothers and trying to seduce one of Drake's friends.

The wind shifted. She inhaled again and her leopard went wild. A male leopard stood only a few feet from her, waiting silently in the trees. *Joshua.* Her leopard clawed at her, edgy, in a dangerously amorous mood. Her hands went to her shirt, opening the first button before she could stop herself.

"Are you all right, Saria?"

She'd never noticed what a sexy voice he had, what a hot male scent. Saria swallowed hard and closed her eyes, trying to under-stand when she was so consumed with Drake how another man might suddenly be so appealing to her. She'd never looked twice at Joshua. It had always been Drake from the moment she set eyes on him. She wanted him, wanted to live her life with him. She craved being in his arms. His kisses. Those mind-numbing, hot, sexy kisses that went on forever. She lost herself in those kisses.

"I need Drake right now. Can you get him for me?"

Her voice didn't sound like her own. Tears burned behind her eyes. She had no escape. She didn't dare go outside where Joshua stood guard. She didn't trust herself to be alone with another man, not while her leopard was in such a sexual frenzy. Concentrating on Drake, the taste of him, the way he looked at her with his golden stare, helped to steady her.

"He's on his way. Elijah called the inn and Miss Pauline said he left," Joshua said. He didn't come out of the trees, but stayed a good distance from her. It was clear he was trying to keep her scent away from his leopard, but he didn't abandon her. "Are you afraid?"

"A little. I don't know what to expect."

"The first time you shift is scary," Joshua admitted, his voice matter-of-fact.

Saria knew what it had to cost him to stay

with her and keep talking as if nothing was wrong when his leopard had to be close to a thrall. His calm voice steadied her. Drake trusted Joshua to keep her safe. She would have to do the same.

"You feel like you might be losing yourself, because you have to let go to let your leopard emerge, but you're still there. It's hard to explain until you experience it, but once you're fully a shifter, you're both leopard and human. You draw on each other's strength. It's just that first letting go that is frightening."

"She feels out of control."

He laughed softly. "So does my leopard. Your leopard's chosen Drake's leopard. She wouldn't allow another one to come too close, that's why it's so dangerous. Once she's actually made up her mind, she'll entice every male in sight, but if they get out of hand, she'll tear them up."

"That's horrible." Saria hissed at her leopard. *I knew you were a hussy.* She pushed her forehead against the windowsill, wanting to weep. Her body wouldn't stay still and even the night breeze couldn't cool her rising temperature. "What if he doesn't come and I can't hold her back? She'll have to go into the swamp and I promised him . . ."

"Elijah and I will look after you. We're strong enough to control our leopards."

She didn't want Drake's men to witness her behavior. She didn't want anyone to see her like this. She had no idea what her leopard would do, how far she would go to entice a male to her, but the way her body felt, she was afraid. She needed Drake desperately.

The scent of a female leopard in heat was strong, permeating the dock and trail leading up to the Boudreaux home as Drake, Remy, Jerico, Evan and Jeremiah stepped off the boat. Drake's leopard leapt and roared, so that blood thundered in his ears and pulsed madly through his temples. Almost instantly his muscles began to contort, his mouth filling with teeth. He forced himself to breathe deeply, holding back the change.

Jeremiah stopped dead right there on the dock. Jerico and Evan walked only a few more feet toward the house before stopping. Remy swore under his breath. Drake ignored him and broke into a run.

"She's all right," Remy called after him. "My brothers wouldn't let anything happen to her."

Drake didn't turn around. How could

Saria possibly be all right? Her leopard was throwing off enough hormones to call in every male for hundreds of miles. She had to be scared and embarrassed and what the hell had he been doing anyway? Pauline could have handled the mess at the inn without him. He could have waited for a shower and for Pauline to wash his clothes while they made all the necessary calls to the cleaners. Damn. He'd been selfish, thinking of his own comfort, not Saria's. He knew she was close to the emerging. Hell. They all knew it. His first duty was to Saria. Always. Forever. And he'd let her down.

He burst through the front door, his body so painful and sensitive, he was already tearing at his shirt to get it away from his skin. Saria's brothers jumped to their feet, all looking in rough shape. They had obviously stretched their control to the limit, their leopards roaring with the demand to protect and keep her safe from any strange males.

"Where is she?"

His leopard raked him, desperate to be released, to fend off all rivals for his lady's affection. Drake couldn't help but notice that Joshua and Elijah weren't in the room. And neither was Saria. His throat thickened, changing his vocal cords so that little would make sense but a growling challenge. Heat was already banding in colors and his skin felt too tight around his shifting bones.

"She's in the bathroom at the far end of the hall," Mahieu said.

Drake was already following the scent, aware Remy was right behind him as he leapt the expanse of the hall, landing in a crouch just outside the door. He didn't knock, but jerked it open. Saria whirled around to face him and Drake suppressed a groan as Saria's eyes locked with his. Her irises were nearly gone, ringed now with all gold. She looked frightened, twisting the fingers of her hands together until her skin was nearly white.

Drake couldn't imagine how she felt. Her leopard had to be clawing for supremacy, knowing she was in the vicinity of males. Saria had to fight to keep her body under control when her leopard wanted seduction, plain and simple. Beyond her, out the window, he not only saw, but smelled her two guards. Elijah and Joshua both were sweating, staying as far from Saria as possible. He forced himself to give them a small salute, and nod of thanks, when his leopard raged at their close proximity. His presence allowed the others to get away from her, taking their leopards out of harm's way.

Remy swore under his breath. "You have

to get her out of here before something happens. This is a bad situation."

Saria couldn't have failed to hear her brother. She blinked rapidly, almost as if she might burst into tears. Her eyes were overbright.

Drake held out his hand to her. "No worries, honey, you've waited a long time for her."

"Take him to *Tante* Marie's cabin, Saria. She lets us use it when she's away. It's empty. Mahieu, grab some clothes from my closet. Lojos, food. Let's get it done," Remy instructed.

Saria's fingers tangled with his. He could feel the fur running beneath her skin, desperate to break free. He closed his hand over hers, pouring strength and confidence into his gaze. He winked at her and saw her take a breath, settle, believing in him. Trusting him. As she'd done from the beginning. Saria had given herself to him and in the moment, he realized the enormity of her commitment to him. Saria didn't do things by halves.

For one moment, he could only stand there looking at her — loving her — nearly weak with love for her. He had never considered what it would be like to give himself totally to another person — to trust someone that much. She could break his heart — shatter it into a million pieces. Fear slithered through him for just one moment, but he knew she was in it with him for life because that was how Saria operated. He knew his heart was in his eyes for anyone to see, but there was only Saria looking back at him. Her chin went up and she smiled.

Mahieu thrust a pack at him. It was heavy enough to contain weapons. He tossed the pack out the window and indicated Saria precede him. She practically dove through the window with no hesitation whatsoever. She wanted to be away from her brothers. He wanted her away from everyone. He trusted his men to keep their leopards under control, but this lair was fucked up and the males in it had little control over themselves — let alone their leopards.

Saria ran toward the swamp, her leopard lending her speed. Drake slung the pack around his neck and raced after her.

"I have to get the clothes off my body. I can't stand anything against my skin," Saria said, desperation in her voice.

"We can undress just ahead. Elijah and Joshua left as soon as they saw me with you. They'll hang out around your family home just to make certain we're safe, but we'll have the swamp between here and wherever you're taking us," Drake assured. His voice was gravelly, husky, sawing rather than clear tones.

Saria glanced back at him and hurried into the darkness of the trees. She peeled her shirt from her body in one swift move. He reached for it, folding it carefully and stuffing it in the pack, even as he unlaced his boots.

"Tell me what to do," Saria said. "Hurry. You have to hurry, Drake." Her shoes were on the ground and she was pushing her jeans from the curve of her hips.

"She'll rise, honey, and you have to embrace her. It will be difficult because you'll feel like she's swallowing you, but let her come to the surface. Let her have her form. You'll be there, inside of her, feeling everything she feels."

She was so beautiful, all flowing skin, golden eyes glittering at him with a mixture of fear, excitement and heat. His leopard itched, trying to leap to the surface, but Drake forced calm. This was her first time and he wanted it to be a perfect experience for her. Shoes and clothes were stowed in the pack and slung around his neck.

She suddenly cried out and flung out her hand to him. Her knuckles curved, and beneath all that smooth skin ran something else — something alive and determined to emerge. He couldn't take his eyes from her. She left him breathless. Her body contorted and she went down to her hands and knees. He kept one hand on her shoulder, stroking with his fingers. Her back arched and she lifted her buttocks invitingly.

"Please, Drake," she whispered, an enticement.

Heat radiated from her body. She looked at him over her shoulder, her eyes begging him. His cock was so hard he couldn't take a step. It was all he could do not to slide his hands between her legs and stroke her inviting sex. She was so beautiful, her head thrown back, her buttocks high, her breasts swinging invitingly.

The moment he felt fur sliding over her skin, he leapt back, took a breath and called his leopard. A female leopard was dangerous. Moody. Edgy. Especially in heat. One never took chances. It was all about her. What she wanted — when she wanted. He had only to keep every rival from coming near her — and to keep her safe while he waited for her signal.

Golden fur, dotted with glossy black rosettes, covered the female form. She turned her head and golden eyes blazed at him, a haunting, smoldering fire that sent a shaft of heat rushing through his body to center every nerve ending in his groin. Her spotted coat was one of the most beautiful he'd ever seen. A luxurious, unique, exotically marked fur, the rosettes scattered like stars against gold.

She stretched as roped muscles and strong sinew formed and reshaped her, as she became fully leopard. At once the female cat rolled sensuously, rubbing her head along the ground and batting the air playfully with her paws. She looked at Drake's male leopard with teasing eyes, rolled again as he began a slow, cautious circle around her. Her cat leapt to her feet. She rubbed along trees, sliding her fur over the bark, leaving her tantalizing perfume everywhere for all males to scent. Her call sign. Her signal of readiness.

Drake's male made certain all males knew he was in the vicinity and no one would come near his female without a fight to the death. He followed the female as she went through the swamp, staying close enough to watch over her, but far enough away to keep from getting swiped by one of her paws should she think he was trespassing before she was ready for him. She was playful, then amorous, calling to him, rolling and stretching, each movement more seductive than the last.

They moved through the swamp, deeper into the interior until he spotted the cabin Remy had told him about. He left his mate long enough to get rid of the pack around his neck and then padded after her down to a stream. Vines tangled and knotted over the ground, and moss hung from the tree branches, swaying slightly in the breeze. He saw none of it — yet all of it. He had attention and eyes for his alluring mate, reading her every signal.

His leopard had waited years for his mate, and even now, when she was finally with him, he took his time with her, rubbing along the length of her, not pressing her, waiting for her to signal her readiness. She crouched twice, but both times when he approached, using caution, she growled a warning and leapt up. He simply backed off and continued their amorous games.

She rolled again and stretched, this time coming into a crouching position, her hindquarters raised, tail to one side. The male leopard was on her instantly, blanketing her body, nuzzling her gently, calming her with his teeth along the back of her neck as he entered her.

They spent hours together, the male taking the female repeatedly, over and over, every twenty minutes. In between, they lay together, rubbing sensuously along each other's body. The sun set with the two leopards twining around one another, mating and lying together for short periods of time. Long into the evening the cats continued.

The moon had managed to emerge from behind a growing wall of clouds and then begin to recede when Drake once again took control, forcing his cat to push the female back toward the cabin. Once on the porch, he surfaced, shifting back into human form. Breathing hard, he managed to shove the door open before turning back to the female leopard.

"Saria. I need you right now. Come to me, baby. She's strong, but you're stronger. She's had her time, now it's our turn." He circled his thick cock with his hand. "See what you do to me? I need you, baby. Now. Shift now."

Oftentimes it was difficult to give up the freedom of the cat's form, but Saria immediately obeyed him, shifting and landing in a small heap on the floor in front of him. He yanked her to her feet and nearly threw her against the wall, the leopard's strength still running through his heavily roped muscles.

Saria's breath slammed out of her. Drake's eyes were heavy-lidded, his pupils dilated, nearly black with glittering gold surrounding the lust-filled dark circles. Pure sensuality was carved into the lines of his face, a carnal lust that only made the terrible hunger in her grow until it nearly consumed her.

Saria looked up at him, her eyes drenched in need. She was on fire. Dripping. Hot. She needed his hands on her, his mouth on her and his cock buried deep in her body. "Hurry," she whispered. "Hurry, Drake."

His hands covered her breasts, his fingers tugging and rolling her nipples. Pleasure streaked from breasts to the very core of her, leaving every nerve ending tingling as a strong electrical current surged through her body.

She couldn't look away with Drake's golden eyes locked on hers. He slowly bent his head and sucked her nipple into the heated cavern of his mouth. His tongue teased and danced, licked and flicked until she couldn't contain the dark moans. She wrapped her arms around his head to cradle him at her breasts. When he sucked her nipple tight against the heated roof of his mouth, she nearly screamed.

Her breathing turned harsh and labored

as she fought for air. She was on fire. Desperate for him. "Please, Drake," she whispered, rubbing her body against his, needing relief. She lifted one leg and wrapped it around his hip, pressing tightly against him.

He tugged on her nipple with his teeth, his tongue stroking to ease the tiny bite of pain. A shudder of pleasure slid through her body in a slow tumbling wave. A fine sheen of sweat dampened her rose-petal skin. He lifted his head and looked with satisfaction at her nipples, now dark and straining toward him, pinpoints of need. He cupped the soft weight in his hands and brushed his thumbs over the sensitive buds. Once more fire darted through her to settle into a storm of desire in her core.

She pressed tighter against him, nearly sobbing. "Drake, I can't stand it. I need you inside of me."

"Trust me, baby, you can take it. You can take a lot more," he whispered, flicking her nipples with his tongue. "I intend to have you screaming for me. Besides, I want to eat you up tonight."

Her entire body went into meltdown at his blatant admission. He didn't try to hide the fact that he wanted her every bit as much as she wanted him — or that he was in control.

He picked her up easily and carried her to the couch. It was wide and long and had obviously been used as a makeshift bed. He threw the sheet covering it onto the floor and sank down, with Saria on his lap. His hard cock pulsed against her buttocks and he squirmed until he adjusted her perfectly so he could nestle in the heat between her rounded cheeks. Saria couldn't stop herself from moving subtly, rubbing over the thick length of him while deep inside her body pulsed with need.

His strong fingers stroked a caress from her ankle to her knee. The light touch over her bare skin shouldn't have produced the terrible ache. She groaned softly and bit his shoulder.

"Baby," he said softly. "Have I told you yet that I love you?" He swept back her damp hair and looked into her eyes.

Her stomach dropped. Her heart fluttered. She pressed her lips together and mutely shook her head.

"I do love you, very, very much and I never want to be without you."

He kissed her gently, his lips moving over her face. Each eye. The tip of her nose. The corner of her mouth. His lips rested over hers, drinking in her soft moan, his tongue dancing with hers, stroking gently at first, building the fire until he was devouring her mouth over and over. His hand settled on her nape while he feasted there.

She loved kissing him. Loved the taste and texture of him. The heat. The command of his mouth and the way he consumed her as if he could never quite get enough. She was addicted to him, craving his touch and his taste, and loved that he was the same with her. She relaxed into him, opening for him and he immediately shifted her in his arms, still kissing her, laying her across his body, lowering her head to the arm of the couch.

Drake looked down at Saria, her soft body sprawled across him, completely his to do whatever he desired. The sight of her stole his breath, her eyes so enormous, dark chocolate ringed with gold, very solemn. He stroked his hand up the inside of her thigh, forcing her to open her legs for him. She followed his every nonverbal cue immediately, pleasing him immensely. She was wet and needy, her breath coming in soft, ragged gasps.

He kissed her again, loving her mouth, that soft, hot fantasy mouth. He had received such pleasure when she was inexperienced, her desire to please him more than making up for her lack of knowledge. He loved the dazed, aroused look in her eyes, the need in her squirming body, but most of all the way she gave her body to his keeping.

"You're so damned beautiful, Saria," he whispered, trailing kisses over her neck. "Thank you for being mine." He couldn't help taking tiny bites from neck to breast, his tongue soothing the little stings.

Her skin was amazingly soft and he couldn't stop himself from stroking and tasting and lapping at her sweetness. Her breath came out in a series of gasps, and she moaned, a low entreaty. He loved the heat of her skin. His. All his. He had all the time in the world to drive them both insane with need. His erection felt so full cushioned in the heat of her buttocks and his heart felt just as full, both threatening to burst.

Her soft breasts were thrust upward as she pushed with her heels against the arm of the couch, trying to ease the burning need between her legs. There was no resisting that invitation, and he bent his head to her tight nipple. He flicked it with his tongue and then stroked with his teeth. She cried out, a broken sound of need. He loved that she didn't try to hide what she felt from him, that she gave him the sounds of her passion as well. Her soft whimpers and groans were music, a symphony that added to the heat ever-building in his body.

He licked and suckled at her breasts, raising the stakes, sucking harder, increasing the pressure of his teeth until she was writhing against him. The sensation of her bottom drove him nearly insane with need. The harder he suckled, the more she twisted sensually, her breath coming in gasps. Her skin felt hot and silky as he glided his palm over her stomach to the seething heat between her legs.

"Open your thighs wider for me, baby," he instructed. The scent of her arousal permeated the air. He was hungry for her, for the taste of her, for her cries and pleas.

She obeyed him, opening her body to him, pressing her heels hard against the arm of the couch as his fingers slid into her slick heat. She nearly came off his lap. Her eyes met his with a kind of shock. That dazed look, so hungry and needy, nearly pushed him over the edge of his control. He wanted her to know that he was her true mate.

"We belong, Saria. I'm the one who makes you feel like this. So good, baby. And you're made for me. Your body was made for mine." He couldn't wait another moment. He moved her quickly, positioning her arms above her head, pulling her legs apart so he could kneel between her legs. Her entire body shuddered with a helpless need.

He waited a heartbeat. Two. Until her eyes met his. His fingers brushed over her wet entrance. She moaned and twisted, her hips bucking, following his fingers.

"Say it, Saria. I want to hear the words."

She thrashed under him, her eyes glittering with gold. "Please, Drake, please."

"That's not what I want. Say it."

She took a deep breath to steady herself. "I love you, damn it. There. Is that what you want to hear?"

"And it's forever. We're forever." He pressed his fingers into her, one shallow fiery inch and she gasped, her body gripping at him, desperate to draw him deeper.

"Yes." Her head tossed from side to side and she lifted her hips, trying to impale herself on his fingers. "Just please do something."

He took her with his mouth, his tongue replacing his finger, stabbing deep, drinking at her, licking, sucking, devouring her. She tasted like sweet candy, yet with a tangy bite of cinnamon and he wanted every drop. He lapped at her, holding her legs apart with strong hands, starving for every drop of liquid he could extract with his greedy mouth. Again and again he brought her to the brink while her body thrashed and bucked against his mouth, but he refused to allow her relief.

When she was mindlessly pleading, nearly sobbing, he lifted his head. "Get on your hands and knees."

His voice had gone to a deep growl. Heat ran like a tidal wave through his veins. She complied, her soft skin covered in that fine sheen that made her feel like silk. He didn't wait for her to settle but pressed one hand firmly on her neck, forcing her head down and her buttocks up. He slammed his cock into that fiery inferno, driving through her tight folds almost savagely.

She screamed, the sound vibrating through his body. His thick length stretched the walls of her sheath until he could feel her every heartbeat. She writhed around him, twisting, shoving back when he withdrew and plunged again and again. His hands tightened and he drove into her heat. The position allowed the deep penetration he craved as well as allowing his cock to create a tremendous friction over her sensitive bud.

Her moans rose to a wailing crescendo. Her pleas grew into a mindless, desperate chant of his name and oh-please — oh-please — oh-please. He gripped her hips and surged deep, over and over, driving through her tight, hot sheath. Each hard thrust stole her breath, rocked her body and sent her into another frenzy of gasping chanting.

Her muscles clamped down on him, gripped like a vise, scalding hot, sending ripples of pleasure through him as her orgasm tore through her, taking him with her. Her back arched, her eyes widened and she cried out as the sensation rolled over her like a tidal wave. Her tight sheath dragged his own release from him, a series of powerful contractions that seemed never-ending, pulsing around him, drowning him in pleasure.

Drake stared down at her. Both of them fought for breath. He could barely comprehend what had just happened. The explosive passion between them was unimaginable. He could feel her body still gripping his, pulsing around him. Saria seemed to be drifting, barely aware, definitely uncomprehending. He eased his body from hers, appreciating her small cry of protest.

"I'm heavy, baby," he whispered. He brushed kisses over her chin, the corner of her mouth, her temple. "I don't want to crush you."

"Don't leave me," she murmured.

"It won't ever happen, Saria. I'm very much in love with you. As soon as I have the strength, I'm putting you in bed."

"I could crawl," she offered.

"I don't think that will be necessary. Just give me a minute to catch my breath." He managed to get a hand up to rub the strands of her damp hair between his fingers. She always felt like silk to him. Her skin. Her hair. "Is it so damned hard to admit you love me?"

Her lashes lifted and she stared at him with eyes wide with shock. "Of course not. I'm crazy about you. I just have never said that to anyone. Maybe Pauline — once. Recently. Never as a child. And I don't think anyone ever said it to me."

He suppressed a groan and buried his face against her neck. He should have thought of that. Saying "I love you" had not been a drunken man's priority. When he was sober enough, he taught her to survive, he hadn't taught her how to love. Pauline, maybe, had fulfilled that role in Saria's life, but she'd been careful of being too demonstrative in case Saria's father had stopped the child from coming to see her. Drake hid a smile against her delicious skin. He doubted Saria's father could have stopped her from doing anything she wanted to do.

He pressed a kiss into her throat and lifted his head to look at her again. "I love you. I'm saying it to you. Over and over. And when we have children, both of us will be saying it to them."

"Okay."

She smiled, a slow, beautiful, Saria smile that made his heart stutter and his cock pulse with life in spite of how tired he was. She made him feel alive, in the moment, every second in her company. He kissed his way up her throat to her chin and then to the corners of her mouth. "You're so beautiful, Saria," he whispered before his mouth settled over hers. He meant the inside of her, her character, her soul, her heart. He wasn't a man to give flowery speeches, but she inspired them.

He sucked at her lower lip, and then licked along the seam of her lips until she opened her mouth to him. He blanketed her again, knowing he was in trouble with her. Addicted to her kisses, craving her body, loving her smile, what the hell chance did he have with her? She was going to wrap him around her finger and get every damn thing she wanted.

He lifted his head and glared at her. "We're getting married immediately. I want our child to know we were in love and wanted each other."

"Our child?" she echoed. "We have a long way to go before we have a child."

"*Immediately.* If I'm going to spend my lifetime giving in to you on nearly every issue, I get this one."

She laughed and pushed at him. "You are crazy, Drake. You're workin' yourself into a fine snit for no reason. We'll get married any time you want. I said yes, remember?"

He forced his body to work. "Where's the bedroom?"

She looked around her with a slightly daze expression. "Over there. *Tante* Marie just left a few days ago, so the blankets are still fresh. She keeps them in that closet inside a plastic tub."

He eased his body from the couch, found he could stand and padded across the wooden floor to the room she indicated. "Why do you call her *Tante* Marie? Is she your aunt?"

Saria propped her head on her hand. "In a manner of speaking. Every child called her *Tante* Marie. She's the recognized local *Traiteur* — our healer. She's very good too. Everyone goes to her, all up and down the swamp. The bayous. Even from town. If she can't find the right plant to heal you, there isn't one."

"And she lives here?" Drake tried to keep the shock from his voice. The cabin was very small and obviously old. Everything was very clean, but very rustic.

"She grew up here, went away to nursing school, and like most of us, found she didn't really want to be away. This is her family home and she's comfortable in it. Every few months she leaves for a couple of weeks to visit her sister."

Drake spread the sheets on the bed and added pillows and a blanket before gathering Saria in his arms.

She wrinkled her nose. "I'm all sweaty."

"I like you sweaty. It's sexy."

She laughed and buried her face against his chest. "On you maybe."

He could feel her tongue sliding over his skin, tasting him. His cock made a second attempt to rise to the occasion. He laid her on the bed, drinking in the sight of her, sprawled out, all that soft skin and alluring curves.

She quirked an eyebrow at him, her gaze dropping to his erection. "Really?"

"Really."

"I don't think I can move."

"You don't have to do a thing."

He made love to her gently, taking his time, a slow, languorous expression of the way he felt. Worshipping her. Taking her to the edge slowly, a long eloquent climb as he committed every inch of her body to memory. Every sigh. Every moan. Each sensitive spot. So many kisses, coming back again and again to her wickedly sinful mouth. She was everything to him and he wanted her to know it. He might not be the best at words, but she was going to know she was thoroughly loved by the time he gave her release. She clung to him when her body fragmented and intense pleasure washed over and through her. He stayed deep inside her for a long time, holding her close, reluctant to leave her.

Drake kissed the back of her neck as he curved his body protectively around hers. "Go to sleep, baby."

"Mmm," she murmured drowsily, snuggling closer into him. Her hand stroked over his as he covered her breast with his palm. "My leopard asked me if that was all you had. She pointed out her male had amazin' stamina."

"She did, did she?" Amusement tinged his voice. "He rested for at least twenty to thirty minutes. I'll be doing the same."

He woke her twice more before morning, and once she woke him, her mouth so hot he told her he wanted her to wake him every morning. She just laughed and snuggled back into him, sated for a short while. He figured her leopard wasn't complaining about his performance anymore.

He drifted with the light coming in the window, just holding her, listening to her even breathing, knowing he wanted to hear that soft sound for the rest of his life. Already, he couldn't imagine going to bed without her or waking up to complete emptiness. Rain played music on the roof and the wind drove branches into the house. He could see the mist through the window, turning the world into a glittering silver paradise for the two of them. She felt like warm, living silk, her skin heating his. He tightened his arms around her, laughing softly when his body, of its own volition, began to come alive again. He couldn't imagine that a baby would not be the result of their coming together so urgently. If her leopard had emerged, both of them were fertile, the only time a shifter could be conceived.

Outside, a twig snapped and he went on alert. His leopard jumped, so that his skin itched and his jaw ached. He listened for another moment and heard the whisper of material brushing against leaves.

Drake lifted his head. "Wake up, baby,

we've got company." His fingers tangled in Saria's hair and he brushed a kiss over the top of her head. "Wake up."

Saria nuzzled his neck. "Mmm, a few more minutes, Drake."

"Charisse is outside. We've got to get up."

19

"Just a minute, Charisse," Saria called as she yanked a pair of jeans from the pack her brothers had given to Drake the night before. "Great. These are too long." She wiggled her hips. "And tight. Whose are these anyway? I think some woman left her jeans in one of my brother's rooms and I've inherited them."

"Before you open that door, Saria, you listen to me," Drake whispered, pulling a weapon from under his pillow.

She scowled at him as she fished for a T-shirt. Whoever had packed the case hadn't believed in underwear. "A gun under your pillow? I was too occupied to think about weapons last night. I have no idea where my knife is."

"You should be happy you have a man who puts your safety first."

"I want you to be so crazy out of your mind for me you can't possibly think about safety," she objected.

Drake flashed a rueful grin. "Then I'll admit I didn't think about it until early this morning." He tugged on his jeans, the grin fading. His eyes went dark and somber. "Don't put your body between me and Charisse at any time. Not for any reason. I don't miss, baby, and if I have to, I'll kill her."

The teasing laughter faded from Saria's eyes and she went still. "Charisse would never hurt anyone, Drake. Please don't make things worse for her by lettin' her know you think she's capable of bein' a serial killer."

"I'll do my best, Saria, but you'll have to trust me on this."

She shook her head, opened her mouth to protest again, but then shrugged and hurried out of the bedroom to the front door. Drake followed her, the gun in his hand, finger on the trigger, hidden under the shirt he carried.

Charisse looked as if she'd spent the night crying. She stood looking completely absurd in her bright red short jacket and long black skirt, with red leather boots and a silk black blouse peeking beneath the jacket. Her hair, once a fashionable chignon, had begun to fall out in the rain and wind, so that tendrils fluttered around her face. She had beautiful skin and eyes and the small curls showed her features off to perfection, far more, Drake thought, than the severe, yet fashionable hairdo she chose to wear. Some people considered black widow spiders to be beautiful — he just wasn't one of them.

Saria caught Charisse's arm and drew her inside. "What is it, *cher?*"

Her voice was motherly, soothing, but she did exactly what Drake had told her, positioning herself so he had a clear shot at Charisse even as she took her into the living room and indicated a chair.

"We haven't made any coffee, *cher,* but I'll do that right away. What happened?"

"I made such a fool of myself with Mahieu last night. He was so angry with me." Charisse put her hands over her face and began to sob.

That, at least, was genuine. Drake could always hear the echo of a lie, and there was a distinct odor to lies, but Charisse was telling the truth. He sighed and went to get tissue from the bathroom while Saria hastily put on the coffee. All the while he kept a careful line of fire to the woman — just in case.

Drake perched on the arm of a chair opposite Charisse where he knew he couldn't miss no matter where Saria was if he was forced to shoot Charisse. He handed the sobbing woman a tissue, and shot Saria an exasperated look. She glared at him, clearly on Charisse's side no matter what.

"Exactly what happened?" Saria said.

"I told him I didn't want to see him anymore," Charisse admitted. "I was lyin' of course. Who wouldn't want to go out with Mahieu? He's . . . he's . . . *perfect.*" She wept hysterically.

Saria sank down beside Charisse and patted her soothingly. "We can straighten this out, Charisse, don't cry anymore and let's figure it out."

"You don't understand. There's no way to fix it. I told him to go away. He tried to talk to me and he said if he went, he wouldn't come back. You know Mahieu, he means what he says." Her voice rose in another hysterical wail. "I told him to go."

"I'll never understand women in a million years," Drake groused. "If you didn't want him to go, why would you insist he leave?" When both women looked at him, he sighed. "And don't you own a pair of jeans? You're out in the swamp and you're some kind of fashion model." Come to think of it, each time he'd seen Charisse, the woman was in some kind of fashionable suit. Even on the edge of the swamp, when he'd been on a picnic with Saria. "It isn't practical, Charisse."

"As a matter of fact, no, I do not own a pair of jeans. I'm a woman and I wear dresses or skirts," Charisse said, batting tear-tipped lashes at him, clearly offended.

Drake would have thrown his hands up in exasperation, but he had a gun hidden by his side and didn't have the luxury of expressing his complete frustration with the woman.

Saria gave him one emotion-laden look from under her long lashes, quelling any desire to continue the conversation with Charisse. Saria switched from her, you-speak-again-and-you're-dead look to a sweet smile directed at Charisse.

"*Cher,* why did you decide to pick a fight with Mahieu? You drove him off on purpose. Why did you do that?"

Drake couldn't tell the difference between what he'd asked and what Saria had asked, but Charisse responded with another sniff and more fresh tears. "My mother had her talk with me again. And she's always right. I'm not good enough. Or pretty enough. Your brother is so handsome and smart and could have any woman he wanted. Why would he ever stick with me? He's just us-

579

ing me. The first real woman to come along, he'd leave me and go off with her."

Saria frowned. "That's just not true, Charisse. A man would be lucky to have you."

Drake wasn't so certain. Not with the sure belief the woman was a serial killer and she cried like a child at the drop of a hat. More tears flooded her large eyes and she covered her face, rocking back and forth.

"I'll never have a man. My mother says I don't have what it takes to hold a man . . ."

"Oh for God's sake, Charisse," Drake burst out, driven beyond endurance. "How old are you anyway? Has it ever occurred to you that you're a grown-up and maybe, just maybe, your mother is full of shit?"

Saria gasped. Charisse startled, staring at him with wide, tear-drenched eyes.

"Drake," Saria cautioned.

"Someone has to tell the truth here, Saria. Charisse, everyone tells me you're a brilliant woman," Drake was more exasperated than ever. "You know you are as well, yet you let everyone treat you as if you're a small child that's not quite bright. So your mother says you're not beautiful enough to hold a man like Mahieu Boudreaux. Why in the hell would you ever believe her? Mahieu is a man of principle. Do you think he's after you for your money?"

Two spots of color flamed into Charisse's pale face. "Every man I've ever gone out with has dumped me for my mother. She sends them on their way and crows about it for months."

He heard Saria inhale sharply and he glanced at her. She pressed a hand to her stomach as if sick and he felt an answering lurch in his gut. "Are you telling me your mother *really* seduced your boyfriends?"

Charisse stiffened. Shame crept into her expression. She nodded. "Even in high school. They *always* slept with her. I was never pretty enough, or smart enough . . ."

"That's sick, Charisse. And abusive. If you're so damned bright, how the hell did you not figure that out? Your mother has something wrong with her and she took it out on you. Did you really think Mahieu would sleep with her?"

"*Mon dieu, cher,* tell me you didn't accuse Mahieu of sleeping with your mother," Saria pleaded. "*Please* tell me you didn't do that."

A whisper of unease slipped into Drake's mind and lodged there.

"I did though," Charisse sobbed. "I did and he left. You should have seen the look on his face. He'll never talk to me again. I tried callin' him over and over. I texted him.

He didn't answer. And I went by your house before dawn and Remy said Mahieu never came home." Her sobs went up another notch, reaching a crescendo. "My mother wasn't home either last night."

Drake stiffened, his mind racing, fingers of fear creeping down his spine. "I need you to calm down for me, Charisse. Stop crying. You won't be of any help if you keep crying." That terrible thought continued to drift unchecked through his mind. Impossible. Totally impossible. Yet that little tendril of suspicion refused to go away. "Is there a phone in this cabin, Saria?"

"Yes. Cell phones don't work here."

"Call Remy and tell him to get over here now," Drake said. "Tell him to send the team to Fenton's Marsh. I want them to spread out and look for any signs that someone has been there. And tell him to bring the photos you took out there."

Saria's eyes met his. "Mahieu's all right?" She couldn't hide the question in her voice, or the sudden fear streaking across her transparent face, nor did she ask why he wanted the photographs of dead bodies.

Charisse gulped, her eyes widening until they looked like two drenched pansies pressed into her face. "Of course he's all right. Why wouldn't he be all right?" He saw her intelligence then, the quick mind fitting pieces of a puzzle together. "What's goin' on? Tell me right now if it has somethin' to do with Mahieu."

The crybaby was gone. In her place was a thinking, sharp woman. She brushed away the tears and looked him right in the eye. "Tell me."

"What do you know about opium?" Drake asked, his voice quiet.

Saria had leapt to her feet, but she paused, turning back toward them. Charisse blinked. Frowned. Her gaze never left Drake's. She leaned toward him. "Quite a lot, actually. I study plants, but what would that have to do with Mahieu?"

Her voice was quite steady. Almost a challenge. As if he dared accuse Mahieu of anything and she might leap forward and claw out his eyes.

"Where are the soaps made for your company?"

Charisse frowned. "In New Orleans. We have a factory right there."

"Do you ever go there?"

"No. I have nothing to do with production. I work in my own laboratory developin' scents. What does this have to do with Mahieu — or opium?"

"Do you, personally, grow your plants?"

"In the greenhouse only. I experiment with developin' different hybrids for scents there."

"And the gardens in the swamp?"

"We have workers for that."

"Who? Specifically?"

Charisse frowned. "I don't know. We have a foreman. I don't talk to him myself. Armande or my mother handles that. I have enough to do in the laboratory. In any case, I never go out in the swamp. Sometimes I meet Saria at the picnic area and . . ." Her gaze darted to Saria. "And Evangeline meets me there."

"But never men."

"In the swamp?" Charisse's horror was genuine. She looked down at her clothes and gave a delicate shudder. "Never."

"What about when you allow your leopard out?"

She flushed a deep red. "She's never come out. That's why my mother said I was useless. Armande has a leopard, but mine has never emerged. I tried to tell my mother she was there inside of me, but my mother is embarrassed and humiliated that I can't shift. She says I'm a disgrace." Charisse gave a little sniff.

"Charisse! Focus on what's important here," Drake commanded. If she was telling the truth, and her voice held a ring of truth, then she couldn't possibly be the killer. The serial killer delivered death with the suffocating bite of a leopard. "I can assure you that your mother's opinion of you isn't worth shit. Saria, call your brother and get that team out into the Marsh."

"Mahieu?" Saria's voice was steady.

"The team may just save his life. Get moving."

Saria nodded and picked up the phone.

"Are you goin' to tell me what all these questions are for? This sounds like an interrogation."

"Believe me, Charisse. If I have to interrogate you, I won't be so fucking gentle," Drake snapped. "Someone is using your soaps to ship opium out of the country. They also have at least one local connection they supply, but more likely there are more."

Charisse sat up straight, her face going pale. "That's impossible. You're crazy. Our business is family owned and completely legitimate. I can't believe you would make such an accusation. Saria! Did you hear him?"

Saria put down the phone after talking to her brother and turned back to Charisse, leaning one hip against the table. "I heard him. I led his men through the swamp the other night, running to catch up with a boat. The Mercier boat, and they docked at *your* dock, Charisse. The Tregre brothers had delivered a shipment of soap in the middle of the night."

"No. No way." Charisse shook her head. "The Tregres have worked for our family for a long time. They work out of New Orleans and take the shipment to the docks, where they are inspected carefully. If there were drugs, the dogs would pick up the sce . . ." She trailed off, her face going dead white.

There was no way she could fake the color of her skin. Her brain was working things out, seeing possibilities and putting the pieces together, but Drake might have to concede he was way off-base looking at Charisse and that would mean that niggling suspicion was growing into a major scare. Because if he was right, Mahieu Boudreaux might already be dead.

"That's right, Charisse. You're the genius with scent, aren't you," Drake pressed her. He leaned close and looked her right in the eye, forcing her to lock gazes with him. "Tell us about the scent that inhibits others, even leopards, from tracking by scent."

Charisse shook her head, her fingers twisting tightly together until her knuckles were white. "You have it all wrong, Drake. Saria . . ."

She tried to turn her head, tried to escape the ever-tightening noose, but Drake refused to let her off the hook. "Damn you, don't look at Saria. She can't help you. Did you or did you not, develop something that inhibits the ability to smell, or perhaps deadens every scent gland?" he snapped.

Charisse drew herself up abruptly, her childlike expression going cool. "I don't have to stay here and listen to these accusations. I think the next time you talk to me, I'll have a lawyer present." She started to rise.

His low growl of pure menace rumbled through the cabin, stopping her. "Sit down," he snapped, his eyes going pure gold. "You're leopard, Charisse. You belong to a lair. I am the leader of that lair and as such, I am the only judge and jury and executioner that you or your family will ever have. There is a death sentence hanging over your head and as much as it would pain Saria, I will destroy your entire family for the preservation and good of the lair."

He raised his voice. "*Look* at *me,* not Saria. She can't save you. You need to convince *me* you have nothing to do with this mess, and right now, honey, it isn't looking all that good for you."

Charisse's hand went defensively to her throat. There was no getting around the ring of truth in Drake's voice. He heard Saria make a small, protesting sound, but he didn't look at her. She was going to be his wife. She needed to see the reality of what their life was like. Amos Jeanmard should have been cleaning up his lair years earlier. Regardless, it was all there in this dying lair, the depravity, the sickness and the greed for power and money. If he had to kill this woman, he would do so and without hesitation.

"It's not what you think. Yes. I experiment all the time with scents and the by-product of this very new scent I was workin' on turned out to have an unusual, very unique aspect to it."

Her voice changed completely again, Drake noted, suddenly animated, her eyes bright with eagerness. For the first time he felt he was looking at the real Charisse Mercier.

"I'd never seen anything like it. Not only was there no scent, but it consumed every other scent around it. Can you imagine the uses? I haven't perfected it yet, but I think it will be amazin'. Think of all the people with allergies to scents and that's just one use. I've been experimentin' with ingestin' it. That seems to yield the best results, but I have to study side effects."

"Charisse." Drake needed to bring her back to the reality of what was going on. Her brain had flipped a switch to pure scientist and she was no longer talking to him, rather talking aloud to herself to find a solution for some problem she'd obviously encountered. "Who else knows about this scent-masking product you've discovered?"

She frowned at him. "No one. What I'm doin' in the lab stays there until I have it ready to be tested and I register it."

"Not your brother? Your mother? You don't confide in them when you make a discovery?" he prompted, managing to keep from shaking her.

She licked her lips and her gaze slid away from his. "No."

He leapt to his feet, his leopard so close to the surface neither woman could fail to see him. Glittering eyes fixed and dilated, a predator's stare locked onto prey. He towered over Charisse. "Don't you fucking lie to me. Do you think this is some kind of a game? I'm *commanding* you to tell the truth, as leader of this lair. You're not protecting anyone by not telling me, you're simply getting yourself into hot water."

Saria surprised — even shocked — him by not leaping forward to try to protect Charisse. He glimpsed her pale face and tight fists out of the corner of his eye, but she didn't say a word or make a move. He knew how difficult it had to be for her not to defend or try to protect her friend. She believed in Charisse, but maybe, like Drake, a building dread and worry for Mahieu was drowning out all reason, because he was damned sure, Saria's brother was in trouble.

Charisse trembled visibly. "If I tell you, you'll think my brother is guilty of all this. The opium, whatever else is wrong, but he would *never, never* betray me or our family. Armande is vain and sometimes selfish, but he isn't a drug dealer. You don't know him. He wouldn't ever do something like that."

"Just like he wouldn't hunt Saria through the swamp with a gun?" Drake spat out.

"Okay. Okay, I can see why that would make him look guilty to you. It was a terrible mistake. A misjudgment. He has a very bad temper, I'll admit that and he lets Robert talk him into things. Most women fawn all over him. He's handsome and charmin' and used to gettin' his way in all things. He's mama's golden boy, yet he still lives in hell. You have no idea what it's like to grow up with her."

Charisse clapped her hand over her mouth and her expression once more became that of a child's. Drake nearly groaned. Charisse had obviously been taught to keep all family secrets and just that small admission was a terrible sin.

"You're not going to hell for telling the truth," Drake pointed out. "I don't have all day, Charisse, and Remy will be walking through that door any minute. If he thinks Mahieu is in danger, he won't be nearly as gentle as I've been."

"I don't understand," Charisse wailed again. "What does Armande have to do with Mahieu's disappearance?"

"Did you tell him about the nonscent you were developing?" Drake roared.

"Of course I did, he's my brother and he fronts our business. Whenever I have a breakthough that may make us a great deal of money, of course I share it with him."

"Anyone else?" When she shook her head, he persisted. "Your mother?"

"My mother isn't in the least bit interested in anything I say or do. She could care less about any of my discoveries. Was she in the room when I told Armande? Possibly. We often talk in the evenin' when we're together, but I can't remember exactly when I told him about it."

"Is Armande your half-brother? Is he Buford Tregre's son?" Drake watched Charisse closely for the answer. She would know by scent, even if no one else could detect it.

She looked more shocked than ever. "No. Armande isn't his son." She looked down at her hands. "I know Mama was sleepin' with Buford, and he often beat her, but she always went back to him. But I know he's my full brother. He smelled just like daddy."

"And the flower? The Leopard's Lover flower?"

Charisse flinched. Her eyes went wide and her mouth opened in a perfect round O. "How do you know about Leopard's Lover? No one can know about that. We stand to make millions of dollars with that scent. I haven't quite perfected it yet, but I've been workin' on it for literally years. I'm close, and if I get it right, we'll be set for life and I'll be able to really pour decent money back into our community where it's needed. No one knows about that flower or the scent."

"The flower is growing wild in Fenton's Marsh and along the Tregre border and on their property." Drake waited, watching her face carefully.

Charisse sagged back in her chair, a look of utter horror on her face. She shook her head. "No. That can't be. That's a hybrid, not indigenous to our swamp. It can only be grown safely in the greenhouse. I've taken extra precautions. I have a special room in the greenhouse for it alone. You have no idea how much money that plant is worth — or how much damage it might do not only to our environment, but to people — our people — to shifters." She kept shaking her head, in genuine shock.

Drake had to believe her. She hadn't been in the swamp, or Fenton's Marsh, or she would have known the plant had escaped the greenhouse. By her own admission she knew Evangeline, but she claimed she met her in the Mercier picnic area, not in the swamp itself.

"Remy's here," Saria announced and headed to the door.

Even then she was careful to remember his instructions. Drake could have told her it was no longer necessary. Charisse Mercier hadn't killed anyone. If she'd picnicked with a victim in Fenton's Marsh, she would have seen Leopard's Lover, her engineered hybrid. But someone who had been in the greenhouse had carried seeds on their shoes or clothing and left them along the Tregre border as well as in the Marsh.

"I know you think Armande . . ." Charisse began.

Remy burst through the cabin door, nearly knocking Saria over. He caught her to steady her, his face grim. "Mahieu isn't answerin' his cell. He didn't come home last night. Where is he, Charisse?" he demanded.

"She doesn't know," Drake said. "It isn't her. Nor did she know about the opium. Was Armande home last night, Charisse?"

"Stop askin' me about my brother. I'm tellin' you, he has nothin' to do with opium. Talk to our workers. Neither of us have much to do with the outdoor gardens."

"But you both go to the greenhouse," Drake persisted.

"Armande is proud of my work. When I ask him, he always comes to see the new plants."

Remy stepped forward and thrust several photographs into her hand. "What about these? Do you think your brother had anything to do with this?"

Charisse looked down at the first picture in her hand. Her entire body went rigid. Still. She made one inarticulate sound, every vestige of color draining from her face. Twice she tried to speak before she managed to get the words out. "I know this man. Is he dead? *Mon Dieu.* He looks dead. I went out to dinner with him a few months ago. Armande introduced us. They were friends from college. He stood me up on our second date."

She swallowed hard and looked down at the second picture. A small scream escaped her and she threw the photographs back at Remy. "Why are you doin' this to me? I went out with him four months ago. We had three dates. He was a nice man. Who did this?"

Saria instantly went to her friend and sank down beside her to take her into her arms, rocking her back and forth. "I'm so sorry, Charisse. I'm so very sorry."

"You think someone is goin' to do this to Mahieu? Because of me? Is this about me?" Charisse raised her head from Saria's shoulder and looked Drake directly in the eye. "You don't believe my brother did this because of me, do you?" There was horror in her eyes, in her very tone. She looked on the verge of fainting.

"I don't know, Charisse, but someone is killing these men and if you are the connection," Drake said, "and you're also the connection to the opium . . ."

Charisse covered her face with both hands. "This can't be happenin'."

"I want you to look at some other photos as well," Remy said, his voice much more gentle. "There's been a series of murders around New Orleans. All female. Their bodies were dumped in the bayous and swamps and around the river. I just want you to tell me if you know any of these women."

"I don't want to look," Charisse protested. "I can't. You're tearin' apart my life and I won't have you accusin' my brother of runnin' drugs or worse, killin' people." She kept her hands clamped over her face and began to weep, a low heartbreaking sound.

Both Remy and Drake opened their mouths but abruptly closed them when Saria imperiously held up her hand to silence them. She stroked Charisse's hair with gentle fingers, making a soft, soothing sound. Drake couldn't help think how she would look calming a distraught child.

"I need you to think of Mahieu, *cher.* If you know Armande didn't do any of this, you have nothin' to worry about, but Mahieu could be in terrible danger. You don't know, Charisse, perhaps there's a stalker out there, someone who is tryin' to make it look as if Armande or you is the guilty party. Please look. It may help us find my brother."

Charisse very slowly lifted her face from her hands and looked up at Saria. The two women exchanged a long look before Charisse finally nodded very reluctantly.

Saria smiled with encouragement at her and held out her hand for the photographs. Remy gave them to her.

The two women looked at the first picture of a woman's face, obviously dead, her features delicate, hair spilling around her like spider webs. Charisse sniffed and shook her head. Saria showed her the next photograph. Charisse gave a small cry and flung herself back against the sofa, trying to retreat from the dead woman.

"That's Lucy. Lucy O'Donnell. She was datin' Armande. He told me she left town abruptly, that her mother was ill." She looked up at Saria, a lost little girl. "I want to go home. I feel sick."

Saria handed the photographs back to her brother. "Drake will get you a glass of water and we'll go in a minute, Charisse. You didn't kill those men, and it's just as probable Armande didn't kill those women."

"He wouldn't," Charisse said. "He isn't like that."

"He attacked Saria in the grove just outside of town," Drake said, trying not to snarl. He glared at Saria. He didn't want her giving Charisse false hope.

"What?" Charisse's eyes widened. She took the glass of water and drank most of it before turning her gaze back to her friend.

"He wouldn't."

Remy and Drake exchanged a long look. Charisse was lying. She knew all about Armande attacking Saria in the grove.

Drake deliberately loomed over her, knowing he was intimidating with his leopard riding him so hard, furious that another man had dared to put his mark on his female, and worse, had hurt her in the process. Saria sent him a look that clearly told him to back off — which he ignored.

"Before you get yourself into more trouble, Charisse," Drake cautioned, "you might remember I'll know if you're lying to me. I'm not all that happy with any member of your family."

"*Mon dieu,* Drake," Saria burst out. "Stop threatening her. Can't you see she's scared enough? You've told her about the opium and the serial killer and now you're practically accusin' her brother. Back off."

Drake looked at Saria's face. She was nearly as pale as Charisse. These were her friends. The interrogation was almost as difficult on her as it was on her friend. He wanted to gather her into his arms and hold her close. "I'm sorry, baby," he forced himself to say, although he wasn't as sympathetic toward Charisse as he should have been. She didn't seem to have the same loyalty toward Saria as Saria did toward her. There was no doubt in his mind that Charisse knew damn well her brother had attacked Saria.

Charisse ducked her head again, looking ashamed. "I'm sorry, Saria, I really am. It's my fault. I talked him into it."

There was a long silence. Drake didn't realize for a moment that he had snarled, the menacing sound filling the room and freezing all the occupants. When he looked down, he could see that Remy had thrown out a restraining hand, but had been prudent enough not to touch him.

Charisse trembled, drawing back as far from Drake as possible.

"It's all right, Charisse," Saria soothed. "That's just Drake's leopard gettin' a little upset, no big deal. He knows I'm marryin' him soon."

Remy's eyebrow shot up. "You are?"

"Yes she is," Drake said. "But I'm interested in Charisse's explanation. Why would you encourage your brother to attack Saria?"

"Not *attack* her. You don't understand. Our mother wanted Armande to marry Saria because it was obvious Saria had a leopard. He told her that he didn't love Saria and Saria didn't love him, that they were just good friends. Our mother wouldn't listen. She told him it was his duty. You don't know my mother. She can be quite vicious when she wants something, especially with Armande. She cries and tells him he doesn't love her. She won't talk for days on end. She punishes us for any little indiscretion. She claims we're not loyal and it goes on and on until every moment is pure, intolerable hell."

She glanced at Drake and then looked away. "You have no idea what it was like growin' up with her. Armande was desperate to appease her, so I came up with a plan. I told him if he used the product — we call it IDNS — basically for identification of nonscent — which wouldn't allow even her leopard to scent him, most likely her leopard wouldn't react or accept him, but he could tell mama he'd marked her."

"Show her the scars on your back," Drake snapped.

Saria glared at him. "I don't think that's necessary."

"The point is, he hurt her," Drake said.

"I know," Charisse admitted in a low tone. "He told me. He cried. He said he could barely control his leopard — that his leopard went crazy on him the moment he was close to Saria. He couldn't stop his cat from reacting to her. I hadn't considered that and neither did he. Her leopard didn't rise because she couldn't scent his, and that made his leopard crazy. I should have known, but all I was thinkin' about was gettin' Mama off his back." She looked at Saria steadily. "I'm sorry. Armande was sorry too."

"If your brother was so fucking sorry," Remy snarled, "why did he go after my sister with a gun?"

Drake was very glad he wasn't the one asking, but he would have if Saria's brother hadn't.

Charisse moistened her lips. "His leopard has been goin' crazy lately and Robert's too. It has to be the flowers, they must have been drinkin' together somewhere in the swamp near the flowers. That's the only explanation I can come up with. When I asked him, he shook his head and said he felt crazy inside."

"Where's Armande now?" Remy demanded.

"I don't know," Charisse said. "He went to bed around midnight, but I heard him leave again about five-thirty this morning. I was in my bedroom cryin' and I heard him talkin' on his cell phone and then he walked down the hall and paused by my door like he might come in and talk to me, but he didn't. He went outside and I heard the car start up. I got up, went to Saria's house lookin' for her and then came here."

"Was he acting abnormal last night?"

Charisse shrugged. "There was an upset last night. Mama was really ugly. She was so angry with me for being upset over breakin' up with Mahieu. She broke all the dishes in the kitchen and tore up a sweater he bought for me when it turned cold on a date we went on. She tore it into strips and threw it in my face. She kept slappin' me until Armande dragged her away. Then she began weeping and told him I was embarrassin' her on purpose and ruining the Lafont name. He lost his temper and told her to shut up. Mama went very quiet and wouldn't accept his apology. She just went away. When she's like that you never know what she's goin' to do. He went to his room and I went to mine."

The niggling suspicion in the back of Drake's mind blossomed into a full-blown certainty. *She tore it into strips.* A woman's rage. A female leopard's rage. Saria's clothes had been torn into strips. His clothes had been torn into strips. He'd believed the men coming to the inn to drive him from the lair had done it, but ripping up clothes wasn't a man's temper tantrum — it was a woman's.

Not Armande. *Iris.* Iris Lafont-Mercier. She had taken care to keep the inn from burning down even while she tried to murder them all. She had access to the coffee to put the drug in it. She knew the security code. She worked at the post office where she could hear all gossip, keep an eye on everyone and intercept Saria's letter. She was a jealous, perverted woman, fit for being the mate of a man like Buford Tregre. The man had spurned her because she couldn't shift. He'd taken another woman as a mate and taunted Iris with his vicious depravity. She'd married the man whose property neighbored his and taunted him right back with her own brand of depravity.

Iris had despised her daughter and worshipped her son. She'd seduced and killed Charisse's boyfriends and slaughtered Armande's girlfriends. She'd even corrupted the family business in the hopes of ruining her daughter by framing her for the opium placed inside the perfumed soaps. Drake had to be certain, but Iris had to have her own secret workplace, close to home, probably close to Charisse's laboratory so suspicion would remain on Charisse.

Iris had given Leopard's Lover to her sister, one of her only real mistakes. She'd been the one to spread the seeds through Fenton's Marsh when she killed Charisse's boyfriends and along the strip between Mercier and Tregre land when she went to meet Buford, which, if he was right and they were mates, would have been often.

Saria made a small sound in the back of her throat. Her face was so white it was nearly gray. That was his woman. Smart. Quick on the uptake. She'd come to the same conclusion as he had.

"Mahieu," she whispered.

Remy shook his head. "Don't worry about him, *cher,* he's leopard. None of these people ever saw it comin' and had no chance."

"We need to go the Mercier house so we can be certain," Drake cautioned. "The team's at the Marsh, baby. If there was any sign of someone murdered, they would have found it by now. And Mahieu would never meet her alone in the marsh. You know he's smarter than that."

"Charisse, we need your permission to search your house and the grounds," Remy said.

Charisse looked up with tear-drenched eyes, glanced at Saria and then nodded.

20

Behind the magnificent mansion that had been built as an obvious showpiece, the crumbling remains of a long-forgotten plantation home lay partially buried by the creeping vines and heavy brush of the swamp. Charisse's laboratory had been constructed in part of the foundation of the original plantation house. Most of the earlier structure was crumbling and eaten away by worms or rotted by the dirt and vines of the swamp as it reclaimed its land.

Charisse used sections of the older house to connect between the greenhouse and her laboratory. Their contractor had preserved one long room to serve as a hall between the two new buildings. Not only did the long room keep the rain off, but it gave Charisse a large storage area for the equipment both for her laboratory and greenhouse.

Drake led the way through the laboratory

to the storage room, heading toward the greenhouse. Obviously the killer had spent time in the greenhouse and it was possible they could find something to lead them to wherever the opium was being placed in the soaps that had been manufactured in town.

"Wait," Charisse whispered as they moved through the darkened storage room. The early morning light couldn't penetrate the layers of dirt and grime on the windows. She stepped out of the line and placed her hand on the wall. "Can you smell that? Blood. I can smell blood. It's faint but it's this way."

"That's a wall, Charisse," Remy felt compelled to point out.

She shook her head. "I used to play in there when I was a child. It's a hidden passage that was for the servants long ago when this area was a plantation. There's a narrow hallway that leads downstairs to a rambling, condemned series of rooms that had been used at one time to house slaves. I haven't been down there for years, but I can smell the blood. I'm certain, Drake."

A chill went down Drake's spine. His leopard was close to the surface, yet he hadn't scented the blood. There was no doubt in his mind that if Charisse said she smelled it — that she did — unless . . . He didn't want to think he was wrong about her and she was leading them all into a trap. He glanced back at Remy and nodded with his head, silently telling the man to bring up the rear — to keep his eye on Charisse.

"You do know Iris Lafont-Mercier can't possibly be the killer, right?" Remy whispered as they waited for Charisse to locate the hidden door in the wall. He drew his gun. "She can't shift. The killer is a shifter. You just pointed the finger at Mama to get Charisse to allow us to search her property right?"

Drake glanced at him over his shoulder. "I'm leader of the lair, not the police, Remy. I don't require or want permission to search anywhere in the lair. I'd just do it."

There was a bite to his voice he couldn't help. Remy should have taken over leadership of the lair, but instead, Drake was stuck with it and Drake didn't shirk his duty. He'd taken on the responsibility and that meant cleaning it up. He had no doubt he was after a very clever killer and right now, his radar was shrieking at him that he was leading Saria right into a trap. Iris didn't need to shift all the way to be the killer. A partial shifting was unusual but certainly happened when bloodlines weakened.

Charisse found the mechanism for opening the door. Drake waved her back and stepped into the darkened, dirty hallway. The scent of blood was stronger here, wafting up from below. He could smell a mixture of fragrances and an elusive scent his leopard cringed away from.

Saria stepped into the space behind him and inhaled sharply. "I smell Mahieu — and Armande. They've both been inside this passageway recently."

"Baby, maybe you should . . ."

"Don't say it, Drake. Don't."

No. She wouldn't stay behind no matter how bad it got. Saria had too much backbone for that. He could hear her heart thundering in her chest, her ragged breathing. The smell of fear coming off of her was strong. She was terrified for her brother, but she wasn't going to hide upstairs while he checked to make certain Mahieu was alive. Drake stopped abruptly at the top of another narrow staircase.

"Those stairs are in disrepair," Charisse said. "No one ever comes here."

There was an absence of spiderwebs and the steps had been repaired in places. Still, it looked as if a few of them might crack under a man's weight. Drake tested each step cautiously. There were seven and they wound around a pillar down into another room and with each stair, the scent of blood grew stronger. Vines from outside had reclaimed the structure and pushed through the slats so that the swamp grew inside, snaking up the walls to the ceiling and down along the floor.

Long tables spanned the room. Small, fancy boxes and colored tissue paper were crammed in the garbage cans. Remnants of perfumed soaps and stems of withered plants were strewn around the floor as if they'd fallen and no one had bothered sweeping up.

"Here's where they packed the opium into the soap," Remy whispered.

Charisse made a small sound and leaned down to examine a crack in the table. When she would have touched a small, hardened bead caught in the crack, Remy stopped her, touching her hand and shaking his head.

Drake halted just past the second table. Fresh blood smeared the edge of the table, a bloody handprint where someone had grabbed the table to steady themselves. His heart plunged and he couldn't help the small glance he spared for Saria. Her gaze was fixed there. She couldn't fail to scent her own brother's blood. The scent of Armande Mercier was strong in the room.

There was no doubt he had been in the stuffy room quite recently.

An open door on the far side of the room led to another hallway. Wood rot and vines crept through the cracked siding. As with most dwellings in the area, the house had been built a good seven feet above ground, allowing for the water that poured into the area each season, flooding the land continually. The hall led down to the space below.

As he approached the room, Drake scented a leopard's lair. This one was damp, dark and smelled overwhelmingly of depravity. Every leopard could smell corruption to some degree. This lair stank of it, of an evil, immoral degenerate. This lair had been used in more than one life cycle, home to a cruel, cunning monster or monsters.

As he took another step, Drake caught the coppery scent of blood, a man's cologne and fear. He moved in silence, his leopard lending him stealth as he rounded the corner and caught sight of Armande crouched over Mahieu. One bloody hand ground into the wound in Mahieu's belly, while another gripped his throat. Across from the two men, Iris Lafont-Mercier stood with a tear-streaked face, one hand extended pleadingly toward her son.

Remy shoved passed Drake, gun in his

hand and leapt toward Armande. Charisse screamed and leapt after him. Although her leopard hadn't emerged, there was no doubt that she had one rising close to the surface. She covered the distance in a single leap, trying to shove Remy away from her brother. Simultaneously, Iris was on her daughter, jerking her backward, dragging Charisse with her, a razor-sharp knife against her throat.

"Mama, no!" Armande begged, trying to roll out from under Remy.

"Don't you dare!" Drake roared. His weapon was absolutely steady.

Charisse squeezed her eyes closed tight, not daring to breathe. Hatred filled the small room. Remy and Armande remained crouched beside Mahieu, working furiously to stem the flow of blood.

Saria moved out from behind Drake, into the center of the room. Iris's green-yellow eyes tracked her, filled with loathing. She snarled, exposing long canines. Her gaze followed Saria's every movement, focused with a predator's stare. Saria took another step to her right, forcing Iris to turn slightly to keep facing her.

Drake's mouth went dry. He had no doubt that Iris was an expert with a knife. Saria was deliberately putting herself in harm's way. One toss of the knife and Saria was dead. Iris would still have weapons. The others thought she had no leopard, but it was evident to him from the scents in the lair that her leopard was strong. She might not be able to fully shift, but some with weakened bloodlines could partially change and her leopard was filled with hatred, giving her the strength for a partial shift.

"Did you think you could hide from Drake, Iris?" Saria asked, her voice low. "You looked to that old man Buford for strength. He was an old fat slug, takin' advantage of any woman he thought was weak. You loved a coward. You admired a man who raped and beat women and you thought that was strength." She poured disgust into her voice, not just disgust, but amusement, as if she was secretly laughing at Iris.

Drake knew what Saria was doing — goading Iris into staying completely focused on her. She knew Iris, they lived in a small area, and were in each other's lives. She knew her vanities, the things that would make her lose her ability to think beyond what Saria taunted her with. She had accessed the situation the same way he had. Mahieu needed immediate medical attention, and Charisse was going to die if they didn't kill Iris first.

"You hated your daughter because she was everythin' you aren't. She's beautiful and intelligent. She's worth millions of dollars and she brought fame to a name you despise. You hated your husband because you couldn't hold him," Saria continued. "Everyone knew it. I heard whispers when I was a child. He wasn't faithful to you, was he? You couldn't hold a man like that. You couldn't hold either of them, could you? Buford or Bartheleme."

Drake waited for the perfect shot. *Another inch, baby. I need her to turn another inch just to be certain.* He could make the shot if there was no other choice, but she still might be able to slice through Charisse's throat and she was vicious enough to take her daughter with her just for spite.

Iris bared her teeth and a slow hiss emerged. "I was the one who had affairs, not that idiot of a husband. He didn't think I was clever. Only Charisse. Always his precious Charisse. If Charisse is so beautiful and intelligent, how come every one of her boyfriends slept with me? How come they all did anything I asked of them? Charisse is so damned stupid she didn't even know what was happenin' under her nose."

"The opium? You and Buford cooked that

up between you."

Drake was so proud of Saria's steady voice. She spoke as if she'd known the truth for years, as if she wasn't guessing at all. She took another step toward the right and her hand slid down to the knife at her belt.

His heart jumped, but he didn't move. Didn't blink. Just waited for that one moment that was certain to come. *Not too close,* he silently advised, wishing he could leap in front of Saria, but he had to trust her — trust her leopard to protect her. Iris was insane and her leopard was just as mad. There was no telling what she would do now that she was cornered.

"Stupid girl. Buford and I made so much money right under her uptight goody-goody nose." Iris's gaze shifted just for a moment to the moldy chests stacked to the back of the room. Vines climbed around them, but each one had a brand new lock. Her treasures. "We fucked in Bartheleme's bed all the time and even in her bed. She never knew, not even with her precious nose — the nose her father wanted to insure." There was such a mixture of loathing and contempt in her voice, Charisse began to weep.

"Maybe you did," Saria conceded, "but you needed the nonscent Charisse developed, didn't you? Buford used you for his own gain. While he was fuckin' you, he was doin' the same to a hundred other women."

"Whores. They were whores throwin' themselves at him. I killed them and left their bodies to rot with the gators."

"Please. Please." Armande wept. "She needs help."

Drake would bet his last dollar that Buford had given Iris gifts and she kept them here, in her lair. The money from the opium was kept in the cases until she could filter it through businesses in town or more likely — to implicate Charisse — the perfume store.

"Mama, please," Armande pushed to his feet and held out his hand to his mother. "You don't know what you're doin'. You don't know what you're sayin'."

"You shouldn't be here," Iris screamed at her son, her face darkening to rage. She shook Charisse, her grip powerful, the thin veneer of civilization completely gone. "Why did you come with him, Armande? You ruined everythin'. I could have fixed this mess, just like I've been takin' care of the messes the two of you have gotten into. Those disgustin' girls, none of them suitable. What were you thinkin', Armande. You would have disgraced the Lafont name, matin' with one. Your child needed to be a shifter."

Saria let out a tinkling laugh. "You're still quotin' Buford Tregre. He raped dozens of women. He laughed at you. Threw you away. And yet you choose to revere him. You're twisted, Iris. *You're* the disgrace to the Lafont name, not your children." She poured amusement into her voice, a taunting, deliberate goad designed to needle Iris. "Trottin' after him was so pathetic, wasn't it? Killin' all the women he made love to? You couldn't stand the thought of him wantin' those others. You just weren't good enough, were you?"

Easy baby, Drake tried to caution her. Iris was working herself up to a killing spree.

"He wanted me. He couldn't leave me alone. They were *nothin'* to him, just like the women Armande used."

"He wanted you so much he wouldn't be seen in public with you," Saria persisted. "You snuck around and he used you in the swamp, in the dirt and muck, hidin' you from the world because he was so ashamed."

Oh, God, she was pushing the woman too hard. He could see the smoldering fury burning behind those yellow eyes. All traces of green were gone and the gaze was fixed on Saria. Iris had forgotten Charisse, and

616

her daughter was watching Saria for a sign. Charisse understood the gravity of her position, unlike Armande, who Remy continued to restrain, even as he kept pressure on Mahieu's wound.

Drake's stomach dropped. Mahieu. Saria could smell his blood. From where she was standing she could see his wound — knew just how desperate the situation for him was — and she was doing more than setting Iris up for his shot. She was maneuvering her into the corner. She intended to end this as quickly as possible — and in any way she could — even if it meant attacking the woman herself.

"When the world finds out about Iris Lafont crawlin' after Buford Tregre, killin' his women, killin' her son's women and so desperate she had to stoop to seducin' *boys* her daughter dated and then killin' them, everyone will laugh every time the name Lafont is mentioned."

Iris shrieked, spittle flying from her mouth. Her face contorted, elongated, teeth filling her mouth and fur mottling her skin.

"Drop!" Saria called, throwing herself to the side with amazing speed.

Boneless, like a supple cat, Charisse slid to the floor as Iris hurtled the knife at Saria. Simultaneously, Drake squeezed the trigger.

A single hole blossomed in the middle of Iris Lafont-Mercier's forehead. She lay on the dirt floor in a crumpled heap, looking small and somewhat macabre with her face half leopard and half woman.

Armande screamed, but he rushed to his sister, leaving his mother crumpled on the floor. He gathered Charisse into his arms, their sobs filling the small space. Saria sat on the floor looking up at Drake, sorrow in her eyes, blood dripping from her upper arm.

"She was fast," she admitted.

Drake was on her in seconds, clamping his hand over the wound. It couldn't have been more than a flesh wound, but it was terrifying to him.

"Call an ambulance," Remy commanded. "We need it now."

EPILOGUE

"Are you going to say somethin'?" Pauline asked.

Saria looked at Drake, tears swimming in her eyes. He looked so handsome in his tuxedo, the cut of the jacket emphasizing his wide shoulders and deep chest. Saria Donovan. There was no hyphenating her last name, although she had teased him that she wasn't certain she would change her name to his. He had given her that golden, glittering glare that always sent a multitude of butterflies winging away in her stomach and she'd laughed at him.

Saria swallowed hard and looked down at the deed she held in her hand. Her wedding present. Pauline had given her the inn and the surrounding acres of land as a gift. An incredible, impossible-to-accept gift. She held the deed out to Drake. He took it slowly, as if the paper might explode in his hands.

"Pauline," he began and then cleared his throat and looked at Saria as if for help.

Saria shook her head, tears spilling over. "I don't know what to say."

"You're my girl," Pauline said. "My only child. I have no other heirs. I want you to have this place. Amos and I will be livin' close, at his home. You don't need to keep it as an inn. Originally it was a home and it wants children fillin' it. I want to come here and sit on the porch and rock my grandbaby. That's my dream now, Saria. I want you to stay close. It's an old woman's hope, and selfish of me, but I love you and the thought of you goin' off too far . . ."

"That's not going to happen," Drake assured, wrapping his arm around Pauline's shoulders. "I promised you I wouldn't take her away from you and I meant it. I'm taking her to the rain forest on our honeymoon, but I promise we'll be back soon. I've got a lot of lair business to take care of."

Amos grinned at him, the faded old eyes sparkling with mischief. "Better you than me."

Drake sent him a scowl, but refrained from speaking when Saria stepped hard on his toes. If Pauline was Saria's surrogate mother, then Amos was signing on to be her father and she wanted to make it plain to him that nothing was going to mar Pauline's happiness again. She'd gone through enough with losing her sister and finding out the woman was a serial killer. Saria didn't want anything else bad to ever happen in Pauline's life if she could have any say in it.

"Who will look after things while you're gone?" Amos pursued.

"Joshua. He's planning on taking his uncles to task and cleaning up his family's home and legacy. The other members of my team will stay and of course Saria's brothers will be on hand should anything go wrong while we're gone," Drake assured.

"How's Mahieu?" Pauline asked, glancing over at the man seated on her couch.

Wedding guests milled around, allowing Saria to catch only glimpses of her brother. "He's much better. It was touch and go for a while, but his leopard is strong and he's healing faster than anyone thought he would."

"And Armande?"

"He was so distraught over his mother. He had become suspicious that she was ill, I think both Charisse and Armande were suspicious," Saria admitted gently. "When Charisse broke up with Mahieu, Iris called him and wanted him to meet her alone to talk. He called Armande and asked him to be there when he met Iris. Armande saved Mahieu's life. If he hadn't been there, Pauline . . ." She trailed off. "Armande and Charisse are good people."

Pauline patted her hand. "I know they are. I love them both very much. They need time to get over all this. I should have stepped in a long time ago when I saw how my sister treated Charisse. The poor girl lived with persecution and abuse for years."

"It's over now," Drake said.

His voice was so gentle it turned Saria's heart over. She leaned into him, uncaring of her beaded gown. Drake immediately swept his arm around her waist and leaned down to brush kisses down the side of her face.

Charisse had been her maid of honor, but Armande hadn't come to the wedding. He'd chosen to go to the rain forest where he could breathe a little and think things through. Now that Charisse was safe, he didn't have to watch over her so carefully. He blamed himself for the deaths of the men and women his mother had murdered. He'd known she was ill, but had no idea of the extent of her madness.

"Come dance with me," Drake murmured in her ear.

She kissed Pauline. "Thank you," she

whispered. "I've always loved the inn. You know I do. It's always been a sanctuary for me. I'll be raisin' my children here."

"Go dance with your handsome husband so I can dance with my man," Pauline said, patting her hand.

Saria put her hand in Drake's, happiness bursting through her as she fit her body close to his. There was something so sensual, so right and perfect about dancing with one's husband, and she intended to savor every moment.

"I love you," Drake whispered in her ear as he whirled her around the dance floor.

She waited a heartbeat. Looked into his eyes. Let herself drown there. "I love you too."

ABOUT THE AUTHOR

Christine Feehan lives in the beautiful mountains of Lake County, California. She has always loved hiking, camping, rafting and being outdoors. She is happily married to a romantic man who often inspires her with his thoughtfulness. Please visit her website at www.christinefeehan.com.